Praise for Stuart R. West's
Coporate Wolf

"Brilliant. Unique horror humor that still ratchets up the tension and manages to shock. Alternately terrifying, hilarious, and ultimately poignant, you owe yourself to read this book."
–Catherine Cavendish, author of *The Haunting of Henderson Close* and *The Devil's Serenade*

"Howling good horror!"
–Russell James, author of *The Playing Card Killer* and *Claws*

"You've heard of the *Wolf of Wallstreet*. Those greedy guys have nothing on the staff of Lerner Corporation. On a company retreat, Shawn Biltmore is attacked by...a bear? Once he return to work, that's when the wolf hits the fan. Humor mixed with horror is Stuart West's forte. This is another great addition to his wild bunch of books about everything from a haunted mine to a spooky bed-and-breakfast inn."
–Cellophane Queen Book Reviews

And More Praise for the Works of Stuart R. West

Ghosts of Gannaway!

"…the story has some truly scary scenes, it is the slow boil suspense that gets under the skin. I'll be reading more of Stuart R. West!"
–Tom Deady, Bram Stoker Award-winning author of *Haven*

"With *Ghosts of Gannaway*, author Stuart R. West pulls back the skin of 20th Century Americana and extracts a magnificent working-class nightmare. It's the kind of tense, creepy thriller that keeps you frantically turning pages. West's talent and mastery of the craft are undeniably enviable."
–Peter N. Dudar, author of *The Goat Parade*

"Filled with tension, excellent characterization, suspense, ghostly presences, and enough twists and turns to keep you glued to the last page."
–Catherine Cavendish, author of *Cold Revenge* and *The Devil's Serenade*

"Captivating…a ghost story full of surprises."
–Joan C. Curtis, author of *A Painting to Die For*

Twisted Tales from Tornado Alley!

"These tales are top class horror with a smile, which is just as scary as a scowl or a snarl."

–Maynard Sims, author of the DCI Jack Callum series

"West draws upon our worst fears, turns prejudices back on to us, and puts us in situations against all odds as we recoil in horror but rejoice in delight at the intelligence of the writing and aha moments."

–MJ LaBeff, author of the *Last Cold Case* thriller series

"A Midwest fright-fest that will blow you away."

–Russell James, author of *Q Island* and *Dark Inspiration*

"A collection of horrific gems from a unique talent, *Twisted Tales from Tornado Alley* is one to curl up with on a dark night. Just make sure all the lights are on. Oh, and that you know where your cat is."

–Catherine Cavendish, author of *The Devil Inside Her* and *Waking the Ancients*

Also by Stuart R. West

Corporate Wolf

Twisted Tales from Tornado Alley:
A Collection of Short Fiction

Ghosts of Gannaway

Dread & Breakfast

PECULIAR COUNTY

PECULIAR COUNTY

Stuart R. West

A
Grinning Skull Press
Publication

PO Box 67, Bridgewater, MA 02324

ISBN-13: 978-1-947227-62-0 (paperback)
ISBN: 978-1-947227-63-7 (ebook)

DEDICATION

Everybody's got a bit of peculiar in them, but Kansas is swimming in it. To the oddballs, eccentrics, weirdoes and kooks, as long as they're on the good side of things, this book's for you.

To Zak, our beloved dog, who's had a rather peculiar year, one ending in the loss of a limb, but not his spirit.

Thanks to Nora Folan. And as always, a special dedication to Cydney and Sarah—keep being peculiar, my loves!

Chapter One

Hangwell, Kansas, Peculiar County, 1965

"*Help* me…"

It takes a mighty big effort to stir me from my sleep. Grams used to say I slept like the dead, then carried on like it was the funniest thing ever. Given the family business, Dad didn't really find it very funny, just not his cuppa joe, being the proprietor of Caldwell's Funeral Home and all.

But that night, something yanked me from a deep sleep like a battling catfish.

"Help me…"

Quite possibly, I'd been hearing the voice for some time, trying to stitch it into a dream the way folks do while in mid-slumber. But the insistent nature of the cry, the rising panic, forced me awake. I shuffled to the open bedroom window, my feet dusting up bunnies. A breeze set the curtains to sailing. I pinched them aside, stuck my head out. Even with the moon riding high, I couldn't see much, just the tops of the neighbor's corn stalks rattling like a hundred catalogs dropped from an airplane.

"*Help* me."

Nothing but a kid, a boy by the sound of his voice, maybe a little younger than me, possibly just goofing. But I didn't truly think that; nobody could fake being scared like that.

I've always been a curious sort, following in my dad's scientific footsteps. Mostly it's because I'm fifteen, I suppose, trying to get a handle on things, adding to life experiences whenever I can. Either way, nothing was gonna stop me from investigating, 'specially when a kid might be in trouble.

"Help...*please*..."

The kid sounded downright terrified, and I gotta admit, it scared me a bit, too. Not that I'm a scaredy-cat, mind you. But when you live in Peculiar County... Well, let's just say the county's name fits like a glove.

I slipped my overalls over my pajamas. Lately, it'd been raining enough to float an ark, so I capped my feet with boots.

Out in the hallway, Dad's snoring nearly whittled a hole through his bedroom door. Like me, if put to the test, he could sleep through a tornado.

Hardly my first nocturnal visit out of the house, I knew the tread and creaks of the stairwell just fine, the map imprinted in my brain. The moon guided me, shining through the window at the bottom of the steps, as sure-handed as a Starlight Cinema usher with his flashlight.

I inched the front door open. An uppity how-do-you-do wind gust greeted me, whipped my hair back and nearly took the door slamming against the wall. I caught the handle and struggled to shut it behind me.

"*Help*...me..."

Tonight, an unseasonable chill crested the wind, downright unwelcoming. A shiver scuttled down my back, more than just the wind rattling my nerves.

"Please...*please*..."

Now out in the open, I high-tailed it through our yard, across the gravel drive, and into the field next to the Saunders' farm. I didn't know the Saunders well, other than an occasional hand-wave (which they sometimes returned, other times not). I could pick Evelyn Saunders's Sunday bonnet out of a crowd, but that's as far as our country neighborliness traveled with them. Dad had always told me to keep my distance. With a cross face, he'd add, "They're not very hospitable." Then he'd vanish behind his newspaper the way adults have a tendency to do, leaving most of my social education to myself.

'Course this just made the Saunders' farm all the more intriguing.

"Help me! Please, don't let..."

The pleas had turned downright horrific. His voice lifted in the night like a heated barn-cat.

The wooden fence separating our properties had seen finer days, weathered down to splinters and loose two-by-fours. I managed to un-hinge one of the boards, swung it down, hiked a leg over, and followed through.

More wind kicked up, setting the stalks to waving. Leaves whispered to one another, sharing secrets. Telling stories better suited to the golden light of day.

Taller than me by a good couple of feet, the corn giants hovered over me. As I entered the field, they crowded in.

"*Help* me!"

The stalks' reaching fingers hid the moon's brilliance. I couldn't see for beans. But the boy's voice cried out louder. My heart likewise thumped to beat the band.

"Oooohhhh...*help me*...please..."

Tears flooded his voice now, his words garbled. Terror struck a spark in me, urgency suddenly crucial. I wanted to help the boy, get it over with, leave the field.

"*Eeeeeeee...*"

His sudden scream—pitched high enough to hurt a dog's ears—plugged ice into my veins. The voice echoed next to me, above me, behind me. Everywhere. I twisted in a circle, closed my eyes, honed my hearing the way hunters sometimes do. Leaves scratched my arms, poked at my face. Corn stalks shook, knocking around like dancing skeletons.

"*Help me!*"

Closer, the voice so close now, I could almost—

"*Help!*"

The boy burst out of the stalks, nearly plowing into me. I shrieked, pasted my hand over my mouth but good. As I suspected, the boy was young, probably eight or nine, maybe a shrimpy ten on a good day. Dressed in nothing but filthy underwear.

Breathless, we stared at one another. His small chest heaved out, sunk back into his bag of bones. Raccoon-lined eyes filled with fear, distrust. Moonlight fingered in through the stalks and touched him with an eerie blue color, a color I was right well-accustomed to: the inescapable color of death.

He stuck out bony arms, palms up, shaking worse than ol' Hyrum Thurgood's three-day tremors. We stood that way for a spell, before I mustered up courage to speak.

"Are you in trouble?" I whispered.

His entire body trembled. His fingers clawed up and stuck, the way heart attack victims shuffle off.

Never one for playing with dollies, a sudden need to protect the boy, to mother him, took hold of me. I wrapped him in my arms, held him tight. Tried to quell his shakes and make them my own.

"Please…" he whispered, "please, help me…"

"Help you *what?*" My voice rose just a hair, nerves grinding down.

A sudden moan—not unlike a freight train—supplied the answer the boy couldn't. The inhuman sound hitchhiked along a frigid wind gust, rode the cornstalk tops, and crashed toward us. Louder and louder, hell-ishly so. My chest thrummed, pounding with fear.

In my arms, the boy jerked straight up, stiff as an ironing board. His eyes rolled back into his skull. Spittle bubbled at his mouth and drew down his chin.

Madder than hell, the earth pounded. The heels of my boots shook, tremoring up into my molars.

Thrum…thump…thump…

The sound of a giant in the cornfield, racing toward us, ready to bring down his Paul Bunyan ax to cleave us in two.

Thump…thump…tump…

"It's too *late!*" The boy's eyes remained locked into his head. His voice climbed to shriller heights. "He's coming!"

I wanted to grab his shoulders, shake some sense into his head. Tell him everything would be all all right. Truth be told, though, it would've been a lie, a parental lie. Every bit as terrified as him, I knew we had to skedaddle. *Now.* His hand in mine felt cold as a winter's day, but I clung onto him regardless. Unsure which way to go, lost in the cornstalk maze, I whirled in a panic-driven circle, swinging the boy with me. Because whatever approached seemed to be coming from every direction, an army of beasts now.

I picked a dirt row, any old row, and wrenched the boy behind me.

Exploding footfalls drew closer, louder. Behind me, the boy murmured, crying nonsense. Next to us, stalks tumbled and crashed.

Tump…thump…thump…

Louder now, heart-bursting, bladder-pushing closer.

Like an arrow shot straight into my heart, a scream arose. One the likes of nothing I'd ever heard before. And living in a funeral home, I've heard lots and lots of mournful screams.

I let go of the boy's cold, cold hand. Clamped my hands over my ears.

One last blast of wind knifed down our path, targeted me. Lifted me off my feet and tossed me into the cornstalks. Woozy, I shook my head, sat up.

The wind stopped. As did the screaming. No more crazy, thunderous footfalls either. Absolute silence.

Likewise, the boy had vanished.

On sea-faring legs, I managed to get up. For the longest time, I stood still. And listened. Other than the banging of my heart into my ears, I heard nothing. In fact, the entire night had stilled, quieter than…well, quieter than death.

In a loud, hoarse whisper, I called for the boy. Poked around the field a bit looking for him. No sign, no trace, nothing out of the ordinary other than a few trampled stalks.

As if the boy had never existed, and maybe he hadn't either.

Folks always say life is different in Peculiar County. More than ever, I suspect death is, too.

Chapter Two

"Morning, Dad." At the kitchen table, our usual morning ritual, I dragged a chair out and sat down. "How'd you sleep?"

"Like an angel."

Well, I didn't rightly know how angels slept, found it strange Dad referenced a celestial being seeing as how he didn't put much stock into whatever came out of the Bible. In his line of work, his controversial beliefs made for some mighty uncomfortable business meetings. Of course, everyone in town knew Oscar Caldwell's beliefs, hardly a secret. Yet, he always provided practiced comfort to the bereaved, gave appropriate lip service to an afterlife when the need arose.

"What about you, Dibs? How'd you sleep?" Judging by Dad's hangdog, tired smile, I reckoned he hadn't heard my late-night outing. Frankly, I was half-convinced it'd been a nightmare myself.

"Just fine."

"I made breakfast for you." Dad peered over his newspaper and nodded toward the two cereal boxes on the table: Shredded Wheat and Raisin Bran. Dad liked regularity in his humor just as he did in his morning constitutionals.

I spilled some Shredded Wheat into a bowl. "Dad… Did you hear anything last night?"

"Hmm?" The paper came down. Folded neatly, set aside on the table. "Heard anything? Did something happen I should know about?" Behind his dark-rimmed glasses, his eyes fluttered, his confused look when logic failed him.

"No. Reckon I just had a bad dream."

"That's all those spooky books and movies you like. You know I've warned you about them."

Dad didn't truly disapprove of my penchant for all things eerie and otherworldly in entertainment, not really. After all, he was always the first to point out the spooky movies playing at the Starlight. Sometimes I suspect he says things just 'cause that's the way parents are expected to act.

Since he appeared to be in a particularly chatty mood this morning, I decided to test potentially disturbing waters.

"Dad, what do you know about the Saunders next door?"

Dad's brow scrunched up. I knew the look, every wrinkle tucked with concern. He sighed. "Why are you asking about them?"

"Well, you always say asking questions is a good thing. About things I don't understand." He gave a stiff nod. "A while ago, you told me I should steer clear of the Saunders 'cause they're inhospitable. I was just wondering if that's the only reason."

His gaze dropped to the table. After several false starts and stutters, he found his words. "There's just…something not quite right about them, Dibs. You know how people in Peculiar County talk. I'm not one to gossip, but word is, some strange things befell the family years back."

"Like what?"

"It doesn't matter. It's just idle gossip. Nothing more. We Caldwells don't go in for that sort of thing. Still, it's always best to err on the side of caution. I'd give them wide berth."

In other words, end of discussion, the way adults finish uncomfortable conversations, satisfying only to themselves. Dad didn't usually react like that, education and enlightenment usually high on his agenda. Of course, considering his non-answer, I now deemed the Saunders' past well worth looking into.

Obviously wanting to tiptoe back into safer waters, Dad asked, "Dibs, can you take your bike to school? I've got a morning appointment."

"Dad, I usually ride my bike. Who died?"

"Hmm? Oh, ah…" He faltered, his mind elsewhere. "Missus Pedersen. Lived on the other side of town. With her son and his wife?"

I didn't know Mrs. Pedersen from Adam, but as small towns went, I'd heard of her. "Tell her loved ones I'm mighty sorry for their loss. How'd she pass?"

He cleared his throat. "Natural causes."

I don't reckon Dad put any more stock into "natural causes" leading to death than I do. Particularly in Peculiar County, where death comes a-knocking in an anything but natural manner.

* * *

Just over three miles provided a lengthy bike ride to Hangwell High, but I didn't mind one bit. Particularly on beautiful, crisp fall mornings. I enjoyed watching the evolution of the seasons, caught before the seasons traded out. Leaves burned orange, still clinging to mother trees. The air never smelled fresher, revitalized, change on the tip of the wind. Temperatures remained at a perfectly comfortable sixty degrees or so, the best sorta bike-riding weather.

At any given opportunity, I sped through town on my beautiful Raleigh bike. A gift from Dad on my twelfth birthday, I maintained it in prime condition, all slick straight lines and a healthy, rich aqua color (none of that sissy pink stuff for me, thank you very much). I loved showing it off, riding the country roads, careening through downtown (comprised of three blocks of stores, a café, the lone bar in town, and the cinema). On my rides, especially the leisurely ones, I learned a lot—some might call it eavesdropping—about Hangwell, Kansas, and its inhabitants. For such a small town, Hangwell surely did harbor its fair share of secrets.

That morning before I set out, I walked my bike past the Saunders' farm. Similar to our homestead, a long gravel drive set their home off the road a ways.

His ball cap tipped ever so slightly over one eye, I recognized Devin

Meyers. In that peculiar, waddly way of his, back and forth and a bit ducky, he sauntered toward his barn—a red one, of course. When it came to barns, I don't believe I'd ever laid eyes on any other color than red, an unexplainable small town law, I wouldn't doubt.

On the porch sat Devin's sister, Evelyn, still as a portrait in her rocking chair. Always dressed to the nines, Evelyn Saunders looked fabulous in her movie star dresses and perfectly rendered make-up. I knew for a fact she rarely left home, so I'd always wondered who she dolled up for. Maybe she had a crush on Odie Smith, the postman, the only other person I'd ever seen come within spitting distance of her farm.

I hopped my bike, ready to venture forward. As an afterthought, I raised my hand in a forbidden wave to Mrs. Saunders.

Took a while, my hand just stuck up in the air, but I finally won Evelyn Saunders's attention. As if it hurt, she worked that hand up, gave it a little shake. And I moved on.

For a good portion of a mile, I bumped across the gravel, dust chasing me like smoke from a forest fire. At the intersection of Oak Grove and our unnamed road, I slid my bike into a sidewinder stop. Pebbles spat up, dinging against the bike's frame. This time of morning, I pretty near had the roads to myself, or at least pretended to, showing off a bit for my imaginary, adoring friends.

True friends tended not to last long, wore out faster than cheap sneakers. Can't say if it was a bug in my personality or something else, but I suspected Dad's business played a part in my loner status. Snotty girls at school tended to flock toward kids born of bankers, pharmacists, and a whole lotta farmers, rather than taking up with the mortician's daughter. Weirder than a two-headed cow, I was fine with the whole pecking order of my school universe. Deep down, I knew it wouldn't last forever, knew things would change once I left Hangwell for college. The silly little girls weren't my cuppa tea anyhow.

And I always had Dad. Everyone knows family's forever—or at least what amounts to forever in terms of a lifetime.

Besides Mom, of course.

After checking both ways for traffic—not that I couldn't fly by most of the old pick-ups without breaking a sweat—I wheeled onto Oak Grove and really set my tires free. Recklessly, I careened down the hill, my short-cropped hair flicking up at the sides. I used the momentum, built on the speed necessary to mount the upcoming hill.

Up ahead lay downtown, the heart of Hangwell. Main Street, of course, was where the money-makers, the real business contingent of Hangwell, took up roost. Bank president Terrence T. Thomason (his father a master of alliteration) was bent over in front of his bank's door, keys in hand, opening up for the day. Alternately the most well-liked and most reviled man in town, folks often didn't know where they stood with the banker. Like the wind, he could come calling either way, fore-closing at a whim or handing out a loan on his more fair-weather days.

I whizzed by him, tossed off a wave and a howdy. "Morning, Mister Thomason!"

He started, straightened. His impressive belly kept him centered, all things balanced. He hollered, "Morning, Dibby! Careful how you ride!"

A grim reaper of the banking trade, Mr. Thomason hadn't seen fit to come calling on Dad yet, our death business healthy and doing just fine. I imagined the bank and our funeral home would probably be the last two businesses standing in Hangwell, even after the advent of an atomic bomb.

I zipped down the street, past *Carol's*—the finest and only diner in town—and flew by the aptly named *Tavern*, closed until late afternoon. As one might imagine, the *Tavern* had proven to be a strong spot of con-tention amongst the townsfolk: the Baptists wanted it shuttered perma-nently and the Catholics didn't mind it as long as it stayed closed on Sun-days. Even though the two reigning groups of religion both followed the peaceful teachings of Jesus, they couldn't get along worth a spit, more than once nearing fisticuffs. Regardless, the *Tavern* was here to stay. A loyal group of farmers—led by crickety ol' Hy Thurgood—saw to that, keeping the bar's doors open unto the wee hours.

The competing churches, Hangwell Baptist and The Holy Mary Shrine of God Catholic Church, sat catty-wampus across from one another making for some interesting showdowns come Sundays once both churches let out.

The post office flashed by, as did the Hangwell Public Library (a place where I hung my boots on many a day). Ever regal, the Starlight Cinema stood tall and proud, vigilant over the rest of the two-level brick and glass buildings. Its marquee—unlit and less glossy by day—proudly heralded the upcoming *The Curse of the Fly*, the third in the series, already planned on my agenda come opening night.

Next to the cinema stood the town's sole hotel, The Lewis and Clark. Lots of folks doubted either Lewis or Clark ever set toe into the dusty, two-story establishment, but try telling that to the proprietors, the crabby-as-could-be Clarks. Harold Clark even claimed to be a descendant of his famous namesake, another point of controversy. Still, visitors didn't have much choice should they choose to stay over in Hangwell.

Rodney Simonson, Hangwell's pharmacist, busied himself sweeping off his drug store's stoop. Dressed in his form-hugging, white pharmacist's smock, he turned and swirled with his broom, practicing his much-bally-hooed prowess on the dance floor. I'd had many an encounter with Mr. Simonson, usually with gosh-awful-tasting results. He loved to ladle out syrups with gruesome ingredients. Still, as Dad said, he's a man you wanted on your side should the fever claim you. In my younger years, I fretted over that, wondering just how in the world things could possibly get worse than Mr. Simonson's latest concoction.

"Morning, Mister Simonson!"

"That it is, Dibby." He maintained his typical sleepy monotone, better suited for Dad's line of work. Maybe they were in secret collusion, Mr. Simonson hastening Dad's flow of business with his vile line of prescriptions.

The combination police and fire station sat on the very edge of down-town, strategically placed to watch over the entirety of Hangwell. While strange occurrences and unexplained disappearances were all too common in Hangwell, our actual crime rate stayed low. Things as they were, there didn't appear to be much call for more than Sheriff Grigsby and Fire Chief Wakuna. More often than not, they'd trade hats, help one another out in a pinch. Other than tending to an occasional rowdy good time down at the *Tavern*, most of their job consisted of strolling downtown or checking into the odd animal mutilation. And eating lots of pastries at *Carol's Diner*.

On the other side of Main, on Hollow Crick Road, smaller stores and businesses, a service station, a seed-and-feed store (the porch always full of big men with little ambition), Doc Bracket's little office, and a couple of other odds and ends comprised the rest of downtown.

On occasion, I'd ride down Hollow Crick, too, but nothing gave me greater satisfaction than watching Main Street wake up.

I left the business district, came upon my old grade school, the un-imaginatively titled *Main Street Grade School*. The school opened up an hour after the high school did, so the parking lot and the playground sat nearly empty. Except for Odie Smith, the one constant in my morning rides.

Odie swung on the swing set, his legs lifting, folding. The bars wob-bled above him, the chains rattled in his hands. Not fat by any means—maintaining good shape via his daily postal delivery routes—the swing set nonetheless hitched a fit beneath his adult weight. As always, he held his breakfast sack in his lap, never straying from his two muffins—corn and blueberry—purchased from *Carol's Diner* the night before.

Like his name, Odie made for an odd sight, but the townsfolk let him be, pretty much a tradition.

"How's breakfast, Mister Smith?" I yelled.

"Never better! And I told you a thousand times, Dibby… Call me Odie!"

Mr. Smith was the only adult who didn't stand on tradition by hav-ing kids refer to him by his proper name, but I just couldn't bring myself to do it. Maybe when I turned sixteen in a couple of months.

The high school just ahead, right before Main Street petered out into endless farmlands, I pushed myself faster. The school bell clanged. Kids separated from mulling about the flagpole and sitting on the front steps. I burst onto school property, skidded to a stop. Behind the front fence, I stashed my bike into the rack and ran into school before the second bell rang.

Just in time, the way I always did it.

* * *

As the class-bell triggered, I slipped into my seat. Mrs. Hopkins favored me with a sour eye. Wrinkles wadded up her face, pruned too long in the sun. One of the class cut-ups had once likened Mrs. Hopkins to an old tree's core, with each wrinkle representing another year she'd spent teaching. Personally, I had no foul with my tenth-grade teacher, even though I suspected she nurtured a deep-down dislike for me because I didn't dress like the other girls.

That sat just fine with me. Rocks settled in all paths from time to time.

As usual, Mrs. Hopkins led us through the *Lord's Prayer*, something Dad had ranted against for years, an irritating sore spot to him. To avoid a level of embarrassment I never wanted to visit, I constantly calmed Dad down before he stormed my school in outrage.

Mrs. Hopkins stood, cleared her throat like a grinding tractor engine. "Quiet, class!" When my classmates ignored her, she turned a fine shade of red. "I said *quiet!*" Her ruler whacked down hard on her desk, her third one this school year. Her methods were effective, though. Fear tamed even the football goofs.

"Today, we have a new student joining us. Principal Brining is currently—"

The door opened, slammed with a loud *thwack*. A long, lanky boy slouched in, cheeky in sunglasses. He stood, surveyed the class, slowly taking us all in like he'd never seen such a strange sight.

But he conjured a new sight, one dreamed up in Hollywood.

A turtleneck sweater hugged him, lucky garment. His mop-top of brown hair drooped onto his collar, over his sunglasses, just like one of the Beatles. Faded jeans fit tight, then ballooned into bell bottoms.

He dang well knew how to enter a room. No one said anything, even Mrs. Hopkins was at a loss for words. Classroom fashion styles—pencil skirts and tapered slacks for the girls; checkered shirts, slim trousers, and hooded pullovers for the boys—had just been rendered extinct. A new breed walked the earth, an absolutely dreamy one.

Granted, the pickings in Hangwell had always been slim at best, but this was the first time I'd ever immediately gone head-over-heels for a boy; a bell-clanging, siren-whistling crush that made me feel stupid and silly. Part of it was the boy's freshness, I'm sure, not a bit stale. I knew this, intellectually I did, yet I still couldn't repress my loosey-goosey urges. I scrunched down in my seat, suddenly very self-aware of my overalls and plaid shirt.

A few of the girls, including the inexplicably popular and monstrous Suzette, went aflutter. Excited whispers bubbled over into titters, a bunch of chickens het up by the wolf at their door.

Appearing on the verge of a heart attack, Mrs. Hopkins strode across the classroom. Her ankles cracked in metronome precision until she stopped in front of the new boy. She yanked off his sunglasses. "Master Mackleby, I presume."

"You presume right." Without his sassy sunglasses, he looked even cuter. Eyes as brown as caramel, they'd easily melt in the sun. He grinned, displayed a smoker's yellowed teeth, but I reckoned even Adonis had a flaw.

"We do *not* wear sunglasses inside the classroom, Master Mackleby." Mrs. Hopkins snapped back to her desk, deposited the glasses into her drawer of collectables. "Class, this is James Mackleby. He'll be joining us for the near future. Please have a seat…next to Miss Caldwell."

Of course, the seat next to me was always vacant, which never bothered me one iota. I rearranged my preferences, straightened up a bit in my chair.

Fluidly, James slid into the next desk, everything about him understated and easy. He looked around, his gaze eventually landing on me. Caught me red-handed staring at him. I jumped, nearly yelped, and fled to the safety of my English book. But his gravitational pull proved magnetic, same as that ol' moth drawn to his light-bulb doom.

When I dared look his way again, James flashed the prettiest color of yellow teeth I'd ever laid eyes on.

And I do believe I flooded redder than Mrs. Hopkins on a sun-baked day.

* * *

School proved to be particularly trying. Especially with James—*James:
even his name sounded like a poet's*—next to me, his charisma smoldering, burning the edges of my thoughts. I felt his heat as surely as I did the last hot
days of summer.

As soon as the final bell mercifully released me from my suffering, I
made a beeline straight to the bike rack. I dared one last look over my
shoulder. The wolves had moved in on the meat, Suzette leading the
pack. Hungry, they circled James. Suzette toyed with her blonde locks,
tilting her head in that dopey, beyond-lazy way that every boy found
alluring.

I'd almost made my escape, vowing to put a little effort into my
wardrobe tomorrow, when a voice called out, "Hey!" A rich, deep voice
of culture from lands far away.

Oh my gosh, oh my gosh, oh my gosh…

I stood, straddling my bike, feet anchored to the ground, head shooting for the clouds. My mouth hung open, ready to catch flies. "You talking to me?"

"Sure am." James broke from the pack, jogged toward me. Just like
a movie star, he swept his hair aside, slipped his sunglasses on. Stroked
the handles of my bike. "Boss bike."

I didn't know from "boss," but I intuited it as a good thing. "Thanks.
It was a birthday gift. You know…until I drive." Wishful thinking, of
course. But I thought it sounded kinda mature.

"That's mine over there." He pointed to a road-beaten, black bike,
patched together with rust and stickers.

Without trying to offend regarding his eyesore of transportation, I
offered, "I reckon it is."

He laughed. "It's kinda a wreck, I know. I'm James." He stuck out his
hand, took off his sunglasses to show who he really was. A move I much
appreciated.

I accepted his handshake, gave it a firm up and down, the way Dad
had taught me to do regardless of gender. His grip felt warm and nice. "I

know. I'm Dibby. Dibby Caldwell."

"Yeah, I caught your last name earlier. But 'Dibby'? That's kinda… weird."

"I suppose it is, as I've never met another Dibby. I've always suspected my folks made a mistake on my birth certificate. Meant to call me Debby. But the name just stuck."

"I'm glad it did. I mean, your name. I like it."

"Thanks." The boy was full of compliments. Good manners suggested I return some, but I couldn't, not without unleashing a vapid, giggly teen. "So…why're you here?"

"Finer learning, I guess."

"No…I mean, why'd you move to Hangwell?"

"Oh…well, Dad's an agriculturalist. An expert on mechanized milking or something dumb like that. The government hired him to run a milking parlor in Durham. That's the next—"

"Yep. The next town over."

"Yeah. But there wasn't anything in Durham. I mean, no schools, no available homes, not even a hotel. So Dad packed us up, moved us to Dullsville, Kansas."

That struck a nerve. Hangwell may be many things, but dull didn't suit it. "That's my town you're disregarding."

His hands went up. "Hey, everything's copacetic. I didn't mean anything by it. It's just…well, hell's bells, we're staying at The Lewis and Clark Hotel until Mom can find us a house. Place is the pits. And some damn dog keeps barking all night. Guess I'm tired."

"Welcome to Hangwell. And it 'pears you've met Mittens."

"Mittens? That's a cat's name."

"Not this critter. It's a dog. Well, I s'pose I should say it used to be a dog. Now it's the dog's ghost haunting the hotel."

A slow grin hauled James's cheekbones high. "Come on… I'm no rube. I'm from Los Angeles! There's no such thing as ghosts. Especially a ghost dog. With a cat's name."

"Say what you will, but there's a lot about Hangwell you don't know. Mittens belonged to Harold Clark's grandfather. You probably met Mister

Clark?"

"The guy with the bushels of hair sticking out his ears?"

"That'd be him all right. Anyway, legend has it, Mittens—a Dober-man by breed—used to bark up a storm day and night at the hotel. Just a-barking away at nothing, not a thing folks could see anyway. Closed doors, empty halls, as if he saw something that wasn't there. Then one day Mittens up and disappeared." I snapped my fingers for effect. "But folks could still hear Mittens barking away at night, fit to raise the dead. They could never find him, though. Just heard his barks coming from the walls and the basement and the attic. Everywhere at the same time, yet no-where. To this day, folks hear him bark. Me? I never heard ol' Mittens, but that's more than likely 'cause I never had reason to stay over at the Lewis and Clark. I'm surely not gonna disregard the legend outta hand."

James's striking, yet dull eyes finally alit with a eureka moment. "I saw the dog's photo in the lobby! Big framed photo. I just thought it was a—what's it called?—double exposure. Because I could see right through the dog."

"That'd be Mittens."

"I'm still not buying it. Is this some kinda town initiation or some-thing?" He shook his shaggy head, not yet ready to accept the peculiar side of Peculiar County. "You pulling my leg?"

He needed a tour guide, and it appeared that particular job would have to fall on me. "Hangwell's no ordinary town, James. Your education's gon-na have to travel further than Missus Hopkins's class."

"You gonna play teacher?" His sunglasses went back on. So did his arrogant—and altogether irresistible—bad-boy smile.

"Reckon I am." Daring, at least for me. I sped away on my bike, teas-ing him, grinning, inviting him to chase me.

Chapter Three

We got sidetracked. Headed toward downtown, James fell behind. On Hollow Crick Road—just one block north of Main—he hollered after me. I wheeled my Raleigh around. Out of breath, he'd stopped, now walking his bike up the gravel drive between the fortress-like oak trees guarding the cemetery.

I turned back and rode into the wooded cemetery grounds. James had staked out a piece of shade, flat on his back beneath the "Judge's Tree." Plum tuckered out, his chest heaved up and down, one hand gripping the wheel of his carelessly slung bike, the other shielded over his eyes.

"I'm not used to tough bike rides in Los Angeles," he said.

"Spoiled rotten city slicker." Carefully, I laid my Raleigh down, far from the Judge's Tree. Even though I wasn't prone to superstition—regardless of what happened last night—it never hurt to be cautious.

I sat down next to James, keeping a leery eye on the Judge's Tree at all times.

He reached into his sock, pulled out a beaten package of Lark cigarettes. Before he could strike a match, I snatched the cigarette away from him.

"Hey, what're you doing?"

"Saving you."

"From what?"

I sighed. The boy seemed several loads light in the head. "First, smoking's bad for you."

"That's not what the commercials say." He scoffed, swept his hair out of his eyes, a rebel looking for a cause.

"Have you ever seen someone die from cigarettes?"

He thought about it. "No. Have you?"

"Yup. Seen a lot of dead bodies."

"Really? What a gasser! How? Where?"

Although most kids my age find Dad's vocation distasteful, James appeared far from being like most kids. "I live in a funeral home. Dad's a mortician."

"He makes dead people pretty and ready for burial and stuff?" I nodded. "Cool! Can I come over?"

In the past, Dad had been particularly touchy about allowing me into his basement workshop, let alone any acquaintances, few as they may be. On the rare occasions Dad had allowed me into the forbidden basement, he'd cleaned up ahead of time, nary a corpse nor drop of blood on display. Disappointing and boring hardly did it justice.

So, in the spirit of exploration, late at night I'd had to venture forth on my own to view Dad's latest works in progress. Of course, Dad had always made a strong case against the perils of smoking, but once I snuck down and saw ol' Jeb Wells's green and emaciated corpse—a victim of smoking cancer—laid out and open like a human book, I became a believer in the health hazards of smoking.

As much as the thought of inviting someone into my world—especially someone like James—sounded mighty enticing, I put my foot down. "Dad doesn't let me near his work lab. He dang sure won't let you visit."

"Come on… Please?"

'Course, he had me at begging, his brown, puppy-dog eyes hard to ignore. "Let me think on it."

His eyes slipped from sleepy to red hot. "Man, that'd be a gasser!" To celebrate his perceived victory, he stuck another cigarette between his lips.

"Uh-uh, nope." Again, I snagged it. This time I snapped it in half.

"Aah! Why'd you *do* that?"

"I told you, I'm trying to save you."

"Everybody else smokes. Just go with the flow, baby."

I tried to ignore how he'd addressed me as "baby," I truly did. No one'd ever called me that before. In fact, I'd never heard anyone speak quite like James before, his hip language lifted from beatniks on TV programs.

"Not only is it bad for your health, you could get in big trouble smoking here in Hangwell."

"Yeah? Like how?"

"Sheriff Grigsby, for one. He doesn't much cotton to kids acting like adults. Besides, you're breaking the law. You'll end up in jail, and I don't mean maybe."

"Ahhh, I'm not afraid of the heat."

"You haven't met our Sheriff, then. And you oughta respect where you are. If you insist on smoking, I'd be real careful where you do it."

"What? Here?" As if just noticing his surroundings for the first time, James looked around. His jaw near loosened once he saw the Hangwell Cemetery 100 feet or so beyond the Judge's Tree. "This place is really gone, Dibs! I love cemeteries!"

"First lesson, look above you. Best respect the Judge's Tree, if you know what's good for you. Don't litter. And for Pete's sake, don't smoke around it."

James looked up at the skeletal remains of the Judge's Tree. Since I'd been knee-high to my dad, I'd never seen the old elm sprout any leaves. The gnarled trunk had three central knots: two blank eyes and a silent, ever-screaming, ever-tortured mouth. Arms branched out, bent like elbows. Smaller fingers achingly reached for the sky as if a bandit had poked a gun at the tree's back. While the Judge's Tree remained barren of foliage, the old branches never rotted or fell off, either. Still alive, just not very happy about it, I reckoned.

"Yeah, big deal. It looks like the pits. So what?"

"You're looking at the tree that gave our town its name. It's called the Judge's Tree. Used to be Hangwell's hanging tree."

"Cool!"

"Ol' Judge Wilbur—no one's ever told me if that's his first or last name, you know how adults can be—ruled this town before it was known as Hangwell. He was a hanging judge, a fearsome one. Judge Wilbur, he didn't see color, not like most folks did back in the day. Well, I s'pose he did, but it didn't matter two hoots and a holler what color folks were to him. Judge Wilbur hung 'em all up on this very tree. You name 'em—bandits, gunslingers, Mexicans, coloreds, folks he didn't like, folks he tolerated just fine—he hung 'em all. Set some sorta record in the Midwest from what I understand. He hid behind his robes, claimed he wanted justice for Hangwell's townsfolk. Maybe he truly did. Surely, he did, even if just a bit. But folks say that after a while he developed a real taste for killing. Enjoyed watching the men sway, wetting their britches like toddlers. Liked hanging a lot.

"Anyway, when he wasn't busy hanging folks—and he hung 'em well, hence our town's name—people say he was the meanest ol' coot to ever walk the prairie. Rail thin, wild gray hair strung out like cotton candy, bush-like eyebrows, a nose as big as a hawk's beak, he bullied his way into town leadership. Suggested the name Hangwell. It stuck like molasses."

"So what happened to him?"

"Story goes late one night some ol' drunk found him hanging from his own tree. Tongue out like a dog, eyes rolled up into egg-whites. Just swinging in the breeze. And they say the knots in the tree took on a different look. The mouth changed into a smile. Happy to welcome Judge Wilbur among its victims."

"Wow… But the tree's not smiling now," said James.

"That's 'cause the Judge's body went missing. The town undertaker had him all boxed up and ready to send off the next morning for burial. But that morning, the Judge was nowhere to be found. They never did find him."

A slow smile crawled across James's face. "C'mon, you're pulling my leg again. You don't really believe all this ghost stuff, right?"

Therein lay the question I'd been pondering since last night.

"I don't know what I believe, tell you the truth. Some folks believe in God, and that's just fine. Some believe in other things that have no explanation. My dad believes in things only science can set right."

"Geez. Sounds like my old man."

"C'mere." I got up, walked over to the cemetery. We entered the graveled walkway, stone teeth grinding up the sides. Crooked tombstones jagged up as if the dead were mighty restless beneath. I stopped in front of an old, rusted, chest-high spiked fence. Whether intended to keep trespassers out or the dead within, I reckon I didn't care to know.

"Everyone in here was hung by the Judge." I took a moment, respectful of the dead. "That's why it's gated off from the rest of the cemetery."

"'Cause people were ashamed of the Judge hanging them all?" asked James.

"Heck no! Folks around here just don't wanna disturb all this dead riffraff. Keep 'em dead. Last thing they want is a buncha dead bandits and ne'er-do-wells running rampant through town."

"And they believe the dead can come back? Has everyone here flipped their lids?"

"No. But folks don't like taking risks. Not when there's so much talk. Because where there's a lotta talk, there's a tendency of a kernel of truth behind it. You go outta your way to walk beneath a ladder?"

James shook his head, quietly taking it all in.

Beyond the fence, I saw something that didn't quite sit right by me. I unlatched the gate and entered the guarded section. James followed, no longer so eager for the macabre. "See this here?" I picked up a nearly skull-sized rock that'd tumbled off a mound covering one of the gravesites. "Folks placed all these rocks on top of the graves for a reason. Now, I'm not saying it's a good reason, or that it holds its weight in water. None of that, not for me to say. But sometimes tradition's all a gal can put her faith into."

I replaced the rock, careful not to tip the rest. The notion struck me the rock might've been disturbed due to forces beyond our ken, but I didn't mention that outlandish fear aloud. No sense scaring James away. With a backward step, I dusted my hands on my overalls.

We left the hanged men's cemetery and strolled through the outlying field. A comfortable horse's tail shake away from the ghosts—real or imagined—we sat. Although James appeared not ready to accept Hangwell's strange and colorful history, I had a real urge—a solid hankering—to burden someone with what happened to me last night.

I told him the story of the boy in the cornfield. Ordinarily, I'm a tight-lipped cuss, keeping everything bottled up inside. But for some reason, I felt I could trust James.

To his benefit, he didn't neigh like a horse. "So…you're telling me the kid was a ghost?"

"Didn't say that at all." I shrugged. "I'm just recommending you keep an open mind in Peculiar County. I don't care how you city boys do it; things are different here."

"There's some sorta explanation. I mean, other than the kid being a ghost." James had cut out his hep-cat patter, clearly set straight by my tale.

"You sound like my dad. Guess you're a scientist's kid, too."

"Ah, my old man lives in Dullsville. But your old man sounds really hep. He's got the best job in the world."

"He's still a dad. Sometimes he understands, sometimes he doesn't. But at least he tries." I stood. "Earlier you asked me if I believe in ghosts. Truth of the matter is I'm not quite ready to pin a tale on any ol' donkey just yet. But one thing I rightly do believe in is evil, nothing supernatural about it." I spread my hands wide. "We got evil here in Hangwell. Lots of it just boiling beneath the surface, ready to spill over." I called out the Judge's Tree. "And just as I'm sure as shooting ol' Judge Wilbur was evil to his rotten core, I think something bad…*real* evil happened to that boy in the Saunders' corn field. I aim to find out what that was. 'Cause I will not abide by evil, particularly against children. Not if I can do anything to stop it. So…you gonna sit there all day in your fancy bell-bottoms and smoke your big city cigarettes, or you gonna get up and help me find out who that boy was?"

He jumped to his feet, grinned like a cat who'd stumbled across a bird's nest. "Homework can wait."

* * *

Next to the stone gargoyle perched up beside the Hangwell Public Library steps, James stopped and slung his bike to the ground. Ever vigilant, ol' Stoney (as he'd been called forever) appeared scornful, his face knotted with irritation at those folks who didn't heed library rules. Or so library lore would have it.

"Cool," said James. "Is he trying to scare people away from reading?"

I parked my bike in the rack behind the sidewalk. "He doesn't stop me from coming," I said. "I figure ol' Stoney for a saint of reading maybe."

"I dunno. Something's keeping people outta here. Don't see a whole lotta cars."

True enough. Folks didn't visit the Hangwell Public Library nearly enough, which suited me just fine. I had the pick of the litter of books.

"Now, don't hang your jaw when you meet Yvette and Miriam." Ahead of James, I raced up the stairs, giving no further explanation. Some things make more sense experienced.

The high ceilings never ceased to inspire awe, something more apt for a fancy church in Italy. Slightly dropped lights provided dim illumination. The second floor—not much more than a narrow walkway ringed with books and a railing—stood high and empty; my favorite area, the fiction section. Old books smell musty to most folks, I reckon, but to me the odor promised grand adventure and visits to unexplored worlds.

As watchful as ol' Stoney, Yvette and Miriam stood side by side behind the front counter, one thing you could always count on in Hangwell.

"Good afternoon, Dibby." Yvette didn't smile. The Sooter sisters rarely did. Best you could expect was a nod of acknowledgment. In keeping with tradition, Miriam, her hand gripping her sister's arm, nodded.

"Afternoon, Miss and Miss Sooter. This here's my friend, James. He's new to school."

Clearly uncomfortable, James sorta shuffled, stuck his hands in his pockets. I suppose that Big City living didn't quite prepare him for everything after all. Eventually, he managed, "Um, hi."

Miriam gave her sister's arm a couple squeezes, then a short pinch.

"Yes, the Mackleby boy," said Yvette. "We'd heard your family had arrived." With a finger, she pushed up her dark glasses, and I rightly hoped to high heaven they'd stay put. Once, and that was more than enough, I saw her without her dark spectacles. When I returned *Huckleberry Finn* one day late, she whipped off those glasses and leaned over the counter. Her eyes were solid white, unnaturally snowy. Those unseeing, white globes seared a brand of shame onto my soul. Never again did I return a book late.

James said nothing, just looked at the sisters in turn. I struggled to keep a boot-kicking grin from surfacing.

On the other hand, Miriam gandered at James for all she was worth. She tapped out a secret code, one known only to the Sooter sisters, on her blind sister's arm.

"Miriam wants to know when the rest of your family will visit the library, James." Yvette tilted her head, caught James in her blind, yet uncannily accurate, sights. Although blind, sometimes I suspected Yvette possessed better vision than an eagle.

"Well…my dad's pretty busy with the dairy project and—"

"I *see*."

And I dang near thought she could see James all squirming and roping a finger around his turtleneck's collar.

"Very well then," sniffed Yvette, "what can we do for you today, Dibby?"

I could tell the sisters had already cast James aside as a book-avoiding heathen and focused their attention solely on me. Although Miriam never spoke (and whether she physically couldn't or just chose not to provide gossip for the phone party lines across town), her eyes spoke heaps. Today, they flowered big and watery and full of more empathy than a convent of nuns.

"Well… I have a different matter than usual to tend to today. I—"

"Dibby…" Yvette leaned over the counter. Her glasses slipped, just a bit, but enough to stiffen my spine in panic. "Have you lost your reading copy of *Frankenstein*?"

"No, ma'am, not at all! I'm nearly done with it! And I'll be sure to have it back a day early!"

"That's fine, Dibby, that's just fine." Miriam nodded in agreement. "There's nothing worse than a tardy reader, isn't that right, Miriam?" Again, Miriam agreed.

Frankly, I could think of a right good number of things that might be considered worse than bringing a book back late, but I knew better than to argue with the keepers of the castle.

"So, then…what is it today, Dibby? We finally received a copy of *To Kill a Mockingbird*, along with several new mysteries."

"That sounds swell. But, honestly, I'm more interested in some town history. Of Hangwell."

Usually the library keepers enforced a quiet-as-Miriam standard, the sisters on guard against uncouth snickers and whispers. But today, my request dropped an eerie, total silence over the entire building. Silent as a morgue, and I should know.

"I…see." This time Yvette didn't sound so much like she *did* see. "And what kind of town history are you looking for, Dibby? And may we ask why?"

Honestly, I'd never met with such inquisitiveness from the Sooter sisters. In my years of visiting, they'd bent over backwards to suggest books, help me root out things I might like, even daring to recommended books some might consider more adult than my age-set. But now I felt like I'd stumbled onto a hornet's nest and the sisters wanted to stir it up. I couldn't quite put my finger on why, but I figured it best not to tell the sisters the entire truth.

"We're working on a school project. Digging into Hangwell's past events and history. Right, James?" Dumbfounded, James didn't help, didn't utter a word. "I'm looking for something fairly recent, maybe the last ten to twenty years?"

Miriam narrowed her usually friendly eyes, glanced sideways at her sister. Through a series of taps and squeezes, she communicated a message. And I rightly didn't believe it to be of the friendly sort.

"I haven't heard of any such school project, Dibby." Yvette set her already hairline lips even tighter. "Surely, I would've heard of such a project. I think there's more here than meets the eye." As if in threat—a dang terrifying one—Yvette slowly reached for the bridge of her glasses.

"No, ma'am." I felt like the Sooters had inherited ol' Judge Wilbur's hanging robes and I'd been sentenced to death. Of course, I didn't want to lie to them, not one bit, but I'd already jumped into the deep end of things and couldn't dog-paddle out. "It's an extra credit project, Miss Sooter," I said. "That's probably why the other kids haven't been at it yet."

"Why, Dibby Caldwell, since when did you need extra credit?" The tone of Yvette's voice lightened a bit. So did the slant of her sister's eyebrows.

"You know me," I answered. "I'm just fixing to get the best high school transcript possible."

Academics before everything else, the Sooter sisters smiled. "We always had you pegged as a bright one, Dibby," said Yvette. "One who—*ahem*—shouldn't resort to words such as 'fixing.'"

"Yes, ma'am," I muttered.

A natural response I positively couldn't stand, my cheeks flushed red, hotter than bare feet on asphalt. The thought of James seeing me this way really flame-broiled my cheeks. I glanced at him, quickly turned away. Grinning that grin, the one he wore so easily, he wouldn't take his eyes off me.

"All right, then…" This time, Yvette grabbed Miriam's arm. Together, the sisters walked along the counter to the swinging gate. "Follow us."

James and I followed the sisters, hustling to catch up. They moved as one, a three-legged race, in perfect unity. Years of experience had taught them the lay of the land well. Even with their handicaps, they effortlessly swam around book carts, scooted errant chairs beneath tables, picked up fallen books. Far in the back of the building, they led us to a door, one I'd never noticed before.

Periodicals had been painted onto the rippled glass inset into the door. Side by side, the women pushed through the door, and we followed. Now the smell of ancient paper nearly set my stomach to roiling, no longer a nice, inviting odor at all. I felt like an explorer opening a long-closed, suffocating tomb. Stacks and stacks of yellowed newspaper were stuffed into nearly a dozen wooden bookshelves, the shelves sagging mightily beneath the weight. Along the wall, thick binders lined more shelves.

The sheer amount of information available threatened to overwhelm me and send me screaming toward the simpler pleasures of fiction. I should've expected as much, though. Hangwell'd never been a simple little town.

"If you could narrow down the era, Dibby, we could point you in the right direction. Over here you'll find back issues of *The Hangwell Gazette*." Miriam displayed an animated arm as her sister directed. "Not sure how much history you'll garner from those, though. Not actual journalism in our opinions." They both sniffed, haughty as all get out. "Along the wall…" With a flourish, Miriam unrolled her arm. "…you'll find some of Hangwell's town records that we've managed to accumulate and preserve." Yvette tapped her chin. A frown drew down her mouth. "Unfortunately, they're a bit spotty at best. I'm afraid if you'd like a full recounting of our history, you may have to visit Town Hall. Although, since the fire a few years back, I'm afraid Mayor Hopkins says a lot of the official records have gone the way of decent music."

"This'll be fine, ladies. Thank you kindly," I said.

James just took it all in, his square shoulders sagging at the thought of the research ahead.

"Now, Dibby, I'm sure I don't have to tell you this, but unlike our loaner books, these records are one of a kind. You may not take any of these from the library." She stood akimbo, knuckles burrowing into her waist.

"I wouldn't think of it."

"As much as we'd like to stay and help, we've a very busy, busy day ahead of us." The women tittered for some unknown reason. "Please put everything back in the order you found it. Needless to say, be careful. Handle everything with delicate fingers. This is history that simply can*not* be replaced."

"I understand."

"Very well. Let us know if we can be of further assistance, Dibby." They turned on their sensible, flat shoes. "*James*." Yvette bid adieu to him in an icy voice, polar caps practically forming on the tip of her nose. The sisters breezed out the door.

"You can close your mouth now, James," I said. "Ain't very becoming."

James did as told. "Man! I thought I was gonna go ape! What's with—"

"Hush! The sisters have great hearing."

"Oh, sorry, yeah… But, c'mon, what's the story there?"

I shrugged, easiest shortcut to a long explanation. "They're sisters, of course. Been librarians for longer than anyone can remember, the way I hear it. Yvette's blind, Miriam doesn't speak. Together, they got more senses than you and me and the rest of the whole dang town."

"You mean…like, they have superpowers or something?"

"Or something. Look, you're new here, James. You got to start looking at things a bit differently than you're accustomed. You'll get used to it. Everyone does."

"I guess." Although he looked doubtful, flummoxed. "We're not really gonna look through all these papers, right? I mean, it'll take forever."

"You don't have to if you don't want to. But I'm gonna. 'Til I find what I'm looking for." I pulled down the closest paper, sat down at the center table, and began poring over the yellowed newsprint. With a light touch, I turned the pages, avoided ripping them down the folding points. Like James, I began to feel the futility of it all.

James sighed, grabbed a newspaper, sat down next to me. Did a fair share of grousing, too. "Dibby, do you even know what you're doing?"

"No. Doesn't mean I'm not gonna try. Shut your hole and look for anything Saunders related."

Endless farm reports, weather forecasts, town fair events, and the occasional passing of an elderly citizen provided much of the Gazette's keen eye for news. As much as it pained me to say so, James was right. Forever felt like a mighty long time.

"Geez Louise, Dibby, hasn't Hangwell ever heard of microfilm?"

"Reckon not. Or maybe the Sooter sisters don't want to change with the times. You get a lot of that in Hangwell, folks hanging on to the past."

"Huh. This is for the birds."

Boredom snatched the wind from his sails. He took to whipping the brittle pages harder, brisker, faster. His sighs grew louder and longer, similar to Mrs. Hopkins whenever she slapped down graded papers onto students' desks.

"So…one of the sisters said the mayor's name is Hopkins?" asked James.

"Yup."

"Is he related to our teacher?"

"Yup," I answered. "They're married. Turn to the paper's indicia."

"The what?"

"Turn to the inner page of the paper."

James did and read the minute accreditation out loud. "'Earl L. Hopkins: Editor-in-Chief.' Huh. The same as the mayor?"

"The very one. Mayor Hopkins is a man of many hats."

"I'll betcha he only prints peachy news about his mayoring."

I folded the paper, gave him a mighty strong stare-down. Although what James had said about Mayor Hopkins had been speculated upon many an evening during Dad's cocktail-fueled rants, Hangwell was still my town, and I didn't cotton to a newcomer from the Big City trying to cast aspersions about it.

"What? What'd I say?"

"You don't know beans about Hangwell. Or our mayor. Don't just assume stuff. It can whip back on you like a rattlesnake."

"Geez, sorry I opened my yap." James retreated back into his newspaper. "Hold the phone!" He slapped a finger onto an article. "I think I found something."

I leaned in next to him—not too closely—and got a good whiff of his smell. Stale cigarette smoke, sweat, a bit of musk, all boy. Repellent, yet attractive at the same time. I forced James from my mind, focused on the article.

Buried on page three, next to a cake recipe and an advertisement for Dad's services, a sad and small headline read, *Saunders Boy Goes Missing.* At the top of the page, I noted the date as May 21, 1953.

Again, there didn't seem to be a whole lot of reporting, but the gist of the story stated that Evelyn Saunders's eight-year-old son, Thomas, had run away from home. I checked the address, and sure as shooting, it was the homestead next to mine. The reporter managed to nail down a quote from Sheriff Grigsby:

> *"...Sadly, several children have run away from Hangwell during my tenure as Sheriff, I'm sure most of them wanting to go out and experience the big old world for themselves, little Thomas Saunders being another sorrowful case. We all know the Saunders family has had a rough patch of it lately, and Evelyn Saunders surely don't need this. Not now. I won't rest until I find Thomas Saunders and bring him home to his momma."*

Mrs. Saunders had either refused to comment or the reporter had rightfully respected her privacy during her time of sadness. Either way, the story made it sound like Thomas had hightailed it away several nights before the story saw print.

I reread the story again, committing the details to memory.

"You think this was the boy you saw in the corn field?" asked James.

"Could be. Maybe not. Hard to say from that blurry, ol' photo."

"Did he look like he was eight years old?"

"I reckon he could've been. But it was late, dark, I was half asleep, and everything just happened so fast. Almost like a dream if—"

I shut my yap. Colors unexpectedly rippled across the closed door's dappled glass. We had company. Whoever it was—and I suspected one of the Sooter gals—stood stock still, just listening in. I nudged James, pointed toward the door, jutted a finger up to my lips.

Already James had struck me as a boy of action more than a planner, the kind of boy who could get a girl into trouble if she didn't take precautions. What he did next proved me a highly accurate judge of character. Fast as a jackrabbit, he made a beeline for the door. The person behind the door swam away, the rippled glass pattern settling back into dull gray. James yanked open the door. Shadows and dim light greeted him. He turned, grinned, shut the door.

When he sat back down, I lowered my voice into a whisper. "Now we have a place to start."

"I guess."

"I wonder what became of Evelyn Saunders's husband? Thomas's father. It's funny he's not mentioned in the article."

"Yeah, where's the kid's old man?"

"Well, he's not there now. At the Saunders' home, I mean. Just Evelyn and her brother, Devin."

"So, Thomas's dad is dead. Or divorced, maybe." James shrugged. "Not so weird these days."

"But…my dad never even told me Evelyn Saunders had been married, let alone had a kid."

Disbelief widened James's eyes. "C'mon! Parents never tell the truth."

Actually, I thought my dad did. Prided himself on it, truthful as ol' Honest Abe himself. Sure, I suspected Dad withheld details on occasion, the way protective parents carry on at times. Nothing unusual there. But come hell or high water, Dad always leveled with me. "It just seems weird my dad never mentioned Evelyn's husband. Or what happened to him. Or that they had a boy gone missing."

"Man, get with it, Dibs. Parents lie."

"Not my dad." I shook my head, unable—unwilling—to believe it. But I knew, deep down in my bones, something smelled funny about the entirety of the situation next door, and I aimed to get to the truth of it. "Let's look through the papers after the May twenty-first one, see if we can find out anything else. Or if they ever found the boy, dead or alive." It sounded grim, putting words to it. But the more weight I gave the matter—and after last night's visitation—the boy's fate didn't seem so unresolved to me. Seemed fair time to start calling a ghost a ghost.

On tiptoes, I reached for the next handful of papers. Discouragement packed a mighty punch. "No!"

"What's wrong?" James joined me by the shelves.

"The library's missing…about six months of papers after Thomas's disappearance."

"Huh. Weird." James scratched his mess of hair and yawned. Pretty much done for the day, I reckoned.

"It's more than weird," I said. "Seems mighty convenient."

"Well…as you said, we got a place to start." James went back to the paper spread out on the table. He lifted the page that contained the article, flattened a hand next to it.

Horror struck me as I realized what he planned to do. "Stop! Don't you dare!"

An innocent shrug belied his criminal intent. "Gonna take the evidence we found." He faked a loud, cartoon sneeze ("*ah-choo!*") and ripped the ancient newsprint. With a dopey grin, he folded the paper, stuck it into his jean jacket pocket. "What? What'd I do?"

"Dang it! You don't wanna get on the Sooter sisters' cross side, James!"

"Who? Them?" He tossed his thumb toward the door. "Ah, what're they gonna do? Hiss me to death?"

"You never been on the end of their scorn before! They're mighty scary and a whole lot stronger than most folk give 'em credit for."

James's smile faded, just a little. Then, like everything, he tossed all worry away with an arrogant chuckle. "Ah, I'm not afraid of those ol' biddies. They can't—"

The door cracked open. James uttered a decidedly effeminate "*Eek.*" My stomach bounced.

The Sooter sisters stood in the doorway, small chests soldiered out, shoulders back at attention. The color drained from their faces; they looked as if someone had run over their dog, then backed over it again.

Quickly, I slapped shut the mutilated newspaper. In my trembling hands, the paper rattled like a playing card clipped to bike spokes. "Um, hello there, ladies. Gosh, where'd the time flit off to anyway? We found what we're looking for. Thank you again for—"

"What're you up to, Dibby?" asked Yvette. "Maybe something… *untoward?*"

Spoken like Vincent Price on an especially sinister day, Yvette sent the fear scurrying down my back. To steady my hands, I leaned them on a shelf and tried to clear a hole for the destroyed paper. My throat dried up, a lump the size of a golf ball wedged in tight. Finally, I managed to slip the paper into the stack, then tended to straightening the corners.

With a deep, calming breath, I turned. "No, ma'am, nothing untoward.

Just researching our project. Finding items of local color and interest to—"

"How come some papers are missing?" James slouched forward, hands dug into pockets. So insolent and so utterly different than the other boys I knew. Still, I wanted to throttle him to within an inch of his life.

As if their posture ever needed readjusting, the Sooters stood even taller, even straighter, their bodies and faces aligned in painful-looking straight lines. "Why, whatever do you mean?" Yvette snapped the words out. Miriam's ever-watchful eyes studied us.

I scooted close to James, jabbed a hopefully surreptitious elbow into his side. But the damage had already been done. "Well, after May twenty-first, nineteen-fifty-three," he continued, "there's, like, six months of missing newspapers. Just wondered how come."

The sisters didn't move, Yvette didn't utter a sound. Stood still as sleeping cows. They didn't like being challenged, I reckoned, particularly in their own domain. Finally, Yvette broke the stand-off. "Is that a fact? We'll have to look into this. Isn't that right, Miriam?" Miriam nodded. "What, pray tell, could possibly have interested you in those missing months, if I might ask?"

"Nothing, not a blessed thing," I said. "We just noticed it, thought it a little funny since everyone knows the Sooters run a very efficient library." One thing I'd learned over the years: playing up to adults always carries the day.

Just not today. "Clearly, a mistake has been made, Dibby. As I said… we'll look into it."

I took Yvette's prim delivery as a departure of sorts, and frankly, I couldn't wait to leave the suddenly dark and very claustrophobic confines of the periodical room. Through the lone window, the sun seemed to fade fast as dusk claimed its portion of the day. Shadows crawled across the sisters' faces. Outside, trees danced and bobbed in a mighty wind that had lain dormant until now.

"Well, I'll be," I said, "it's nearly supper time. Dad'll surely have a fit if I'm not home in time."

"As well he should." Yvette forced it through clenched teeth.

"Thanks again for your help. Much appreciated. I reckon we'll be on our way."

I didn't even wait for James. I brushed by him, bumped into his shoulder (maybe a little too forcefully), and hightailed it straight through the large main room and out into the fresh air. By the time James shuffled out the door, I'd already straddled my bike.

"Wait a minute," he said. "What's the hurry?"

I wheeled my bike around to face him. "I happen to like visiting the library, James! Now you may've made it impossible for me to show my face around there again!"

"Whoa, Nellie. Hold your horses. I don't see why you're so jazzed up. I was just trying to help you get—"

"Into trouble?" I stood up, planted firm feet on the ground. "I don't cotton much to trouble. Maybe you were a delinquent back in the Big City, but—"

"A delinquent? Me?" Both thumbs turned toward his chest.

"Yes, you!" Out of frustration, I scrubbed the air, realized the futility of my hissy-fit. James needed *Dick and Jane* reader-level illustrations. "In the future, don't embarrass me or break the rules or—"

"I embarrassed you?" His eyes went a little soft around the edges.

"Okay, maybe that's a little harsh, but honestly, James, just follow my lead. 'Til you get to know the ways of our town a might better. Is that too much to ask?"

"I guess not. But…what's really got you so jazzed? I mean, you're, like, jumping at shadows and everything."

Only then did I realize I *had* become spooked. Frightened of two ol' ladies who I'd come to liken as friends, if not mentors. "You shouldn't have asked the Sooters about the missing papers."

"Why not? You wanna find out about—"

"They *lied*. And that don't sit right."

"I've said it before, adults lie all the time, Dibby."

"Not the Sooters. Not when it's about their library. There ain't no way in Heaven or Hell or wherever you like to believe, the gals would make a mistake about missing six months of newspapers. Just not possible. Not them. And they flat-out lied about it."

"I still don't see what the—"

"I gotta go, James. I'll talk to you tomorrow." I pedaled off fast, a tornado of confusion whupping up behind me.

When I glanced back to wave a more amiable farewell to James, I spotted the Sooter sisters from behind a library window, shoulder to shoulder, glowering at me. And Yvette's dark glasses were in her hand.

* * *

In bed, I tried to invite sleep by way of reading. The words on the book's pages collided, meshed together, stirred into alphabet soup. Many times I found myself re-reading sentences until I finally gave up the ghost, turned off the lights, and waited for the real ghost to reappear.

I'll be hanged (and I reckon I hadn't oughta say that, not in Hangwell) if I ever nodded off. But sometimes tricks of the mind can fetch one over on you, particularly when you're rafting in that eerie boat between waking and sleeping lands.

Regardless, by the time the boy's—Thomas's—cries started, I'd already slipped out of bed and slipped one boot on. Aided by an earlier pot of coffee and a lot of gumption, I dressed in a jiffy.

"Help me...*pleassse*..."

I assumed the haunting—if I truly had to hang a title on it—was happening again in the same spot. In no time at all, I proved my assumption correct.

Deep in the cornfield stood Thomas, his back turned toward me.

"Thomas?" I said. "Is your name Thomas?"

Trembling, he spun around. Moonlight sparked life, awareness, into his eyes before they washed out again, dull as clay marbles. His unnaturally pale white skin radiated in the darkness. He stretched his arms out toward me, aching for comfort.

Then the horrible pounding started again. Corn stalks rattled, stirred by the wind. An inhuman howl whipped into a frenzy, the carrier unseen, but its presence felt. The field waved. Husks dropped beneath the intruder's stampeding arrival.

On my knees now, I crawled toward the boy. Pulled him in tight. My fingers froze at the touch of his bare back, so I hugged him all the tighter, sharing my body warmth.

I whispered, "Thomas?"

In the crook between my shoulder and neck, I felt his little chin nod. I stroked his hair, tried my best to ignore the approaching beast. If I showed strength, Thomas would surely take strength from me. I swathed him in hugs and coddled him with words of comfort even though they didn't do much to quell my own fear. I told him everything would be all right. But things wouldn't be. I knew it as I knew the back of my hand.

But to set things right for Thomas, to find out what happened, I had to see. Wait it out and witness the horror soon to be unleashed.

"Hurry, Thomas, tell me…what happened to you?"

The train from Hell chugged along. A near-to-ear-bursting whistle rose. Next to us, stalks toppled, the dark storm rolling in.

I took a stab in the dark, figured I couldn't possibly be physically hurt from a ghost.

But sometimes reason's not worth risking your life over.

"*Run!*" I screamed. With the strength of a grown man, Thomas broke free of my bear-hug and dove straight through the facing stalks. I tore out after him.

Protruding stalks and husks slowed me, but Thomas ran like the wind itself, turbining a clearer path in his wake.

Behind me, panting rose, fuming from a great beast's nostrils. Wind squalled, circled us. Leaves lifted, swirled. Hot, fetid breath blasted the back of my neck, filled my nose with the stench of rot.

"Run! He's *here!*" Screaming for all his worth, Thomas's pace didn't lag. From the forest across the road, bats took wing, eclipsing the grand moon. Creatures hooted, cawed, and skittered away to safety.

Yet the beast kept coming, mowing down stalks with ferocious ease.

Bam…bam…bam…

Tempted to turn around to see our pursuer, I figured it for a fool's choice. It'd slow me down, drop me in the monster's killing path.

Thomas broke away and didn't look back. Just vanished back into the shadows from where he came.

Behind me, something swished. Close enough I felt a rush of air on my neck.

Zzzzz…shissss…

I didn't have to look. Terror, auditory cues, filled in the blanks. Just like the Grim Reaper—and for all I knew, that's what it was—the monster swung its scythe, plowing the fields of life. Keen on harvesting my soul and adding it alongside Thomas's.

I picked my legs up higher, tried to follow in Thomas's shorn path. The air sliced behind me. Closer…closer…ever closer…

The blade bit into my back. Just a nick. But the sharpness of the instrument, the severity of the blade, drew a line of pain.

I stumbled. Went down on my side. Crashed into stalks.

The beast's footfalls stopped. But its overheated gasping didn't. Above me, in the dead dark, hoarse gulps strained for breath.

One final gasp. A big one, as if preparing to exert a last strenuous effort.

Darkness swallowed me whole.

Chapter Four

When I looked in the mirror that morning, I reckoned I needed to quit spending my nights in the Saunders' corn fields. I looked a mess and a half. My eyes, motion picture ghoul eyes, gave me a scare. Black circles blemished my pale skin, not the way I cared to be noticed.

The way I had it figured, the trauma of last night gave me such a fright that I passed out. Didn't wake up 'til first call of the rooster. Still early enough to slip back inside before Dad crawled out of bed.

For my troubles, all I managed last night was Thomas's verified identity. Well, that and the realization ghosts can indeed hurt the living. The cut on my back proved that theory beyond a doubt. Dad always preached to believe in absolutes. "The facts never lie," he'd say. I wondered what he'd make of a factual ghostly wound. Plain and simple, he wouldn't believe it. Can't rightly blame him, either.

But there sat the proof on my back, a little forget-me-not from the world beyond. The cut itself wasn't bad, just about an inch-and-a-half long. Not too deep, the bleeding had long clotted. I'd had worse paper cuts. Still, even in the bright light of morning, the thought of what had cut me shook me head to toe.

Now, I'd be a downright liar if I claimed all of last night's sleeplessness rested primarily on the ghosts in the cornfield.

Don't reckon I realized that, either, until I found myself almost absentmindedly applying make-up. I'd worn make-up before. Usually on the rare occasion I went to church or out to dinner with Dad. So I kept it around, waste not, want not. Just hadn't had much call for it lately.

Yet, even though I looked like The Mummy, ol' Imhotep himself, this morning I wanted to present myself in a different light.

Because of James, dammit.

I'd been more than curt with him yesterday, maybe a little scratchy around the edges. But I certainly wouldn't mind enlisting him as a partner in solving Thomas Saunders's presumed death—if I hadn't pushed him away. 'Course, the fact the partner in question was cute played a part in it all, too.

Shameful, I know.

Beleaguered, I stared into the closet full of nice clothes, left-behinds from Mom. All of them stylish, even by today's ever-changing standards. I'd never worn Mom's pleated skirt before—never dared to—mainly because ghastly pink drenched it, the color the awful Suzette swaddled around herself. I knew pink represented femininity, but based on Suzette's ridiculous airs, I associated the awful color with poor character more than anything.

Today wasn't the day to try out the pleated skirt. Not even a cute boy made wearing pink palatable.

Tapered slacks in a perfectly inoffensive teal color would do nicely, a middle-of-the-road compromise I could live with. I paired it with a white shirt and a sorta mustard-colored pullover that clung to the neck.

As I modeled before the mirror, I turned every which angle, agonizing over my bold rebirth. While I'd never fetch the Most Alluring Beauty prize at a fair, my mirror managed not to break either.

I returned to deliberating over the make-up. Clearly, the eyeliner was too much, probably even against school code. In the bathroom, I scrubbed and scrubbed until the flesh around my eyes went from black to red. Even worse, it made me look like I'd been crying, something I'd never allow Suzette and her little hellions to see, not in this lifetime.

Angry, nervous, I scrubbed and started over. Finally, I got the base right, the foundation of my face. Mom's long-abandoned hairspray filled the air and hardened my hair into place. Playful and daring, I puckered my lips into a red oval and kissed the mirror. I giggled at the left-behind prints, perfectly molded. My mind wandered, and I allowed it to indulge in what it'd be like to press those lips against James's. Of course, he'd have to give up smoking. Kissing an ashtray sounded like it'd leave a lot to be desired.

Before I chickened out, I grabbed my books and rumbled down the stairs.

In his usual spot, behind the cover of the *Gazette*, Dad munched on cereal. For some reason, he rarely used milk. As a result, our breakfasts always resulted in loud affairs.

I planned to rush through breakfast, hoping Dad wouldn't draw aside his shroud of newsprint.

"Morning, Dad." I filled my bowl, less than the usual amount.

"Morning. Sleep well?"

"Like a baby on a log."

He chuckled at my mixed metaphor, the way he always did. The paper accordioned together, the pages met. As the paper drew below his chin, he took a long look at me.

In the hallway, the clock ticked. Inside my chest, my heart tocked. Finally, he grinned. I mighta understood his reaction better had he gone the other way.

My cheeks and forehead reached mercurial and dangerous levels of heat.

"My, my, my, you look nice today, Dibby."

I shrugged. "Thanks."

"Any reason in particular?"

Before he began that odd ritual parents enjoyed, belittling their children about crushes and what not, I bottled his mischievous genie. "There's some kinda school photos today or something. For the yearbook. Just thought I'd try and make an effort."

His smile turned warm, far from condescending. "It's a mighty fine effort, Dibby. You look very pretty."

By now, my cheeks probably matched the bright rose red of my painted lips. I employed my other battle tactic: switching topics. "Dad?"

"Hmmm?" He settled the paper down, crossed his legs. Attentive parent position.

"Are you keeping something from me about the Saunders next door?" I needed to force Dad into talking. Eventually, he'd come around, he always did, even if it took some coaxing. The lessons we both learned over "the birds and the bees" debacle were hard to forget. Although he'd been more mortified and embarrassed over that particular talk than me, he discovered I never let go of my inquisitive nature.

"*Again* with the Saunders. Dibby…why're you so interested in them? Why now?" Lines scrimmaged across his forehead. "You've lived here fifteen—"

"Almost sixteen."

"…*fifteen* years and never showed a wink of interest. Now, suddenly, they're …the Beatles or something."

"I wouldn't quite—"

"Just put the Saunders out of your mind. Leave them be."

"*Why?* What's—"

"Just *listen* to me." He achieved that intimidating lower tone, rarely used and one not to take light-heartedly. He retreated behind his newspaper.

"Fine." I left my cereal unfinished and emptied the remains into the sink. At the door, I figured I'd give him one more shove. Make a fast getaway if I needed to.

"Dad, did you know Missus Saunders had a son? An eight-year-old?"

Time may as well've stopped. The newspaper, usually so crinkly in his hands, drew taut. From behind the paper, he said, "Have a good day at school."

As I walked to my bike (no running, not in my fancy duds), an unsettling notion dropped on me. Maybe James was right about parents and their penchant for lying to their children.

* * *

The farther I rode, the more uncomfortably my girly attire fit. The pants chafed my legs, wanted to ride up into tender parts. Worse, my clothing choice gnawed at me, a less-than-reassuring start to my day. Sometimes a small itch could grow into a festering pimple.

Lost in worry, I nearly had a head-on collision on Oak Grove Road with ol' Boot Gunderson, Hangwell's telephone operator.

Boot seemed an odd name for a man who had two legs, but only one arm. A victim of the Big War (although I'm still unclear as to which big war Boot fell victim to; he purt near seemed old enough for either), he'd left his arm overseas, but not his uniform. Every day about this time, Boot hightailed it to work on foot, marching down the road to imaginary military anthems, dressed to the nines in his army uniform. He'd been the telephone operator in Hangwell since the phone had been invented, I reckoned, alternating with Gretchen Singer, a notorious busybody.

But if you ever needed to know someone's business, know where they were at a certain time of day or night, you rang up Boot and he'd set you straight. Thanks to the party lines prevalence throughout Hangwell (again, another antiquated item that could use modernizing), Boot could tell you in a blink where so-and-so was. One of Hangwell's most colorful, yet creepy, citizens, I generally tried to steer clear of him. I s'pose Boot was harmless enough, but he gave me the willies, and not the good Starlight Cinema kind either.

Just a foot or so away from Boot, I dragged my heels to a hesitant halt. He reached over and snagged my handlebars.

"Well, now, Dibby Caldwell, as I live and breathe!" One eye squinted like Popeye, the other sized me up. His sea-salty chortle just added to the cartoon caricature. "If you're not a living doll this morning. What's the occasion? Hah?" He lifted a hand to his cauliflower ear, cupped it. "Huh?" Everyone knew you had to raise your voice to the heavens when speaking to Boot, which made him an odd choice for phone operator.

"Morning, Mister Gunderson. Just on my way to school."

"Looking like that? You gonna kiss the boys and make 'em cry?" Another bray.

I reckoned if Dad hadn't instilled a good dose of manners in me, I might've planted my foot right on top of his. But, frankly, I didn't want to touch him, not even with my shoe.

My skin crawled like a kazillion ants. I wanted nothing more than to get away from him.

I tried a smile, found a grimace winning out. "No, sir. I wouldn't do that. Just…going to school. Picture day."

He stepped back, surveyed me again top to bottom. "Yessir. Purty as a picture you are." His lecherous smile dropped. Tar-discolored fingertips massaged his whiskers. Then he leaned in close to lock one open eye on mine. "Listen to me, girly. You be careful out there. Ya' hear me? I reckon Hangwell's not nearly as safe as some folks make it out to be. I know things. I hear things. Purty thing like yourself 'specially oughta be careful."

"Yes, sir." My voice quivered, my usual angry or frightened response. I managed to wrest control of my handlebars, then quickly got my bike up to speed. "Gotta get to school," I called back.

"You hear me, Dibby Caldwell? Just mark my words! You be careful!"

I pushed my pedals harder, leaving Boot far behind. Hearing about the hidden dangers of Hangwell from the man I believed responsible for a good deal of them seemed about as fruitful as spitting in the wind. Then again, "Never judge a book by its cover," Dad always said. But sometimes it's hard to ignore a moldy, sodden, rotten cover.

My first day as the new Dibby Caldwell hardly kicked off in the rip-roaring sensation I'd imagined. I suppose a silly part of me, the goofy, little, head-in-the-stars schoolgirl, expected there to be a coming-out party of sorts, a belle-of-the-ball scenario, nothing but flying doves and long-belled trumpets and a stuffy ol' British guard announcing my glorious arrival. All of the incredibly silly, little girl stuff I thought I'd put away a long time ago, along with my teddy bear, nightlight, and Mom's departure.

More than ever, I considered wheeling back around, zipping home, and changing into my overalls or jeans. Something that felt natural, that wouldn't draw attention.

What was I thinking?

But it'd mean passing by creepy Boot Gunderson again, something I'd rather not do more than once a day.

At the last minute, I decided to bypass Main Street and instead high-tailed it down Hollow Crick Road, the less-traveled street one block over.

Unlike Main Street, the shop proprietors of Hollow Crick opened up a bit later, something I had counted on. Of course, the corner gas station seemed to never close; Darryl Mooney was out in his flawless uniform pumping gas and talking up a mean streak from the back end of a customer's Buick. He hollered something unheard to me. I poured on the speed and buzzed right past him with a wave.

Round the corner I flew, cut back to Main, and came up on the grade school.

Part of the architecture, Odie Smith sat in his preferred swing, nibbling away at his muffins. He risked loosening a hand from the swing's chain to pitch up a fast how-do-you-do.

I stopped, dropped my feet. Waved. And honestly considered riding up the hill to have a chat with Odie. Next to Boot Gunderson, Odie Smith was considered the second-best fount of information on town legend, past and present.

Except for one other townsperson, of course, and the less said about her the better.

But unlike Boot and the woman who shouldn't be named, Odie was a friendly sort, a non-scary fella, the kind of guy you'd see sitting in church every Sunday and helping ol' Mrs. Pederson (before she died, natch, and I harbored no doubt Odie was already planning to be a pallbearer at her funeral; he was at practically everyone else's) cross the street.

"Morning, Odie," I called out, remembering to call him by his first name, "you got a minute to—"

"You look fetching this morning, Dibby! Got a new boyfriend?"

With that tossed out on the wind for all of Hangwell to hear, I re-directed course and went to school. Wished I woulda cut for the day and gone fishing instead.

* * *

Late as usual, I wheeled right up to the rack and jumped off. At the first bell, I raced up the steps. Outside of my classroom, I straightened my slacks before entering.

First thing I saw pretty much set me crashing into an iceberg. Suzette hovered over James at his desk, unashamedly flirting with him. Fluttering those goofy—clearly fake—eyelashes like bat wings and playing with the silly baby doll bow holding up her ghastly pink potato-sack jumper. She knew how to utilize her long, blonde hair and whipped it around, making sure it grazed James's face.

Then all heads turned toward me.

Upon seeing me, Suzette opened up her big mouth. She released a whoop akin to a pig realizing it's bacon day. Her lacquered claws came up, pointing at me.

"What happened to you, Dibby?" she screeched. "Did someone hit you with the pretty stick?"

A bout of laughter infected the room. Suzette's foul cronies formed a supportive circle around their leader. I burned hot, boiling in a stew of embarrassment, humiliation, hurt, and anger. Anger not only at Suzette and her stupid followers, but at myself for ignorantly believing I could dress-up without being put on parade. Mostly, though, I hated myself for trying to change into one of *them*.

The laughter continued, a record stuck in a groove.

My fingers curled into my palms. The power of my fists took up a mind of their own, ready to share some anger. Flabbergasted and useless, Mrs. Hopkins stood before the chalkboard, pointing stick in hand.

More insults were hurled. But they flew past me, my mind and ears pretty much blockaded.

All that mattered was James. His brow furrowed as he stared at me. While he hadn't joined the hyena-like caterwauling, his response seemed far worse. As if disappointed, he shook his head, held a suppliant hand out toward me in a *What in the tarnation did you do to yourself?* gesture.

Rather than pounding some humanity into Suzette, I backed up onto the high road and skedaddled out of there. If they wanted to suspend me for cutting class, I'd smile, curtsey, and help them fill out the paperwork.

Anything would be better than facing the classroom again. And James's clear disenchantment with me and sudden infatuation with the fanged she-devil, Suzette.

* * *

Never a body part to beat around the bush, my gut made a strong case for James's betrayal. But my gut tended to be one of the more traitorous parts of my body, leading me astray on more than one occasion. On the opposing side, my brain argued that Suzette was just flirting with James, no two ways about it.

But honesty's the best policy—so Grams used to tell me, at least— and if I couldn't be honest with myself, then I may as well give up, crawl in bed, and let tears wash me away. Either way, tossing a fit hardly seemed like the answer.

Childish pettiness aside, I suppose I had no claim on James, no stake on his heart. We hadn't even gone on a date and most definitely weren't going steady. I'd known him all of one afternoon.

So why had his flirtation with Suzette plugged my heart full of lead? Just more silly, hormonal stuff, the junk of those creaky, ol' Harlequin romances at the library.

I laughed, pretended like logic had worked its miracles again. But it hadn't.

Fact of the matter was, I couldn't deny the allure of deep, brown eyes, a strong chin, and a roguish smile. And James had all of that and a dollar.

Not to mention he'd shown interest in me. For a change, *me*.

Still…

Slowly, I crept my bike down the road toward our house. I truly hoped Dad had been called away. Not that I ever wished for folk to die for personal gain, mind you. That'd be tantamount to flipping nickels with ol' Death himself, and I'd come close enough to that last night, thank you very much.

I just didn't feel up to one of Dad's heartfelt talks, usually designed to wring tears from at least one of us. Not to mention the unfortunate, but understandable, fact that I'd cut class.

Fate smiled kindly on me. The drive sat empty, Dad's hearse gone. I sped across the gravel, bumped through the yard, and hid my bike behind the house. The longer Dad suspected I was at school, the longer I had to build a stronger defense for myself. Maybe catch up on some much-needed sleep, too.

As I stood next to Evelyn Saunders's corn field, curiosity lured me in. A quick look around didn't mean much as I couldn't rightly see over the tall stalks anyhow, but I figured if Devin Meyers had been out working the field, I'd at least hear him or see some stalks swaying.

On tip-toes—not that it mattered a hoot-and-a-half, it just felt right— I crept toward the rotting picket fence, stepped over the fallen slat, and snuck into the field. In the daylight, the crops adopted a healthier persona. Alive under the sunlight, the greens appeared more natural and the yellows provided a lovely contrast. At first the sun-licked rows threw me off track, but soon enough I stumbled upon my well-trodden path from the night before.

Maybe my stubborn nature just wanted to confirm I hadn't dreamed the entire ordeal, or maybe I hoped to find more clues, but I was drawn to the field as surely as a child is drawn to candy.

I felt a pang of guilt, just a smidgen, when I realized the extent of the damage I'd caused last night. I'd trampled more stalks than I'd imagined. They lay broken and wounded, sad amongst their healthy brethren. The spot where I'd toppled was easy enough to find, the shape of my body (and do I *really* look like that?) outlined by surrounding, standing stalks. Down on my knees, I looked closely at the ground. I found my footprints, one fitting my foot like Cinderella's slipper. But further searching turned up nothing. Ghosts didn't leave behind footprints.

A sudden, tuneless melody nearly shuttered my heart.

I jumped to my feet and listened.

Not very far away, most assuredly in the corn field, the whistling grew louder. Stalks whisked, someone brushing gently past them. Briefly, the whistling stopped. A man grunted. Not a grunt of anger or dismay, rather it carried the calm of a man perplexed, working things out in peaceful solitude.

The whistling resumed, the man not too terribly fraught. But very much coming my way.

I had to get out of there.

Carefully, I stepped over the stalks that lay in my path. Thirty feet or so of field stood between me and where I'd entered. The dull white of the fence glowed beneath the afternoon sunlight.

Two rows over, I saw Devin Meyers's ball cap bobbing along with his peculiar waddle. I dropped into a squat, made like a four-legged varmint. On all fours, I followed the dirt-packed row to freedom.

"Well, I'll be…" Devin said it under his breath, a man nonplussed. No doubt seeing the damage I'd perpetrated in his field. Carefully, he divided a path through the stalks, entered, headed in my direction.

Ten more feet to the fence…

Devin Meyers stepped into the row behind me.

I leaped for the fence, stuck myself in between the slats. Mr. Meyers gave me an eyeful.

Fast on my feet, I reversed direction and pretended I'd just climbed into the corn field.

"Oh, you gave me a start," I said, by no means a lie. "You must be Mister Meyers. I'm Dibby. Dibby Caldwell, your neighbor next door." I approached him, hand out. Without saying a word, he tilted back his ball cap to fully gander at me. After he wiped his hand on a red handkerchief, he accepted my hand in his. I gave the shake my all, showed Mr. Meyers some steel. Pumped up and down, then released.

"Well, good morning to you, Dibby." He grinned, showcasing tobacco stains and damaged gums. But it was a friendly enough grin, a right neighborly one. "I've seen you around, sure, but I reckon we've never had the privilege of actually meeting."

"Reckon you're right, sir. I hope you don't mind my intrusion, but I swear I saw a coyote dash in here just now. Thought I'd shoo him away. Now I know they're primarily carnivores, but if you listen to legend, they'll take to corn like it's dog food if given the opportunity."

Mr. Meyers tipped his head back and laughed at the sun. "Sounds to me like you're a well-educated young lady. Speaking of which…" He lowered his head and his eyelids drooped in a suspicious manner. "…why ain't you in school?"

"Oh…well, I was feeling under par, so they ran me and my germs on home." I shuffled, stuck my hands in my pockets. Toed the dirt. Adults knew how to make kids feel guilty. Whether they actually were never seemed to rightly matter.

"Looks like you were par enough to go coyote hunting."

I shrugged. "I'm feeling better. I just didn't want the coyote to damage your corn stalks, healthy as they look and all."

Suspicion slipped away into a sort of Santa Claus gentility. He took his hat in hand and allowed me a better view. Grime covered his forehead and cheeks. Sweat drove it into small black tears of mud. His hat line divided fish-belly white skin from sun-bothered flesh. Small, animal-like eyes kept on the prowl, skittering this way and that, but not without kindness. A wealth of wrinkles rode his forehead, surrounded his eyes with tough leather, more proof that he fought a losing battle with the sun. Strands of hair stretched sparingly across the top of his head, while bushels of it stuck to his temples and sprouted from his ears. As I'd only known him from a vague boogeyman status, his gentle nature caught me off-guard.

He fanned his hat back and forth, trying to beat the heat. "I appreciate that, Dibby, I surely do. But I don't reckon your papa would look kindly on your crawling through my fields and hunting for coyotes. Particularly when you're sick."

"It's no problem at all, Mister Meyers. I'm glad to be of help."

"That damn, ol' coyote—'scuse my French—must've got to some of my stalks." He worked his jaw back and forth as if searching for a forgotten lump of chew. "Plum done tore 'em up to hell and back."

Guilt saddled up on my back and rode me hard. "I'll be glad to keep an eye out for the coyote, Mister Meyers. Shoo 'em away with Dad's rifle should I see 'em prowling around again."

He took a step toward me. Again, he wiped his hand on his kerchief. Then ruffled my hair as if I was a toddler, a boy one to boot. "I 'preciate that mightily, Dibby. I surely do. But…it ain't your place to be doing a man's job. And I suspect your papa wouldn't take kindly to you doing me any favors either."

When on fishing expeditions, sometimes the pole dang near baits itself. "I doubt that. My daddy loves helping people."

As in the Wolfman movies, Mr. Meyers's face transformed, step-by-step. First, he grimaced. Then he chuckled, just once, dry as the desert. Gazing down at his feet, he kicked at the dirt. When he looked up again— still not at me—he appeared lost, eyes clouded by memory, somewhere else entirely. Squinting hard, as if locking up some base emotion.

More than a bit hesitant, he said, "I'm mighty sorry, Dibby, but it just ain't my place to tell you why your daddy might find issue with you being here." Turned on a dime, he mussed my hair again, and I really wished to high heaven adults would cut it out. "Now you run along home, you hear me? Thankee kindly for the heads-up on that ol' coyote."

He stuck his arm out, finger pointing, showing me the way home.

* * *

I've read that catching up on sleep is like snipe-hunting, nothing more than a myth. But the second my head hit the pillow (after scrubbing off the make-up, of course), the wonderful shut-eye that followed surely felt like catching up.

While the ghosts took a holiday, the caller at the doorbell surely didn't, ringing away like Sunday church bells.

Half awake, I sat up. An opossum had crawled inside my mouth and died, leaving me parched and gummy. I didn't want to see anyone, but the afternoon caller's persistence couldn't be denied.

Bing-donggg…bing-donggg…bing, bing, bing…

Honestly, I'd rather have smothered myself with my pillow, but Dad would never forgive me if I'd become his next customer. Or if the visitor was a customer in need of Dad's services.

After I hauled myself out of bed, I glanced in the mirror and frowned at the silly cowlicks poking up in back. I looked a fright. Rubbing sleep from my eyes didn't do anything to diminish my appearance. Beauty sleep appeared not to shine on me.

Quickly as a brain bothered by fog would allow, I jumped into regular folks' clothing.

If a door-to-door salesman stood on our stoop, I vowed to run after him with a pitchfork. My hand on the doorknob, I snuck one last peek in the mirror hanging in the foyer, frowned again at my image.

But at least it was the real me. None of that childish make-up and clothes to impress a boy.

I whipped open the door, nearly squeaked like a mouse caught in a trap.

Bent forward, James appeared confused, doorbells apparently non-existent in Los Angeles. Poker-faced, he straightened and said, "Dibby." Not a salutation, no excitement, just a factual statement.

Panic set my body to full alert. I performed an impromptu dance-step, ending with an awkward pat at the damned cowlick on the back of my head. Not that James noticed. He just sorta looked around, peered over my shoulder.

I struggled to think of something witty to say. I came up with, "What?"

A smile wiped away James's dim-witted appearance. "You feeling okay, Dibs? Man, you cut out fast. I got worried."

The hallway clock chose that inopportune time to chime three o'clock. James should've still been at school, just getting out. "What about you? Shouldn't you be at school?"

His jean jacket shoulders pinched up with a shrug, stayed that way briefly before falling back in place. "Hey, you know, study hall. I don't need study hall. I bugged out. Everyone was buzz, buzz, buzzing about you. Thought I'd, you know, check up on you." Another shrug, a poor substitute for emotion.

"You're gonna get in trouble, James. Especially as a new—"

"Hey, no sweat. Trouble and me, we're no strangers. But I couldn't help it, practically up a tree all day long about you. I mean, you show up, then beat feet." He knew how to use his eyes, leaned in with the practiced soul of a puppy dog. "So, you okay?"

"Right as rain. No need to worry 'bout me. I can take care of myself."
It seemed silly, standing there, having the conversation in the doorway,
but I felt guarded. And I'd already let my guard down with James.

"I know you can, Dibs. But…why'd you wig out?"

"I did *not* wig out, nor did I bug out, or whatever you wanna call it!
I left because I plain and simple wanted to! And I don't owe you any
explanations, and I don't mean maybe!"

"Okay, geez, don't blow a gasket. I didn't mean anything. Really. I
was just worried about you, that's all."

"Didn't look like it to me." Immediately, I wished I could lasso the
words right back in.

"What?" Like a tortoise-slow sunrise, realization dawned on him.
"Oh… Oh. You mean Suzette?" He grinned, and I surely wanted to turn
that upside down. "She's nothing. *Pffft.* I knew girls like that back in L.A.
They're a dime a dozen, those broads."

Seeing as how I practically needed a slang dictionary to decipher
James's odd speech, I intuited enough to realize I may've jumped the gun in
my assumptions. Just a bit. "Looked to me like she was right special to
you this morning."

"Hey, she's nowhere! I can't help it she wouldn't leave me alone.
The minute I got there, she was on me like white on rice. Nothing to it,
baby."

Of course, my heart pitter-pattered. In a good way. But I knew he
was slick, too slick. A boy to watch out for. The kind Dad told me to stay
away from. Which, I suppose, made him that much more exciting. "You
telling me the truth?"

"Nothing but." He held up three fingers, waffled with a fourth, absolutely messing up the Boy Scouts' sign. "Come on, Dibs. Like I said,
those girls are so…Dullsville. They're all the same. All stylish clothes,
fancy make-up, giggles all the time. Just…phony, phony, nothing but
baloney, dig?"

I dug all right. But he was doing a right good job of shoveling it
even deeper. "I'm sure Suzette and her little hellion squad had nothing

but awful things to say about me."

His hands went up, neither confirming nor denying. No matter. I knew the truth. After one day, I could read James's body language. Nervously, his finger ringed his collar.

I let him off the hook. "Let 'em gab. They'll be that way their whole lives."

"Yeah. I think so, too." James looked up at the sun, drew his arm across his forehead, clearly not used to the Midwest heat. Might do him a world of good if he reconsidered wearing his jean jacket all the time. "Hey, can I come in, Dibs? Maybe get a glass of water?"

He'd earned passage. "I suppose so. But if Dad comes home, you might wanna hightail it outta here."

"But I thought your ol' man sounded like one of the good ones."

"He is. But trust me, if he catches a boy here, he'll grill you like a hotcake. A nice and toasted one."

He said nothing, just breezed by me. "Ah, I know how to handle adults. No sweat."

While I didn't necessarily buy into his secret mastery of the world of adults, he was definitely dead wrong about the "no sweat" part. He looked soaked through to the bone. "I'll get that glass of water. If you're so hot, you might take off your jacket."

He shrugged. Kept it on. For a boy who claimed he didn't care about the appearances of the tarted-up girls at school, he sure put a lot of thought and care into his looks.

When I came back with the water, he'd taken up residence on the den's sofa, one arm draped over the back of it. He patted a hand on the cushion next to him. I ignored him and sat down in Dad's recliner next to the sofa. Over the coffee table, I handed him the glass.

Disappointed, his cocky grin slipped away. He hid it well behind the glass as he gulped down the water.

"So…your Dad's gone? I mean…not like he's 'gone'." He wiggled finger quotes. "Gone like he's not here now?"

"I said he wasn't here, didn't I?"

"Fab! Can I see where he works?" James shot off the sofa.

"That's not a good idea. I gave it some thought and it's just not worth the trouble."

"Ah, c'mon, Dibs, your old man'll never know. I won't touch a thing, I swear."

"Dad made the rules to—"

"You're kidding, right? Let me clue you in on something. The squares wanna lord it over us with their rules. No rock 'n' roll, no fun, no nothing. That's the only kinda life they know. But times are changing. You need to live life a little, baby…"

He rattled on like a beatnik poet, going round and round and headed nowhere. But he had a point. Maybe it was time for me to explore my world a little, branch out from beneath Dad's protective wing. Earn my own adult wings and learn to fly. I faced a mighty perplexing crossroads. I was the only one who could make my adulthood happen, yet Dad seemed pretty adamant about keeping me underfoot as his little girl.

As I tuned back into James's goofy soap-boxing, I'd made up my mind.

"…squares, baby, nothing but squares." Out of breath, James drew a lopsided square with his finger. "S…q…u—"

"Fine. Let's go."

"What?"

"I said, let's go. Don't stand there gawping. You wanna see where Dad works or not?"

"You're the ultimate, Dibs. Let's beat feet!"

"Hold your horses." I stuck an authoritative hand high. "I've got some ground rules—"

"Always rules," he grumbled.

"You can't touch anything. And you can't ever, *ever* tell anyone. If we hear my dad coming, you're gonna hightail it out the back door. You understand?"

He nodded, held up his half-way Scouts sign again.

"All right, then. Let's go." I gave the hallway clock a glance. 3:32 p.m. Of course, that didn't mean beans when it came to Dad's work schedule. Some days he'd be gone all day, others he'd slip out for fifteen minutes. I'd struck the match, though, ready to play with the fire. While

I knew this particular fire could likely burn, a larger fire blazed within me, smoldering with excitement.

Down the main hall we went, past the kitchen, and into the extension wing my ancestors had started years ago.

"Man…this place is like a maze or something. It just keeps going." Clearly awed, James craned his head around, taking in the sights like a kid visiting Disneyland.

"When my great grandfather started the funeral home, it was only 'bout half this size. My relatives just kept adding on and built this new wing to accommodate the flood of new customers."

James laughed. "I guess there's no shortage of old geezers kicking off around here, huh?"

"It's not just the ol' folks who up and die in Hangwell."

That put his laughter on the skids.

We turned the corner into another hallway, leaving windows with hints of sunshine far behind. I reckoned Grandpa figured the dead didn't need sunlight. The lighting grew dim, small bulbs dangling at evenly measured intervals. James stopped to look at the array of photos lining the wall.

"Who's this?" He pointed toward Grandpa standing in front of an early incarnation of our home, chest out, and thumbs hooked behind his suspenders.

"Grandpa. The second Caldwell in the funeral home business."

"Boss! You gonna take over the business some day?"

My immediate post-Hangwell plans had been set in stone and definitely not the tombstone type either. "Heck no! I can't wait to leave Hangwell and go to college."

James just nodded. I imagined he hadn't heard me, completely entranced by the surroundings.

I pushed through a set of swinging teal doors. Beyond the doors, a cement ramp descended at a slight decline.

"Too, too much," said James. "Why the ramp?"

"There used to be stairs, but Dad thought it took too much effort hauling bodies up and down them. So he poured the concrete and built the ramps."

"Wanna race our bikes down here?"

"Over my dead body." Recognizing my faux pas, I knocked on the wood paneling, not caring to rile things up. Just a precaution.

The paneling—the last of the homey touches—gave way to red brick walls. James trailed his fingers down the old and seen-better-days walls. "Man, these are cold."

"Today they are, but not always."

"Really? Why?"

"On the other side's the oven. Where Dad cremates the bodies."

James yanked his hand away as if bitten by a rattler. As much as he huffed and puffed, I wondered if he was truly prepared for the sights ahead.

Around the corner, we descended a second ramp leading to the bottom level. The floor leveled out into a space large enough to wheel bodies around on a gurney. A solemn wood door, reinforced with steel, stood to the right. Ahead of us sat two swinging doors, well-used and worn down. Color had drained from the original teal color of the doors, leaving them an appropriately death-like gray. The sheen of the metal door plates had worn off, buffed into blandness. Fingerprints smudged the plates while dried specks of blood dotted the door bottoms.

I took James through the single door first.

"Wow." Truly astonished, maybe in reverence to the recently departed, James's voice melted into a whisper.

"This's the crematorium. Over there's the oven," I said.

Slowly, James crept toward the filthy and scuffed oven door set into the brick chimney. As if afraid of what he might see on the other side, he made several jackrabbit starts and stops before peering through the little porthole window.

"I can't see anything."

"'Course not. It's not fired up. Even when it's on, there's not a whole lot to see. At least that's what Dad tells me."

"How's it work? I mean, how does he burn the bodies up? Can we open it?"

For the most part, I noticed James's hep lingo had fallen by the wayside, maybe sticking closer to his true character. And I liked what I saw, no putting on airs, no bluster, just up-front and honest.

"I'm not gonna do that. But…let's see what I remember about it…" 'Course I remembered. Just like James, the crematorium held a special fascination for my macabre sensibilities, too. "After preparing the body, Dad sticks it in a coffin or container. Then a trolley wheels the body into the retort, which is the chamber where the fire fries 'em to dust. The walls are made of layers of heat-resistant bricks, so the whole house doesn't go up in smoke."

"I betcha the fire gets hot. Really hot."

"Dad used to use coal, but that was a lot more work. He switched to propane not too long ago. In the olden days, back in Grandpa's days I reckon, they used to just heap the bodies on a pyre. Living with a mortician, I learn a lot. You should see the newsletter Dad gets." I rolled my eyes. "Wasn't 'til this year, in fact, that the Catholics finally lifted a ban on cremation. Dad says that's why the town Catholics don't cotton too much to him." I moved around the corner to the control panel on the wall. "The big green and red buttons are pretty much self-explanatory, I reckon."

Flames seemed to dance in James's pupils, the green button an alluring temptress. Before he gave in to his delinquent calling, I dragged him out of the room.

Still in a dumb sorta daze, he asked, "How do you want to die? I mean, when it's your time?"

He lobbed the question at me from left field. I'd never given such notions much deliberation, not at my age. Frankly, it spooked me a bit that James had.

"James, we're still young. We don't need to be thinking of such things. Now, over here—"

"But, Dibs, we could go just like *that*." He whipped a hand up and snapped his fingers. "I mean, any of us, no matter our age. Even if we're in great shape or whatever. *Any* of us." He gripped my arm, held it firm. Glared at me with the conviction of ol' Judge Wilbur.

"I understand what you're saying. I surely do. But I'm not gonna live my life that way, looking for the Reaper over my shoulder, worrying every li'l wart and bump and pimple to death. That ain't living life at all. That's just waiting. Now, leggo my arm."

He let go of my arm but appeared to still be hanging onto his dark thoughts. He rubbed his chin, stared at the swinging doors before him, but I had no clue what he really saw.

I'd never met anyone so dark before, young or old. Frankly, James scared me. Just a scooch. And it also made him that much more fascinating.

'Course, we were definitely in the right auditorium for such debate. "James…why are you like this?"

"Huh?" Clarity parted the dark clouds in his eyes, a welcome respite from the stormy weather. "Ah, forget it. Everything's copacetic, baby. What's in here?"

The change happened fast. Contrary to what I'd thought earlier, I welcomed back James's big-talking, hep-cat persona. At least this side of James appeared to embrace life.

I led him through the double swinging doors and flipped the switches on the wall. Overhead, fluorescent lights snapped to life, flickering like a silent lightning storm. The room radiated with a pale yellow color, anything but natural.

"Dad's workshop." A nice way of hanging flowers on an ugly mule. Dad did everything down here from preparing the bodies for burial or cremation to shaping them into fair viewing again. It was no secret Dad could apply make-up tenfold better than I could, a fact that left me a might bit jealous. Sometimes Sheriff Grigsby called upon Dad, inquiring as to the cause of death in a suspect case. What that entailed only led to nightmares, 'specially when I looked at some of the tools hanging next to the sink, particularly the one that looked like giant hedge clippers. Sometimes, late at night, I imagined Dad cutting into one of our late neighbor's chests, just chopping away. In my mind, I heard an awful crunching sound, a horribly similar noise to Dad's gnawing on his dry cereal.

In fact, for what I imagined to be the messiest job in Peculiar County, Dad somehow kept his work space cleaner than freshly hung linen. He always lined up his tools, biggest to smallest, orderly like so much of his life. On his cart sat all manners of scalpels, something he called a trocar, various ointments and disinfectants (both for him and the deceased, I assumed). The sink, longer than the tallest fella Dad had ever buried by a foot, remained sparkling, fresh-out-of-the-box-looking. Not even the drain in the bottom or the small crevices trailing to it looked used. Of course, it never stopped me from imagining what kind of body fluids made the long trawl to the sewers below.

Next to the sink stood the gray chugging beast of an embalming machine that had scared me to death as a child. Still did, not that I'd tell a soul. But sometimes in my bedroom three stories above, I could hear the machine gobbling blood and spitting back embalming fluid, which carried a particularly nasty odor. On occasion—sometimes seemingly just out of the blue—the fluid's smell stuck on my skin and clothes. Other times, I imagined the machine as a living beast, my dad doing its evil bidding by supplying it bodies. It'd shake back and forth, the tubes snaking from it, wiggling to and fro like living limbs. The metal grate grew giant gray teeth. The knobs above transformed into cold, dead eyes, not unlike monstrous "googly eyes," the pupils rattling around in the other-worldly orbs. Dad had never let me see the machine actually operate, nor did I care to. In my mind, I'd witnessed more than enough, honest truth.

However, those were the ruminations of a child's imagination. Nothing I needed to worry about any more. On my few visits down to Dad's workshop—at least the supervised ones he knew about—I'd never seen a drop of blood.

"Man, it's freezing down here." Even though clad in his jean jacket, James rubbed his arms.

"Yup. Dad likes it that way. Keeps the bodies preserved for as long as possible."

James forgot about being cold, turned left and right, searching for something, and I had a good notion what that might be. Where I'd draw the line.

He strolled over to Dad's workbench, admired the various sharp-edged tools adorning the wall. Next, he hunkered down, pored over the contents of the cart next to the bench.

"What're these for?" A line of silver bells, each with a red ribbon threaded through the top-loop, caught his eye. Anywhere else the bells' sole purpose would be to gussy up Christmas. But not here. Not at Caldwell's Funeral Home.

"It's kinda silly, but Grandpa used to tie them onto the bodies' toes."

"Why?"

"'Cause back in the olden days, it was harder to tell if bodies were actually dead or not. So, if the toe started wiggling, the bell started jingling, and the corpse started singing."

"Nuh-uhhh! Your old man ever hear any jingling? Wait…did he ever bury anybody alive?" I felt like snapping James's jaw closed and nailing it shut, his behavior a might bit ridiculous.

"Not that I've ever heard."

"Huh." Disappointed, James raced toward the opposite wall, the one I wanted to keep him far away from. In front of the walk-in freezer, he stopped, his hand wavering over the door. "Is this…" He latched onto the protruding handle. Ready to pull up on it.

I raced across the lab, grabbed his arm and flung it away. "I told you not to touch anything!"

"Come on, Dibs, just a look," he pleaded, reaching for it again. "I won't tell a soul. Scout's—"

Again, I yanked his arm down. His nonsense had worn me slick, and I just wasn't in the mood. "You're not looking in there, James."

"But that's where the dead bodies are, right? I just want a quick peek. Then I'll—"

"I said no! Besides being disrespectful to the dead, you're also disrespecting my wishes!" Aggravated, I stuck my hands on my hips, gave him a stare down, and wouldn't back down come hell or high water.

Finally, he waved a flag of surrender. He sunk his shoulders, tried to work his pouty, soulful charm on me again. But I held firm.

A sudden, unsettling notion fairly gob-smacked me. *Maybe James has more interest in the funeral home than me.*

"We're going back upstairs now. Then you're going home."

"But, Dibs, I didn't mean to—"

"I don't rightly care what you meant to do. You ever hear that actions speak louder than words?"

With one last, forlorn look at the hypnotic freezer door, James skulked out ahead of me, his head hanging low. "Sorry." He said it like a petulant child, just giving service to the words and not really meaning them.

And, dad gum, if I didn't feel like his mother in that instant, wanting to tan his hide 'til he screamed for mercy. Not exactly how I'd fancied myself with James, but then again, my fancy seemed fairly unreliable lately.

"Just go." Before I pushed through the swinging doors, the left one swung inward and thumped James's forehead. He staggered back, his arms propelling for a smooth landing.

Dad breezed in and, just as I had, stuck his hands on his hips. Through clenched teeth, he said, "*Dibby*. Who's your little friend?"

Chapter Five

'Course I'd heard about deer caught in the headlights, and now I knew how the poor varmints felt. Trouble awaited me, no doubt about it, but gauging Dad's reaction, I couldn't quite measure the magnitude. Dad always believed in keeping public displays of emotion on the quiet side of never.

I doubted a fanciful fabrication would help me now, so I played innocent. "Oh, hey there, Dad. I was just showing James here where you work. I reckoned you wouldn't mind as long as we didn't touch—"

"Of course I mind, Dibby. I mind a *lot*. You know the rules." Quietly, Dad simmered, a sneaky teapot.

"I'm sorry, Dad. I—"

"We'll discuss it later. Again…who's your little friend?" He sized James up like a side of beef ready for the smokehouse. He tipped a smile, a knowing smile, the kind that said, "Aha! Young love in blossom." Unlike a lot of parents, Dad didn't lean toward embarrassing me very often, but every once in a blue moon, when he did, he did it up grand like a Fourth of July celebration.

I folded into myself, looked at my feet, and willed them to whisk me away.

To my surprise, James swooped his shaggy hair from his eyes, stepped forward, and jutted out a hand. "How do you do, Mister Caldwell? I'm James. James Mackleby. I'm new to Hangwell. My parents just moved here."

The cat got Dad's tongue, something I didn't see often. Speechless, he shook James's hand.

This new James took the wind right outta me, too, his hep lingo and brooding attitude gone the way of the wild. Minus the haircut and clothes, he could've passed as the most Baptist boy in Peculiar County.

"I apologize for visiting your workshop, Mister Caldwell," James continued. "Dibby said you wouldn't approve. It's all my fault. I twisted her arm. You see, my Dad's a scientist, too, and I've got a learning nature just like him."

Dad nibbled at the bait, and James reeled him in. Still shaking James's hand, Dad said, "Oh, you're the new Durham agriculturalist's son. I've been wanting to meet him."

"I'm sure he'd be pleased as punch to meet you, too, sir."

They may as well've been pumping a two-handled railroad cart the way they worked each other's hands, grinning at one another. All but forgotten, I rolled my eyes. Enough was enough.

"Um, Dad…I think James needs to get home," I said.

"Hm? Oh, right." He released James's hand. "You tell your folks I'd like to have them over for dinner some night. I'd love to pick your father's mind. I find his line of work fascinating."

"I'm sure he'll feel the same way about your work, sir." James showed real cheek by flashing me a wink. If Dad saw it, he overlooked it. "I'll tell him about the invite."

"Thank you, son. I look forward to it."

"Come on, James. You gotta get home in time for supper." Anxious to be done with the boys' appreciation club, I nudged James with my elbow.

"Bye, Mister Caldwell," James called back as I rushed him out of there.

Burning bright and red—a boy had never winked at me before, let alone in front of Dad—I drove James fast and hard up into our proper home. Right now I just wanted him gone before Dad set into questioning his intentions with me.

At the front door, James laughed.

"What's so dog-gone funny? Case you haven't realized it, I'm in a mess of trouble."

"Ahh, don't sweat it, Dibs." His hair flopped back into its natural state. "I got your old man eating outta my hand."

"I wouldn't be so sure about that. He's no one's fool."

"Hey, everything's spiffy. I'm telling ya, don't sweat it. I know how to handle squares."

"My dad's not a square." Actually, he very well could be, but he's *my* square dad, and we Caldwells stick up for one another.

"Easy, easy, I'm just pulling your crank. I didn't mean nothing."

I opened the door. A last-second decision, I gave him a shove to hasten his departure.

He tottered onto the porch and swung around. "Hey! I said I didn't mean anything by it."

I followed him outside, planted my feet, and tried to grow a couple inches taller. "Say my dad's not a square."

"Fine. He's not a square." The words fit right, just not the manner in which he delivered them. He huffed and groaned and swaggered back and forth.

In my best Mrs. Hopkins manner, I waggled my finger in his face. "You're darn tooting he's not. And what in the world were you trying to pull anyway?"

"What?" He splayed his hands. "I didn't do nothing. If anything, I got you outta trouble."

"You're…impossible! You breeze into my town—my school—with your hep language, your gang clothes, your cigarettes—"

"They're not gang clothes."

"…and you make me break my dad's rules and—"

"I didn't make you do anything."

"I ain't done yet! And you get me into trouble with Dad, and everything about you is just a buncha phony baloney! I don't understand you!"

"Welcome to my world." With a great deal of showmanship and a little bit of resolve, James sighed and lowered himself down to the front steps. He pulled his knees in close and hugged them, tucking himself into yet another James persona, one I hadn't seen before.

Now I felt bad about my verbal licking. James certainly knew how to wring the previously unknown nurturing side out of me.

I sat next to him. "James? I'm sorry I lost my temper. It's just… You know, I'm used to a certain way of life, my life. And 'cause of that, I reckon from time to time, I'm not the easiest person in Peculiar County to get along with. Just ask that nasty ol' Suzette."

He looked at me. A bit of a smile curled up. "What's the deal between you two anyway? I mean, you and Suzette?"

"Well…there may well be strange creatures roaming the hills of Hangwell, but Suzette's about the most monstrous of them all. Don't get dragged in by her false face. Her expensive braces hide fangs of the sharpest sort."

James laughed. So did I. Already the air felt lighter and a whole lot fresher.

"I won't let Suzette kill me," he said.

"Really, James… Why do you talk the way you do? Carrying on like you don't give a whit about anything but being 'hip'? Right now you seem normal. And I like who I'm chatting with."

James's gaze traveled out across the Saunders' cornfield, his eyes at a late-afternoon squint. His Adam's Apple bobbed. Dimples formed, pulled taut in a painful-looking manner. He swallowed, took a deep breath. And ricocheted back into put-on airs. "It's just who I am, baby."

Overlooking his disappointing answer, I had to admit whenever he called me "baby," it made all the hep talk just a little more tolerable.

"I don't believe that, James. I mean, maybe how you act's a small part of you, but it's not *who* you are."

"I dunno…it's just how kids talked back in L.A. You'd never guess it, but I had a hard time fitting in back there. And more than anything, I really wanted to belong, y'know? So I started talking like everybody else. I dunno…" He shrugged. But beneath that nonchalant façade, I understood his hurt and confusion. Something I knew a little bit about.

"I've felt the same way, more than I care to think about."

We sat for a spell, together in nice, companionable silence.

Finally, he said, "Now I get to ask you a question." When he placed his hand on my knee, I nearly jumped out of my skin. "Why'd you dress up for school this morning?"

I'd fairly hoped he'd forgotten about that. But he wasn't about to. He just kept grinning, waiting. And I reckoned since he'd bared a bit of his soul to me, it seemed only fair I give back a bit. Something I wasn't used to doing. Ever.

Of course, I couldn't tell him the entire truth. About how I wanted to capture his attention. If he didn't feel the same attraction I did, he'd laugh me into the deepest ostrich hole this side of Africa.

After giving my answer the consideration of a golden-tongued lawyer, I said, "I s'pose I have a hard time fitting in with the rest of the girls. They don't give me the time of day or even particularly like me. I guess I just wanted to see what life was like in their pencil skirts and fancy dresses and silly make-up."

"Yeah? And how'd you like it?"

The question riled me up, and I couldn't rightly say why. Possibly because I was mad at myself, mad for dressing up for stupid reasons. I took a deep breath, the way Dad taught me to do.

James diffused my anger by launching into a high-pitched giggle. So spirited and heart-felt and contagious, I had no recourse but to join him.

I rocked and laughed, a right good feeling. Tears squirted from my eyes, the welcome kind. In hindsight, my morning situation seemed ridiculous. In fact, the entire day had been funny and strange and, here on my porch, I'd found a decent way to alleviate some of that tension.

Laughter, like all good things, fizzles. For the second time, James dropped his hand on my knee. And again, I darn near took off like a bottle rocket. "Hey, Dibs… I like you just how you are. The way you dress and everything. Really. Don't change to be like one of those other stupid girls."

His eyes met mine. They flitted back and forth, certain, than not so certain. Even dreamier up close than I'd remembered. The air took on life, darn near electric. Fine down on my arms stood, tickled my skin. It felt like a moment in the movies when lovers just mutually know the time's right. But I couldn't be sure, surely didn't want to make an embarrassing mistake that would define the rest of my high school life.

His gaze dropped to my lips, then moved back to meet my eyes. He leaned in closer. Absolutely no misreading his intentions now.

Scared like the dickens and two times as excited, I closed my eyes.

The front door cracked open behind us. My eyelids whipped up.

This time, Dad didn't look nearly as keen on seeing James.

"James, I believe it's *beyond* high time you got on home for supper," he said.

* * *

Of course, Dad and I'd already fidgeted through "The Talk," so I didn't think I'd get a reprisal, but I could tell he was itching to have a chat of some major discomfort. Prickly in his body, his clothes, he wouldn't stay still, scratching everywhere like he'd fallen into a particularly aggressive sort of poison ivy.

Most of our talks were conducted at the kitchen table, but tonight Dad decided to bypass that and adjourn to the sofa, where all of our monumental decisions were made. For an irritating length of time, Dad cleared his throat, revved up his motor, then patted the well-worn cushion next to him.

"Have a seat, Dibby."

"Yes, sir." Tail between my legs, I scampered toward him. I didn't fear my due punishment for allowing James downstairs. No, sir, that'd be a cake-walk compared to the notion of discussing my first near-kiss. I thought the world would be better off if we pretended it hadn't happened.

"Dad, I know I'm not supposed to go down to your workshop uninvited, especially with a friend. I'm—"

"You know the rules, Dibby. I have to say I'm a little disappointed you disobeyed them."

"I'm sorry." And, boy howdy, did I hate disappointing Dad. The few times I'd managed to do so, he carried that sad look in his eyes for days, a badge of shame that tugged mightily at him. Like he'd let me down, too.

"I just want to make sure you understand the rules I make aren't… arbitrary. You know what that means, right, Dibby? Arbitrary?"

"Yes, sir. It means there ain't no form or sense to it."

He patted my head, usually kind of patronizing, but here I took it as a sign things weren't nearly as bad as I suspected. "Good girl. And don't say 'ain't'."

"Yes, sir." Best to keep my lips sealed and sail through it. Loose lips sink ships after all, the first time that nonsensical adage ever helped me in life.

"Anyway, I don't make up the rules just to be mean. You know I trust you, right?"

"I do."

"But I don't want you—or any of your little friends—getting hurt in my workshop. There're sharp and dangerous instruments down there, not to mention the fireplace."

"I told James not to touch anything, Dad. It's—"

"I know, I know, James has a scientist's curiosity." Dad smiled, catching that far-away look in his eye again. "I certainly understand an inquisitive nature. I do. Still…we can't risk anyone getting hurt, especially down there. By my instruments or the fireplace or…" His words drifted off. Confusion wrinkled his face like he'd hopped off the train of thought. He looked at me, brow brought low and serious. "Being around corpses is not a place for children."

Besides the fact he still insisted on referring to me as a child, I rightly suspected he had something else on his mind, something dark. Thoughts ran scattershot, a particularly scary place given my penchant for horror films and books, not to mention that given any ol' day, a dead person was like to be found lounging in our basement.

"Dad, I'm almost sixteen. I'm not really a kid anymore."

Unexpectedly, he hugged me. Tight. "I know that, sweetheart. Now more than ever."

I deemed that a sorta unspoken nod toward James and hoped it wouldn't become more specific.

"Um…Dad?" While he'd wedged himself into a downright sentimental mood, now seemed as good a time as any to spill the rest of the beans. "I oughta tell you something so you don't hear about it elsewhere. But today, I wasn't feeling right, so I left school."

"Were you sick?"

"No. Well, sorta. You know…women problems. I didn't have my product with me and felt embarrassed, so I high-tailed it home."

He continued to cradle me in his arms, the way he hadn't done in a coon's age. Like he wanted to stall my growth, forever crush me into fifteen. "Oh…well…do we need to go into town, pick up some items at Simonson's?"

"No, I've got everything here."

"Right, right. Ah…will you need a note tomorrow then?"

"Probably be for the best." My surefire get-out-of-jail-free card always worked with Dad. The menstrual cycle. As a scientist used to cutting up bodies, a woman's natural body functions somehow mortified Dad like no tomorrow.

Out of nowhere, Dad blurted, "Is James your boyfriend?"

"Dad!" I heaped on a whopping dollop of outrage. "James is new at school, didn't know anybody, so I felt sorry for him. We're friends, I guess."

That appeased Dad enough to release his bear hug. We both sat back, took deep father and daughter breaths.

"So," he said, "I guess we don't have to talk again about…you know."

"No, Dad, we don't have to talk about it again." Turnabout's fair play. My turn to make Dad squirm. "Lessen you want to, of course."

"No, no, if you're okay with everything, I'm okay. Still…if James or any other boy should, ah, try anything…fresh with you, you'll let me know, right, Dibby?"

"'Course I will." *Not in a kazillion years.*

"That's fine, that's just fine." While we considered the stuff neither one of us wanted to talk about, Dad managed to circle his way around to another uncomfortable topic. One we never discussed, and for good reason. "You know, sometimes I worry about you, Dibby. Ever since your mom…"

As usual, Dad choked up. I reckon it's one of the reasons we never talked about her.

I ended the conversation before we got carried away on a flood of tears. My arms tossed around his neck, I said, "I love you, Dad."

In a weak, somewhat garbled voice, he managed, "Love you, too, Dibby."

* * *

Another fairly restless night followed. I lay awake half-way expecting another ghostly visitation. But the ghosts played nice and decided to take the night off from a-haunting, and that suited me just fine.

I had other things on my mind: how I'd face Suzette and her little hellions in the morning, and, more importantly, how I'd react toward James. I didn't know whether to be a mite bit embarrassed or sky-high over our near kiss.

My life had suddenly grown very complicated.

Sometimes I longed for the ignorance of childhood.

In the morning, my overalls and flannel shellacked me with a nice coating of normal. As I tooled down Main Street, folks hardly gave me more than a fleeting notice. Business as usual, the way I liked to conduct my life.

Back in his swinging saddle, Odie Smith high-kicked his boxy, hard-heeled shoes (torturous footwear for a postal route, I imagined) up to heaven and back. He flew so high on the swing I fairly expected to see him wrap around the top pole. But Odie knew his limits, knew the safety confines of the swing-set. Years of practice had honed his peculiar talents.

"Morning, Odie!"

"Morning, Dibby!" A muffin gripped in one paw, the other freed in a wave, only the forces of gravity kept Odie pinned to the swing's seat. Upon downswing, he latched back onto the chain.

With extra minutes to kill, I rode up the driveway, then walked my bike through the grade school's rough-and-tumble yard.

"Why don't you pull up a swing and join me on this beautiful morn?" Odie jerked his chin toward the swing next to him. A gentle breeze bobbed the swing to and fro as if occupied by a ghost. Something I had on my mind.

"Reckon I will." I lay my bike down and hitched up next to Odie.

"I must say, Miss Dibby, you sure looked mighty purty yesterday, yesiree." He squirreled a good chunk of muffin into the side of his mouth and spoke through the other side. Crumbs flecked his lips.

"Well, it was picture day. Ol' Missus Hopkins told us to wear our finery."

"That a fact? Huh. I hadn't heard hide nor hair of such an event."

For all the nice things small-town living had to offer, privacy didn't qualify as one of them. Everyone knew everyone's business. Just a matter of time before news of my would-be romance with James got out, I supposed. Then again, teen matters rarely ranked high in adult gossip. Thankfully.

I shrugged, let that work as answer enough to Odie's roundabout query. I didn't want to dig a graveyard of lies. "Odie, everyone around says you know just about everything regarding Hangwell and Peculiar County."

"That's right." He nodded, pride in his grin. "Some rightly refer to me as the town historian."

"I reckon not much gets by you, past or present," I said, slathering on the butter.

"Reckon you're right."

"If you don't mind, I'd like to jaw a little bit with you."

Immediately, Odie slipped into a suspicious look. Word around town had it Odie owned the worst poker face this side of Clemmett County. With eyes narrowed to slits and a lower lip enveloping his upper, I could plainly see why everyone wanted to play cards with him. "Say…is this about that history project of yours I heard about, Dibby?"

Proof that Odie was the man in the know. "Yes. Well, sorta."

"The Sooter sisters done filled me in. I have to tell you, Dibby, they was a might bit leery seeing as how they hadn't heard about such a project from Missus Hopkins."

As Odie had already grown suspicious, I just tossed my question right out there. "Odie, what do you know about the Saunders family?"

Reet...reet...reee...

Odie's legs quit kicking. He tucked them beneath and dragged the tips of his shoes in the dirt until he stopped. White knuckles gripped the chains. The swing seat finally quit squeaking, and the chains stopped rattling. He just plum stared at me.

"Now, Dibby...I haven't said boo to anyone about your history project being a fabrication. I figure it ain't my business and seemed like a harmless enough li'l white lie. But why in the world would you want to know about the poor Saunders family?"

"Well...I *don't* have a real reason, but I was a tad bit curious as they're my neighbors and all."

Odie shook his head, inhaled deeply. "Dibby, you don't wanna go sticking your nose into the Saunders business. It's not your concern, 'specially for someone of your age. Nothing for a young girl to worry her head about. Why, you oughta be thinking about going to the Spring formal, kicking up your heels, dancing with cute boys and—"

"What happened to Missus Saunders's son, Thomas?" Dad would tan my hide for interrupting an adult, but frankly, my patience bucket had just about run over. Everyone wanted to paint me as a pretty li'l flower, and in so doing, tell me nothing.

For a moment, Odie's lower lip trembled. His appetite folded, unheard of. He tossed the rest of his uneaten muffin into the grass. Birds migrated toward it. "Dibby, just let poor Missus Saunders be," he said, quiet as a whisper. "Woman's had her share of hurtin' without it being brought up again. The past is the past."

It seemed to me that everyone in town—every adult, at least—had taken it upon themselves to dictate my concerns. "I'm not just being nosy, Odie. They're my neighbors. I thought I'd get to know them a little—"

"Some things just shouldn't be known." Without so much as a parting nod, Odie left his swing. As stiff-legged as a man on stilts, he hurried toward his mail truck.

"Why won't you talk to me about them?" I called out.

He stopped, stiffened, my words striking his spine like a bullet. He swiveled around, looking very un-Odie-like.

Panic messed up his face. Fear pushed him close to an unpredictable edge. He came at me fast, scary fast. I nearly took off a-running in the other direction. Right in front of me, he stopped and bent over. In a hushed voice, he said, "Thomas Saunders ran away. No one ever heard a word again from him, nary a peep. It's all very sad, frankly, and I don't think it'd be right of you to go stirring up memories again. End of story." Through clenched teeth, he growled. Hardly the face of the friendliest man in town. I felt chastised, ashamed. Frightened. And dying of curiosity. Of course, I didn't want to end up like the cat who'd squandered all his lives, but by my count, I still had several to spare.

"Too many kids done gone missing already," Odie hissed as he briskly walked toward his truck. "And I don't like thinking 'bout all the stories pertainin' to them, neither."

None of my questions had been answered, but more had certainly been raised. Just like the hair on the back of my neck.

* * *

In the school office, Mrs. Hemsworth grabbed Dad's note. Over the top of her cat eye glasses—which I always thought looked kinda funny as an accessory to her floral, form-fitting dresses—she glanced at it and nodded briskly. She handed back the note and excused me with a royal flourish of her wattle-heavy hand.

Just like Dad, the "time-of-the-month" excuse worked wonders on Mrs. Hemsworth. Her eyes always grew frightful and worried whenever a student evoked menstruation. Like the gypsy woman in *The Wolfman* movie, she referred to it as "the curse," acting as if she might catch it. I suspected her window for the "curse" had long since closed, rendering her heebie-jeebies all the more puzzling.

Outside my classroom, I took in a deep breath and prepared to face my daily tormentors. And James.

Three minutes 'til the second bell clanged, everyone appeared to be in a particular flurry today. Most of the action orbited around James's desk. Suzette, of course, stood front and center, her followers flocking toward her.

At the center of the commotion, James provided pull, his hands flailing above the clustered girls' heads. Given the clucking of the girls, no doubt James was regaling them with amusing anecdotes.

My own center—my perilously perched heart—sunk. James's actions didn't align with his words from yesterday.

I felt duped in the worst way, a silly girl lured in by a nice smile and deep eyes and broad shoulders. Then I rightly put things into perspective. James's smile was a smoker's green, his eyes captured the intelligence of a cow's, and his shoulders didn't hold a candle to Suzette's man-back.

I hurried to Mrs. Hopkins's desk and handed her Dad's note.

"I see," she sniffed. "We were quite worried about you, Dibby. Quite worried. Next time this happens, please see the school nurse."

Eager to sit down in relative invisibility, I nodded and hurried toward my desk.

Suzette and her gang separated from James. Once Suzette caught my eye, she gave me one of those haughty up-and-down looks that came second nature to her. "Well, looks like you're back to wearing stylish farm-wear, Dibby," she said.

Burning like a hay-stuffed barn, I sank low in my seat and felt even lower. I couldn't even look in James's direction. Let Suzette listen to all of his stupid gibberish if that's the way he wanted it. I resolved myself to a life alone.

But Suzette just wouldn't let up. "Are those hand-me-downs from your grandpa, Dibby?"

Clear as a motion picture, I envisioned myself launching across the room and popping Suzette in her expensively put-together mouth. Sure, the braces would hurt—quite a bit, I reckoned—but they also might serve as brass knuckles and really gum her up good. Briefly, I weighed the merits of suspension versus common sense.

The other girls tittered at their ringleader's harsh and cruel taunts. I scrunched farther down into my seat. An elbow on the desk, my face resting in my hand, I tried to hide my shame. And tether my growing fury.

"Well, I'm darn glad you came to your senses, Dibby," continued Suzette, "and settled back into your regular hired-hand clothing. I mean, honestly…what in the world possessed you to dress like you did yesterday? You looked like an icky old man had dressed you. You looked like—"

Sometimes common sense ain't all it's cut out to be.

Like a rocket, I launched out of my seat. I might've yelled, or maybe that'd been someone else. Jet fuel propelled me across the classroom. Suzette's awful face, painted and twisted into a scowl, drew closer and closer and bigger and moon-sized ugly. My rocket-fist landed on her mouth.

One punch put things right. As Suzette went down, screams soared high. As I sorely expected, my knuckles had taken a sound beating. But it was well worth it.

As in the movies, I threw up my arms. Waiting for arrest or a show of victory, I didn't rightly know, but it just felt like the right thing to do at the time.

Mrs. Hopkins rushed toward me, her voice like a wah-wah trombone. In a heap of chiffon and bows, Suzette boo-hooed a river. She held a petite and painted hand over her mouth. Blood spilled between her fingers, perfectly complementing her barn-red lipstick.

Finally, I glanced at James. He smiled and gave a sort of dumb, slow nod.

I couldn't quite pinpoint how I regarded his reaction. Either he approved of my handiwork or he was a big jerk. The truth probably lay somewhere in between.

* * *

The four of us sat in a row, Principal Brining's firing squad line-up.

Other than a few huffed, irate words, Dad hadn't really said much to me since his arrival. Later, in the privacy of our home, I fully expected to hear more words, the kind he used whenever he stubbed a toe.

On the other hand, Mrs. Keating—Suzette's mother—had quite a bit to say.

"Mister Brining, just look at my daughter. *Look* at her," Mrs. Keating ordered with the force of a drill sergeant.

As instructed, everyone gandered at Suzette. Next to her mother, the little blonde terror snuffled like someone had torn the arms off her prized dolly.

The Devil's voice inside of me said, "*Yeah. Just look at her. Attagirl, champ!*" But I buried that voice when Dad gave me the evil eye.

"Yes, Missus Keating," Principal Brining said, "I'm aware of Suzette's injury. She's been thoroughly examined by our nurse and—"

"I would hardly call Missus Hemsworth a qualified nurse, Mister Brining!" Mrs. Keating leaned in, narrowed her eyes. "She's your front-desk woman!"

Principal Brining spread his hands. "I'm afraid small towns have small ways. But there's no damage to Suzette's teeth, and her braces appear to be intact as well. I'm sure—"

"I barely hit her," I muttered.

"Quiet, Dibby," hissed Dad. Tonight, no amount of hugs or professions of love would bandage these open wounds. "I think you've caused enough trouble for one day."

I folded my arms, snorted.

"You see what I mean, Mister Brining!" Mrs. Keating stuck a bejeweled finger toward me, one I was sorely tempted to bite. "This…this little *monster* shows no remorse or—"

"My daughter's *hardly* a monster, Missus Keating." Dad found a new target for his ire and it pleased me to no end. "Now, granted, I admit what Dibby did was wrong, but it wasn't entirely unwarranted. It's my understanding your daughter is quite the playground bully—"

"Dad, we don't have playgrounds anymore."

"—and Suzette's been acting mean and provoking my daughter for some time. Before we start calling names, Missus Keating, I believe it might behoove you to look into your own daughter's appalling behavior." Very much an anti-violent man, Dad nevertheless came to my rescue, even though my punching Suzette surely put his moral fiber to the test.

The funny thing is, I'd never told Dad word one about how Suzette had tortured me over the years. Maybe adults paid a little more attention than I gave 'em credit for.

"Why, that's preposterous," said Mrs. Keating. "My daughter's an absolute angel, a—"

"More like devil-spawn," I whispered.

"That's enough, Dibby. Don't make me tell you again." Dad glared at me, then switched to Mrs. Keating. "Now, by all means, have a dentist give Suzette a full examination and—"

"I certainly intend on doing that," snipped Mrs. Keating.

"—we'll pay for any damages. *If* there are any damages. And I'll see to it that Dibby is fully reprimanded for her behavior—"

"Her *beastly* behavior."

Dad glowered at Mrs. Keating. I hoped he'd expend all his glowering before we got home.

"And I fully expect you to do the same for your daughter, Missus Keating. If I hear Suzette's returned to her same bullying ways after this…well, we just might find ourselves having a long chat."

And I knew how Dad liked to chat, his version of a sock to the mouth.

Suzette bubbled over anew. Her claws reached out for her mother. Mrs. Keating kept her daughter at arm's length, probably not wanting to soil her Jackie Kennedy dress with Suzette's blood and tears. Instead, she consoled her daughter with a dainty fingertip pat on the back. The apples don't fall far from the tree, so I've heard, especially the sour ones.

Poor Mr. Brining just sorta looked befuddled, at a loss as Dad and Mrs. Keating commandeered his meeting.

Mrs. Keating said, "Mister Brining, I certainly hope you'll suspend, if not expel, this…this…*girl*." She refused to look at me, let alone address me by name.

Mr. Brining hemmed and hawed like a donkey refusing to go down in a mine. Finally, he said, "Missus Keating, I'm afraid I've heard several eyewitness accounts regarding Suzette's occasionally less than…civil behavior."

"You're telling me you knew about this bullying?" Dad jumped up on that ol' soapbox and stood tall. "And refused to do anything about it?"

"Well, you see…it's not all that simple." While Principal Brining blathered on, Suzette just kept a-crying, giving me a mighty headache. I was sorely tempted to hush her up the hard way.

"Both Suzette and Dibby are two of our finest students," continued Mr. Brining. "They both achieve high grades. I'm afraid if I suspend one, I'll have to suspend the other. Frankly, I'd rather not do that. It'd be a mark on their permanent records."

Of course, I'd heard about the mysterious permanent record, a document carrying so much secret heft and weight it may as well be locked up in the Pentagon. One of these days, I'd like a gander at mine just to see what the adults were all on about.

"That's preposterous," spat Mrs. Keating. "This girl assaulted my daughter! You can't possibly let her actions go unpunished! Why, it's simply barbaric!"

Brining's hands went up again, patting the air and putting out fires. "As I said, Missus Keating, if I suspend Dibby, I'll need to suspend Suzette as well. I don't think any of us want that." He waited for someone to object. I highly doubted they'd take my vote into consideration.

"Now, I've been reading about several new methods of dealing with disciplinary problems," said Mr. Brining. "Positive, instead of negative, reinforcement. What I propose is that Suzette and Dibby apologize to one another. Shake hands, smile, and repeat it in front of their classroom. Then, for one week, they'll stay after school and work together—as a team—helping Missus Hopkins with various classroom chores."

I groaned. This sounded a whole lot worse than suspension. Of course, Suzette responded with another blubbering fit. Once again, the strange world of adults had no idea the torture they'd be inflicting on us.

"Is this amenable to everyone?" Mr. Brining eyed us all with lifted eyebrows and higher expectations.

Dad sighed, the first to answer. "It sounds more than fair to me."

Mrs. Keating chimed in. "As long as…that girl never touches my Suzette again. Why, do you have any idea how much her braces cost? It took—"

"I already offered to pay for any damages," said Dad. "*If* there're any damages. And I'd like to see a printed estimate and bill, should it come to that."

"*Fine.*" Mrs. Keating crossed her legs, looked away.

"Girls?"

Dad nudged me.

"*Okayyy,*" I groaned.

"I guess," spat Suzette.

Suzette and I stood, faced one another. "Reckon I'm sorry if you are," I said.

"But I didn't do anything!"

"Suzette! Apologize now," demanded Mrs. Keating. "Even though we both know you didn't provoke this attack."

Suzette stomped her little Cinderella slippers. Through glassy eyes, she glowered at me, then wiped her nose. And stuck the offensive paw out to me.

Not to be outdone, I hawked into my palm and slapped it into Suzette's.

"Dibby," yelled Dad.

Suzette wrenched her hand away, held it close to the bow tying her stupid head to her stupider body.

"What? It's like a blood oath," I said, full of innocence and secretly proud of myself.

I suspected the adults in the room were fed up with us by now. They hurried the meeting to a conclusion.

The little demon princess and I glared at one another again before Dad gripped my hand and dragged me away.

And on that fateful day, an unholy alliance was born.

Chapter Six

Dad tossed my bike in the back of the hearse. After he jumped in, he chunked the door shut. Didn't say a word, just stared straight ahead. Centered on James, straddled on his bike, looking back at us.

James raised a hand, heart-breaking almost in its hesitant nature, almost like saying "goodbye."

And after what I'd done today, I fully suspected it was a forever goodbye. Dad intended on locking me in my room and swallowing the key 'til I hit old maid-dom.

"Is *he* the reason for your behavior, Dibby?" Dad set free his quiet, scary voice, and I much preferred just plain quiet. "Did you get in a fight over that *boy*?"

"Who, James? No, Dad, he had nothing to do with it." I stared at Dad, waiting for acknowledgment, any kind whatsoever. He just pulled out onto Main, eyes set ahead as if looking at me would turn him into stone. "And it wasn't really a fight," I added beneath my breath.

That got his attention. "You'd better start showing some remorse, young lady, and I don't mean maybe! Except for school, you're grounded for two weeks. I mean it, no lollygagging, no hijinks, no cutting of school, and definitely no fighting!" We traveled on in silence until Dad nearly shattered my eardrums with a sudden shout. "I'm absolutely *beside* myself!"

That's one of those adult terms I've never understood. Physically, I sat beside him. But beyond the literal interpretation, I took it to mean he didn't know what to do. And that bothered me. A lot.

If parenting downright spooked Dad, the thought absolutely terrified me. He always knew all the answers. Of course, he never told me as much, not a peep about his unspoken fears. But by piecing things together, picking up on little tidbits dropped in our chats, watching Dad's behavior, I put meaning to the anxiety he couldn't verbally express: without Mom around, he worried he didn't know how to raise me, felt like he was doing a poor job of it.

And more often than not, the blame fell back on me.

"Dad…I'm sorry. Honest. It's just…I dunno, I lost my temper. I know it was wrong—"

"Well, you're right about that!"

"And I swear I won't do it again. I'm really, really sorry."

"You're gonna be sorry, all right!"

After he stewed a bit, he settled into a calm. His shoulders sloped, his hands relaxed on the hearse's wheel. "I hear you *say* you're sorry, Dibby. I just… I don't know what's gotten into you lately."

"Dad… I'm okay, you need to know that. And it's not anything you've done. You're the best dad in the world." I spread my hands far. "I'm just growing up. That's all."

"Fighting's hardly a sign of maturing, Dibby."

"I know. But…sometimes you just have to stick up for yourself."

He nodded. "Like I told you. But there are ways to do it without fists."

"Okay. Pinky promise." Quickly—Dad didn't dare relinquish the steering wheel for long—we linked pinkies. "And you know it's true…about your being the best dad in the world. Everything I know, everything I do, who I am…is because of you. 'Cept, of course, for hitting ol' Suzette."

He smiled. If he didn't so firmly believe in the nine and three o'clock method of both hands on the steering wheel, I sorely think he would've reached out to take my hand in his.

* * *

Tip-toeing toward midnight, a sound stirred me awake. Lately, I'd taken to sleeping in my clothes in case Thomas Saunders came calling again. I bolted outta bed like it'd been tipped over and ran to the open window.

"Hey….hey, Dibby! Psst… Oh, hey!" Below, James just smiled at me. Torn between excitement and anger—the way James always sparked my battery—I jutted a finger to my lips.

"Quiet!" I spat. "You're liable to wake the dead." Just to make sure he hadn't, I peered into the cornfields behind him. All seemed quiet and down-in-the-earth. "I'll be down in a jiff."

Kinda silly and probably moot, I quickly checked my image in the vanity mirror. Doggone cowlick just wouldn't ever behave. I licked my fingertips, patted the hair down to no avail.

Mercifully, James hadn't stirred Dad or the dead. I bypassed his bedroom and snuck outside.

When James saw me, he may as well have been calling the cattle home, loud as a rodeo. "There you are! Hope you got your winks—"

I strode straight up to him and clamped my hand over his big trap. "Shut your hole! Dad's sleeping and I'm in enough trouble already." An obedient nod. I released him. "What in Sam Hill are you doing here this time of night? No one's up but ghosts and the bad element."

James looked around, eyes wide. "Um…are they out? The ghosts?" He shook a thumb behind him at the corn field, not nearly as calm as he pretended.

"I don't think so. At least not that I can tell. What're *you* doing here?"

"Kinda a funny story. See—"

I could tell it was gonna take a while for him to spill his guts, so I took him by the hand, led him down the yard nearer the road. Far enough away to speak freely, we stopped beneath the large oak tree.

"Now we can talk. But keep your yapping down to a dull holler."

James swept his hair from his eyes, gave my hand a little squeeze.

Honestly, I didn't even know I was still holding onto him, it felt so natural. But now that he called attention to it, I pulled away. "Tell you the truth, Dibs, I was sorta outta my tree about what you did at school today."

"It's my cross to bear. I'm a big girl."

"Well, if I didn't know that before, I sure do now. Wow, that was really something. You really put Suzette's lights out." He grinned. Wan moonlight struck his teeth just so, turning them an even deeper shade of yellow, corn yellow.

"Not proud of what I did, James. It was wrong. Even if the little hellion deserved it."

"Yeah, right. But, man, what a gasser!"

"Is that why you're here? To pat me on the back for laying out Suzette? I done told you I'm not proud of it." Truth be told, I was proud. Just a little bit. But no doubt that was my ol' childish self rearing her ugly duckling face. "Besides, from what I saw today, you were getting along just fine with Suzette, flirting up a storm. Why don't you go call on ol' metal-mouth and leave me be? Just get up on your bike and hightail it outta here. Now, go on. Git." I stuck my arm out, pointing the way.

"Hold your horses. I told you I don't even like Suzette. I mean, other than a friend, maybe. Besides…it's you I'm here for. Not her."

"*Why*, dammit?" What I really wanted to hear. What I needed to be convinced of.

"Well…" He shrugged. "I didn't want to call you or anything, make things worse with your old man. And I couldn't sleep. That damn ghost dog whining and making a racket and everything. Anyway, since I got my own room, it was easy to sneak out. I was worried about you."

"I don't need your worry. Got plenty of that myself. Get going."

"Just hold on. Lemme tell you what I did… Now, I'm no rat-fink, but after school I went into the warden's digs, told him how Suzette was calling you names and stuff. Told him you didn't deserve to be kicked out."

Other than Dad, no one'd ever really gone to bat for me before. It felt good, knowing I wasn't alone, that someone looked out for me. Then again, Dad had warned me about boys carrying loaded smiles, loaded compliments, and overloaded hormones. I still didn't know if I could trust James. Especially since he always appeared friendlier with Suzette than he lead me on to believe. After a lifetime of distrust, being on-guard comes naturally.

"Did you really do that? For me?" I asked.

"Sure did."

"Well…what did Mister Brining say?"

"Told me to get outta his office. Said he'd handled it."

"Yeah… He handled it, all right. I've gotta make best friends with Suzette."

"What? Brining's outta his tree!"

"I guess."

"Can you do it?"

"I dunno. I'll find a way. Reckon I always do."

James sat down, his back against the tree trunk. I sat next to him, putting a bit of trunk between us.

"So…what'd your old man do to you?" he asked.

"Two weeks grounded. And somehow I gotta help pay for Suzette's metal teeth if I hurt 'em."

"Man…oh, man…"

A breeze gusted by, rattled the leaves above us. Shadows painted a mosaic of dark and moonlight across James's face, daubing him in even more mystery.

"Well…what're we gonna do about, you know, Thomas's ghost and everything?"

A mighty fine question, one I'd been asking myself before I got into this stupid Suzette mess. "Reckon there isn't much we can do for a coupla weeks. Unless we go out at night, see what ghosts we can stir up."

"Okay." His eyes lit up.

"I'm kidding. We can't sneak out every night looking for ghosts."

"Don't see why not. You're doing it already."

He had me there. But they hadn't been planned ghost hunts. Rather, the ghosts had drafted me into duty. "That's about as poor an idea as I've ever heard, James. Besides, we need to do more investigating, talk to people. No one's up at night. 'Sides, Dad and your folks would find out we're traipsing through the night in no time."

Then I thought of ol' Hettie Williquette. Someone I highly suspected would be awake during the wee hours. But the thought of talking to her, even under the comforting sun, scared the dickens out of me. And I knew enough about James by now to know he'd jump at the chance to talk to a bona fide witch. I kept my trap shut regarding Hettie.

"Ah, still stuck in Squaresville." He leaned over, dug into his pocket, and pulled out a bent cigarette. He slipped it between his lips, then fished into his pocket for matches.

I plucked it from him and snapped it in half. "I'm *not* stuck in Squaresville."

He looked at me in wide-eyed disbelief. "Not *this* again."

"My boots are firmly planted in reality, not your make-believe Squaresville. Neither one of us need to go looking for trouble."

As soon as he pinched out another crooked cigarette, I broke it, and boomeranged the broken halves back to him.

"Dammit! Quit breaking my bogeys!"

"If we wanna stay outta trouble, we'll start here."

He closed one eye and peeked into his nearly empty, well sat-on package. "But…I'm about out. You can't break any more."

"Sure can."

He groaned, rightly tucked the package into his jacket's pocket. "Give me one good reason why we can't we go out at night. I can break outta my hotel, no sweat. It'll be fun."

James practically bent over backwards for fun. But he couldn't understand that Thomas Saunders's murder was about as far from "fun" as one could get. Furthermore, what Odie'd said kept circling the drain in my head: *Too many kids done gone missing already.* Maybe what'd happened to Thomas could just as easily happen to us.

"James, I'm not fiddling around here. I need to know if you're fully committed to finding out what happened to Thomas Saunders. Things could get dangerous." I set my lips firmly, gave him a good eyeful.

"Hey, easy, easy. I wanna help you. I like danger. About time something cool happened in this burg."

I sighed. Absolutely irrepressible. "Just keep what I said in mind, James."

In the distance, a critter howled, something I couldn't identify by sound. Nothing new under the moon in Hangwell, though.

"What was that?" asked James.

"Who knows?" I decided to embellish a bit, maybe shake some sense into him. "Here in Peculiar County, you're liable to hear lotsa strange things. I suspect it might be a devil hound. Maybe a werewolf." I couldn't hide my grin. Maybe Odie Smith didn't have the rottenest poker face in town after all.

"Ah, now you're putting me on."

"Caught red-handed. Still…you can't deny Hangwell's weirdness. You're already well-acquainted with Mittens, the ghost dog. And the Sooters sisters."

"Yeah, completely cuckoo. So…you know about werewolves and stuff?" I nodded. "Well…I was wondering… You know there's a horror film, *The Curse of the Fly*, coming to the Starlight Theatre and—"

"Yes." I blurted. "I'd love to see it! I loved the other *Fly* movies, too!"

"Really? I mean, you'll go with me?"

Reality crept up and slapped the upside of my jawbone. My newly grounded status hardly made allowances for movies. In a way I felt a trifle relieved. I'd never been on a date before. I needed some time to get my toes wet before diving head in. "Oh, wait…I'd really like to go with you. But I can't. I'm grounded, remember?"

"Oh, yeah…right. *Hell.*"

Disappointment deflated him. There, in the dim moonlight, beneath the tree, he looked much younger than the way his swagger and bluster aged him. I felt awful, both for him and for me.

"Well…maybe the picture will stay in town for a couple weeks." But I knew that wouldn't be the case, not with horror pictures. Around here, the Starlight scooped in all the kids for one weekend, then the movie'd blow outta town like the wind. "Or maybe…maybe I could ask Dad to make this one exception." Honestly, it sounded far-fetched. While, on occasion, Dad had given me leeway—I suspected out of his deep-rooted parental guilt—socking Suzette seemed fairly irredeemable, even to me.

"Really? That'd be fab."

"I can't make any promises. But it surely won't hurt to ask. As long as you stay out of trouble, too."

"Yeah." As if I'd reminded him of his bad habits, he plucked out his rumpled cigarette package again. "They got any cigarette machines in this town?"

"Well… There's one down at Daryl Mooney's service station—you know, the Sinclair—but ol' Daryl keeps a tight eye on doings. He wouldn't cotton to a minor buying cigarettes. And, don't quote me on this or anything as I never set a foot inside, but I'm willing to bet dollars to donuts there's one at the *Tavern*. But you don't wanna go in there. Probably couldn't anyway."

This time James really deflated. He groaned, raised his hands to the sky. "What'm I gonna' do?"

"Sounds to me like not much choice other than quit. That advice's on the house."

"I guess." He snatched the last cigarette from the pack, quickly jabbed it between his lips. Just as quickly, I plucked it away, gave it what for.

"Nooo," he cried. "That was my last one!"

"Good. You ever kissed an ash tray?"

His cigarettes forgotten, he grinned. "No. Have you?"

"Absolutely not. Disgusting."

"You ever kissed a boy who smokes?"

"No. That's even more disgusting."

"Wanna' try?"

"I reckon I might."

The conversation happened so fast, I couldn't keep up with my mouth. But it felt right.

He leaned in. So did I. His fingers caressed the bottom of my chin, playing over the little scarred reminder of when I cracked my chin open as a kid. Self awareness of my flaws kicked in. But if he noticed the scar, it didn't seem to phase him.

Our lips met. A gentle and smooth kiss, not at all the roughhouse, back alley, and dive kissing found in movies. I followed James's lead, explored his lips with mine. To get closer, fit more snugly, I angled my head. His other hand rested on my shoulder—when it found its way there, I couldn't rightly recollect—and he massaged it.

My heart banged away. Breathing turned locomotive. Plumes of his breath warmed my cheek. I pressed harder, wiggled to and fro. His slightly smoky breath didn't matter one whit.

Warmth spread through my body, tingles from head to toe, and nearly exploded at the physical center of myself.

At that moment, I had no idea how this would end, how I *wanted* it to end. For all I cared, we could've kissed all night. Time had crashed to a halt and politely waited for us. Nothing else in the world mattered but now.

Yet, as if from a well, Dad's voice hollered up, full of warnings about the dangers and complications and mysteries of sex.

Even though my body felt ready to chug down that track at full speed, my mind stepped on the brakes.

With a hand on James's chest, I broke the kiss. And opened my eyes.

James's eyes twinkled, of course, their usual way. I reined in my galloping breath, tried to wrangle my runaway heart. And I grinned, a full-on, stupid, jack-o-lantern grin.

"Gosh." That's all I said. All I could come up with after being immersed in a lifetime of witty cinema repartee. Anything fancy alluded me. From the looks of James, he'd been stricken with the same, not unpleasant ailment.

"That was nice," he said.

"Yep, surely was. Except I was right."

"About what?"

"Kissing you was like putting my mouth on an ash-tray." With that, I hopped up and clapped imaginary dust away from my hands. Hoping

James would get the picture that the deed was done. For now.

He joined me and reached for my hand. Somewhat skittish—and I rightly couldn't be sure why, either—I pulled away and kept my hands clasped tightly beneath my chin, the way I'd seen the girls at school do while flirting. And now I sorta understood it, too. It was a mighty effective form of defense and offense at the same time.

Without saying a word to one another, we strolled back to my house. I jumped up onto the porch and whispered, "I'll ask Dad about the movie."

Deciding that was about as good a farewell as I had in me, I hurried inside, and quietly closed the door. On tiptoes, I looked out the small door window. James stood there, dumbfounded, another deer caught in the headlight. Then he waved. And got on his bike and rode off into the dark of night.

* * *

It took some fine finagling, but I finally convinced Dad that fresh air and sunshine would benefit me if I rode my bike to school. Of course, I had to promise not to make any other stops, a promise I fully intended to keep at the time. But if the road to hell is paved with good intentions, the road to good intentions is surely pocked with pot-holes.

Of course, since I'd just won a minor battle, I didn't dare ask Dad about the movie this weekend. Winning that war would require more stamina, none of which I had now.

Regardless of my dog-tired body, sheer excitement powered my brain. I pedaled through town, straight down Main Street, delivering greetings with a little more pep in my voice than usual. I didn't even mind the occasional odd stare, figured I near earned it by socking Suzette. Nothing could dampen my day, a glorious one. Funny how a kiss could flip things sunny side up.

"Dibby? Dibby Caldwell!"

Right away, I recognized the voice, damaged by years of cigarettes, whiskey and barking orders. Never before had he called me out, and it set me on edge. But it was a voice I'd be wise not to ignore.

I braked and wheeled around. Sure enough, Sheriff Grigsby stood in front of Simonson's Drug Store, hands set to the side of his mouth as if to holler at me again. Behind him, Fire Chief Wakuna—his ever present companion—strutted out of the store, shadowing the bigger man.

"Morning, Sheriff Grigsby! How-do, Chief Wakuna!" Rather than going over to them, I sat perched on my bike, hoping to get on with my day. But the Sheriff—the world's biggest pear—strode across the street, huffing and puffing. Clearly, he had something on his mind other than chatting up the weather.

Wheezing like a squeaky gate, the sheriff fanned his face with his hat. Although 75 degrees out, he looked like a man who'd just crawled out of the Sahara Desert.

As his usual wont, Chief Wakuna took forever and a day crossing the street. Despite his giraffe-length strides, he lived life at a decidedly easy-going pace, the polar opposite of the sheriff.

Sheriff Grigsby still couldn't muster the air to form a sentence.

"Morning, Dibby." Chief Wakuna stuck his hands in his jeans pockets. A light breeze blew his open flannel shirt back over his t-shirt and lifted his long hair. I'd always been secretly jealous of his thick, lustrous locks, by far the best in Hangwell.

"Morning back to you, Chief. Sheriff. Just on my way to school. Can't be late."

At long last, the Sheriff's breath topped off. "Well, now, Dibby, I certainly don't want to contribute to your being late to school. I understand you're already in a mite big heap of trouble."

"I wouldn't say 'heap'," I suggested.

"Fact of the matter is, I'd like to make sure you don't add anything onto that ol' heap you seem gosh-durn hell-bent on building for yourself."

"That's powerful nice of you, Sheriff. But I fully intend on staying on the straight and narrow."

Typically, Chief Wakuna said nothing. A man of few words, he never beat around any bushes unless they tumbled in his way. If he knew what the sheriff wanted, he didn't show it. But that didn't mean a thing. Unlike

Odie Smith, Chief Wakuna enjoyed the reputation of being the man no one in town wanted to play poker with.

"Dibby, it's come to my attention…well, this matter gets a little tetchy, if you know what I mean…" I didn't, but the sheriff tapped his temple as if he had everything under control upstairs. "I done heard you made up some nonsense about a non-existent history project. One regarding the Saunders family."

That wasn't the only thing I'd fabricated. A fake cough covered my nervous gulp. "Oh, we were just fooling around, Sheriff. We didn't mean anything by it. Honest."

"By 'we,' I take it you're referring to the new Mackleby boy? The one living over at the hotel?" The sheriff framed a sour face as if a bug'd flown into his mouth, his distaste for James obvious. Knowing the sheriff, I fully suspected James's long hair provided the reason.

"That'd be James, sir. Since he's new, I thought I'd show him around."

"Now that still doesn't explain why you're running around lying about school projects. That just doesn't sit well with me. How 'bout you, Chief?"

"Mm."

"But the thing that strikes me as odd, Dibby…" continued the sheriff, "…the thing that just sticks in my craw and won't let go…is why in the world would you be having fun at the expense of the Saunders family? That seems a bit cruel given their history."

He waited for my response, stretched back and stood tall. A bullet of sunlight pinged off his sheriff's star.

I weighed my responses. On the one hand, it seemed like the sheriff might be the most knowledgeable person regarding Thomas Saunders. On the other, I reckoned I was much too young to end up in his hoosegow. All over a stupid lie over a stupid, made-up school project. "Sheriff, I surely meant no disrespect. I was just curious about what happened to Thomas Saunders. Seeing as how Missus Saunders is my neighbor, I didn't want to say something off and stick my boot in my big ol' mouth."

Just when I thought the Sheriff had blustered every shade of red, he turned heart-attack purple, the color ol' Fred Landry assumed when he dropped dead last year. His lips drew into a tiny, colorless, draw-stringed bag. "You listen to me, young lady, and you listen good! Tommy Saunders ran away from home years ago and it done tore his momma up. He just up and ran off to make good in the big city or join the circus or some other starry-eyed notion. Either way, what he done was a huge disrespect to his momma and now I see your heading down that same path. Missus Saunders has had enough heartache. I suggest, and this is a strong suggestion…" His stubby finger nearly poked me in the eye. "…that you never mind about the Saunders' past heartbreak and go live your li'l girl life. Like a normal girl."

That didn't set well with me, but I let it be. Decided to press my luck. "What happened to Thomas's father?"

"Why don't you ask your daddy about *that*." Spittle flew from the sheriff's mouth.

"My dad won't talk to me about the Saunders." My voice sounded small. I felt like a little girl, the kind the Sheriff wanted me to be.

"For damn good reason, I imagine!" The Sheriff straightened, took a breath, then snorted it out toward me. The minty odor of chaw, mixed with onions, filled my nose. "Just leave things alone, Dibby. I mean it." He brought back his long finger of the law. "Or I might just have to look into that accusation that you defiled and stole from the library. Now get on to school. Git!" He slapped my back tire as if it was a horse.

I didn't stick around, no moss on me. I pedaled fast as my legs could work. A safe distance away, I looked back. The two men hadn't moved from the center of the street. They held court, imposing as all get out, arms folded and shoulders back.

Further on down the street, two women stood side-by-side, shoe to shoe, arms interlinked. Watching me. Or at least one was watching me.

The Sooter sisters—as James would say—had rat-finked on me.

Shadows drew fast over Main Street, very wrong for the time of day.

* * *

It seemed all of Hangwell's townsfolk had been picked up by a twister, stirred, then dropped back down on their heads, everyone acting a might odd. A funny feeling, adults rarely gave me the time of day, let alone considered me the center of their storm.

Even Odie Smith had abandoned his breakfast swinging post. Surely, a prophetic sign of the times.

As I pulled my bike into the school rack, I took a long look at the sky above. Blue skies forever cottoned with a few clouds. It surely didn't look or smell like a brewing storm. But it felt that way.

I barely made it into my seat before the bell rang. Classes proved endless, the monotony broken only by furtive glances and coy smiles shared with James.

Aggravating to a fault, I couldn't even get a word in with James. Because of Mrs. Hopkins's rigid structure, even our lunch period was highly regimented, assigned seats and no talking. Now I truly knew how those star-crossed lovers, Romeo and Juliet, felt as dark forces conspired to keep them apart.

Surely melodramatic, but as I couldn't concentrate on classes, I had to occupy my time somehow.

Of course, you can't have good without evil. Suzette and her evil battalion of Barbies were at it again, stabbing me with eye daggers and blatantly whispering about me. Years of that behavior, though, had forti-fied me with the skin of an armadillo.

Still, I dreaded the inevitable end-of-day public apology, worse than seeing the dentist over in Durham.

The time came. I braced myself. In front of the class, I stood next to Suzette. Not too close, though. I didn't want any of her rubbing off on me.

"Class, Suzette and Dibby have something they'd like to share with you." Mrs. Hopkins beamed like we were two of the cutest puppies ever witnessed. "What do you have to say for yourselves, girls?"

Silence. I wasn't going first. I figured Suzette felt the same.

A dead heat, Mrs. Hopkins called the tie. "Suzette, do you have some-thing to say to Dibby?"

Suzette studied her stupid shiny shoes, just swaying back and forth. She smiled, big and metallic, a demonic smile of trickery. "Yes, I would. I'd like to say I'm sorry..." The pause lasted longer than the entire agonizing day of class. Her painted fingernails flew to her mouth to stifle a not-so-subtle giggle. "...that Dibby hit me!"

Not to be outdone, I shouted, "And I'm mighty sorry I didn't sock you twice!"

The class erupted. Hoots and hollers and two-fingered whistles rooted for another round of battle. Outraged, Mrs. Hopkins stood, her eyes twin eggs and her mouth wide enough to fit 'em both in. She smacked her yard stick against the chalkboard, screamed for the class to settle down. Over the barnyard calamity, her shouts went unheard.

The final bell, however, accomplished what Mrs. Hopkins couldn't. Bloodlust forgotten, my classmates barreled out the door. The last one out, James shot me a wink, followed by a small hand-clap, the kind usually reserved for polite social functions.

The consequences be hanged, I felt empowered. Based on Suzette's hideous, metal-covered smile, she felt the same way. I caught her eye, smirked. Laughed. Just couldn't help it. So did Suzette. Whether a shared laugh or mocking laughter, I couldn't rightly tell, but it just seemed like the only response to a silly situation.

On the other hand, Mrs. Hopkins appeared less than tickled. Her yardstick still beat the tar outta the chalkboard and she gave us a grimace that could mortify babies.

"Girls...that's *not* what had been discussed." When she spoke, her lips remained locked just like a ventriloquist. "Apologize...this instant! Or you *will* be suspended."

Since the last sunrise, things had changed for me. Yesterday at this time, I wouldn't have given two hoots and a holler if I'd been given the school boot. But that meant three days without seeing James.

Begrudgingly, I turned toward Suzette, grumbled, "Sorry I socked you yesterday."

Suzette adopted the same put-upon, stomach-growling tone. "Sorry I made fun of you."

"There. That wasn't so hard, was it?" Sunshine informed Mrs. Hopkins's smile. "Now, girls, I want you to act together and clean the chalkboards and erasers. I'll be stepping out for a spell. Can I trust you girls to behave like young ladies on your own?"

"Yes, Missus Hopkins," I groaned.

"Very well. You'll find rags in the sink. Your future relies on this, girls. We wouldn't want bad marks on our permanent records now, would we?"

"No, Missus Hopkins," I bellyached.

Already reaching for a cigarette inside her purse, Mrs. Hopkins fled in a hurry.

I've never understood the reasoning behind cleaning chalkboard erasers. Seemed to me like a fairly futile exercise. The next day, the erasers would be full of chalk again. Some of the boys in class actually enjoyed banging the life out of them, and I had to 'fess up to banging things around (like Suzette) did hold a certain charm. Still, cleaning things just so they can get dirty again seemed an uphill battle.

From a bag beneath her chair, Suzette pulled out an apron. It draped her full-length. Like a Mummy, her wrappings dragged the floor.

I laughed, pointed at her. "Are you wearing a mop?"

"At least I care about my appearance. Maybe you should try it sometime." A trollish sneer gummed up her face.

"I tried, remember? Didn't make a lick of difference. You made fun of me when I dressed up. And you belittle me when I don't." The absolute nonsense of it all struck me. "You and your little hellions want it both ways and neither way far as I'm involved." I shrugged. "I don't care." Although, I reckon I did. Just a bit, but I'd never let Suzette know that.

"Cry me a river." She balled a hand in her eye and rubbed it.

"No, thank you. You did enough crying yesterday to last a lifetime."

That righteously shut her maw. At the sink, she wet down a rag. When she finished, I did the same. I set to work, mindlessly scrubbing the board. Humming just to keep my mind occupied. We managed to stay out of each other's paths, until we met at the middle of the chalkboard.

"*You* like the Beatles?" she asked incredulously

"You talking to me?"

She stomped a foot. "There's no one else in the room, Dibby! You were humming—if *that's* what you call it—*I Wanna Hold Your Hand*. I can't *believe* you like the Beatles."

I hadn't even realized the song I'd been humming, not consciously. "You gotta monopoly on the Beatles? Sure, I like 'em. Like 'em lots. Unlike you, though, I don't paste my walls full of pictures of them, praying for them to notice me."

"You're weird."

"You're stupid."

A silence fell over us. Frankly, the never-ending battle just ate up too much energy. I took back to humming, turned it up a bit.

"*Must* you do that so loudly?" Suzette screeched. "You're gonna call the cows home!"

"Well, it got your attention, didn't it, Bessie?"

She sighed, the fight gone out of her. Probably because she didn't have her flock of geese to impress. And I had to confess, it made her a lot less interesting. "You're *really* weird," she said.

"Better weird than one of the same ol' lemmings," I volleyed back.

"That doesn't even make sense."

"Don't strain your brain."

"So…who do you like? I mean in the Beatles? *This* should be rich." She rolled her eyes. If they stuck that way, I vowed to attend church regularly again.

"I like them all. Duh."

"I mean, which *one* do you like?"

I gave it some thought, first time really. To me, the Beatles were nearly indistinguishable in their dark suits and black mop-tops, a collective, unattainable group. Nearly fictional. I didn't care. The cutest Beatle in my mind was my would-be bug, James. But to tell Suzette that would be to hang a target on my back, proclaiming, "It's Dibby hunting season!"

Instead, I answered, "I guess I like the cute one." Let her gnaw on that a while.

"Me, too." She stopped, looked at me, dumb eyes wide.

Before I embarrassed myself with my lack of Beatles knowledge, I left the topic behind. "Why do you do it anyway?" I asked.

"Do *what?*"

"Why do you try to berate me every time I turn around? I can't remember ever doing anything to you. Matter of fact, I seem to recall we played together in grade school."

She rolled her eyes again. "That was back in kindergarten, Dibby! Grow up!"

"You're the one dressed up in baby doll clothing."

"And you look like Farmer Leroy who—"

"You'll end up marrying," I finished.

"You're so…so…darned aggravating!"

"So that's why you try to beat me down, Suzette? 'Cause I aggravate you? According to science, the world doesn't rotate around you."

"*See?* See *there?*" I didn't. But I rightly felt we were finally getting somewhere, rather than trading insults and punches. "That's what I mean about you. You're *weird.* Maybe if you acted normal—like a regular normal girl—people wouldn't make fun of you all the time!"

I considered her argument. Didn't like it one iota, no sir, not a bit. "You never took time to get to know me, Suzette. And, frankly, if it takes being like you and the others to be your friend…no thanks. I reckon I'm okay with our relationship just the way it is."

"There's nothing wrong with me and my friends." She wrung the rag in her hand. Water dripped onto her polished shoe. Her face scrunched up. "*You're* the one who's weird! Not me!"

"We'll just see 'bout that in ten years when you're still living here, kissing on ol' Farmer Leroy, and slopping his pigs supper."

Apparently, I struck bone. She came at me with two chalk erasers, her mouth twisted and ugly. Hardly fearsome looking, just a little dolly in a too large apron, near sobbing, prepared to felt me to death.

She brought the erasers together with a surprisingly mighty clap. A cloud of white dust rose, surrounded me. I coughed. My eyes irritated to the point of tears. But not so much I couldn't find my own weapons.

Determined to storm down clouds of dust upon my nemesis, I banged my erasers together. I blew into the resultant cloud, unfortunately getting a bit of backlash. But Suzette got the brunt end. Snowy dust caked her hair and face 'til she resembled a powdered donut down at Carol's Diner.

She squeezed out a girly "ooh!" As she reloaded, she scribbled a piece of chalk over one of her erasers. Then she whomped 'em together.

Like Old Man Winter, we filled the classroom with blinding snow, the fall-out hard to breathe through. We took turns chasing, both of us screaming. Most surprising, laughter stitched up my belly.

I held up a hand, halted our impromptu battle. Our battleground lay in shambles. If we didn't do something about it soon, we'd be topping that heap of trouble Sheriff Grigsby warned me about.

"Come on!" Eyes running like leaky faucets, I waved Suzette over to the windows. Together we opened them, the kind that opened bottom out to keep kids locked inside. Panting, I stuck my head outside. Next to me, Suzette did the same thing.

My eyes cleared a bit. I looked over at Suzette. With our hands and heads hanging out, we resembled witches clopped into the stockades of olden days. Again, it tickled my funny bone and apparently struck Suzette, too.

"So," I said, facing the back field, "you don't like me 'cause I'm different? I don't rightly think that's fair, Suzette."

She let out a cleansing sigh. "I guess I just kinda thought…you were fine with it."

"'Fine'?"

"You know…how we act around each other. We each do what we do. It's just the way it is."

"I never considered it that way before. And you know what? Now that I've considered it, I reckon it's the dumbest thing I ever did hear."

Laughter ruled 'til we sucked up our share of fresh oxygen.

"Missus Hopkins must be taking the longest cigarette break in school history," said Suzette.

"Sure seems that way."

I don't know what came over me. Maybe the fact I'd cracked Suzette's mean, icy exterior put me a bit at ease. Or maybe our adversarial relationship had just grown old and tiresome. Could be, now that I had her vulnerable, a prisoner locked up next to me, I could pick that pea-brain of hers.

More than likely, I'd just banged up against a dead end and had nowhere else to turn.

"Suzette, you ever hear tell what happened to Evelyn Saunders's boy, Thomas?"

Like a prairie dog vanishing inside his hole, Suzette withdrew back into the room. On the way, she banged her curly-haired head on the sill, which brought a grin to my face. I wiped it clean before I reentered the room.

Even through the chalk dust, I could see Suzette was a right shade whiter than usual.

"Why on earth do you wanna know about *that?*"

"Because it matters to me, okay? And not a single adult in town will say boo about it."

Regardless of the still cloudy classroom, Suzette took a seat and motioned for me to join her. "Could be the adults are right for once," she said.

"So *darn* frustrating!" I tossed up my hands and dropped into the desk facing her. "All I wanna know is what happened to Thomas! His daddy, too. But no one—"

"I know what happened." Suzette lowered her voice, uncustomary behavior. Usually she shrieked everything out like a vulture cawing after prey. And she looked frightened to death. The same precious look I committed to memory right before I walloped her.

"Then do spill," I said.

"Dibby, I don't understand why you wanna know—and I don't care either—but you best be careful. Again, I don't care about—"

"Just tell me!"

"That ol' witch Hettie Williquette fixed Thomas Saunders's wagon. Gobbled him up like candy."

Of course, I'd given Hettie a fair dose of consideration. Everyone in town considered her, it'd be dang foolish not to. Hangwell's resident witch, Hettie'd provided many a sleepless night for children throughout the years. The stories were endless, every one growing bigger than well-kept stalks of corn. As a kid, I regularly checked under my bed at night for sightings of Hettie and her crooked visage. When I saw her at the drug store, I'd scurry away to a different aisle before she swept me away on her broom. Kids knew well enough to stay out of her pasture, off her front porch at Halloween, and out of her path for fear she'd cast the evil eye on you.

Like she did to ol' Hyrum Thurgood.

Everyone knew Hy liked to tip at the bottle, no secret there. But rumor had it he made the mistake of saying some mighty disparaging words about Hettie down at the Tavern. Once word got back to Hettie (and 'round here, word travels faster than electricity), ol' Hy found his big toe rotting away, the end shriveled up like a sun-baked walnut.

"Suzette, I know you can't grasp much, but surely you don't think Hettie Williquette ate Thomas Saunders."

"I know it as gospel. You just sit there on your high horse, Dibby Caldwell, but I know what I know."

"How do you know?"

"Angela told me. Saw it with her own eyes."

Right when I felt near to gullible, Suzette lost her credibility. Just one rung down on humanity's ladder from Suzette, Angela spent most of her time gossiping and spinning mighty tall tales. "The day I start believing Angela Brader is the day I—"

"Angela saw Hettie eat Gordon Turndell."

I blinked, tried to clear the outlandish imagery from my mind.

Of course, everyone knew Gordon Turndell. Or had known of him. The high school senior with a face chiseled out of granite and a chin that could slice through wood was hard to miss, all the girls ga-ga for him. Successful at everything, Gordie made the grades and conquered the football field as the Hangwell Lions' star quarterback. With two months to go until fetching a diploma, it seemed highly unlikely he'd turn his broad-shouldered back on such a promising future, but that's exactly what he did. Just up and packed a bag and took off without so much as a peep or goodbye to anyone. Just like Thomas Saunders. Those in the know—and by that, I mean the regulars down at the Tavern—reckoned it was just a case of a boy's wanderlust, the way cats are prone to. But when Sherriff Grigsby was called upon to investigate and came up with no satisfying answers, people talked.

Or more than likely, they whispered, the way of Peculiar County.

Although I down-right despised Suzette, I never considered her particularly naïve. "Come on, Suzette. Hettie Williquette didn't eat Gordon Turndell! Angela saw no such thing."

As Suzette nodded, her goldie locks bounced over her shoulders. "She surely did. The night before Gordon went missing, Angela was out riding her bike, and she saw Gordon's car pull into Hettie's drive. She dumped her bike in a ditch, hid behind the front hedges, and watched Gordon stroll right on up to Hettie's front door."

"And Angela just happened to be riding her bike by Hettie's house? Out in the woods? Alone, late at night?" I sighed, long and dramatically. "Everyone's scared to death to even be in the same town as Hettie, let alone her neck of the woods."

"Well…truth be told, Angela might've been following Gordon, since she was sweet on him."

"That sounds about truthful."

"Anyhoo, when Hettie opened the door, she grabbed Gordon, and swung him into her creepy ol' house. Angela decided to take a closer look. She snuck up to Hettie's porch and heard screaming. Terrible noises! She took a gander through the window. Ol' Hettie had taken off Gordon's clothes and had him on the floor, just gnawing away at him. Biting his neck, his man nipples and, um, even…" Beneath the chalk dust, Suzette's cheeks reddened. She cradled a hand around her mouth, whispered, "…his man parts."

"Ew. Um…were they having sex?"

Clearly, the idea of sex seemed to startle Suzette more than a flesh-eating witch. She formed that gawd-awful figure eight with her mouth. "That's disgusting, Dibby! Blech!" She stuck her tongue out between prissy, pursed lips. Gave her head a right shake as if clearing thoughts of sex away might keep her mind pristine forever. Seemed to me if Mrs. Keating hadn't had "The Talk" with Suzette yet, it surely shouldn't fall on me.

"Fine, Suzette. So Angela saw Hettie doing that to Gordon."

Solemnly, she nodded. "Gordon was never seen again."

Frankly, banging erasers had proven more productive. "How do you figure Thomas Saunders ran afoul of Hettie?" If ol' Hettie was favoring young men with sex—the imagery a might bit disturbing—that didn't explain what she would've been doing with a younger boy.

"Well… It's just a fact that Hettie eats all the runaways. Been doing it for years."

"Good grief. It's more than likely those kids did run away. Who wouldn't wanna leave this town behind in the dust? So, that ain't no fact about Hettie, Suzette! Hell, it's hardly even a good rumor."

Again, Suzette screwed up her mouth. "You cursed! I'm gonna tell—"

"Oh, go tattle on your own time. In the meantime, I'm trying to find out what happened to Thomas Saunders. I think someone killed him. And I don't reckon it was Hettie Williquette, either."

"I know she did it. I truly do."

"*How?*" With Suzette, it proved worse than wrenching teeth, maybe my actual next move.

"'Cause Momma told me so. She says Hettie eats all the bad kids. They don't run away, that's just a nonsense story everyone made up. Momma told me to stay far from Hettie's, and seeing as I'm no fool—"

"Beg to differ."

"…I listen. Momma also said Hettie did away with Thomas's father, Hedrick."

"What?"

"Before Thomas Saunders went missing, his daddy, Hedrick Saunders, used to pay Hettie visits. Everyone thought they were in cahoots over witchcraft. It's no secret that when Hettie runs dry of kids, she takes to eating cats. Hedrick Saunders used to bring her cats for her supper."

I'd heard the rumor, and frankly, I didn't discount it out of hand. Like any small town, Hangwell has its fair share of stray farm cats roaming the countryside. You can't swing a…well, a cat, for fear of hitting one. At least that used to be true 'til a couple years ago, when the cat population done fairly dried up. Naturally, the blame fell on Hettie. A lotta disgruntled farmers blamed her for crops faring poorly as well.

"So…if what your mother says is true—"

"It is."

"…whatever became of Hedrick Saunders?"

Suzette guffawed, very un-girly-like. "Hettie ate him. Duhhh! Just how slow *are* you, Dibby?"

To answer her properly, I tilted my chair back, grabbed two dirty erasers, and clomped them together mightily below her nose.

Chapter Seven

At long last, Mrs. Hopkins returned, miraculously pleased as punch over the thorough job we'd done. Outside, Suzette's mother, Mrs. Keating, sat behind the wheel of her big, ol' Lincoln Continental, scowling like a rabid badger. By way of parting, I managed an almost amiable chin jerk toward Suzette.

Behind me, laughter belted out. Half-hidden beneath the shadows of an elm tree, James lay in the grass, his bike next to him.

"You look white as a ghost," he said.

"You're a real cut-up, James, a real comedian." I patted my shoulders, clapped my hands. Chalk dust rose. "The rewards of hard work." Worn out, I dropped into the grass beside him.

"So…how'd it go? Did you get into another brawl?"

"No. Not really. Just chalked each other up a bunch. It….well, it didn't pan out like I expected."

"You buddies now?"

"Never. Just…I dunno, I reckon maybe the world's big enough for both of us. Forget all that. What're you doing here? Don't you ever crack a book?"

"Sure do. Every night, I crack 'em against the hotel wall trying to shut that damn ghost dog up." He stood, stretched. His t-shirt came untucked, exposing a tanned, taut belly. "Let's beat feet."

"Can't. I'm grounded, 'member?"

"Oh, yeah, right. You ask your ol' man about the movie yet?"

I stood. "Not yet. One thing at a time. I sorta need to handle Dad with kid gloves."

"Yeah, sounds familiar. But, hey, you gotta go through downtown anyway, right? We can go together."

"I reckon there's no harm in that."

Dusk already seemed antsy, battening the sun down before its time. As we walked our bikes down Main Street, our shadows stretched as long as our limited time together.

"Not to change the channel or anything," he said, "but…what happened to your old lady? You never talk about her. Did she…um, die?"

Rude and to-the-point, but I figured it best to put a tail on the situation before James heard about Mom from someone else. Particularly from one of the more judgmental Hangwell folks. "Tell you the truth, I don't know where she is now. And, frankly, I don't rightly remember her much. When I was just a little gal, no taller than your hip bone, she took off. Just up and left one night without so much as a 'boo'."

James stopped. "Oh…wow. Sorry she finked out on you. What a drag. Why'd she leave?"

"Not real sure. I ask myself all the time."

"What's your old man say about it?"

I shrugged. "It's something we don't talk about. Not that it'd bother me, I s'pose. As I said, I don't remember much about her. Just the idealized notion of her more than anything, I guess. You know, the kind of mom who wears aprons, hums a lot, shows you make-up tips, cooks up a storm…that kinda thing. But…it bothers Dad. So, I just leave it be. Some things are better off buried, I reckon."

"I'd be…you know, off my rocker trying to find out why she left. Did they get divorced?"

"Dad doesn't even know where she is to get the procedure handled, the papers signed. Or maybe he's waiting for her to come back…some day." I swallowed, my throat parched as a gulch. Maybe the topic bothered me a bit more than I let on.

Silent for a spell, we walked our bikes side-by-side down Main Street's sidewalk. More than happy to change the subject, I asked, "What're your folks like?"

"I dunno. The usual, I guess. They're so square, their edges are sharp. My old man's Uncle Sam's soldier, you know? And my old lady spends a lot of time locked in her hotel room, doing who knows what. When they're together, they fight and scream a lot. I kinda wish they'd just get divorced."

"Careful what you wish for." Turns out James and I had a lot in common, our folks an unhappy bunch. For those still present, at least. "I'm sorry they're not happy, James. But…be thankful you have a mother."

He didn't say anything, just shuffled along. I ambled ahead a ways before I realized he was no longer beside me. Stopped in front of Simonson's Drug Store, he gazed into the display window. Mr. Simonson's year-round train set had captured his attention. Railroad cars trundled through a cave, up a grassy hill, and hooked around the figure eight layout. Various candy and drug boxes stood about like odd trees and three-dimensional billboards. A BB gun, several board games, an odd-looking rubber device that looked like it'd hold a gullet full of water, a pair of crutches, old time remedies, and flavored cough syrups padded out the crowded panorama. Other than the sheet of snowy cotton Mr. Simonson painstakingly set beneath his display come every winter, the items rarely changed, a rare comfort in Hangwell.

The window reflected James's image, his consideration not on the moving train after all. Turned away, his shoulders hitched up—hiding in plain sight—he dabbed a finger beneath his eye.

I moved in closer, touched my shoulder to his. We stood that way for a bit, a more effective tonic than words. I grabbed his hand, gave it a squeeze, let him know I understood. Pretty much like the Sooter sisters, if anyone could read my physical short-hand, I reckoned James could.

His sudden vocal outburst startled me. "Hey, I'm starving! How 'bout some chow?"

"I can't. I gotta get home. Besides I don't have any money."

"No sweat, my treat!" Excited now, a complete turnaround, he dragged me into Simonson's Drug Store.

The little bell above the door *ding-a-linged*.

Behind the counter, Mr. Simonson looked up, all nose, brush mustache, glasses, and business. Sometimes it tickled me wondering what he really looked like behind his Groucho-styled disguise. "Why, hello there, Dibby Caldwell." Always my full name, the way he addressed everyone. "Surely Dibby Caldwell's not due again for more feminine products just yet?"

Oh, dear Lord, no!

Flames of scarlet shame spread across my forehead and my cheeks. Busy studying the colorful candy bar displays, James hadn't heard Mr. Simonson, or at least had the common decency to pretend not to. I set my brow to a very serious position, shook my head with grim determination, hoping Mr. Simonson would realize his mistake.

"How's your daddy's corns coming along, Dibby Caldwell? Still setting him to ache at night?"

I gladly embraced the world's second worst topic of conversation. "I do believe Dad's corns are going the way of the do-do, Mister Simonson. This here's my new friend, James Mackleby. He's new to town."

"Ah, yes, James Mackleby. Your father's Robert Mackleby, I presume. It's a pleasure to meet you, James Mackleby."

By way of hello, James gave a curt nod, grunted, a bit sullen. His hair swooped down, animated, announcing the scary-for-adults length. For someone who prided himself on his ability to communicate with adults, James appeared far from photo ready.

I hurried toward him, nudged him. Dense as all get out, he still didn't understand what he'd done wrong. "Say hello in a proper fashion," I whispered, and it surely got my dander up I had to do so.

"H'lo."

His hands full of candy bars, he shoved them toward me. "You want one of these?"

Absolutely befuddled by his sudden mood swings—his actions now bespoke of a sugar-addled child—I shook my head. "Dad doesn't like me snacking on candy. And I really gotta head home."

"Oh, right, sure. Let me lay down some bread." His arms full and spilling over, he rushed toward the counter. I scooped up a fallen *Baby Ruth* bar and followed.

As Mr. Simonson rang up the bounty of candy, he commented, "My, oh, my, James Mackleby, you'll rot your teeth out, you surely will."

"Fab!" James grinned. "Then my old man won't have to get me braces."

James attempt at humor soared over Mr. Simonson's flat-topped head. The pharmacist frowned at me as if I'd been in charge of James and had let him out of his cage. "Will there be anything else today, James Mackleby?"

"Sure. A package of Kents. No filters."

My world tipped sideways, then sprung a leak. My stomach flipped. Lunch swirled, swooshed, threatened to revisit. The unspeakable done, James had hogtied me into being his accomplice in crime.

Mr. Simonson appeared appalled, lower jaw set to wobbling. James just kept grinning, the grin I now felt stupid for once considering charming.

"I think not, Master Mackleby." I knew we were in trouble—acres worth of trouble—when Mr. Simonson resorted to James's surname. "I hardly 'spect you're twenty-one, let alone sixteen if a day."

"Hey, back where I come from, they—"

"And where is that, Master Mackleby? Hooliganville? Crime Alley? Dibby Caldwell, I'm surprised at you! Why, wait until I tell your poor daddy about this…this…" Mr. Simonson fumed. Steam practically whizzed out his ears, his words stoked on coal.

"I'm sorry, Mister Simonson. Honestly, I had no idea what James was up to. It won't happen again." I grabbed a good handful of James's jean-jacket back and dragged him toward the door. He tottered after me, arms flailing every which way.

"Hey! What about my candy?"

"Shut your pie-hole," I hissed. "Right now you best just hope to get outta here afore ol' Sheriff Grigsby comes around." To the pharmacist, I called out, "I apologize again, Mister Simonson." I didn't stop until I'd scooted out the door and shoved James toward his bicycle.

"Dibby, what—"

"Oh, shut up, already! I can't believe you did that, especially since I already warned you *not* to. And now I'm your…your criminal accomplice!"

James looked at his feet, feigning a lost little boy. "Sorry. I just thought—"

"No, you didn't! You *never* think. And that problem's gonna get you in deep, deep trouble, James! It's time you bellied up to the truth. You ain't smoking cigarettes in Hangwell no way, no *how*. And if you don't wise up? Hangwell's got a way that'll come back and bite you!"

Finished leading my angry Main Street parade, I ignored all of the gathered gawkers and hopped onto my bike. I zipped past Mildred Clark, narrowly missing her as she swept the sidewalk in front of her hotel. I swerved around Mr. Thomason, the banker, as he left Carol's Diner. Across the street, Sheriff Grigsby stood big and large, glowering at me.

Eyes locked straight ahead, I fled downtown. The Hangwell communication highway traveled even faster than me, and Dad had probably already heard about my new life of crime.

"Dibby! Hang on," James called. "I'm sorry! You're right, I didn't think!" His words panted out, ho-hum and tired. "Wait!"

Once I cleared the business district, I pulled my bike sharp. The tires skidded, my feet trawled dust. As I watched James struggle to catch up, I wondered just how many chances I'd give him, if he was worth all the trouble.

Like a judge holding court, I set my arms on top of the handlebars.

"I'm sorry, Dibby. I didn't mean to get you into trouble. Sometimes I just do stuff…stupid stuff…"

"Sometimes, 'sorry' doesn't make things right. And I got to thinking… Were you trying to use my good reputation in town to help you get your damn cigarettes?"

"No! I'd never do something like that to you, Dibby. Scout's honor." Again, he made the faulty Scout's sign, fooling only himself. "Look… If you want, I'll make everything right. I'll explain to the old coot in the drug store that you had nothing to do with it. I'll even talk to your old man and tell him—"

"You'll do *no* such thing. You've done more than enough damage. When word gets back to Dad, I'll be grounded for two lifetimes. And I'll *never* find out what happened to Thomas Saunders!"

"What can I do to make it up to you, Dibby? Just say it. Anything."

And there, sitting on his bike, eyes sorrowful, and voice choked with big clots of regret, I believed him. Either that or he'd mastered a lifetime's worth of swindling.

"Right now, just…just don't do anything. But if it comes down to it, I ain't falling on this sword for you."

"Sure thing. I'll kiss-up to whoever I have to."

"How 'bout you start by knocking off all your hip play-acting? My dad'll see right through your phony baloney."

"I'll do it. You'll see."

Under the sun's heat, I percolated. Before reaching boiling point, I turned my temperature down to an even-keeled simmer. "You aggravate the tar outta me, James Mackleby."

"That's because you kinda like me, Dibby Caldwell." His smile, the one that could conquer cities, came back. "I kinda like you, too."

So help me, he was right. About my liking him. But he hadn't earned any sort of recognition of the fact. Far as I was concerned, he still had a good long haul to make things right with me.

"Don't you ever, *ever* try anything like that again. Not with me around. I won't stand for it."

"Got it."

"You're just lucky I need your help. 'Til you prove yourself worthy, you do as I say."

"I'm at your service, m'lady." His hand rolled away beneath his chin in what he considered a gallant move. Rather it looked like he'd just swallowed a mouthful of hot peppers.

"Tonight, I need to go see someone, a trip I'd be rightly stupid to make by myself."

"Yeah? Who's doorbell we gonna ring?"

"A witch's."

Crickets chirped. Cicadas buzz-sawed. From a distance, a cow lowed.

Finally, "Fat city!"

* * *

Not for a minute did I buy into Suzette's stupid little Grimm-minded tale of a boy-eating witch, but one thing life in Hangwell had taught me. Behind every fanciful beanstalk of a tale, a deep seed of truth had been planted. I had no idea what the best, if any, method would be to approach scary Hettie. I didn't much take to the notion of banging on her front door and inquiring if she ate Thomas and Hedrick Saunders. But I suspected she knew something about their disappearances, maybe even acted as a participant in their fates. Either way, I'd be highly negligent if I didn't pay a visit.

I just didn't care to do it alone. Particularly if Hettie had a mind to stir me into Dibby stew. Silly, of course; nothing but a kid's campfire notion. But there wasn't a single, silly thing about missing—possibly dead—kids.

Lost in thought—dawdling a bit and hesitant to face Dad—I pedaled back and forth across the gravel road in a lazy pattern. In front of the Saunders' homestead, I dropped feet and anchored them. The Saunders' mailbox flag sat down, Odie's postal run completed.

Far off down the drive, Mrs. Saunders sat on her porch, rocking her life away. In the distance, I heard evidence of her brother, Devin, pitching up the earth on his tractor.

And Dad's hearse was nowhere to be seen.

Surely Fate had aligned everything properly, a winning shot in a game of pool. I'd be a right fool not to act upon it. Before my brain could caution against, I acted. I grabbed the mail in the box—mostly catalogs and the urgent, no-nonsense typefaces of overdue bills—stuffed them in-to the bike basket beside my books, and tread down the Saunders' pebble-covered driveway.

Halfway down the drive, I regretted my impulse, considered turning around.

Slowly, Mrs. Saunders stood. A breeze, one conjured by magazine photographers, drew her floral dress tight around the perfect hourglass of her body. As if saluting me, she tented her hand over her eyes and watched as I drew closer. From a small table beside her, she grabbed a tall glass, and sipped from one of those fancy straws, the bendy kind. She sat back down. Legs that I envied, crossed.

Near the porch, I hopped off my bike, toed down the kickstand. Nervous, I walked toward the porch, the mail offered out at arm's length as if gifting the Queen of England.

She didn't move, didn't lower her movie-star glasses. Her stoic demeanor rivaled Mount Rushmore.

"Ma'am." Stupidly, I curtsied. "I, um, well, I thought I'd bring you your mail."

"Isn't that nice?" While not overflowing with joy, she didn't sound quite ready to fetch the shotgun either. In fact, she didn't sound much of anything.

"I'm your neighbor, Dibby." I tossed a thumb back at our house. "Next door? Dibby—"

"Dibby Caldwell. Yes, I know." Nearly as slim as her waistline, a smile tightened. Honestly, I didn't know how she kept such a trim figure. Far as I could tell, she didn't do much of anything other than sit and drink. Maybe long-term rocking had its benefits. "Why, I haven't spoken to you since you were just a babe."

I had no idea she even knew who I was, let alone spoken to me before. "I reckon you'll forgive me when I say I don't remember meeting you."

She melted, just a bit. A corner of her mouth hitched up. Wrinkles rippled, the first indication she was somewhere around Dad's age. She gestured toward the rocking chair next to her. "Of course. Join me for a sit."

Strangely mesmerized under her spell, I accepted, all haste to get home forgotten. Under no control of my own, my legs bounded up the three steps. Like a tummy-ache, loose floorboards rumbled. Worn but solid, the cloth bottom of the chair sagged. No doubt Devin's chair.

Palm up, her hand went out. It took me a tick to understand what she wanted. I handed over her mail. "Thank you," she said.

"You're welcome, ma'am."

"Please…call me Evvie. That's what my friends call me."

Again, I wasn't near comfortable addressing adults that way, but I certainly didn't want to look a gift horse in the mouth. Maybe Evvie'd just flat out tell me what happened to her boy. Seeing as how we were friends and all now.

"Evvie, it is." I stuck my hand out. Hers lay limp in mine, weak, cool from her ice-filled glass. "I s'pose I oughta apologize for not coming to visit before now. Not very neighborly of me."

"Don't you worry, Dibby. I imagine your pa had something to do with that. Frankly, I'm surprised he's let you come visit."

"Oh, sure, Dad… Well, he just…" Tired of lying, tired of digging myself deeper, and just plain tired, I stopped talking.

Evvie laughed, three tired, insincere notes. "It's fine, don't you worry about hurting Evvie's feelings."

It didn't take a detective to figure out bad blood percolated between Dad and Evvie. Bad blood I hoped to spill. "So were…*are* you and my dad friends?"

"We were. First person I met when I moved here. But that was a lifetime ago." She sucked through her straw. An ice cube clinked against the side of her glass. "People change. So do lifetimes." She swallowed, then grimaced as if the liquid burned.

"I surely do understand. About change, I mean. Seems like the world's always on the move and I'm pushing on in the other direction."

Again she laughed: *Eh, eh, ehhhh.* "That's the beauty of youth, Dibby. Live it best you can and don't squander it."

Over the past several days, I'd had my fair share of strange encounters with adults, but this one took the cake. Evvie carried a mule's load of philosophy on her back, but not a lick of it made much sense.

I tried to ground our conversation a bit. "I met your brother the other day. Out in your cornfield. I was trying to spook away a coyote."

"Hm. That's funny. Devin never said a word about it."

She started rocking in her chair again, the way old folks carried on at times, spouting wise and waving away the flies.

Unexpectedly, she jerked forward, and pressed her sunglasses on top of her blonde crown of hair.

I nearly yelped. Bloodshot red, sorely so, her eyes looked a sight different naked. Wrinkles surrounded them, marching inward with age. Fading sunlight struck her line of vision, causing her to wince. The flesh around her eyes appeared red, too; swollen from crying, perhaps. Her true age now lay revealed, nothing glamorous about her.

"You look like her, you know," Evvie said.

"Pardon me?" I'd heard her but didn't know if I cared to hear more.

"Your mother. Emily. You look like her." She reached out, folded a lock of hair behind my ear. Smiled. "There. Yes… You look the spitting image." Her head tilted, that condescending manner in which adults consider kids. "Same mouth, same eyes. Something about your…facial structure."

"Thanks. I guess." She took to stroking my cheek next, a very uncomfortable feeling. I didn't know what else to do but sit and take it. We must've looked quite the pair, the owner and her lap dog.

Mercifully, she rounded up what little sense she still possessed. "Oh, my! Where are my manners?" She pulled back, dropped her hands on her knees. Her fingertips slid between her locked knees as if to keep them from getting away. "Would you like a cold beverage?" She swirled her glass. Ice cubes rattled.

"Yes, ma'am, that'd be nice." Actually, I didn't want a drink, my bladder near full to bursting as it was. But I figured it might gain me entry into her house. Why that seemed important, I couldn't say. It just felt right.

"I have lemonade." She frowned. "I'm afraid it's not home-made."

"That'd be fine, Evvie. Could I also bother you to use your washroom?"

I may as well have asked her if I could move in. Her face pulled and tugged as if her innards were boxing at her skin. Finally, she settled on a barely present smile. "I suppose there'd be no harm in that. But please… don't make a mess, dear."

"I'll treat it like my own washroom."

"That's…what I'm afraid of."

I pretended the insult flew over my childish head and followed her toward the front door. As soon as I'd stepped inside, the screen door slammed behind me with an alarming firecracker bang.

A hot wave of electricity crackled around me. Hundreds of tiny needles nipped at my flesh. Unnatural humidity pushed down. Similar to what I'd experienced during my two cornfield visits with Evvie's son, I wondered if Thomas's ghost had joined us.

Something brushed my neck, a slight, cool breath. I turned, half expected to see Thomas. Maybe Devin playing at being quiet and creepy. No one—or nothing—stood behind me. Just the huge, ol' mess of the room.

Now I've seen clutter-bugs before, my grandpa, for one, coming to mind. But the Saunders had him beat by a country mile.

In the front room, boxes upon boxes piled high on one another, threatening to topple if you looked at 'em just so. Knickknacks, figurines, doilies, ashtrays, miniature lamps, dog-eared paperbacks, decorative dinnerware, matching glasses, metal toy tractors, and things I didn't recognize occupied every nook and cranny. Thick burgundy drapes captured mustiness as if the Saunders collected that, too. An errant ray of sunshine provided a stagnant pond for dust mites to swim in.

An odor struck me as a might bit peculiar, if not altogether unpleasant. It took me a while to place it, a memory from my childhood: fried chicken cooked to a char, the way Mom used to do it.

This time a hand landed on my shoulder, all too real. I let out a little yip.

"My goodness," said Evvie Saunders, "I didn't mean to give you a fright."

"I'm fine. I just…I guess I need to use that washroom."

"Of course, of course." Quickly, she snatched her hand from my shoulder as if afraid she might jiggle loose my bladder. "Follow me."

Expertly, Evvie navigated between the clutter, careful not to bump into anything. She led me down a hallway, her ankle bones snapping like fingers. Photos hung along the wall, some yellowed with age, others of a more recent vintage. None of them, not that I could see, were of Thomas.

Evvie pushed open a door and stepped back. "I'll be right out here if you need anything."

She meant it, too. After I shut the door, I heard Evvie on the other side, impatiently shuffling, her breath batting up against the woodwork. When I sat down on the toilet seat, the air whooshed out beneath me, a cushioned model. My bladder locked up. I gave the toilet a good flush anyway, washed my hands.

Evvie practically fell onto me when I whisked open the door. Over my shoulder, she gave her washroom a peek. "We didn't make a mess now, did we?"

"No, ma'am, we didn't." I didn't rightly understand how I could've possibly made a mess that would rival the rest of the house, but it wasn't my place to ask.

"Very good. Let me get that glass of lemonade for you then. Follow me, this way."

I suppose she was afraid to set me loose, maybe fearful I'd get lost in the maze of clutter. She maneuvered back to the living room and situated me close to the front door. "Now you stay put. I'll be right back."

She left, humming a tuneless ditty. Again, I felt something at the back of my neck, almost a tickle. Alive, my skin crawled, ready to move with or without the rest of me.

Something pressed into my back. No malice, no harm, but a strong prod of a finger. I swung around, saw nothing. It did it again, this time to my belly. I took a step backward. The pokes kept coming, clearly directing me somewhere. I handed the reins of my body over to my unseen copilot. Once we started working in tandem, it became easier. The ghost corralled me toward the fireplace.

Several framed photographs sat atop the fireplace mantle. Unlike the ones in the hallway, these had recently been dusted.

The first photo displayed Evvie, much younger, standing next to a man in military uniform. His arm around her, his shoulders stretched near the width of Montana. He had kind eyes but a mean-looking mouth, a jaw that could crack walnuts. And I imagined that his large brow—eyebrows sewn together—might cast his eyes a turn angrier once downturned.

No doubt Evvie's husband, Hedrick.

Next to this photo sat a smaller, sadder one of Thomas. Except for his full set of clothes, he didn't appear that much different than how I'd seen him in the field. Posed in front of the Saunders' home, his eyes—very much his daddy's eyes—fixed on something in the distance. Worry troubled his gaunt face, his thin scribble of a mouth bothered. He looked lost, a little boy dwarfed by things bigger than him, things he was powerless to control let alone understand. Worse, he didn't look comfortable at home at all.

My heart bled for Thomas. Possibly attributable to his ghostly presence, I felt he'd had a troubled childhood, one that ended in even more troubling ways. Felt it bothering my bones.

At the far end of the mantle, another photograph lay on its belly. Dust blanketed the back of the frame. I reached for it, hand shaking. Electricity tingled down my spine. Sudden heat flushed over me. Sweat broke out on my brow, my face clammy. I thought I might faint, chunk my head on the fireplace's brickwork.

"What the *hell* do you think you're *doing?*"

My body snapped back together, limbs on the ends of rubber bands. I turned, saw Evvie holding two glasses. An obviously very angry Evvie. The whites of her eyes glowed. A feral scowl exposed clamped teeth.

She clacked the glasses down on a rare bare spot of property. "Get away from there now!"

"Yes, ma'am. I…I'm sorry. I didn't mean to—"

"You need to head on home now." For a woman of such natural composure, she radiated intense fury. "Go on then… Git!"

It didn't take a boot up my backside to get me gone. Still, I didn't like leaving on such a downturn. At the door, I said, "Evvie, I honestly meant no disrespect. If I upset—"

"It's Missus Saunders." She slammed the screen door, then the front door sealed like a tomb.

Fast as I could, I hauled out of there, running alongside my bike 'til I reached the road. On the short trip home, one thought kept niggling through my mind:

I sure would like to know who that last photograph featured, I surely would.

* * *

Minus his usual *Hangwell Gazette*, Dad sat hunkered down at the kitchen table. Word had already reached him about my mishap at Simonson's Drug Store.

"Dibby…" When he raised his head, he looked like an older man. Usually his glasses covered some of the worry lines around his eyes, some of his sadness. Today, he held his glasses, twirling them by the temple tips, swinging in the wind like I was surely about to do. "Please tell me you don't smoke."

I sat down. "'Course not, Dad. I'm no dummy. I'll never forget those pictures you showed me. Of all those cancer victims. That was all James at the pharmacy, and believe you me, I gave him what for about it, too."

He just nodded, either too tired to press or taking me at my word. "Where've you been since then?" He looked at his watch, the one that'd been passed down through several generations of morticians. "You should've been home at least a good hour ago."

Maybe Dad saw me next door. Maybe not. But if I ever intended to leave my bedroom again, I'd better stick with the truth. In a round-about way, of course. "Well, you know I had to help Missus Hopkins after class."

"How'd that go?"

"About as well as could be expected, I suppose. And I guess you heard that James accompanied me down through Main Street."

"*I'll* say." He rapped his fingers over the Formica tabletop.

"And then, when I was on my way home, I saw Missus Saunders… You know, next door?" 'Course he knew her. A little bit better than I'd ever suspected from what Mrs. Saunders had hinted at. "She hadn't yet fetched her mail, so I thought I'd do the right thing by her and bring it up the drive."

Dad's face tightened. His hands roamed through his thinning hair, drawing the sides out like a circus clown. "Dammit, Dibby! How many times have I told you to stay away from that woman? Her and her no-good brother, Devin!"

"I'm sorry! But I just don't understand what harm could come from bringing a woman her mail. Honestly, you won't even tell me *why* I'm supposed to stay away from her! And 'less you do, I can't see any reason to do so. She's just a sad lady, a little kooky maybe, but she's just sad. Sad about her son and—"

Thwack!

Dad's coffee cup jumped, and I matched it, bounce by bounce. His fist came down on the table again. I'd never seen him lose his temper like this.

"*What* do you know about Thomas Saunders, Dibby?"

Bravely, I stood my ground. "What do *you* know about him, Dad?"

Just like in one of those hokey ol' westerns, we stared at one another, itching for the first person to make a move.

Dad drew first. "Dibby… Thomas Saunders ran away from home a long time ago. In 1953, to be exact. So goes the official story." He took in a mighty big sigh, blew it out. His attention safely focused on his coffee cup, he ran a finger around the rim. "That's all you need to know about the situation."

"But…you said the 'official story'. Like that's not the truth."

"Who's to say what really happened?" His eyes lifted, met mine. Sadness tinted them red, and they glimmered under the light. The most haunted I'd seen him since the early days, right after Mom left. "Between you, me, and the walls, I've long suspected foul play came of the boy. But I've nothing to back up my theory. And that's really all you need to know about the Saunders, Dibby. I apologize for not trusting you with…my reason for wanting you to stay away from that family. But I'm the adult here, and I expect you to abide by the rules. That's all the explanation I owe you." He didn't blink, didn't move. Dang near looked like a wax figure, just like outta that Vincent Price *House of Wax* feature.

"Dad…was Thomas Saunders murdered?"

His head shook. "Dibby, I really don't wish to discuss this further."

"But, what if—"

"That's enough." He reclaimed himself, gestured upstairs. "Go do your homework."

As I hurried outta the kitchen, I heard him opening the tall cabinet—the one where he kept his not-so-secret supply of hooch.

* * *

"Help me! Please! Help…"

Accustomed to practically sleeping with one eye open, I got out of bed quickly, one more time down the rabbit hole. Even in a half-asleep state, I quietly flew down the steps and was out the door in seconds.

Tonight, the cornfield absolutely clamored with the ruckus of ghosts. The corn stalks seemed taller, more menacing, rattling like maracas in the agitated wind.

"Please, help meee…"

The moon was only a sliver-full tonight, so I couldn't see beans. But Thomas's mounting hysteria drove me toward him, his fear at a high. Hackles rose across my arms. I swung my heavy-duty flashlight up, ticked it on.

Ahead and on either side of me, stalks stirred and slashed at one another. I hightailed it down the middle, keeping to the dirt path. Thomas's pale form dashed in front of me and dove into the opposite row. Stalks snapped and broke in his attempt to hide.

"Thomas!" A whisper at best, but I couldn't risk giving away Thomas's location to his pursuer, even if history was bound to replay the scene over and over. I turned the flashlight off. Thomas's ghost image bounced across my eye's memory.

The beastly, always unsettling roar rose. But tonight, it sounded different as well. Almost like it'd been slowed down a spell, the voice deepened, words nearly formed through guttural and long, drawn-out growls.

Trapped in the middle, I could either go right, pursue Thomas, or wait and see who came crashing out from the left.

Stalk tips vanished, toppled, marking the beast's speedy approach. One after the other they fell, *crack, crack, crick…* Moving closer.

Closer.

Scared, I froze in a bout of panic. I'd learned ghosts could physically harm me. I didn't know if they could kill me, but it aimed to follow.

Yet, I had to see. I had to see what happened to Thomas. I had to see his pursuer, his killer. I had to help the boy in any fashion I could.

Crack…crick…tack…

The destruction of the field drew closer. Beneath me, the earth shook. Tremors traveled through the earth's core, wormed up into my feet, zipped up my legs, and attacked my full bladder.

Ready to jackrabbit away, my legs refused, kept me planted. I swung the flashlight up. Ready to use it as a weapon for all the good it'd do me. The final stalk toppled. It fell toward me, and I elbowed it out of my line of sight.

Then…. Nothing. A preternatural quiet as if I'd been snatched out of the real world and deposited into an eerie afterlife. Silence reigned.

I flicked the flashlight on, sprayed the beam from left to right. At first, the light swept right on over a tiny, huddled figure. Startled, I brought the beam back around and lowered it. Another boy, this one's hair as blond as the fallen corn he crouched on. Just as pale as Thomas, maybe even a tad younger, and just as frightened. His bony hands reached toward me.

Behind the boy, a dark figure swiftly approached. The blond boy melted into living shadow. Then drew within the earth, sucked right up as if ol' Scratch had grabbed his ankles and pulled him into Hell.

The new figure stepped into the arc of light.

"Boo!" he said.

I yelped, dropped the flashlight. It lit up James's black and white sneakers.

"Dang it to hell, James! You dang near set my hair to gray!" I felt like hefting up that flashlight and clubbing him with it. But my first priority lay in settling my hammering heart. "What're you *doing* here?"

"Hey, don't flip your wig." He grabbed my shoulders. I wriggled out of his touch, plainly not in the mood. "'Member? We had a date tonight to go see the witch's pad."

"Guess I fell asleep. But why are you in the corn field?" I took to shuddering, not in a cold sense either. I rubbed my arms up and down.

"I tossed some pebbles up into your bedroom. Figured that's why you left the window open. Then I heard something in the cornfield. Like quiet thunder, sorta. Thought I'd take a look, see some ghosts."

"Well, not only did you scare the tar outta me, you spooked the ghosts away, too."

"What? That's bananas! I chased the ghosts away? I missed 'em?"

"I kinda think they don't want you to see them. When you came lumbering into the field like an elephant, they vanished. Done packed up and went home."

"Dammit."

"I'll trade you any ol' day. Now, hush before you wake my dad."

* * *

Thin, blue clouds cut away at the sliver of moon, sailing fast, as if something big and unspeakable had blown them from its monstrous maw. On our midnight bike ride, I took to shivering like I'd come down with the pneumonia. But germs weren't the culprit behind my chills.

A couple times James offered up his jean jacket. Tempting as it was, I declined, not wanting to be beholden to him for anything. Even though the offer gave me kinda a nice, warm feeling, the chills stuck, riding piggy-back through the moonstruck roads.

Just to hear a voice in the dead of night, I told James about my visit with Evelyn Saunders, my talk with Dad, and the mystery of the second ghost boy in the field.

"Huh. Who do you think the kid was?" His tortured lungs huffed, panting like an overheated dog.

"Beats the dickens outta me. But I aim to find out."

And that was pretty much the extent of James's interest in all things mysterious and ghostly. He had other things on his mind, things of a personal nature.

"So..." he gasped, slowing down on his bike, "...is your old man ready to kill me? For the smoking and all?"

"I dunno. He's hard to figure at times. Might go either way."

"Man..." James slouched over his handlebars, almost laid out on them.

His knees jacked high to keep up with me. "So, has he said anything about the movie?"

I sighed. "Haven't found the right opportunity to ask him yet."

"Oh."

"I will, though. Just gotta find him in the right mood."

We left my road behind, wheeled onto Oak Grove Road. Across the smooth pavement, we made good time.

Along the road, limbs waved at us as we sped by. Tree trunks creaked with stiff rheumatism. Leaves shook. Branches stretched. Whispers rode the wind, passed from tree to tree, limb to limb, secrets buried with fallen leaves.

An owl hooted, twice, three times, had its fill, then stopped. Some kinda varmint squealed, a rhythmic *ai-ai-ai-aiii* that could've been a war cry from a different time. Deep in the woods, a coyote gave voice to his hunger. Maybe he found it, too. A horrible cry went up, then cut off abruptly. Birds, bats, other critters I didn't like to ponder too much, took flight, blotting out the meager moonlight.

"Hey! Hey, where ya going?" The voice cracked like a thin sheaf of ice at the end of winter.

James gasped, whirled his bike around. He over-compensated and buckled onto the road.

"I said, where the hell you going this time of night?"

I couldn't see him, but I sure as shooting recognized the sour voice of Boot Gundersen.

Beside James, I pulled to a stop. He looked up at me, dazed, yet with a silly *I'm-too-hip-to-hurt* grin.

"A little late for you to be out, ain't it, girly?" Beneath an oak tree, a red ember lit up, a wink from the Devil himself. Boot stepped out of the darkness, bringing a fair share of dark with him. On stiff legs, he climbed down and up the roadside ditch. As he approached, his military boots clacked across the pavement. He tossed his cigarette to the road, snuffed it out with his foot.

Caught red-handed, I improvised, something I'd grown good at lately. "Oh, hey there, Mister Gundersen. You gave me a start. This here's my friend, James. He, ah, needed some emergency studying tonight for a big test at school."

As Boot stepped closer, shadows carved away from him. Wrinkles mummified his features. "James, huh? The Mackleby kid?"

James stood, pulled his bike up to lean against. "Yes, sir. I was just, um…seeing Dibby home."

Boot scratched a sandpaper cheek. "That doesn't fit one bit. Nosiree! You was heading the wrong direction. Way I figure it, you think you can put one over on ol' Boot, that's what I figure. Boot Gundersen, he knows everything!" He jabbed a pinkie into his ear, gave it a squeaky twist. "I know for a fact you're s'posed to be in bed at the Lewis and Clark. And you, missy!" He turned a shaking finger on me. "You're grounded for a good spell, if not longer."

The response I formed in my head tended to lean anywhere but lady-like. But I couldn't afford to have Boot rat me out to Dad. I didn't care to be grounded until menopause.

"You caught me red-handed, Mister Gundersen." I tried on a smile, but it didn't fit very well. My lips quivered, wouldn't hold. Boot Gundersen never failed to give me the heebie-jeebies. "I'm just…doing a favor for a friend. Someone who needs my help."

His finger jabbed out in an accusing manner. "You ain't fooling me, li'l lady! I know exactly what you're up to. Matter of fact, you got the whole town up in arms about your inquirings and carrying-ons. Me? I think it's about goddamn time someone tried to find out the truth about the Saunders boy. But I'm telling you, missy, for your own good, you just let it be. Let someone else go digging up graves. Ain't for you; not a sweet young thang like yourself."

Every time I think I've built up a tolerance for Boot Gundersen, he does something to turn that goodwill around. Still, it wouldn't do any good to rile him up now. Not when he appeared to be the only other person in town after the truth.

"Mister Gundersen…do you know something about Thomas Saunders?"

"Yessir, ol' Boot knows lots and lots. If it's said over the phone, I store it away up here." He tapped a gray temple. "Mind like a steel trap. *Snap!*" Boot brought up a knee and thwacked his one hand down on it. "Now, I reckon all I hear is rumor, nothing but. But I'm informed enough to make my own conjectures. Ol' Boot's got his ideas." Open-mouthed, he leered. Strands of saliva stretched between his lips.

"What might those ideas be, Mister Gundersen?"

"You wanna know, li'l lady? Be glad to tell ya. But you gotta do me a favor first."

Although afraid to ask, I figured things couldn't get much worse. Then again, my mind hadn't been working at peak lately. "What kinda favor?"

"Dibby," said James, "I don't think—"

"You hush, boy!" Boot's command—no doubt learned during whichever war he served—ordered James into silence. "You let the li'l lady make up her own mind about things. Missy, you wanna know about Thomas Saunders, you come visit ol' Boot up at my place. Then I'll tell ya what you wanna know." Just like his hound dog, Queeg—curiously bearing only three limbs as well—his tongue lolled out of his mouth.

"Well now, Mister Gundersen, I do rightly appreciate your offer, I surely do. But I reckon you of all people know that I can't get there, not while I'm grounded."

He scratched his beard, gave it some consideration. "There is that, I s'pose. But you seem like a resourceful gal, missy. You're out now, ain't ya?"

"Come on, Dibby, let's go," whispered James.

"I'll think about it, Mister Gundersen." *'Course I won't!* "Only if you promise not to tell my dad you saw us out tonight."

Boot drew a big ol' "X" across his torso. "Cross my heart, hope to die," he said. Hope flooded his rheumy-looking eyes. His smile showed teeth sacrificed at the altar of tobacco, fried foods, and liquor. He swayed his one hand, graceful as a professional golfer, ushering us on our way. "God speed then, li'l lady. Just be careful who you trust. Folks ain't right in Peculiar County."

Isn't that the truth?

James walked his bike up next to mine, again whispered, "Dibby, let's beat feet. *Now*."

With a wave and a hidey-ho, we cycled our legs as fast as possible away from the strange, possibly dangerous Boot Gundersen.

As soon as we were far enough away, James asked, "Man, what's with that scurvy square?"

"That's ol' Boot Gundersen. He's one of our two phone operators. He's kinda creepy, but Dad says he wouldn't hurt a fly."

"Your old man hasn't seen *Psycho,* then. Old fart's a pervert! If I hadn't been here, who knows what he would've tried to do? You can't go to his shack, Dibby. Tell me you won't."

"Why, James Mackleby," I batted my eyes the way I'd seen Suzette do it a zillion times, "I didn't think you cared." I tossed in the whole Mc-Coy, awful Southern belle accent and all. And felt dumb as a bag of rocks for my efforts. I reverted to normal. "Ol' Boot can't do much damage, no how, not with just one arm."

"If you go, I'm going with you."

"I can look after myself. But if I need help, I can't think of anybody I'd rather have along."

Lately, I didn't know what'd come over me, but I felt changed, a different person at times. I stopped my bike, waited for James to catch up. Considered rekindling our romance, right then, right there. Kisses are a lot like chocolates: you can't just settle for one.

Finally, James rode up next to me. Beneath the moon's glow, he searched my eyes. Glanced down at my lips. Shorthand if I ever saw it. Over our bikes, we awkwardly leaned toward one another.

Then something swept over us, something large. It zipped away fast. A mighty back draft pulled me into James. Together, we tumbled down to the pavement, a mess of bikes and limbs.

Darkness dropped over us. I looked up into an unexpected lunar eclipse. A hovering presence, something massive, something not quite human, blotted out the moon. It gobbled oxygen, the sky, the world as I knew it, and I was beginning to think I didn't know it very well at all.

Like a land-locked fish, I gulped at the air. The sky creaked. Ancient bones folded with leathery snaps. The shadow lifted. It flitted away, the moon briefly silhouetting expansive and huge wings. Then, as if yanked away on ropes, the creature vanished.

The air cleared. So did my lungs. My mind didn't. James's definitely didn't as he still stared slack-jawed at the sky.

"Welcome to Peculiar County," I managed. "Now get offa me."

Chapter Eight

We'd already lost enough time, so I figured I'd get right down to business. "Before you ask me what that was, James, I couldn't tell you. I've never seen it, nor could I even venture a guess."

"But…but it—"

"In Peculiar County, sometimes it's just best not to think too much about things. Many folks—'specially adults—find it's a right nice plan for a happily-ever-after life here."

"That's what everyone does? Just not think about all the creepy stuff? I mean, sure, there's the ghost dog—and I'm still not convinced that's on the up and up—and then there're your ghosts, but, you know, they're—"

"Wait a minute! You don't believe in my spooks? You think I'm fibbing?"

"No, no, nothing like that! It's just… I can, you know, sorta understand ghosts. But I can't even imagine what just happened to us. Or why. How do you guys put up with it? I mean, live here and everything?"

I shrugged. "You adapt, I reckon. A lotta adults are beyond being able to do such a thing, set in their ways as they are. So they choose to ignore what's plain as the nose on their face. The kids, though, they're a might bit more open to such things. I used to kinda fall somewhere in the middle. Dad taught me to believe in science, the facts of things. Concrete reasons behind anything that doesn't quite fit. Thing is, he picked a really weird town to live those lessons. Or I guess he didn't really pick Hangwell. His great-great-grandpa did. Still, I'd be a darn fool if I didn't buy into some of the weird, otherworldly happenings in Peculiar County."

"Man, I'll say."

"Now…you ready to go home, pull the blankets up over your head, and hide? Or are you ready to go look in on a witch?"

"I don't think we're in Kansas anymore, Toto. Let's go see the Wicked Witch of the West!"

I groaned. Years of outsiders' stupid Kansas jokes never grew easier to tolerate.

While no one considered Hangwell a big town, the bike ride ahead of us was formidable, nonetheless. Hettie Williquette lived on the outskirts, her spooky abode hidden in the sticks. As the night—morning, now—drew on, our pace lagged, especially James's.

We peddled through downtown, quite a different sight in the wee hours. Every light had been doused, the Lewis and Clark Hotel tucked into a comfy darkness I envied. I figured at least the lampposts would still be blazing, and I figured wrong. Another penny pinching, purse-tightening ploy by Mayor Hopkins, that no-good so and so, as Dad liked to pontificate.

Shadows crawled out of shadows, making me reconsider how many different shades of black might actually exist. My imagination reached out and set up shop in alleyways, peeped out from around corners, and slithered behind drawn shades, a might bit scarier than the truth. Then again, normal rules never did apply, not in Hangwell.

We zipped past the grade school. A ghost had taken up Odie's swing. It wobbled about drunkenly as if Odie'd just left it, and maybe he darn well had. No one knew the solitary mailman's nighttime routine. In fact, now more than ever, I wondered if any of us in Hangwell truly knew our neighbors.

We left Main Street and sped by Hollow Crick Road. Chills chased after me as I snuck a quick peek—not too long, mind you—at the Hangwell Cemetery. Full of piss and vinegar tonight, the wind dosey-doed through the Judge's tree's naked limbs, whistling quite the jaunty melody. Clearly just a trick of my overheated imagination, I swore I glimpsed a silhouette of a man performing his own swing dance at the end of a rope. He spun, bounced, ended with a little bow before dropping slack.

I set my gaze ahead and didn't look back.

We buzzed through the southern farmlands out yonder, destined for the desolate woods that might even give the stout Hansel and Gretel reason for pause.

Now out in the boonies, I slowed, gathered my bearings. Not many folks inhabited the area, practically forgotten by the more prosperous townsfolk. The powers that be—"the righteous Mayor Hopkins, that S.O.B." according to Dad—didn't deem the little dirt roads worthy of names. But I recognized the road Hettie lived on, could find it blind seeing as how it proved a worthy challenge for any kid worth her salt growing up in Hangwell. And in the woods' darkness, we may as well have been blind.

I flicked on the flashlight and tried to steady it inside my bike basket. It didn't produce a straight-on beam but provided an ample, if unsteady, source of light.

We turned left on Dead Man's Slip (a moniker the boys at the Tavern had deemed worthy of this orphaned road), deadly enough in the rain, drop the temperature a bit, and it well earned its name. Untamed by automobiles, the narrow dirt road proved rough riding.

"Wow, this is…a gasser." Big shot words, but James's voice folded into an unsure child's. Dang near shaking in his boots, he studied the alien environment. Trees hulked over us, edging in when you looked in the other direction.

The sounds, though—especially the unidentifiable ones—were what set me to my bike seat's edge.

Cries, hoots, bellows, barks, clicks, caws, hums, and nearly audible whispers—punctuated by nerve-rattling sibilant *sssssssssss's*—followed us deep into the woods. A network of varmints announced our arrival, passed it on, animal kindred to Boot Gundersen's telephone board. But something else seemed at play, something unnatural riding upshot over the proceedings.

James looked fit to be tied. Truth be told, so was I.

Down a hill we raced, mounting speed to tackle the last incline. At the top, I stopped. James walked his bike up the last several feet, drinking in great mouthfuls of air and thankful for it.

Hettie Williquette's clapboard of a rat-trap house nestled snugly in the center of an odd clearing. Guardian trees formed a near-perfect circle around the witch's abode. Only a fool doubted the trees' true intent, or so said ol' Hy Thurgood. Often, when deep in his cups, Hy spoke of how he once saw the trees come alive, dancing to beat the band. Most folks had a hard time separating the truth from Hy's fevered benders in a bottle. These days, though, I tended to lean toward Hy being the savviest man in Peculiar County.

Although no one ('cept for kids, of course) ever dared venture near Hettie's land, her house remained an ongoing topic of dismay for town meetings, particularly the Baptist and Catholic contingent. They proclaimed the house a disgrace to the good moral fiber of Hangwell (questionable) and an eyesore (hit the nail on the head).

Faded shutters of a now-indiscernible color sagged to one side, putting me in mind of Aunt Gertie's face after her stroke. Paint had long fled the walls, worn down to wood. Brick columns struggled valiantly to hold up the roof covering the front porch, but it sloped madly toward the right. Weeds you could get lost in rose up around Hettie's house, a minor beard of color. I long suspected a strong gust of wind might just flatten Hettie's house into a pancake. But against all odds, against all elements, it kept standing.

And bursting with life, too, by the looks of things. On the porch, in what passed for Hettie's yard, and deep in the weeds, strolled a legion of cats. All kinds of cats, calico, Siamese, bobtails, long haired, short haired, no haired (quite a disturbing sight), cats I'd never seen before nor could I hook a name on, cats that'd surely been stirred to life in the magic of Hettie's cauldron.

Until now, I hadn't realized the rest of the wood-living varmints had quieted around us. Even creepier, the cats remained solemnly, spookily silent as the proverbial church mice. A couple glanced at us, then dismissed us as if bored.

Usually, country wild cats kept on the move, leaping out of garages and barns, then spinning away in a blur of bothered fur. Other than a wayward flick of the paw here or there, a swish of a tail, or a few mute yowls, Hettie's feline zoo stayed impossibly inert.

"Wow…"

That's all James said, and it pretty much encapsulated my thoughts, too.

"What do we do now?" he whispered.

A fine question, one I'd burned a lot of gray matter over. Unfortunately, I still hadn't come up with a decent answer. Standing in front of Hettie's frightening hovel in the dead of night certainly didn't encourage my exploratory nature.

Yet Hettie's home lit up like the lights of Las Vegas, an invite—a dare—of sorts. Even the small attic above blazed with fire, an orange inferno brilliance poring through the tiny porthole window.

Unhealthy black smoke rose from the chimney. And something smelled, off and rank, something I didn't want to lend a whole lot of thought to.

I considered heading home, the sensible thing to do, particularly on a school night. But ever since James's arrival, maybe due to his wild-side influence, I've felt a calling of a different variety other than sensible.

Next to the road, I leaned my bike against a tree, faced it north should we need a fast getaway. Quietly, I snaked my way through the trees toward the house. Stealthy, one with the shadows, I edged closer. James followed with the nerve-grating grace of a rhino, crunching up leaves and bashing into bushes. The cats paid no heed to his ruckus, and thankfully, Hettie didn't either.

Mismatched stacks of brick and rock propped up the leaning side of Hettie's house, a patchwork foundation. I tip-toed up three wooden steps, warped and cracked like desert ground, to her porch. Behind moth-eaten curtains, I caught movement, flesh-colored flashes.

Music swelled, hypnotic. Chanting of a foreign nature, if I had to put a name to it. A voice rumbled low, then lifted a few steps above high-pitched. It struck me wrong, my cavity zinging like I'd chawed down on tin foil. To block the headache-inducing sound, I clamped my hands over my ears.

The noise affected James even harder. From behind a tree, he'd fallen to the ground. He winced, released his hands from around his ears, then gave me a finger meets thumb-tip, "a-okay" sign.

The caterwauling stopped. My ears quit ringing. Tenderly, I touched both, inspected my fingers for blood, but they came back dry.

I tiptoed around the porch cats. Tested my weight on the unforgiving floorboards. They squeaked and tattled. While softer now, the music from within covered for me.

Dizziness swept over me. The floorboards seemed to pitch and sway, a ghost ship moored in the woods. I saw double, triple, a world of porches shimmering off of one another. I clomped a hand—couldn't be helped and hoped it wasn't heard—beside a window and waited for the world to simmer down.

It did. Or could be I just got used to it.

Inside, the chanting continued. I peeked into the nearest window but couldn't see past the filthy, soot-covered curtain. My feet slid—assuring a steadier hold—toward the next window. Behind the grungy curtains, orange and red and yellow lights danced as if the house burned. Maybe plum dropped into Hell itself.

Through the narrowest parting of curtains, I got a gander, more than I'd bargained for. Lit candles formed a circle around the largely barren room. Wax melted onto the hard wood floors. In the middle, Hettie Williquette sat, naked as the day she was born. Cross-legged, hands on knees, centered within a crudely scrawled six-pointed star with a chalked circle enclosing it. Her bosom pulled down to her belly. As if tetched, her head swayed, her bun of hair bouncing to and fro.

But her eyes, Lord, I'd never seen anything like those.

They'd rolled up into her head, the best way—the only natural way—I could explain it. Big and white as bone, they stuck that way, too, not at all like that stupid Donald Johannsen fixing his eyes all funny to scare the girls at school.

Hettie didn't blink, not once. Blind, she saw nothing, yet observed everything.

Fascinated yet stomach troubled, I couldn't pull away.

On Hettie's body, a roadmap of squiggles, shapes, figures, and things that defied description had been inked in black. Several snakes seemed to writhe across her sagging breasts, then merged into one. A jag of dark lightning appeared on her cheek, then came alive, striking other parts of her body. It crawled down her neck, shot down over the hills of her breasts, and vanished into the valleys of her nether regions.

Blood wept from her eyes. Then it downright gushed out, spilling onto her body.

I locked a scream down tight with my hand. Too scared to run. And mesmerized, positively glued to witness the next unfolding atrocity.

Only then did I see the bowl in front of her. Not a witch's cauldron, by any means. More like an ornately designed pot with two handles. A crude, horrific tableau wrapped around the pot: definable figures killing one another by stabbing, strangling, tearing off limbs, and methods of death beyond my ken to imagine.

Black smoke rose from the pot and billowed into the room. Just as suddenly, the smoke folded back on itself, compressed, and dove back inside its original dwelling.

Hettie reached inside—deep, deep inside, up to her shoulders inside, farther than the physical limitations of the pot could possibly allow inside—and pulled out a squirming critter by its leg. One of its six legs.

I choked back a scream and nearly gagged on it.

The critter wasn't of a nature I'd ever seen, even in the movies. The six legs waggled from its black-furred body. The oval-shaped head turned, rotated an impossible 180 degrees. Two eyes set aside its head, all too human-looking eyes. And it looked right at me.

A shriek escaped me, loud and uncontrollable.

I tottered, dizzy again. Drawn back to the window—*I don't wanna look, I don't wanna look, please don't make me look...I absolutely have to look*—I bent down. The curtain whipped back.

Thwump.

The tip of mad Hettie's nose flattened against the dusty window, her eyes still turned up inside her skull. Her mouth opened wide, wider, too wide to be humanly possible. I stared into her maw of blackness. Deep within, things squirmed, itching to come out, things I had no earthly desire to witness.

I screamed again.

Whatever smidgeon of humanity that still resided in Hettie must've pitied my absolute, pants-wetting terror. She closed her abyss of darkness. Thin slices of lips needled together and made a smile. One that said, *Now, I'm going to eat you, my pretty.*

With her crooked finger, she scrawled a message for me in the window's dust: *I see you.*

Just like in the cartoons, I cycled my legs, working 'em fast, but I couldn't move. I twisted, nearly tripped on a calico cat nuzzling up against my legs. I hopped over him.

A massive black ball of fur dropped from nowhere, clumped onto the porch. The floorboards trembled. I've seen some plumpers, but the biggest cat I'd ever laid eyes on—tiger size and then some—glowered at me with green eyes. A spoon-sized tongue lapped a hungry circle around its mouth.

Mrraowww…

More of a roar than a meow, the cat's yowl sent the whole porch—possibly even the house—to pitching.

The front door opened with a *thwack.* Hettie, dressed now in a buttoned-up dress belted around the middle, held up a thin arm. Her crooked finger pointed at me. Everything about her was crooked: just like her house, her posture skewed to the side, her nose crept to the right, and her limbs connected to her lean frame with sharp angles and mean twists.

Out of my mind, I screamed again. Babbled nonsense. "*Sorry, sorry, sorry, I'll never do it again, I swear, sorry, sorry, just please don't eat me…*" On and on I went, my head and words mushed into a stew of terror.

Somewhere far away, I thought I heard James holler my name. Could be the monster cat said it.

Hettie smiled her crooked smile, kept that crooked finger hooking all the way to Hell and back.

Mind over matter, I forced my legs to work. I leaped over the tiger-cat, hurtled off the porch.

The ground rushed up. Knees bent, feet assured, I landed. Immediately, I sprung off into a sprint, dodging trees left and right. James stood by the road, waving my flashlight around like a loon. Urging me to run faster.

Behind me, the cat-thing growled, deep and throaty and hungry as all get out.

I glanced back, wanted to know where Hettie was. She hadn't moved. Frozen on the porch, finger crooked.

I'm gonna make it!

Just another 75 feet to my bike.

My arms flailed, beating the air.

In front of me, Hettie stepped out from behind a massive oak tree. Smiling. I whipped back around. Impossibly, she stood on her porch, too.

My feet tangled. I crunched down at Hettie's booted feet.

Before I succumbed to the powers of the witch, Hettie Williquette, I thought: *Maybe I should've pursued stupid, girly things after all.*

* * *

My head hurt. The desert had migrated into my mouth. Every little joint and inch of flesh banged away at its individual nerve ending, sending a message that pain belonged to the living.

As I rejoined the living, I wondered if I'd drawn the short straw. First thing I saw was ol' Hettie hovering over me, warts and all. Her mess of black and white scraggly hair had escaped the tightly drawn bun, sticking out of her scalp like straw from a broom. Hettie let out a crow's caw.

"Well, lookee here," she said. "Little Dibby Caldwell's back amongst the living."

I sat up, attempted to get my bearings. Held captive in a small room, Hettie's bedroom from the looks of things. The bed I lay on felt like the springs would bounce me right through the window, and I surely wished it would.

"Um, yes, ma'am. You know who I am?"

"'Course I do! Not much gets by me. Folks round here think I'm tetched, crazier than a loon." She tapped a graying temple. "But I've got the sight of the third eye."

Only third eye I've ever had the acquaintance with was a pimple planted smack-dab in my forehead, but that was neither here nor there. "I'm mighty sorry, Miss Williquette, for looking in your window."

"And what was it you were hoping to see?"

"Tell the truth, I'm not sure. I just figured you might be able to help me. About Hangwell history. All the other adults 'round here don't like to chat about it much."

"I see." One of her eyes widened to the size of a golf ball, making it that much easier for her to see. Or hex me with her evil eye. "And what *did* you actually see through my window?"

"I…I don't think I rightly know, ma'am."

She cawed again, tossed her head back. "'Course not, you little git! I knew you were coming, my cats done tol' me as much. I mixed up a little spell, I did, thought I'd teach you a lesson. Don't always trust what your eyes show you."

While what she said provided a bit of sorely needed relief, I didn't know whether I believed her. The horrible things I saw seemed pretty real, not the results of some witch's spell.

A large, yellow cat jumped up on the bed, gave me a sniff, then ske-daddled into the room's corner.

"Claw seems to think you're trustworthy, girl," said Hettie. "Me? I tend not to trust someone sneaking around and peeking through windows. You want something from me, you ever hear tell of knocking on a door?"

Now that she'd put it in such no-nonsense terms, I honestly didn't know what in the world I'd been thinking. And I told her as much.

She responded with another deep-rooted laugh. "Guess we'll chalk it up to the innocence of youth." Again, she glared at me with one large, accusatory eye. "Even if you were trespassing."

"No, ma'am, that wasn't my intention, not at all. I rightly do apologize again for my mistake. It's just…well…I didn't know how to talk to you." I didn't much fancy telling the local witch she scared the daylights outta me, so I hoped my mighty sorrowful look would do the talking.

She waved a hand. "Piffle. If you listen to everything folks say about me, you'd think I was the Devil herself."

"Well…your reputation does mightily precede you."

"Yes, indeedy, it does." She rocked, holding onto her bony knees. Just as long as she didn't fix to cook me, I much preferred this whimsical side of her. "You're friends with those two ol' coots, the Sooter sisters, aren't you?"

"Well, I don't rightly reckon I'd consider us friends, but I do frequent their library on occasion."

"Next time you see those ol' bats, tell 'em I'll see 'em in Hell."

'Course I wouldn't deliver that message, but I told Hettie I'd give the librarians a nice howdy-do from her.

"Better then what they got coming to 'em. Now, then…what is it you wanna know?"

"I'm fixing to find out what happened to Thomas Saunders, Evelyn Saunders's boy. And her husband Hedrick."

That stopped her rocking. Even the cats seemed to stiffen.

Hettie's eyes narrowed. She tapped a bent finger on her chin. "My, oh my, isn't this interesting? And why in the world would you be looking to dig up that ancient history?"

Out of all the adults in Hangwell, I imagined Hettie Williquette—town witch and devourer of children—might be the only one to give my supernatural tale credence. "'Cause I've seen Thomas's ghost. Couple of times."

"You don't say…" She gave me a mighty long and disturbing look. "Where'd his ghost visit you?"

"In the Saunders' cornfield."

"I see." And every time she said she saw, I truly believed it and wished to Sam Hill she'd take that ol' evil eye of hers off me. "That should tell you a little something right there, Dibby. Where you saw Thomas."

Once again, I got spoon-fed the hazy, unclear treatment adults favored. "Why can't anyone just come out and tell me what happened to Thomas? Everyone just pats me on the head, tells me to never mind, just scoot on about my business, and leave such grown-up notions to adults! No one tells me anything! Thomas is visiting me for a reason! Why? And why now? What *happened* to him? What happened to his *daddy? Dammit!*"

A week of firsts, this one nothing to cheer about: cursing in front of an adult. But, dad-gummit, it felt great to unleash my frustration. And, if anything, Hettie looked like she enjoyed my slide into the dark side. Her smile grew wider and rounder. She sat down beside me, close, fetid breath close.

"Let me tell you something, girl… That Saunders family is an odd bunch." Talk about the pot addressing the kettle. "Bad things follow them around like shadows. Did you know Hedrick Saunders came to see me? Afore he went missing?"

"I, ah, think I mighta heard something about that."

"Surely, he did. Scared outta his wits—what little he had—he came around, asking me to intuit something for him. Told me he'd pay me a healthy wage, too. Wanted me to ply my witchcraft." Open-mouthed, she gawped at me. Tickled, almost.

"Um, did you?"

"Hell, no! Why in the worlds would I wanna help a man who'd never said boo to me before?"

"What'd he want to know?"

"If Thomas was his child. His natural offspring." Again, she seemed to be testing me. Close to me and still coming, practically in my lap now. An odd odor of herbs and spices and something sour rolled out of her mouth.

"Well," she continued, "good Samaritan that I am, I took pity on Hedrick. And told him li'l Thomas Saunders had a different birth daddy. Hee! Ol' Hedrick just took off like a shotgun blast. 'Course he wasn't seen again after that night." She scratched her whiskers.

"Who was Thomas's real father?" I asked.

She chuckled. "Now that would be telling, wouldn't it? You see, I know things, quite a few things, I do. 'Specially 'bout that cursed Saunders clan. Let me ask you something, Dibby… Do you *really* wanna know what happened to Hedrick Saunders?"

I inched back, afraid to speak, scared. Not only of Hettie, but of the answer to the Saunders mystery. At long last. But if her sadistic grin was any indication, I didn't know if I was quite ready.

"Are you absolutely *surrre* you wanna know what became of Hedrick Saunders, Dibby?" Long and teasing, her words resembled a cat's purr. She scooted in closer, so close I literally had my back against the cold wall. I nodded.

Eyes tapered to slits, she said, "You might not like what you *hearrr…*" Words all sing-songy, she grinned, pleased with herself.

"I need to know." My throat and mouth dry, I barely formed the words.

"This is your last chance, Dibby. One final opportunity to just pick yourself right up and get on home without—"

"Just tell me!" I hollered.

"Why, Dibby…everybody *knows* Hedrick Saunders up and ran off with your momma."

Hettie's laughter exploded, flinging shrapnel into my world. My stomach roiled. The witch's cackling ballooned into the room, taunting me about my mother running off with the man next door. How she left me behind, unloved like a red-headed stepchild.

The secret Dad wouldn't tell me.

Hettie held her gut, guffawing, lolling around next to me. I hoped she'd choke on her laughter.

In a white-hot burst of heat, I bolted off the bed, ran for the door. Sweat-covered, my hand slipped from the handle. On the second attempt, I lassoed it and threw the door open. I made a beeline for the front door, stumbled into furniture, uprighted candles that snuffed out onto the floor. Hettie's incessant laughter chased after me.

"Your daddy ain't told you the truth about your *momma*," the ol' witch gleefully cried out. "That's rich! You come back again and I'll tell you *all* 'bout poor, li'l Thomas Saunders!"

I threw open the front door, then threw up on the front steps.

Winded, I fell onto my hind quarters, just dropped right down onto the porch. My world spun out of control, and any control I thought I had over my life flipped over into a lie.

"Dibby?" From out of the shadows, James cautiously approached. "Hey…you all right?" With one eye glued on Hettie's front door, James bent over, shook my arm. "What happened? Are you okay?"

'Course not, you damn fool, I wanted to yell. But I didn't. Instead, I just nodded, said, "Let's get outta here."

As we wheeled down the road, I could still hear Hettie's cruel laughter and taunts. Like spicy food, they stuck with me well into the wee hours of morning.

* * *

For the first bit of our long trip back, I didn't say a word, not a peep. Even though he was chomping at the bit to find out what'd happened, James must've realized my need for quiet. Finally, on the last leg, nearly home, I hopped off my bike and walked. James did the same. And I told him my story. All of it.

"Wow. That's terrible, Dibby. I'm sorry."

I shrugged, carried big shoulders, and didn't do right by them. "It wasn't what I thought I'd find out."

"Your old lady just up and left with the neighbor? Never said goodbye or, you know, left a note or anything?"

"I reckon there's a lot 'bout her leaving I don't know about. I was young, three years old. My recall isn't what it oughta be. And Dad…he never talks about her. All I have really are these vague memories. How Mom was perfect. But then reality's gotta way of sneaking up and pulling the rug out from under you. What I really remember…was Mom not talking. Not doing much of anything. I think…the last time I saw her was at our kitchen table, just bawling her eyes out."

James stopped, put an arm across my back. I rested my head on his shoulder.

"I really don't feel up to snuff. I don't wanna talk about this any-more, James."

He nodded. "Copacetic."

I girded myself, took a couple of breaths, then moved on. "Hey, what happened to you back at Hettie's? When she grabbed me?"

"I…ah…I kinda hid back in the woods. I was watching the house, looking for a chance to rescue you."

"You mean you were scared and high-tailed it for cover. My hero."

"Come on! I was really trying to—"

"Wet your britches."

He sighed. "I'm *telling* you I was—"

"Never mind. So…what did you see out there? I mean, from the moment I got up on her porch."

He paused but continued to walk his bike along Main Street. Finally, he said, "Dibby, I don't know what I saw. Really. I kinda…maybe I don't wanna think about it too much."

And maybe he was right. Finally learning how to cope in Peculiar County.

"So, what're we gonna do now?" he asked, clearly relishing a change of topics.

"As much as I surely don't ever wanna visit that ol' witch again, she told me to come back in regards to Thomas Saunders. I just wish there was someone else willing to tell me the truth."

"I guess there's that Boot guy," said James.

"You kidding me? I'd rather go with Hettie."

"Whatever you do, I'm going with you. You can count on me, Dibby." Moonlight caught in his eyes, illuminated his commitment. For a moment, I wanted to be bold, grab him, continue where we left off the other night. But the news of my mother—not to mention my sick breath—washed such notions away.

We neared the Lewis and Clark Hotel. As if on cue, James released a not-so-subtle yawn, his arms taking turns stretching for the stars.

"You don't need to see me home, James. I can manage just fine on my own."

"Are you sure? I mean, it's the right thing to do. I can't just leave you—"

"You've performed enough heroic duties tonight." I laughed. He toed the dirt, his male ego wounded. "You just get on to sleep. Not too much time left in the night anyhow."

Hollow barks bellowed from within the hotel. James jumped as if someone'd stuck a lit match between his toes. "That damn dog!"

"You're finally accepting Mittens's ghostly origins?" I asked.

"Guess I am. Now." He grew edgy, twitchy, searching up and down the street as if afraid something from Hettie's had followed us home. "Anyway…g'night, Dibby."

"Good morning, more like." He leaned in, gave me a quick hug, a buddy hug. A sudden, heartbreaking, puzzling change in our status quo. Then again, we'd both been through a lot tonight. Or could be he got a whiff of my breath, similar to a skunk gone belly-up.

On the way home, I rode fast and hard. I had an abundance of anger and hurt I needed to cast away and better it be through bicycling than taken out on Dad. Even if he deserved it.

Nearing four in the morn, I gave up the idea of getting any shut eye. With a fresh pot of coffee, I set up camp at the kitchen table. Time slowly ticked by as I played out all the scenarios in my head, the many different conversations I intended to have with Dad.

Going on six o'clock, Dad finally shuffled into the kitchen. He saw me, scratched his stubble, gave a half-hearted, tired smile, yawned, then sat down.

I yawned, too, contagious as a cold, and hardly the commanding way I'd wanted to start the proceedings.

"Thought I smelled coffee. You're up early, Dibs." His brow tucked down as he gave me a once-over. "Everything okay?"

"Dad… Why didn't you tell me about Mom?"

Caught off guard, he shook cobwebs from his mind. Then that heavy brow of his dropped with the weight of the world. "What're you talking about?"

"Why didn't you tell me Mom ran away with Hedrick Saunders?" I kept my face serious, my voice monotonic. I wouldn't surrender, although cracks formed along my voice's wall. The unfairness of it all clobbered me. Surely, the onus should've been on Dad to have this talk with me long ago.

Dad looked down at his folded hands, too ashamed to look me in the eye. "Dibby…that's *not* what happened."

"You're just gonna keep on fibbing to me, Dad? I got a right to know what happened to—"

"She didn't run off with Hedrick Saunders."

"Sure, she didn't! How'm I supposed to believe anything you say anymore? Why—"

"It's true because I know where your mother is."

"*Where?* Tell me!"

He grabbed for my hand, and I knew then what he aimed to tell me was much worse than Hettie's version of the truth. "Your mother's in the Lackasaw Mental Facility. An asylum for the mentally ill."

CHAPTER NINE

"Say that again... No! Don't say it again! I don't understand *any* of this! Why didn't you *tell* me? Is she crazy? Am *I* crazy? Am I *going* crazy? Are we *all* crazy in this stupid, dumb—"

"You're not crazy, Dibs." His smile looked like it hurt him, his gums full of splinters. He squeezed my hand. I held on for dear life. The ride just kept getting bumpier. "And your mother's not crazy either. That's... kind of an unfortunate term. Your mom had...*has* issues."

"Issues?" That word was all it took—one lousy little word—to break the wall holding back my tears. "What...kind of issues?"

"She was depressed. Had been for a long time. And it was damn negligent of me to not have noticed it before I did." He sighed, kicked his slippered feet out. Preparing for a long trip down Memory Lane. "For no reason I could understand, she'd become prone to crying fits. She wouldn't sleep. She stayed awake nights, wasting away, sobbing. I tried to figure out what was wrong with her. Studied my medical journals. Even consulted a couple colleagues from college. I couldn't figure it out..."

He swallowed audibly. Wouldn't look up, considering his failure and how his much-vaunted science and logic had failed Mom.

"She took to drinking, too," he continued. "I suppose it was her way of medicating. That's where...those rumors about Hedrick Saunders came from. Everyone knew Hedrick liked to tip at the bottle. Your mom and Hedrick closed down the Tavern many a night. I didn't much care for Hedrick because of it. And…I'm ashamed to say I bought into the rumor, too. About their running away together. You know how tongues tend to wag, particularly in small towns. When your mother left about six months or so after Hedrick did, it didn't take long for the gossip mill to get up to speed. For the longest time, the thought just ate me up. 'Til she called me."

"You…talked to her?"

"About two years ago, I think it was. Took me by complete surprise, just when I'd nearly accepted the fact I'd never see her again. But I was over the moon to hear from her, that she was okay. But she said she wasn't. She'd checked herself into Lackasaw. A mighty big step for her. And after many years of being lost, living by bare means, she was finally getting help. Help I'd failed to provide."

"Can we…see her?" Frankly, I didn't know if I really wanted to. The thought terrified me. Or filled me full of anger. I didn't know what to think, a terrible time to need my mother. "Maybe just a small visit?"

Dad shook his head. "Afraid not. Not yet, at least."

"*Why?*"

"She doesn't want you to see her this way. I tried to tell her it wouldn't matter. But like it or not…it's her decision. She said when she's better… then we could visit. Some day." He spread trembling hands, then closed the gap. "I'm still waiting. But she *is* getting better. Be happy for her, Dibs. She's getting the help she needs."

Not only did that sound like a double-edged sword, but I felt both sides puncturing my heart. How could I be happy for a woman who'd abandoned us? When she couldn't be bothered to tell us why, let alone farewell. When I didn't matter a bit in her decision.

Except, of course, for all those years I blamed myself for her deserting me, wondering what I'd possibly done to make her despise me.

"But…was she unhappy with you? With…me?"

Dad looked at me with mournful eyes. "No. Absolutely not. I mean… yes, we had our fair share of problems in our marriage. But sometimes… people just get sick. Not right in their head. Not crazy, mind you, but…

your mother developed a chemical imbalance in her brain. But Dibby, know this…she loved you. *Loves* you."

Dad enveloped me. I tucked into his warm embrace. Alternately, I bawled, then raged. Wiped my mess of a face, then started all over again.

"Why didn't you tell me?" I warbled. "All this time… I never knew. All this time I've wondered…"

"I know, Dibs. And I'm sorry." Once his voice broke, I knew I'd had it and started another round. "It wasn't fair of me or her. I'm sorry. I guess… maybe I was wrong."

"It should've…been…my…"

"I'm sorry."

We stayed that way for some time. As much as I wanted to be acknowledged as an adult with needs and thoughts and feelings of my own, as much as I wanted the world to finally wake up and see me, tears reduced me back into a child. Helpless in my father's loving arms. And sometimes, no matter how old or mature you are, maybe that's a-okay.

* * *

Dad took pity on me. Red heat splotches from crying speckled my face, a notorious visual sign school bullies were almost supernaturally attuned to recognize. Or maybe Dad realized I hadn't been to bed all night. Could be guilt played a big part in his decision, too. Whatever the reason, Dad considered it best I stay home from school.

Under any other circumstances, I'd do cartwheels over the idea. But it meant not seeing James and I couldn't risk leaving him to the dangerous clutches of Suzette. He could barely look after himself, let alone worry about predators.

We compromised. I told Dad I'd go into school late. He hemmed and hawed and finally relented. I hit the hay.

Sleep came calling, but not for long. Troubled dreams mosied into nightmares, normal folks swapped their skin for demon scales, and my classroom caught on fire. Flames licked the chalkboards and blackened the windows 'til they exploded. My classmates fled while I remained stuck at my desk, unable to move. The classroom tore apart. Nothing more than stage props, the four walls slammed down into dirt.

Dream logic performed its lazy magic and dropped me into the Saunders' now-familiar cornfield.

Thomas Saunders's face—pale as the underside of a slug—screamed at his unseen assailant. His malnourished arms swept up, flinging left and right. Down on the ground, he curled into a pill bug, trying to make himself invisible amongst the corn stalks.

A man's voice rose. Fury torched his lungs. Stalks cracked and caved. They parted. Thomas screamed.

Hedrick Saunders stood unveiled, hovering over his son, panting. Eyes wild. Single brow scrawled with anger. A scythe in his hands, the weapon he no doubt had nicked me in the back with.

I tried to scream but couldn't find my voice.

And I woke, knowing full well that wasn't any ordinary dream. Stalk scratches on my arms provided the proof in the pudding.

Thomas appeared to be growing impatient. Since I hadn't been home last night for our usual get-togethers, I imagined Thomas had contacted me via other methods, stepping up the details in his show-and-tell stories. Attempting to light a fire—literally—beneath my hind quarters. A warning?

Undoubtedly, Hedrick Saunders had killed his own son, Thomas. That much was clear now. But more mysteries remained. What had happened to Hedrick? Why'd he do it? And where did he dispose of poor Thomas's body?

I had a lot to do before my fourth hour class, and little time to do it, even though I sure as shooting didn't want to do it.

In the basement, Dad stayed busy stuffing dead folks with chemicals and what-not, so I didn't bother him. I left silent as my shadow and sped through the outskirts of town.

On Hollow Crick Road, Odie Smith was making his afternoon rounds, delivering mail and hand tosses with equal vigor. Once I caught his eye, he practically dove for cover into his mail sack. His always eager-to-please smile sunk, too. Through my actions, I'd managed to shake the always durable Odie Smith, and it made my skin crawl.

Without James slowing me down, I zipped past the Judge's tree and down into Dead Man's Slip fast as a jackrabbit.

In the daytime, the woods didn't seem nearly as big or scary. Shadows originated from definite sources I could point a finger to. The way I liked things.

Still, the farther I traveled along the narrow dirt road, the more nature conspired against me. Everything hushed again in an unnatural union.

I could've heard a pin drop onto the forest floor. Once I rounded the corner and pumped the pedals up the final hill, things changed. At first, the hubbub sounded like the unleashed sobs of a family viewing a lost loved one. But as I conquered the hill, savage, anguished wails rose beyond any sound a human could make. A clowder of cats sat on Hettie Williquette's sagging front porch. Agitated, their tails switched back and forth. Some clawed at the front door, others stood on their back legs pawing at the windows.

I wheeled up close, much closer than I'd dared come last night on my bike, hoping to quiet the ruckus. But my attempts did nothing but rouse the cats into further distress. The cumulative sound resembled the police/fire department building siren, the one that hadn't gone off since JFK had been shot.

With a gut shot full of dread, I laid down my bike. Carefully, I wove between a porch full of fur. Even though I knew there wouldn't be an answer, felt it in my bones, I knocked on the door anyway. Next, I peeked into a window, saw nothing but Hettie's empty front room. The six-pointed star and candles that had (or might not have) been on her floor the night before had been removed.

The doorknob twisted with ease, and I entered. Can't say what struck me first, not really. But having spent more time around dead bodies than any teenage girl should, I recognized the oppressive and still air, the unnatural, unseen character that seemed to physically accompany dead folk. Maybe it's an acquired feeling or something I'd inherited from Dad; hard to say.

But I knew, sure as shooting, what I'd find in Hettie's bedroom.

For the second time within hours, I emptied my stomach onto the late Hettie Williquette's front porch.

* * *

Out of breath and wild as a hare, I pulled a Brody in the Hangwell Police and Fire Station driveway. My out-of-control skid nearly sent me face first into the gravel. I dropped my bike and ran into the front office. No one sat behind the desk, hardly a surprise. Only Sheriff Grigsby, Fire Chief Wakuna, and, on occasion, Mrs. Hemsworth (pulling double duty from the school office) hung their hats there, and that seemed to be a rare day indeed.

"Hello?" I hammered my knuckles onto the front counter and called out louder. "Hello? Sheriff Grigsby? Chief Wakuna? Anybody? I got a real emergency here! Please, any—"

"Land's sake, Dibby, you're liable to rouse the dead!" Sheriff Grigsby hurried out from a back door. Judging by the way his belt wasn't completely looped, I figured I'd caught him during an afternoon constitutional. Sweat drops licked at his forehead. After he finished his belt work, he pointed a finger at me. "Why ain't you in school, young lady?"

"Dad gave me permission. I gotta report—"

"Let's just simmer down a spell and catch our breath." Looked to me like he needed the breather more than I did. "Now, why don't you calmly tell me what's got your knickers in a bunch."

"I stopped by Miss Williquette's house—Hettie Williquette—out offa Dead Man's Slip and—"

"I know where it is."

"…and I found her deader than a doornail! Just up and keeled over in—"

"Whoa, Nelly!" Hands went up. "You're telling me Hettie Williquette's gone feet-up?" I nodded. He reddened even more, wiped his hand across his forehead. I think I ruined his day, bothering him with a dead woman. Flustered, he turned, yelled, "John? *John!*"

Fire Chief Wakuna stepped out from another door, looking like he'd just woken up from a nap. Then again, his sleepy, hooded eyes always gave him that appearance. At least his eyebrows rose in curiosity. "What's going on?" he asked.

The Sheriff jerked his chin toward me. "Li'l Dibby here claims that ol' Hettie's taken a six-feet-under slumber. Lessen o' course she's pulling my leg. You wouldn't do a thing like that now, would ya, Dibby?"

"No, sir! I surely wouldn't!"

"We'd best check it out, Bill," said Chief Wakuna.

"I reckon you're right. But something appears a mite odd. Dibby, tell me exactly what you saw."

"Well, Miss Williquette wouldn't answer her door and her cats were up in a tizzy outside. I got worried. The door was unlocked. I went in and I found her in her bedroom. On her bed. White as a sheet and eyes fulla milk."

"And you're sure she's dead? Maybe just—"

"I know what a dead body looks like, Sheriff!" I snapped.

"Don't you take that tone with me, missy," he fired back, his finger loaded and ready to shoot. "I'm just trying to get to the bottom of this."

"Sorry… I'm sorry. I'm just shook up a bit, I guess. But I checked the pulse in her neck. Got nothing. Also held my hand over her mouth to see if I could catch a breath."

"You touched her body?"

"Yes, sir. I considered it appropriate in case she was still hanging on. But she's passed, no doubt about it."

Bent down, hands on knees, the Sheriff spoke to me with unnecessary kid gloves. "This is important, Dibby. Did you touch anything else? Anything at all? Try to remember."

Efficiently, I listed everything I'd committed to memory. "When I looked inside Miss Williquette's house, I touched the front window. I banged on the door. I twisted the front door knob, pushed open her bedroom door, felt for a pulse in her neck as I said. That's it. I looked around for a phone to call you but couldn't find one. And there wasn't a speck of blood, not that I could see."

With some bone-cracking effort, the Sheriff straightened. He shot Chief Wakuna a mighty serious look, one that made me feel like I'd just topped the FBI's most wanted list.

"We'd better look into it, Bill," said Chief Wakuna. "You wanna take the fire truck or your car?"

"I reckon my car'll be good enough for Hettie now if what Dibby says is accurate." I rolled my eyes. Neither man caught it. "Dibby…what in the world were you doing out at Hettie's place anyway? That ain't no place for a young girl." He stuck out his lower lip, shook his head, another disappointed adult.

He was about to get even more disappointed 'cause I aimed to lie. "Miss Williquette had asked me to help with some chores out in her field. Cleaning up some of the brush and whatnot. She was fixing to pay me."

"Hettie Williquette asked you to help her." The Sheriff repeated it flatter than a pancake. "Ol' Hettie asked you to do that, did she?"

"Yes, sir."

"Huh." He gave his jowls a good rub. "I find that highly unlikely."

"C'mon, Bill, time's getting on," said Chief Wakuna. "We'd best get on out there."

Exasperated—purt-near the Sheriff's one expression—he turned on the fire chief. "Hang on a minute, John. I ain't done with Dibby here." He plucked out a jangly tambourine of rings and flipped them to Wakuna. "Go bring my car around."

Chief Wakuna said nothing, not unusual, and left.

"Dibby, something about this smells fishy. And I don't like fishy smells, prefer to leave that to the Catholics on Fridays. Why do I get the feeling you ain't telling me ever'thing?"

"I'm not sure, Sheriff. Could be I'm still upset over the entire ordeal, me being a little girl and all." I considered forcing crocodile tears, but honestly, I didn't want to go to the effort. Besides, I'd pretty much drained my ducts earlier.

"It's fine, Dibby." Unexpectedly, he turned fatherly, dropped a bear claw of a hand on my shoulder. Gave me a little condescending pat. "It's fine. Everything'll be fine; you just heed my words. Don't you fret. I reckon it was just Hettie's time, the way God planned it."

"Yes, sir."

But I highly suspected God didn't have anything to do with Hettie's passing. For now, I decided to keep that information locked up tight. The Sheriff wouldn't stand to listen anyway. If I thought he might, I would've been glad to share my other observations I took away from the crime scene.

Hettie'd been fully dressed—not in her pajamas, not in a house-dress—laying on top of her made bed. She hadn't passed in her sleep. Besides, Hettie didn't strike me as the kind of gal to just accept death at face value and wait in bed for it to come snatch her away.

But the thing that really got under my skin, the evidence that Hettie went out fighting, was the little lamp that lay smashed to pieces clear across the room from her body. The lamp I'd noticed on Hettie's bedside table the night before.

* * *

By the time I finally reached school, I may as well not have bothered. With only an hour and some change to go, I couldn't concentrate, my mind elsewhere. On James, among other things, natch.

Out of the corner of my eye, I saw him stealing glances my way, trying his dangdest to snare my attention.

And I enjoyed every second of it. I played like I didn't notice him. Chin up, smile proud, I looked straight at Mrs. Hopkins blathering on about angles or some such geometrical nonsense as if it enthralled me.

I couldn't have James believing me to be an easy mark, just another notch, after all. Besides, the newspaper advice columns always instructed to make the boys give chase.

The final bell rang. As I tucked my books beneath my desk, preparing for another afternoon of torture with Suzette, James swept up behind me.

"Um, Dibby?"

I acted like he'd flown beneath my radar. "Oh, you gave me a fright." Just like I'd seen the silly girls do, I fluttered a hand toward my chest, fanned my face. Something straight out of *Gone With the Wind*. Utterly preposterous.

"Sorry 'bout that. Hey, how come you didn't show up earlier? How'd it go with your old man?"

I lowered my voice. "I'm not sure how I feel about that, tell you the truth. We talked, but..."

He grabbed my hands, pressed them together between his. "James! Not in public," I hissed. I looked up at Mrs. Hopkins, mercifully lost spelunking inside her handbag.

Before I could stop him, James tugged me outside the door and onto the front commons.

"Dangit, James, you know I have detention to get to." I felt my cheeks flush. A few lingering students gawped at us as James continued to hold one of my hands. Part of me—the old Dibby—felt mortified. But the Model '65 Dibby thrilled at the notion of my very first romance, practically wanted to crow about it.

"No sweat. Even Missus Hopkins knows you've got to use the john on occasion, right?"

"Behave. Folks are looking."

"Let 'em gander, I don't care." He swung my hand high, then low, smiling like nothing mattered, and in that moment, nothing else really did. "So what'd your ol' man say about your mom flying the coop with your neighbor?"

"She didn't. I can't get into it now... I'll tell you later." I broke contact, something I didn't particularly want to do.

"Wait! You gotta tell me more!"

I ran up the steps, opened the front school door. Turned, said, "I will, promise. Oh, and I also found Hettie dead." I knew it was a horrible way to leave James, but his befuddled, flabbergasted look could've made the cutest camera snapshot. I stashed it away in my mind's darkroom, thinking of how things might develop between us.

Grinning, I went back to class. Naturally, upon seeing Suzette, my grin struck downward.

"You're late." Suzette didn't look up from her fingernails.

"I'm late? Seeing as how you kick your legs up for all the boys, I rightly imagine *you're* the one who's late." I couldn't believe I said it, a joke as off color as those shared on the *Seed and Feed* store's front porch. But Suzette's look of horror was beautiful, very much worth any price I'd have to pay. Her jaw hung down, her metal works shining like diamonds in the dirt.

"I'm going to tell Missus Hopkins you said that, Dibby!"

"Be my guest. I'm already in detention, can't get much worse."

She harrumphed, folded alabaster arms.

Her standoffishness didn't last. As a person uncomfortable in her own company (couldn't rightly blame her), Suzette always had to jabber away to someone. Even her enemy.

"So. Where were you today?" she asked.

"I had stuff to tend to. Is Missus Hopkins taking her cigarette break?"

"I guess. We're supposed to sweep up and straighten the room."

With Mrs. Hopkins notoriously long smoking breaks, we had all the time in the world. I sat down next to Suzette.

"You know Hettie Williquette died," I said.

"She did not!"

"Surely did. And I found her body."

"You'd better not be lying to me, Dibby Caldwell, and if you're not, you'd better tell me everything." She leaned toward me, cherubic chin resting on her palm.

Seeing as how Suzette'd set me on the Hettie Williquette trail in the first place, I figured I owed her the story. Withholding certain details, of course.

Not wanting to speak ill of the dead, I cleared up a few matters as well.

"So ol' Hettie didn't eat any children, she didn't eat Hedrick Saunders, and she didn't eat Gordon Turndell. She had sex with him, maybe, but beyond that, I reckon she didn't do him any harm."

Suzette sat aghast, mouth open. Then she stifled a giggle, hardly the reaction I'd expected. "Lordy, Dibby, you have the mouth of a sailor."

"I can chew tobacco like one, too."

She gasped. "Really?"

"No, not really."

"You're funny," said Suzette in sorta the same way adults talked down to me. "I mean…other than the way you dress and act."

"And you're about as mean as an ingrown toenail on a camel," I tossed back.

She laughed and so did I. Honestly, my mood soared, high on a cloud, particularly surprising given how poorly the first part of my day had fared. I wouldn't let Suzette sour that mood, either.

"Dibby, I swan—"

"Oh, don't go swanning; you're liable to tear your purty li'l clothes."

"…I *swan* I don't know why in Heaven's name you're so fixed on this whole Thomas Saunders thing. I mean…you didn't know him. We were just kids when he ran away." She sat back, tugging a blonde braid, thinking. I feared she might hurt herself. "Unless, of course, you're *really* a li'l ol' lady pretending to be young. Which is kinda how you look."

"Did you know your momma bought you out of the store? Just took the plastic off the box and set you on her mantle. That's why your head's hollow. Along with your heart."

She groaned. "Why do you always *do* that?"

"'Cause you started it."

"Just *tell* me, dang it! Why does it matter to you what happened to the Saunders boy?"

"Well… Unlike you, Suzette, I happen to care 'bout folks other than myself. I think something rotten happened to Thomas Saunders. Something other than his running away. I know it for fact."

"You're still not telling me how you know."

As much as I despised everything about Suzette, it seemed pretty much a given she'd believe me. She certainly had no problem buying into the child-eating tales of poor Hettie.

"Fine then. Thomas's ghost visits me." I waited for the laughter to begin, her customary fingers-on-blackboard shrieks. When it didn't happen, I finished my tale.

"My gosh… So you believe someone killed Thomas?"

"I suspect it was his daddy, Hedrick."

"And you think someone also murdered Hettie Williquette?"

"I surely do."

"Oh…" I'd rendered her speechless. Something I thought I'd never see.

"You believe me?" I asked.

"Yes. Yes, I do. Unless you're crazy, of course, and I've kinda thought that for a long time, but… I believe you. Could I… Could I come see the ghost?"

An absolutely ridiculous request if I'd ever heard one. I wondered if she hadn't suffered a chemical imbalance of her own. We weren't friends. The thought of having Suzette sleep-over made my gut buck. And, of course, I couldn't conjure up Thomas at will. Regardless, I jumped on that ol' high road. "Not for a while, at least. My dad's grounded me for a spell."

"Well…shoot." The golden girl melted. Strange sadness clouded her fair-weathered nature. Call me foolish, but I felt a scratch of empathy for her.

"I'll see what I can do," I said. "Maybe if I talk to Dad, I can get him to go easy. Tell him you're coming over to study or something. But first, I need to talk him into letting me go to the movies this weekend with James." Rarely had I seized the opportunity to crow, so I flew with it.

Suzette's lower lip fell, trembled. She had something to say, hesitated. She'd never held back before. When her cold paw dropped on mine, I nearly jumped out of my seat. She followed it with a couple of light-weight pats.

"But, Dibby," she said, "James already asked me to the movies this weekend."

Now the crow had been served to me.

Chapter Ten

My stomach clenched tighter than the fist I reserved for James. In her defense, Suzette looked downright sad, hardly gloating, as was her wont to do.

Over the past day, I'd thrown up more than I had since I'd been a toddler and had no intention of stopping.

I felt used, betrayed one more time. The final time.

Somehow, I managed to stand. "Tell…tell Missus Hopkins I had to go home sick. Tell her…I dunno…tell her whatever you want…"

I didn't wait for a response. Frankly, I didn't even remember leaving the room. Far away, a voice as meek as a little girl stuck down in a well, hollered, "I'm sorry, Dibby! Sooo sorry! I didn't know! I really…"

I'd left my books behind and didn't give a tinker's damn. Somehow I made it through the front doors. Fresh air slapped some sense into me, a renewed resolve to never be fooled again. To stop making myself vulnerable.

Then I saw James in the courtyard, arms open. Waiting for me.

Eyes straight-ahead, one scootch from brimming over, I hurried down the steps. I brushed right by him. My shoulder met his with heft. And I kept right on going.

"Dibby?"

I didn't answer him. Wouldn't—couldn't—give in. I straddled my bike, wheeled it back. Behind me, I heard him panting, sneakers clopping down the drive.

"Dibby! Wait a minute!"

Hollering for his life's worth (which, admittedly, didn't amount to a hill of beans), he jumped into my path. He raised his hands like a frazzled crossing guard. I stood on the pedals, pumped them with all my weight. I envisioned running him over, watching his body go sky high, turning head over heel. Satisfied by my macabre daydream, I aimed to make it happen and poured on the speed. His face swam up, the one I'd stupidly been so intrigued with. At the last moment, he dodged right and twisted in a matador's circle. His jean jacket flipped out and grazed my arm.

"Dibby, what the hell's the matter?" Huffing away, he ran alongside me.

I put him far behind me. Then decided the buffoon should be held accountable for his actions, brought to trial inside my courtroom. And so help me, if he dared play big-eyed and innocent, I'd smite him down with the righteous zeal of ol' Judge Wilbur himself.

My bike swerved into a U-turn. Gravel and dust spat up.

"Dibby… Talk to me. What's wrong?" Winded, he caught up. Hands on his knees, he looked ready to toss up into the drive.

Calm as blue skies, I swung my leg over my bike and toed down the kick-stand. As I approached him, he smiled—actually dared smile at me! This changed my tactics. My fist bunched. As I broke into a trot, my fist tightened.

He stood still, an easy target. "Are you okay? I was wor—"

Tumph.

Over the last couple days, I'd fairly well learned that when you sock someone upside the face, it doesn't sound anything like the movies. No firecracker *smack* of fulfillment. But it surely put the spring back in my step as I watched his head turn, his body twist, his arms flail about like a grounded bird. One foot came up, and he went down, flat on his back.

He didn't look so cute on the ground, just kinda pathetic.

"What… What'd you do that for?" He rubbed his cheek.

"Don't you *dare* act like you don't know what you did, James Mackleby!" I stood over him, arms akimbo, not beyond kicking some sense into him.

"I don't! I swear to God, I don't know what I did!"

I looked up to the sky on my right, glanced likewise to the left. "You'd better hope God didn't hear you. I imagine he'll be hurling down a lightning bolt any second now."

"Dibby, just tell me what I did." He struggled to get up.

I wouldn't have it. "You just stay right down there where you belong, you bottom-dwelling, trash-eating, lying catfish! Don't make me sock you again! Although, truth be told, I sorely wouldn't mind having another crack at it."

He stayed put but didn't know when to keep his pie-hole shut. "I didn't do anything! I swear I didn't, Dibby!"

Sure enough, he aimed on playing the wide-eyed innocent to the very end. Shame on him for making me have to say it. "You liar! No-good cheat! You asked Suzette to the movies!"

"What?" With one hand out (more for protection, I imagined, than balance), he made it to his legs. "Dibby, I only asked her because I thought you couldn't go. I didn't think your old man would let you. Then I got to thinking…maybe you hadn't asked him yet 'cause you didn't really want to go with me."

He reached out, grabbed my shoulder, his other hand looking to make them a bookend set. I shrugged free, stepped back.

"Damn you, James. Just…damn you." And damn me for falling back on tears. My hands flew to my face, covered my shame, my humiliation. My naïveté for falling for an absolute cad.

"I'm sorry, Dibby. I didn't mean to hurt you."

"No one ever does! But they keep doing it!" I uncovered my face, drew a shirt sleeve across my eyes. "After my mom left…I didn't trust anyone again. Ever! And just when I was ready to take a big leap of faith on you, James… Well, you betrayed me. Betrayed me just like everyone else…"

"That's…not what I wanted, Dibby. Not at all."

"What about what I want? How come I never get what I want?"

"I still want to go to the movies with you, Dibs. Um…if that's what you want." He tipped his head, tried to raise a smile. His sense of timing needed a tune-up. "I like you… No one else. Honest injun. I only asked Suzette out as a buddy. If that makes you feel any better."

"It doesn't." I pulled back and walloped the other side of his face. "But that surely did."

I hauled myself out of there fast as my Raleigh could fly, leaving James dazed in a cloud of granite dust.

* * *

My studies had been suffering from neglect lately and I didn't give two-hoots-and-a-holler. Frankly, the school should make allowances for affairs of the heart that plummet south. I don't know how folks cope with the aftermath, hardly worth the effort.

I walked my bike up the drive, my mind set on an early-to-bed evening, when I heard a voice holler out.

"Hey there, Dibby."

Devin Meyers stood behind his battered picket fence, looking for all the world like an overstuffed scarecrow. He lived up to the title, too, nearly scaring the daylights outta me.

I gathered myself and returned a greeting. "Hey there, Mister Meyers. Didn't see you standing there."

"Sorry if I spooked you, Dibby. I've been needing to speak to you but didn't want to bother your daddy at work." He gestured toward Dad's hearse in the drive. "Not when he's doing the good Lord's work."

I didn't think Dad would appreciate Mr. Meyers's heavenly assessment of his particular vocation, but I didn't possess the fire to argue the point. "That's mighty thoughtful of you."

"Anyhoo… Seems you're a bit late getting home from school today, Dibby." He leaned his forearms over the fence, clasped dirty hands together. Smiled out of one corner of his mouth, while the other nibbled on a piece of hay. He balanced his cap, tipped it ever so to the other side of his head. Getting serious minded.

"Truth be told, I've been staying after class a bit, helping Missus Hopkins."

"Uh oh. I surely hope you're not in too much trouble."

I shook my head.

As if he'd bitten into a sour walnut, he grimaced. "First, let me just doff my hat to you, young miss, for your bringing the mail to my sister yesterday." True to his word, he swept off his cap, bowed over a bit. A question mark of lonely hair fell from the top of his nearly naked scalp. He swooped it back into place, locked it in tight with his cap. "But…as you mighta figured, Evelyn…Missus Saunders…ain't quite right. Seems your visit set her back a spell."

"I'm real sorry to hear that. I hope she hasn't taken to bed or—"

"No, nothing of the sort. It's just…Evelyn doesn't handle stressful situations very well. I'm afraid I'm gonna have to ask you to not come 'round no more."

"Oh… Would you tell her I hope she gets to feeling better real soon?"

He smirked, gave a put-on nod. He had no intention of telling his sister hear any such thing. "I'll do that, Dibby, I surely will. You take care now." He trawled off through his cornfield, humming that same strange tune I'd heard the first time I'd met him.

On top of everything else, Mr. Meyers's out-of-the-blue request hardly seemed shocking or hurtful. Just another odd adult encounter. I was used to them.

Maybe Devin Meyers did indeed have his sister's welfare in mind by making decisions for her. Or maybe he was keeping her prisoner. Come to think of it, I'd never seen another visitor over there, 'cept, of course, for Odie delivering the mail. And he tended not to linger long.

Something stuck in my craw about our chat, though. When the realization finally smacked me, it set the willies loose: Devin Meyers knew of my comings and goings, right down to my school hours. An unsettling notion if I'd ever had one.

I'd just walked through the door when an engine, one starving for maintenance, rumbled out in our drive. A familiar one, too. I pulled back the curtain. Sure enough, Sheriff Grigsby's ol' green monster of a pickup rolled to a persnickety stop, the tailpipe back-talking with a loud *pop*. In the truck's bed, ropes pulled taught over an object wrapped in canvas and potato sacks. A fairly familiar sight at our home, and a macabre one to boot.

Hettie Williquette had made her first and last house-call to our abode.

Whenever the Sheriff brought around bodies, Dad didn't care for my eavesdropping, but I wasn't about to miss this conversation. Like it or not, I was involved up to my back teeth in Hettie's passing.

I raced upstairs to the landing and tucked in neatly behind the modesty panel of the desk that sat there, my usual spying nook.

Clearly, Sheriff Grigsby didn't know how to move quietly, everything about him a three-ring event. He clomped up the steps to the porch, knocked loudly on the door, then banged away on the bell.

So as not to miss a customer, Dad had rigged the doorbell so a buzzer went off down in his workshop. *Bad for business*, he'd explained with a wry grin, *to keep death waiting*.

Determined, the Sheriff kept on stubbing at the doorbell. From down in the depths of Dad's workshop, swinging doors squeaked like mice. Dad's footsteps clomped up the ramp and down the hallway. The sound carried far, echoing through the ducts and whispering through the vents. I peeked around the desk, saw Dad hurrying toward the front door. In the mirror, he straightened his lab coat, which appeared to be shrinking with age. Nice and tidy now, he opened the door.

"Afternoon, Bill," Dad said as he looked over the Sheriff's shoulder. "I assume this isn't a social call."

"You'd be right in your assumption," said the Sheriff. "Look here, Oscar, I don't know how much you've heard or what Dibby might've told you—"

"Dibby? What's she got to do with this?" Dad's voice raised one octave below panic.

"She's fine, just fine. Level-headed little gal, that one of yours."

"What's this about, Bill? Who's in the truck bed?"

The Sheriff swept off his wide-brimmed hat, fanned his face. "It's ol' Hettie Williquette. Off to meet her maker."

A pause. I could practically hear Dad's logic grinding away, working to fill the gaps the Sheriff wasn't in any hurry to plug. "I'm sorry to hear that… But what's this about Dibby?"

"Well…she found Hettie. At her home up in the woods."

"*What?* That can't be. She—"

"'Fraid it's true. She discovered the body, reported it to us just this afternoon."

Like an ill-prepared student called upon in class, Dad sputtered. "I don't… This is… Sorry, sorry, Bill. I'm afraid I didn't know anything about this. Dibby doesn't talk to me like she used to. She's…hiding things from me."

Fine talk coming from Dad, seeing as how he'd kept hushed about Mom for most of my life.

"Aw, you know kids, Oscar," said the Sheriff. "It's just part of growing up. Stretching their sea legs and all."

"I suppose you're right. Doesn't make it any easier."

"It surely doesn't." How in the world the Sheriff knew anything about kids struck me as plum odd. Far as I knew, he'd never had any children himself, a lifelong bachelor. "But we were the same way as kids. Just hard to remember back then." He laughed, slapped his belly.

"But what was Dibby doing… Never mind. I'll talk to her later." Dad took a breath, put on professional manners. "I assume since you brought Hettie here in your truck, she's one of the sad cases."

"That's about the size of it. Far as I know, ol' Hettie had no living relatives. There ain't no records, and no one in town knows diddley 'bout her either. So…there's no one to pay for a funeral service. If you wouldn't mind…"

"I'll be glad to settle affairs." Dad never said it, but I suspected it pained his wallet a bit to take care of the town freebies. The send-offs weren't elaborate by any means: a nice, simple cremation, ashes spread over the graveyard. Still, time was involved, and Dad always said, "Time is money."

"Me and the rest of the town thank you muchly, Oscar. Now, don't go wasting any more of your resources than necessary. Hettie's death was a plain and simple case of old age."

Dad stiffened. His coat threatened to split at his back. "I understand. I'll see to it."

Even though I had no interest in the family business, I knew Dad's number one rule of death by heart: *Dying from old age is a bunch of hooey, nothing more than a pretty metaphor to cover up what really happened to the body.*

"I can always count on you," said Sheriff Grigsby. "Speaking of which…care to give me a hand?"

"Surely. Let me go get the gurney."

As Dad went back downstairs to retrieve his wheeled stretcher, the Sheriff clumped off outside. I heard Dad throw back the cellar doors—a direct shortcut to outside—and together, they wheeled Hettie down into the workshop.

I waited 'til I heard the truck grumble away before I came up for air. Faster than usual, Dad met me at the bottom of the stairs.

"Um…hey, Dad."

"Hey there, yourself."

Miles of tension stretched between us. I just wanted it done, ready to swallow my newest dose of medicine and move along. "That's a real shame about Miss Williquette, huh?"

"What's a shame is you didn't feel the need to tell me you'd found her body, Dibby."

"I think there's a lotta shame regarding things kept between us, Dad." Without consideration, the words blurted out. Intended to wound. Still very angry, very muchly hurt.

Dad pulled off his glasses, rubbed the bridge of his nose.

"Dad… I'm sorry I said that. I think…there're things I still need to say. To understand. But is it okay if we do it some other time?"

"Absolutely." He looked as relieved as I felt. He pulled me into an awkward hug. Like a rag doll, I just went along for the ride, my arms stubbornly at my sides. "Dibby, I know you've been through a lot today. Are you okay?"

"Hettie wasn't the first dead body I've ever seen, you know."

"That's my girl." He chuckled. Living in a funeral home, you learn to look for humor in the darkest of corners. "But if you need to talk about it, you know you can always come to me, right?"

"Sure." But I didn't really know if that was the case. Not anymore. I used to think Dad was beyond reproach, incapable of lying. But he was all too fallible, just like every adult. I didn't know if I could trust him any longer. I scooted out of his embrace.

"What were you doing way out there, Dibby? At Hettie's place?"

"I was gonna help her clear out some brush and stuff." I'd already set fire to this lie. I figured fanning the flames a bit wouldn't singe anybody's eyebrows. "She was gonna pay me."

"Why? I always give you money for what you need. And, to be honest, Hettie Williquette wasn't known as the friendliest woman in town. I don't want to…falsely accuse you of anything, but I suspect you're not telling the truth."

"Now you know how it feels to be in my shoes."

My second arrow fired. The cumulative effect of today had tightened my bow string and I had to release it.

"Dibby…" His voice cracked, just a hair. I truly couldn't unleash any more waterworks, not today. Besides, we had more pressing matters at hand. Matters that didn't directly involve cutting open our hearts and letting them bleed out.

I did the best thing I could, something very adult like. I changed the topic.

"Dad, there's something you oughta know about Miss Williquette's death."

Taken aback, his eyebrows flew sky-high. "What would that be?"

"Someone killed her. There wasn't anything natural about it."

My third arrow dropped Dad to the bottom step. I sat beside him.

"Tell me what you know, Dibby."

I told him about how Hettie'd been dressed, how the bed was made. He appeared doubtful, but when I told him about how Hettie's lamp had traveled across the room and smashed against the wall, he changed his tune.

"So…you think Hettie threw her lamp at someone? Someone she was trying to fend off?"

"I surely do."

Dad tugged at his lower lip, let it fly back with a *plip*. "Tell you what, Dibby. I respect your intuition. And I trust your instincts. I'll look into it and let you know what I find out."

He coaxd the first, honest-to-gosh smile outta me for hours. "Thanks, Dad." Sometimes it's the little things that matter.

* * *

While Dad was banging, sawing, drilling, Lord only knows what down in his workshop, a ruckus of another sort arose outside. The loud caterwauling set the kitchen windowpanes to jiggling, loud enough to get even ol' Hy Thurgood out of bed before noon.

At the front door, a visitor scratched away at the wood. When I swung the door open, irritation gave way to melancholy. Hettie's cats had gathered on the stoop, come to pay their last respects.

At least thirty felines crowded our porch. They rubbed against the posts and columns, sought comfort by brushing into one another. Furry heads turned up when I walked out onto the porch. Animal town criers, they meowed, chattered, and chirruped. Tails slashed back and forth, swept the floorboards. A funeral parade wove between my legs.

Out in the bushes, leaves rustled. And I swear I glimpsed a large, black mass: the giant, otherworldly cat from last night. Heard him yowl, too, all brass and brumble.

I knelt, gave a good rub-down to those nearest. They flocked to me, the new Pied Piper of cats. Now that Hettie had passed, I wondered if they'd adopted me. Their glowing, haunted eyes seemed to answer in mystical affirmation. Sadness formed their vocalizations, sorrow rounded their eyes. I sat, let them crowd me, felt an affinity with them, all of us aching for devotion.

If the townsfolk of Hangwell had all disliked Hettie Williquette, she sure had nurtured a loving following of a different sort.

Through a narrow slip of the door, I escaped inside and returned with a couple large bowls of milk. The platters were licked clean in no time.

Dad opened the door behind me. "What in the world?"

Sweat darkened his underarms. Other stains soiled his usually pristine lab coat, gruesome blotches I'm fairly certain had originated from within Miss Williquette.

"Say howdy to Miss Williquette's cats," I said. "Holding their very own funeral procession."

"Well, I'll be…" Clearly befuddled, Dad struggled to accept the proof on the porch. Finally, he just shook his head and sighed. "Never let it be said I don't try and comfort all of my mourners. C'mon, Dibs, let's get 'em some more milk."

In the kitchen, Dad said, "You were right. About Hettie."

It didn't surprise me, not a bit, but I acted that way anyhow. Sometimes it's less work to give adults what they expect. "Oh, my gosh. What'd you find?"

"Well…I'd guess Hettie's death happened about twelve to fourteen hours ago."

Not too long after I'd left her home last night. The thought I'd barely missed encountering Hettie's killer—maybe even my own death—dropped the fear of mortality on top of me with the solid load of a piano.

"Even though her eyes had begun to cloud over," he continued, "she had small, burst blood vessels beneath her eyelids. There was also small pressure build-up behind her ears. And I'm afraid to say…she'd wet herself a bit." Dad looked askance, downright silly the things that could embarrass a mortician. "Now, none of that's hardly condemning evidence of a murder. Suspect, sure, but it wouldn't hold up in a court of law. But… I found slight ligature marks—dark brown spots—on her neck and a couple around her wrists. Also, her tongue was enlarged."

"What's it mean?" I asked, but I already knew the answer.

"I believe Hettie was strangled. Coupled with your theory about the lamp being shattered across the room…well… A full autopsy should reveal more."

"What're you gonna do?"

"I'm gonna call the Sheriff, tell him my suspicions, and recommend an autopsy. Whether I carry it out or the County boys over in Durham take care of it makes no difference to me. Just as long as it gets done." Carefully, he handed me two bowls filled to the rim with milk. "Here. Go on and tend to Hettie's friends while I call the Sheriff. May as well get it over with."

Dad rolled his eyes, and I well understood. A cantankerous cuss, even Sisyphus himself couldn't budge the Sheriff once he set his mind to something.

I rushed outside and set the bowls down, spilling a bit in my haste. Again, Dad's conversation with the Sheriff was one I intended to hear.

When I came back inside, Dad had locked down into the living room sofa. Eyes closed—how he dredged up deep concentration—he struggled mightily to keep his voice on an even keel.

"…I know, I know, Bill. It'll be costly… But, frankly, it'd be a miscarriage of justice if we didn't… No, I'm not telling you how to do your job…. No, I don't want your job… Look, I'm just telling you what I discovered… I know you told me not to… There isn't any such damn thing as death by natural causes, and this sure as hell doesn't even come close!" Rarely did Dad blow his top, but whenever he did, animals from miles around burrowed back into their hidey holes. "I'm telling you she was strangled!… All I want to do is conduct a little further… Fine! I'll contact the boys over at County if you won't… Uh huh… Mm-hmm… Of course you'll be the first to know… Uh huh… Sure, you betcha. Thanks, Bill."

Dad hung up. A litany of curses, nearly poetic in its colorful alliteration and impossible body contortions, flew from his mouth.

I cleared my throat, announcing my arrival in the room.

He jumped up off the sofa, turned around. "Oh…sorry, Dibby. I didn't know you were there."

"How'd it go with the Sheriff?"

"Pretty much as I suspected." He swatted the air, chasing after an invisible fly. "Grigsby never wants to do his job. Laziest damn fool in town. Probably why he took the Hangwell position in the first place."

"I don't follow."

Dad fixed me with common-sense eyes. "Because there's rarely ever any murders in Hangwell."

Common-sense eyes or not, I reckoned Dad had no idea what he was talking about.

* * *

The Sheriff relented and gave Dad his blessing to perform an autopsy. The fact Dad volunteered to do it no charge undoubtedly helped sway the decision. The County boys charged an arm and a leg, drawing deep from Hangwell's tax funds.

Like a dog with a bone, once Dad attached himself to something, he wouldn't let go. Over dinner, he grew that faraway look, already planning Hettie's autopsy. Before he'd finished eating, he mumbled an "excuse me," then vanished into his mad scientist's lair. The banging and buzzing commenced, shared through the elaborate duct-work of our patchwork house.

Retired to my room early, I attempted to make sense of the geometry problems swimming in my text book. As my reward, they handed me back gobbledy-gook.

I crawled into bed. Unsettling thoughts burrowed deep and ripped the bandage off my fear.

Why would someone have killed Hettie? Probably because of what she knew about the Saunders boy. I harbored no doubt Hettie and Thomas's murders were connected. And I was smack-dab in the middle of it all, maybe even the reason for Hettie's premature death. I imagined it wouldn't be long before the killer came a-calling for me.

Which meant I had to move the urgency of my investigation up a hair.

I tossed and turned for what seemed like hours but only amounted to minutes. The room's stuffiness kept sleep at bay. I bounced out of bed, trod toward the window, and flung it open. A light breeze lifted the curtains, sent them waving at me.

Satisfied, I dove back under covers. And knew full well why I'd opened the window, nothing to do with having nature at my call. Maybe Thomas would make another nocturnal appearance and I surely didn't want to sleep through it.

But the real reason?

James.

Why couldn't I let go? My mind kept circling back to the stupid, arrogant, cheating, lying jerk. The very cute and charming and irresistible jerk.

I came around to wondering if I'd been a little harsh on him, two punches worth of harsh. And maybe he'd mounted a solid defense for his heinous crime, one Perry Mason himself couldn't have presented better.

Still…what kind of mettle did he consist of if he immediately fell back on the monstrous Suzette just because I hadn't given him a fast answer regarding our movie date? The girl he swore he had no interest in other than as a friend. And who would want her as a friend any ol' how?

I sighed. Whipped down the bedspread so just the thin sheet provided cool coverage. A breeze rolled in, sailing me off to slumberland.

But every time I nearly dozed off, stupid images of James snatched me back from the brink.

Some foolish part of me wanted James to pay another late-night visit. To come calling at my window at midnight, the way Romeo courted Juliet. A tragically romantic relationship. A tale as old as…

Snurk!

Clear thoughts jolted me awake.

Then my round-robin thoughts started bob-bob-bobbing along again…

Of course, I couldn't just flat-out forgive James. Not yet. Well…not completely. Maybe a little.

Dang it, I wanted him to chase me, beg me for forgiveness, plead his undying love toward me. Prove himself. Earn my trust. Be my…my…

Donggg…

Somewhere a bell chimed. A deep clang that resonated long after the clapper had stilled.

Slowly, I rose through the cloudy, thick muck of sleep, swimming to break the shoreline of consciousness.

Donggg...

With an abruptly violent intake of air, I bolt up in bed. A strand of saliva trailed from the corner of my mouth. I wiped my chin, rubbed sleep from my eyes. Blinked. Confirmed my surroundings. Looked at my bedroom window, where the curtains whipped back and forth at a mad rate.

In bare feet, I stumbled toward the window, poked my head out. Beneath a full and bloated moon, the Saunders' cornfield appeared at peace. No unusual movement, definitely no heart-aching pleas from Thomas.

So what shook me from my sleep?

I thought I'd only dozed a few minutes at most. But the clock spoke a different tale. A little after two in the morn, several hours had passed since I'd last looked.

Most definitely something had stirred me out of my dreamless slumber, though. Sleep cobwebs draped over my mind, obscuring clarity.

Something about a bell...

Ting-a-ling...

Barely a sound at all, really, not worth a second thought. It could've been the wind playing outside. Maybe a bell tied around a distant cow's neck. Probably nothing at all, just—

Ding!

There! I didn't imagine it. Faint as a final drop of rain into the gutter, it formed a solid, if slight, sound.

Ting...

Down by my slippers, coming from the vent. On my knees, I placed my ear on the cold, hardwood floor.

Ding-ding!

The sudden sound, sharp as a hand-clap, brought me to my feet. My full bladder pressed against my pelvis. I danced into my slippers and quietly scurried down the hall to the bathroom.

The bathroom's layout memorized, the light stayed off. I sat down to conduct my business. A whiff of air blew through the vent and chilled my feet.

Ching…ding…

I finished, yanked up my pajama bottoms. For now, I left the toilet unflushed. Once put into motion, it sounded like a dinosaur with a tooth-ache, a sound capable of waking even Dad.

Taking my time, I washed my hands. Procrastinating.

Because I knew what caused the sound, knew it deep down, my dread unbearable.

Down below, way below in Dad's workshop, the bell chimed again.

Ting-a-ling…

Summoning me.

As much as I wanted to wake Dad, revert to a scaredy-cat little girl and ask if he'd accompany me, I knew I had to make the journey myself.

Dad's snores sawed out from his room. With care, I lifted my feet, acutely aware of every little sound now. My slippers *shh, shh, shushed*, muffling my footfalls.

Halfway down the stairwell, the temperature dropped. Not by much. But cold enough to raise a goose farm on my flesh.

I followed the hall, trod by the kitchen. Every time I passed a vent—supply or return, high or low, it didn't matter—the bell rang again. Guiding me ever forward.

In the added wing of the mortuary, I pushed through the first set of swinging doors. Behind me, they swung silently, well-oiled. A backlash of cool air urged me on.

Heavy darkness filled the hallway. Blind, I prospected along the wall for the light switch. I found it. Overhead, the three dim bulbs sparked into half-life, a jaundiced color. Alien and hard on the eyes.

Dinggg…

As I descended closer to the source, the bell rang a bit louder. The after-effect resonated longer, a tiny gnat persistently buzzing at my ear.

On the wall, three generations of Caldwells posed in framed yellowed photographs. A sudden draft, alive, rushed up and lifted my hair. Above, the bulbs swayed on their cords like pendulums. Shadows flitted back and forth across Grandpa's photo, setting him to dancing a jig. One second, his foot high-kicked, then falling shadow set him right again. I knew it couldn't be real. But I didn't care to investigate, just in case reality and me had recently parted ways.

At the end of the hall, my foot crunched on a floor-set vent grate. I yelped, stepped back. Cool air whiffed up from it. An orange light flickered beneath the metal grid, burning like a match before it snuffed out.

Ting…dinggg…

Around the corner, I descended the first ramp. My slippers fairly acted like a toboggan and propelled me down the slope at a fast clip. At the landing, I turned my shoulder to take the brunt of my impact into the wall.

Ding! Ding! Ting…

The bell chimed louder, more demanding. Temperatures kept right on dropping, too, but didn't manage to quell my sweat.

The next ramp likewise hurried my descent. My feet slapped the bottom floor. To the right, the furnace. To the left, the swinging doors leading into Dad's workshop.

Zing! Ding-a-ling! Chinggg…

I didn't need the bell to lead me through the right door. Just like in the ol' story, I chose the door with the tiger behind it.

I pushed through the doors. They swatted at my backside, squeaking with mischief. *Eee-hee, eee-hee…*

Down in the workshop, the cold really packed a wallop. I rubbed my arms, stamped my feet. I rode my hand along the wall, searching for the light switch.

Tik…tek…tik…

Fluorescent ceiling lamps sprung to life, duller, deader than usual. Instead of providing warm luminescence, they cast everything in an odd light, everything touched in artificial tints.

Immediately, the strong, familiar odor of ammonia enveloped me. But I couldn't place the other smell, couldn't describe it. If pressed, I suppose I'd catalog it somewhere between sweet and metallic. Sorta the way blood tastes when you prick your finger and suck on it. I'd never smelled anything like it before, not in Dad's workshop or elsewhere.

An overriding smell rode in like fog. A strong, wrong odor that brought to mind mold and rot. A primal scent from a different time or place.

Ching! Ding! Ting-a-ling!

Impatient as a hungry baby, the bell-ringer called.

Click.

The walk-in refrigerator door handle swung up.

Chumpf!

The door released its seal and opened, just a few inches. A pale blue—hardly blue, more like moon-white—cone of light fell across the floor. A swirl of frost slivered out, twirled in the bare luminescence.

Ding! Ding! Ching! Ting-a-ling-aling—

Cut off in mid-ring, the bell silenced. Everything hushed. No sound, not a peep, a tick, a drop. Just the silent shroud of death.

Slowly, I crept toward the refrigerator. Which didn't make a lick of sense as I knew Hettie waited for me. There didn't seem to be any real sense in maintaining silence either. But any noise—even my own—made me want to scream.

Above me, the light flickered off, on, then sizzled like bacon before settling on dark.

My hand gripped the handle. Arctic cold, I wrenched my hand back. I shook it 'til the stabbing needles of cold left. With my shoulder, I nudged the door. It pushed open half-way, then stopped. I followed with a mighty mule kick.

The door opened as far as its hinges would allow.

I took a deep breath, held it. When I exhaled, I spouted out a frozen, visible vapor.

"Hettie?" I whispered.

I entered. To the left, the metal shelves on the wall were unoccupied. On the opposite side, all but one sat empty. A rumpled plastic cloth lay across the bottom shelf.

The eerie blue light had no visible source, but it provided ample light to see by. Maybe too much, considering.

"Hettie?" I repeated a little louder.

In the back of the unit, where Dad housed his supplies, a hanging shower curtain billowed out. Plastic crinkled. Something moved, fluid be-hind the curtain's rippling waves. Not exactly flesh-colored, not much of anything.

Tinggg!

My heart urged me to turn back. Traitorous feet wouldn't comply.

White snails of fingers crawled around the plastic and gripped it. Slow-ly, the curtain pulled back. Rusty rings on a rustier rod squealed: *screeeeeee.*

Hettie stood exposed, naked. Except for the black "X" stitching up her innards. Varicose veins twined her legs. Toes exploded into corns the size of thumbs. Her scrubbing pad of hair stood up on end, a static-raised brush of black and white.

Clouds had moved into her eyes, milkier than when I'd found her, yet intently focused on me. She showed that awful cavernous smile again. Barnacle-like teeth jabbed out of her gums.

Her lower jaw wobbled, then dropped ajar. Not an involuntary move-ment caused by gas either, the way sometimes happened to corpses. She gasped, a hissing radiator.

She took a doddering step toward me.

Ding!

The bell tied to her toe tolled.

Ding-a-ling!

Each step forward took great effort. A kind of ghostly arthritis ham-pered her dead limbs, encased them in cement. When she moved, wood cracked. More wood splintered, her body falling apart. She raised an arm. Dark veins spiraled around it, swimming upstream with determination. They rode toward her sagging bosom, traveled north up her neck, snaked beneath her chin, and set up house on her face.

And still she kept coming.

I managed a step back, nearly stumbled.

Ding!

"Hettie? It's me…Dibby." My voice retreated into a Betty Boop squeak.

But she stopped. Her mouth narrowed. Her eyes swam clear, then clouded again.

"Hettie, I'm mighty sorrowful this happened to you. Can…can I do anything for you?" I didn't know what to say, no experience well to pull from.

Hettie gasped again. Not the spooky hiss from before, but a sudden intake of air, as if she were startled. The noise cut off abruptly, ended in a ghastly wheeze. After all, she no longer had breath to call upon.

"Hettie… Who did this to you?"

Her arm still upraised, a finger cracked out. Pointed at me.

"No… I didn't do any—"

Then I realized she wasn't crooking her digit at me, but rather over my shoulder. Her mouth strained into agony, she continued to gesture toward the wall.

"What? What're you trying to tell me?"

Anger flushed her eyes from cloudy to full-on thunderstorm. And she just kept on motioning that crooked finger.

The air dropped another notch, near intolerable. My breath blew out great streams of frozen vapor.

Behind me, the refrigerator door slammed shut with a *whumpf.*

"No!" Terrified I was sealed inside a frozen coffin, I whirled around.

The back of the refrigerator door crystallized. Ice particles formed and migrated toward the middle. An invisible finger scrawled something inside the ice patch.

A straight line darted up at an angle, another one came down. The line crossed over, and several more built on it until a star stood revealed. A six-pointed star like the one I'd seen Hettie sitting in the night before.

Suddenly, the temperature rose. The image melted away.

"Hettie…I don't understand what—"

When I turned back around, she was gone. The blue light faded. The refrigerator's usual wan yellow light ticked on.

Against the wall, on the lower shelf, a body formed ski-slope bumps beneath the plastic blanket. Hettie's wild hair stuck out the top, her corn-riddled toes the bottom.

The bell had stopped ringing.

The seal on the door clumped. The door swung open. Incoming air provided warm relief with an almost human, yet hushed, sigh.

Ding-a-ting!

The sharp peal of the bell kicked me out of the starting gate. I barreled out of the refrigerator, pulled a sharp u-turn halfway into Dad's workshop, remembering I'd forgotten to close the freezer door behind me.

Bumph!

Hettie took care of it.

I didn't give one whit about making noise now. I rushed through the doors, zipped up the ramps, raced down the hallways, clambered up the steps, and I think I did it all while holding my breath. Dad was still snoring loud enough to wake the dead (and I really hoped that wouldn't become a reoccurring occurrence). In my bedroom, curtains plucked up in front of my window. I closed the window, triple-checked the lock. Tonight, Thomas would have to wait. In bed, I pulled the covers up over my head.

Morning seemed an awfully long way away.

Chapter Eleven

Saturday morn had finally scooted Friday away. Usually I'm over the moon for Saturdays, the only day it's easy to wake up. But today, once the sun came up, I finally felt fit for sleep.

Others conspired against me.

In my fitful sleep, I mistook the non-stop clanging of the doorbell for the small silver bell wrapped around Hettie's corns. I sat up, terrified, the bed sheets sweat-drenched. Once I staked claim to the here and now—the sunshine comforting through my window—I exhaled in relief.

But our Saturday morn visitors were far from relaxed, banging on the bell like there was a three-alarm fire.

Apparently out and about, Dad didn't answer the door, so the welcome wagon duties fell on me. Fully experienced in welcoming mourning customers, I thought I'd dealt with it all. But nothing prepared me for the surprise on our doorstep.

Linked arm in arm, a human pretzel in matching black, ankle-length dresses, the Sooter sisters greeted me with customary, bare-boned nods.

"Miss and Miss Sooter," I said, "what brings you to our neck of the woods?" I'm sure I looked a mess, bed-hair and all. A right good thing, then, only one of the sisters could see.

"Good morning, Dibby," Yvette answered. Miriam nodded, lips set into a prim line of bother. "Is your father at home?"

On tip-toes, I looked out into the drive, verified Dad's absence. "Reckon he's out at work. I'm awfully sorry for any inconven—"

"That's fine. We'll wait." Still hooked together, the Sooter gals railroaded past me. They moved fast, almost as one, and much more graceful than folks with all senses intact. They settled into the living room, taking up but a third of the sofa.

I lingered in the living room doorway. "Um…might be a spell before Dad gets home. If you'd like, I can—"

"No, no, Dibby, we don't want to be any trouble at all. We'll just wait, nice and quiet like. Isn't that right, Miriam?" Miriam agreed. I think. "Besides…it'll give us a chance to catch up. We haven't seen you around the library in days." Their thin smiles were about as sweet as salt-water.

Shanghaied in my own home, I sought cover in Dad's recliner. But I kept my feet on the ground, sat on the tip of the worn cushion, ready to spring away if need be.

"I've been pretty busy with school work and all." That didn't seem to dent their armor. "And, well…Dad grounded me."

In tandem, they tossed their heads back, opened their mouths as if making a discovery of Sherlockian proportions. "Yes," said Yvette, "we've heard something about your troubles with the Keating girl. Caused by that rather unsavory Mackleby boy, we presume." Miriam posed an empathetic face, pursed lips and head tilted.

"No, I shoulder the responsibility." I felt helpless, on trial without counsel.

Yvette smacked her lips. "I certainly hope you don't let that Mackleby boy draw you down the wrong path, Dibby. You've such a bright future ahead of you. It'd be a shame to waste it."

That kind of talk armed the teenager in me. "Well…honestly, ladies, I don't see what James has to do with my future. Or non-future, for that matter. Seems to me—"

"Is he the one who put you up to vandalizing our newspaper?" Yvette scooted forward, Miriam along for the ride. Literally on the edge of their seats now, ready to pounce.

"I didn't take any newspaper article, and that's a fact. Goodness sake, you know me better than that."

Miriam gripped her sister's arm, gave a couple squeezes, a few tugs. Grabbed her ear twice, like a baseball catcher.

Yvette said, "Then how in the world did you know a newspaper article had gone missing, Dibby?"

"Um… Well, folks talk. You know how word gets around here." Words did fly, but I doubted James's wanton act of periodical destruction caught wind with most folk.

"I see." The sisters waited for me to crumble.

I bellied up and played the waiting game. The mantle clock tick-tocked an impatient heartbeat.

Yvette buckled. "Well now, moving right along… We're still curious as to why you're researching the Saunders family. And we know darn well there's no such school assignment involving Hangwell history. Missus Hopkins verified it, of course."

"I do apologize for not being forthcoming regarding that, ladies. Truth be told, I was just curious about my neighbors, the Saunders. Just wanted to get to know them. After all, doesn't the Bible preach to be good neighbors?" I rolled the dice, took a chance. Of course, we Caldwells weren't much for the Bible. But I assumed the Sooters were; everyone else in Hangwell swore by it. And old or new testament, surely a mention was made somewhere about being neighborly.

"That's all very fine and well, Dibby, but you were researching a very specific time period. One involving the Saunders' tragedies. In no way would your knowledge of such matters ingratiate you to the Saunders. Perhaps it would behoove you to leave such things alone. For your own benefit, as well as the long-suffering Saunders family."

This could go on all day. "Honest to Pete, I haven't the foggiest notion what you're getting at. Saying as I was looking into a certain something, maybe the missing Saunders boy and his daddy—and I'm just conjecturing, mind you—but why in the world should my inquisitive nature be a bother to anyone? I'm just a young girl, after all."

Miriam started quaking, a human seismometer. Her fingers squeezed her sister's arm, prompting Yvette to jerk up straight. Miriam laid her head back, gaze poring through the ceiling.

"Miss Sooters? Ma'ams? Are you okay? Should I fetch you some water or—"

"Good morning, Miss Sooter. Miss Sooter." Dad swung in, and a right sight for sore eyes he was. His natural settling calm worked wonders on the three of us. With reverently clasped hands, he addressed the sisters. "May I get either one of you a glass of iced tea? Lemonade, maybe?"

The sisters had recovered, back to prim and proper. "No, thank you, Mister Caldwell," said Yvette. "We're fine as can be."

"I apologize for being out. Business waits for no one." He smiled, waited for the Sooters to acknowledge his mortician's humor. They didn't, of course. I'd warned him many times that vein of humor didn't suit socializing. "I hope this is a social call, ladies."

"I'm afraid we have business to take care of, Mister Caldwell." Yvette looked at her sister, got a nod of affirmation.

It never ceased to amaze me how fast Dad could change demeanor. His brow lowered as did his voice. "My goodness, I'm so sorry to hear that." Dad sat on the opposite end of the sofa and faced them. "Have you lost a loved one?"

"You might say that," answered Yvette, although she sounded a hair uncertain. "It's our understanding you're in possession of Hettie Williquette's mortal remains."

"I am."

"We're here to take her home."

Dad seemed as flabbergasted as I was. His eyes wouldn't stop blinking. "I don't... Frankly, ladies, I don't understand."

"Hettie was our sister."

Just when I thought I couldn't uncover any more Hangwell secrets, another one always happened right along.

Dad had an even harder time hiding his shock. "I had no idea." His clasped hands sunk between his knees, and I thought the rest of him might follow. "Ladies, I'm sorry you're experiencing a delicate and hard time right now, but...I honestly didn't know Hettie was your sister. Please forgive me for being taken aback."

Miriam slashed a hand through the air.

Yvette agreed with her gesture. "There's no need to worry about us, Mister Caldwell. Given the circumstances, your manner's appropriate. I don't believe a living soul knew Hettie was our sister."

I certainly knew of one dead soul who knew, right beneath our feet.

"Hangwell's just full of surprises," said Dad.

"Yes, indeed. Now I'm not one to speak ill of the dead…" Miriam shook her head, mouth buttoned. "…but the reason we didn't trumpet the fact Hettie was our third sister is because we'd had a falling out with her, oh…seems like centuries ago."

And now, seeing the sisters in a different light, I suspected that might not be far from the truth. The librarians might very well be witches, too, living however long witches did.

"I'm very sorry to hear that," said Dad.

Other than book talk, Yvette never struck me as much of a chatterbox. Today, she appeared to be in fine form. "I appreciate that. But we'd said our goodbyes to Hettie a long time ago. You see, without digging into the particulars, Hettie'd decided to pursue a different…course than us. One we didn't approve of."

And I harbored no doubt she meant witchcraft of a dark nature.

Miriam agreed, her head bobbing.

"And we didn't deem it to be anyone else's business but our own," added Yvette.

"I can certainly understand that, ladies," said Dad.

"Be that as it may, our only regret is we didn't get to patch things up before Hettie passed." Yvette's voice straddled the thin line of rock solid and tissue thin. "We would've liked to have made amends, welcomed her back into our fold." Miriam dabbed a tissue behind her glasses and came dangerously close to taking them off. "But now, it seems…we won't have that chance. At least, not now."

I sorely wanted to comfort the sisters, tell them they still had a chance to say their piece to Hettie. As I'd learned last night, just because someone's dead doesn't mean they're gone. Not by a long shot. If my suspicions were on the nose, and the Sooters were witches, surely they'd embrace the notion. 'Course I had to handle Dad with kid gloves. I suspected he couldn't abide by the truth.

"Ladies, I'm absolutely certain you'll be reunited with Hettie someday." Dad handed out consoling words like Halloween candy. Yet, like candy, he didn't have any personal use for it.

"You're correct, Mister Caldwell." Yvette girded her loins, flushed iron into her voice. "We will be reunited again." She placed a hand on Miriam's. "Sooner than you think."

I interpreted Yvette's cryptic statement a bit differently than Dad. He scooted even closer to sofa's edge, serious as a heart attack. Clearly, he believed the Sooters planned on hastening their reunion with their sister by their own hands.

"Ladies… I know you've been dealt a shock. An awful, horrible shock. But please know I'm here should you need to talk to someone. Life goes on even after the loss of a loved one. It may not seem like it now, but given time, I'm sure you'll find happiness again. But for now, you must seek solace in knowing that Hettie's probably kicking her heels up in Heaven now—"

"Highly doubtful," said Yvette.

Dad just shut up. The Sooter sisters were quite unlike any customer he'd ever tended to, I imagined. Since his usual rigmarole didn't appear to work, he changed gears. Finalized matters.

"Be that as it may, I'm sorry for your loss," said Dad. "How would you like me to take care of Hettie's departure, ladies? Would you like a formal burial ceremony or a small, private gathering? Perhaps cremation, that's—"

"No, no, none of that." Yvette seemed ready to get the show on the road. "We don't want any such thing. We're here to take Hettie with us. We'd like her remains, please." She said it plainly, the unfussy nature of someone deciding on a double burger at Carol's Diner.

Dad's sensibilities took another punch. He closed his eyes. Tight. "I don't… I'm afraid I don't understand. You mean you're going to dispose of Hettie's body yourselves?"

"That's correct."

"Well, now… I can't say I've ever run across a situation like this. Frankly, ladies, I'm not even certain it's legal to relinquish a beloved one's remains. Peculiar County has certain statutes that—"

"I can assure you it is legal." Yvette dug into her large purse. She brought out a stack of paper, neatly stapled into a booklet, her librarian training showing. "As you can see, we did our research, Mister Caldwell. I also checked with our Sheriff and Mayor Hopkins. There are no laws explicitly prohibiting such an action."

Dad riffled through the pages, his face blank. "But…may I ask what you intend on doing with Hettie's remains?"

"No, you may not." Yvette sat back, wiggled her fanny into the sofa. Her sister did likewise, two snug bugs in a rug. "We're private people. It's no one's business but our own."

Dad gave up, just breathed out a long, quiet sigh. "Fine, ladies. Let me read through your research, merely for legal reasons, mind you. But there may be another bump in the road."

From behind her glasses, Yvette's penciled-in eyebrows rose.

"Regarding Hettie, I'm in a somewhat sensitive position, but nothing can be gained by beating around the bush. I'm afraid I may have to hold onto Hettie's remains for a while longer."

"Why in the world would you need to do that?"

Dad hesitated, beating around that dang bush he said he wouldn't. "I've, um, done some preliminary studies. But a thorough autopsy has been ordered on your late sister. I'm awfully sorry to tell you ladies this right after—"

"Do you mean to say Hettie was murdered?" asked Yvette.

Dad said, "That's right, Miss Sooter. It looks like someone took her life."

The mantle clock ticked. Yvette and Miriam sat stone-still, still as their library gargoyle, Stoney. Their hands froze on their respective purse handles. Mouths puckered into tiny, colorless hearts. Dad waited. I could dang near hear his sweat drop to the floor. Time stopped. I swallowed. I had no idea how the Sooters would respond, but I hoped it wouldn't be with fire and brimstone.

"Oh, dear." Yvette's voice shattered the fragile quiet. "How many days will it be before we can reclaim our sister?"

Dad wobbled, drunk a bit on Yvette's unexpected response. The sisters appeared to take to murder as a commonplace happenstance.

"I'm not sure, Miss Sooter," Dad mustered. "Could be a couple days or it might run into something longer. But you'll be the first person—"

"This definitely stitches up our plans," said Yvette. Together the sisters sniffed, tossed back their shoulders. "Very well, Mister Caldwell. Please do everything in your power to hurry the process along." They stood, ankles and legs just a-snapping.

"I certainly will, Miss Sooter." Dad stood, too, ready to close with a more appropriate farewell. But the sisters were fast, sidewinder fast, and beat it around the table and down the hallway. "Dibby will see you out," Dad called out.

"That would be fine, Mister Caldwell," Yvette volleyed back.

Near hypnotized by the entire strange encounter, I'd melted into the recliner. Dad cleared his throat to stir me, then jerked his head toward the front door.

I clambered out of the chair and raced through the house.

I needn't have hurried. Blockaded in front of the door, the sisters didn't appear to be going anywhere just yet.

"Let me get that door for you, Miss Sooters." I opened the door, smiled. Ready to see them on their way.

"Remember what we talked about, Dibby," said Yvette. "Stay out of folks' business that doesn't concern you."

I'd heard that back-handed advice time and again and certainly had no mind in heeding it. My timing terrible, though, I did recollect what Hettie'd asked me to tell the Sooters the night before she died.

"Um, there's something you oughta know," I said.

"Yes?"

"I visited your sister, Miss Williquette…the night before she passed."

"Oh?" A sure attention grabber, P.T. Barnum big, I'd earned the ladies' full attention. "And where did you visit with her?"

"At her house, ma'am. I offered to do some work around her fields. She wanted me to say hello to you ladies." 'Course it wasn't exactly the send-off ol' Hettie'd wanted me to deliver, but a fair amount of sugar-coating never hurt anyone.

Yvette harrumphed. Miriam smiled. "Dibby…that's a very kind thing of you to say, but we very well know it's far from the truth now, isn't it?"

I dug a toe onto the floor, locked my eyes down. As I didn't care to stir up Hettie again, I acted like Sweden: straight down the middle.

"Well, those weren't exactly her words, no. But she wanted me to offer you salutations. Of a sort. You were very much on her mind."

Smiles let me know I'd passed muster. "Very well, Dibby. You just heed our words, though, heed them well." With that. the women scuttled away, stiff and starched. Both of them crawled into the driver's side of their ol' fishtailed Cadillac, twenty years old and as well-preserved as its owners.

I shuddered to think what they had in mind for Hettie's body, but frankly I'd be on the upside of giddy once Hettie left our house. And as soon as I thought it, I figured it might not be the nicest sentiment a ghost might lend an ear to.

A light finger tapped at my shoulder blade. I whirled, half-expecting to meet Hettie's awful open-mouthed smile. But I saw no one.

Instead, Hettie's cats greeted me. Now a permanent fixture, they rubbed against my legs, reminded me of breakfast-time.

* * *

In the kitchen, I found Dad struggling with a huge bag of cat food.

"Well, you could've knocked me over with a feather regarding the Sooter sisters. Did you have any idea Hettie Williquette was their sister, Dibs?" He tipped the bottom of the bag up, aiming for three bowls on the floor. A torrent of nuggets rained down, scattering everywhere but the bowls.

"I surely didn't. Might be easier if you put the bowls up on the counter," I said.

He dropped the bag with a grunt of relief. "Could be. Either way, I figure these cats are gonna be around a while. I don't want them in the house, mind you, but as long as you're up to feeding and watering them, they can stay. Can you handle the responsibility, Dibs?"

"Yes, sir."

"That's my girl. Have a seat." He gestured toward our meeting hall, the kitchen table. Honestly, I'd been grounded so much lately, I couldn't keep up anymore if I'd done anything new worth punishing. Dad belly-upped next to me. "Dibby… I know you've been going through a lot lately. Taking on problems and headaches that aren't yours." He reached out for my hand and I gave it to him. "I think…maybe I'm partially to blame. I mean, for the trouble you've been getting into. How you've been acting out."

"I don't recollect you giving me boxing lessons. Wasn't your fault I socked Suzette."

Dad grinned, but I could tell guilt hitched a ride. "No. You know I abhor violence. But…let's just say I'm concerned. With your skipping school, your fights, your—"

"Just one punch, not really a fight."

"…your blatantly ignoring my rules. This new boy…James. Every-thing."

Dad toed at the shoreline of whatever really had him bothered. I truly hoped he wouldn't dive into another Birds and the Bees talk. Once was more than enough.

"Dad, if this is about James… I don't think he's gonna' be pestering me any longer. So you can relax."

Apparently I hit the bull's-eye. He settled back into his chair, sighed. "Oh… I'm sure sorry to hear about you and James." A small smile didn't quite seal the sentiment. "Do you want to talk about—"

"No."

"I'm sorry?" And he did look a bit sorry, too. Puzzled, unable to fix me as he'd always done in the past. "Anyway… I *am* concerned, Dibs. As your father, I'd like to know what's going on in your life."

"There ain't—"

"Don't say 'ain't'."

"...*isn't* anything to be concerned about, Dad. James and I weren't going steady or anything like that. We never got that far. I really don't want to talk about it."

"That's what I'm afraid of. We used to talk about everything. *Everything.* You told me all about your life, asked me questions...we really *talked.* But now... I dunno, you're different somehow. More secretive."

"Probably 'cause I'm not the kid I used to be. Maybe I'm growing up a bit, trying to figure things out on my own."

"I understand that, Dibs." But I could tell he didn't. "Of course everyone grows up. But you've been acting out lately. A lot. That's not like you. You're my golden girl. Always have been, always will be." He let go of my hand and ruffled my hair.

"Dad, I'm the same person. Older, maybe." I grabbed his wrist, brought it back down to the table. "How am I supposed to take on more responsibility, grow as a person, when you won't let me?"

He nodded. "I certainly don't mean to stand in your way. Of course you need room to grow. And now's the time to do it. Now that you're becoming a responsible young woman...experiencing the changes high school life brings. Which is why I've decided to lift your grounding."

In a week of shocks, I considered that the only good one. "Thanks, Dad. I won't let you down."

"I know you won't. But...there're some conditions."

Of course there were. Always. I couldn't wait until the day I made my own conditions.

"First, you're going to have a strict curfew. Weeknights at nine o'clock. Weekends at ten-thirty. And I want to know where you are, day or night. Everywhere."

"I reckon I can abide."

"Second...you need to bring your grades back up."

"My nose is already at the grindstone."

"Third...and most importantly..." He leaned forward, serious. I got a good whiff of mortician's chemicals rolling off him. "...you tell me everything that's going on in your life. The full truth. No more half-truths, no more lies."

It seemed like half-a-step back, but as in any dosey-do, there's give and take in any dance. "I'll put forth my best efforts."

"That's all I can ask for. So, let's start now." He settled back, arms crossed, very much the authority figure again. "*Why* have you been misbehaving lately? Tell me the truth."

Because a dead ghost boy wants me to find out what happened to him, and someone killed Hettie, maybe because I talked to her, and every dang adult in town treats me like a baby, and won't tell me the truth, especially you about Mom, and dead folks come back to life, and James, the boy I thought was downright dreamy, betrayed me and broke my heart into a kazillion pieces, and…

"No real reason, Dad." I topped it off with a shrug.

He sighed, not hiding his irritation very well. "You're already breaking our agreement. There *has* to be a reason for your turnaround in behavior. All of it happened so fast and unexpectedly. I've seen the effect. Now, I want to know the cause. We're creatures of science, biology plain and simple. There's logic and reason behind our behavior. Unless… unless you're experiencing…*issues.*"

Therein lay the root of the problem. The real "cause" for Dad's weird behavior. The insinuation hurt. Then anger reared. Finally, I wondered if maybe Dad's theory was right…and it more than scared the hell out of me.

"So…that's what you think? You think I'm crazy?"

"What? I don't—"

"That's what you said about Mom! That *she* had 'issues,' too! You think I've gone crazy! Why can't I just *do* something without there being a reason? Why can't I just… Dammit!"

"Dibby!"

I jumped up. "I *ain't* crazy. I'm *not* like her. Sometimes…I don't know *why* I do things. Do you? Maybe it's…hormones. Or who knows. Maybe you're to blame! Ever since you finally—*finally*—told me the truth about Mom, I've been wondering if I'm going crazy! And now I *am* crazy!" I wanted to give into tears. But I fought them. Plenty time for those upstairs. When I'm alone.

"Dibby, your Mom's *not* crazy. I *explained* that. And…you're not crazy, either. All I—"

"Then quit acting like I am!" Before I started acting crazier than a bedbug, I high-tailed it upstairs. Dad called after me. Wanting to make things right between us.

But sometimes things are said you just can't forget. Or forgive.

* * *

Ornerier than a caged polecat, I paced my room, tackled my bed, couldn't get comfortable in my own skin, let alone the bed sheets. Reading didn't take either.

In a way, I felt petty, childish for throwing such a tantrum. But I had a big fish tugging on my line, and Dad jerked it clean out of the water. Since Dad told me about Mom, the notion had been lingering like a boogeyman beneath the bed: maybe I'd inherited Mom's craziness.

I rethought everything, questioned what was real, what my mind might've spun. No one else seemed to be bothered by ghosts or dead witches or unspeakable creatures that fly in the night.

And if craziness hadn't already claimed me, it surely would if I kept dwelling on it.

I had to get out of the house.

After a quick change of clothing, a splash of water on my face, a comb through the hair, I felt movie-ready.

I heard Dad in the living room, his newspaper rattling. To get out the door, I had to walk past him. I had no intention to pick up where we left off.

Fast as lightning, I struck. "Dad, I'm going out," I hollered from the doorway.

The feet of his recliner flumped down. "Dibs, can we talk?"

"I can't. I'll be late for the movies."

"Wait! How're you doing? I'm just—"

"Bye. I'll be home by curfew." I hurried out the door, didn't let it smack me in the behind. Honestly, I was fed up to my back teeth with folks, particularly Dad, asking about my mental welfare, walking on egg-shells around me, afraid to tip the crazy girl into a hatchet spree. It set me to doubting myself, looking deep into my brain for broken pieces.

On my bike, I blew through town, my eyes locked dead ahead, my business my own. Caught up in a tizzy, I couldn't really say who I'd passed. The seven o'clock showing of *Return of the Fly* mattered, nothing other, nobody else's problems. My back arced up like a cat, my claws ready to come out at anyone who dared get in my way.

Unusually careless with my Raleigh, I hashed it into the theatre's stand. As always, Benji manned the ticket kiosk. I slid my change through the hole in the window, ordered my ticket. Possibly the slowest man in town, Benji'd been known to create block long lines due to his sloth-like speed, handling every bit of currency like sticks of dynamite. When folks complained, Mr. Halloway, the owner of the Starlight Cinema laughed it off, boasting, "Them long lines makes it look like every picture I show is a top-notch house packer."

"…thirty-five cents, Dibby…forty cents…forty-five—"

"It's all there, Benji, and then some. Just keep the change and I'll be on my way." Antsy, I did a little jig, afraid to run into someone from school. Or James.

"No, no, Dibby," said Benji, "what's fair is fair. You'll pay fifty cents like everyone else, not a penny more. Just wouldn't be right." He squinted at me behind glasses too big for his grapefruit-sized noggin. "Let's see… Where was I? Oh! Forty-five cents…"

"Well, lookie what the cat drug in," said a hellishly familiar voice. I wheeled on Angela, Suzette's first in command. Suzette and the rest of her Lollipop Guild sashayed into line behind her, all frills and bows and gaudy idiocy.

"Looks like you're here with *all* of your friends," continued Angela.

They tittered, cackled, a witch coven in training.

"I thought you were going with James." More laughter, sharp as paper cuts. "What's the matter, Dibby? Did he find out you're really a boy?"

"No. But he told me about your feminine ailment, Angela," I said. "You still scratching down yonder?"

Angela gasped. I grinned, mean and well-earned. My mood demanded it.

"You…you stupid, ugly…stupid *tomboy*!" Angela's fists knotted beside her billowing skirt. The clownish, red color painted on her cheeks spread to her forehead. "You take it back right now!"

"Nope. Why don't you keep your sex disease all to yourself?"

Angela shrieked, came at me with crab-like hands.

"Cut it out!" Suzette stepped between us. "Angela, you leave Dibby alone!"

Dumbfounded, Angela's crayon-encased features crinkled. "But, Suzette, Dibby's icky. We can't stand her! We always—"

"Maybe you better rethink things a bit." Of course, Suzette didn't find her own behavior in need of adjustment, but even babies have to crawl first, I reckon. "All you be nicer to Dibby. She can't help the way she is."

I rolled my eyes, thought they might spill out and continue rolling down the alley. "I don't need your help, Suzette."

She gave me a crooked, sad smile. Her head tilted as if sand weighed down one side, and maybe it did. When she grabbed my hand, I nearly jumped out of my overalls. I much preferred her outright scorn over this baby doll pity.

That's when she really plied her talent for torture. Like a carnival high striker, Suzette whomped a figurative mallet on my toe by whispering, "Are you all right?" A bell clanged in my head.

She'd asked *the* question; the one that would set things rosy side up, fill the world with unicorns and butterflies, and shoo away all the demons. The question that absolved the asker of all responsibility, their task completed, job well done. The question that didn't ever help one damn iota and just made things worse.

"Not a thing wrong with me. I'm right as rain." Not exactly how I wanted to answer, but it seemed a might bit more tolerable than punching Suzette again. Besides, for once her tiny little heart at least searched for the right place. "Thanks for asking."

Ready to make a getaway, Benji still hadn't straightened out our transaction. Naturally, Suzette wouldn't let up. "By the way, James didn't say anything else about taking me to the movies. Actually, he hasn't said more than howdy to me. Can you imagine? *Me?*"

I imagined Suzette spontaneously blowing up, a welcome quirk of fate.

"Suzette, it doesn't matter a pile of beans what James does with his life. And while I appreciate your riding to my rescue, I don't need saving."

"Well…" All bashful and coy, she took to swaying in her party dress, chin tucked to her chest, eyes wandering, acting like she was too darn cute to be held responsible for her abhorrent personality. I couldn't understand why anyone found her behavior adorable. "Just thought I'd try."

Caught up in a storm of confusion, Suzette's followers, minus their leader, circled their wagons. They clucked, tossed up hands, spoke in beyond-rude outdoor voices. I imagined a coup was underway. Now that Suzette had shown a kinder side, her cruel days of dictatorship might be coming to an end.

"…and fifty-four cents!" hollered Benji. "Dibby, you plumb gave me four extra pennies, you did." Oblivious to the confrontation that had happened in front of his ticket booth, Benji scooted pennies toward me. "Let's see now. Onnne…twooo…"

An audience now gathered at my back, I told Benji to keep the change, reached in, and snatched a ticket off the coiled loop.

Beneath the unlit marquee (frugal to the point of Great Depression days, Mr. Halloway never lit the bulbs until after dark), the posters for upcoming motion pictures held me in their sway. Even though I'd wanted to quickly disappear inside, I just couldn't pass up the gaudy, ghoulish delights. One poster displayed a skull shooting light-beams from its eyes, the ballyhoo proclaiming I'd scream once I saw the titular skull. In another poster, Boris Karloff's milky white eyes—not unlike Hettie's from the other night—glowed menacingly. Next to him, a woman in repose (always a woman in tattered clothing) lay waiting for menace to overtake her.

For a moment all my troubles seemed not to matter, my mind giddily anticipating the blood-curdling horror and dreadful frights that would unfold on the silver screen in the weeks to come. Rarely did the movies outrace my imagination, my expectations hard to beat, the build-up just part of the fun. But now that real horror had ensnared my life, any macabre fun had dampened a bit.

I stepped into the theatre. A fascinating mixture of aromas assaulted my senses. The popcorn machine unleashed a smell of salt and butter mixed with feet that'd been marching through the trenches for too long. An overriding odor of water damage and mildew had been stampeded into the ornate, burgundy carpet. The sweat of underpaid ushers practically oozed from the walls. Behind the concession stand, hot dogs rotated round and round on a grill, on the cusp of burning black. But mostly I smelled excitement.

Dressed in his silly, marching-band outfit, Mr. Halloway manned the podium. Curtain ties draped from his chest and waist, matching the ropes strung across the theatre's entrance. "How're you this fine evening, Dibby?"

"Just swell, thanks."

He tore my ticket, handed me a stub. "Don't you go getting too scared, now, y'hear? This motion picture's guaranteed to turn that purty hair of yours white as pillow feathers." Always the same patter, complete with spooky, wiggling fingers. I enjoyed it anyway. Part of the experience of going to the pictures.

Several chandeliers dangled overhead, lending the Starlight that palatial look Mr. Halloway strove for. It worked. I felt a might bit like royalty every time I strolled into the glorious, garish museum of wild adventures, faraway lands, and things that made most people hide behind their hands.

A maze work of fat, purple ropes strung back and forth (for no particular reason I could see) between gold posts. Straight ahead the theatre's main level sprawled out, a place I avoided like the cooties. Suzette and her mindless posse always saddled up there. Instead, I hightailed it to the left staircase (next week, I'd opt for the right side) that wound up into the balcony. I commandeered my usual spot, front row, smack dab center, right in front of the partition to keep rowdy moviegoers and suicides from plummeting to their deaths.

Usually I had the balcony dang near to myself. No exception tonight, only a bald fella behind me, and a couple in the back (who clearly had more on their mind than cinema), kept it from feeling like a private screening. The amorous couple's deep-sea breathing set a pace, ticking down the seconds until show time.

Below, excited voices mixed, rose, shrieked, the crowd anxious tonight. I enjoyed overlooking them, studying folks' top-sides. Tightly coiffed pig and pony tails identified Suzette and her cronies, their dresses flumped out over the seats like parachutes. I recognized several football players from school. They stood in the aisle, punching one another in the shoulder, basically carrying on like monkeys at a zoo.

The lights dimmed. An engine chunked alive. Curtains swayed, then tugged back. I wriggled into the seat, the wood welcoming my bottom like a firm handshake.

Even though I'd outgrown cartoons, if I missed even a few seconds of the opening one, I felt gypped. Woody Woodpecker knocked his way through the opening credits and raised the roof on an unsuspecting walrus, his usual victim. I laughed throughout, maybe not too old for the colorful antics after all.

Someone slid into the seat next to me. A blast of stale nicotine rolled with him.

"This seat taken?" James leaned in, grinning like his charm couldn't be contained. His hair dropped over one eye, mysterious. I imagined he'd posed it so on purpose. In fact, I suspected everything James did he calculated with the meticulous skill of a chess player. I couldn't believe it'd taken me this long to realize it.

"Yup. My date's in the bathroom," I whispered. "Beat it before he beats you." I set my eyes straight ahead, the cartoon onscreen blurring into madcap reds and yellows and blues that didn't register. With James practically breathing down my neck, I couldn't focus worth a hang.

"Come on, Dibs… I know you're too classy to go out with any of those other bozos from school." As if invited, he settled in. His shoulder rubbed up against mine, and he kept it there. Instead of moving away, I shoved him back. No one infringes upon my cinematic territory.

"Do I have to go fetch Mister Halloway to kick you out?" I asked.

"Hey, it's a free world! I'm just—"

"It's not a free cinema. Buzz off."

"Dibby, how long you gonna give me the business? I'm sorry already. I'm so sorry my knuckles are dragging the ground. I—"

"Shhh!" the bald guy behind us hissed.

With a hand beside my mouth, I stage whispered, "Sorry."

"No sweat, Daddy-o," added James.

"*Stop* it, James. I'm trying to watch the show. *Alone.*" The movie started. "You need to move."

"No problem." James got up, stepped over my feet, fell into the seat on my other side. "There. Plenty room for both your date and me." He kicked up his sneakers onto the front railing.

"Don't *do* that," I spat. "Mister Halloway doesn't like—"

"Don't flip your wig, Dibs." More belligerent than usual, he dropped his feet one at a time, clumping them down heavily onto the floor. "Listen, I get you're still mad at me, but I wanted to explain. It wasn't copacetic, not a bit, that I asked Suzette out, too. She was, you know, just a back-up plan. I kinda thought you didn't dig me or something."

Boys can be so stupid, and then there's James. "You think I go 'round kissing any ol' boy just for the fun, sport, and amusement of it?"

He shrugged, bobbled his head up and down in a simpleton's manner. "I dunno…"

The fact he'd even leant the notion serious consideration couldn't go unpunished. I hauled off and smacked his shoulder.

"*Ow.* Dammit, what was *that* for?" He rubbed his shoulder, playing it to the hilt.

"Oh, shut up, crybaby. You know I can hit harder than that."

"Shhh!" Clearly at the end of his rope, the bald man leaned far over the seat in front of him. "I'm trying to enjoy the picture!"

"Don't sweat it, chrome-dome," said James. "I can tell you what happens. See that guy?" He pointed toward the screen. "He's gonna turn into a fly, kill some folks, then take a dirt nap."

"James!" This time I punched him like I meant it.

The bald man stood, shook his head. "Why, I never! Dibby Caldwell, your father'll hear about this!" He shook a finger at me, and only then did I recognize Farmer Gentry from the other side of town. "Kids today! I swan..."

"Sorry, Mister Gentry," I whispered.

He griped all the way to the balcony exit. From the stairwell, his voice grew even more indignant.

"Dangit, James, look what you did!"

James laughed, determined to drag me down his wayward path to ruin. "Ah, I'm glad ol' chrome-dome flaked off." He turned around. The hot and heavy couple hadn't come up for oxygen yet. "Looks to me like they know where it's at." His eyebrows wagged up and down.

"If you think I'm gonna kiss you again, you got another thought coming! Besides, you just ruined the movie for me, too!"

"You kidding? I haven't seen it. It's just, you know, all horror pictures are like that."

"Will you just shut your pie hole and leave me alone?"

James fell silent, a long stretch for him. But it didn't last. "Really, Dibs, you're the only girl for me. You—"

"Mm-hmm. Sure. Heard it all before."

"You're the absolute ginchiest. I don't care anything about that stupid sosh, Suzette."

"Uh-huh. Once a liar, always a liar."

"It's true. I'll do *anything* to prove it's you who I like. Anything. Just ask."

I fairly wanted to see if he'd take a head-dive off the balcony for me, true devotion and what not. But I didn't cotton to answering a lot of Sheriff Grigsby's questions. "You can start by putting a cork in your hole."

"I can do that." James dropped a hand on my knee and plastered on a serious face.

"Final warning, James! I'm gonna go get Mister Halloway if you don't... James?"

His hand on my knee went cold, freezing through my overalls. Still cutting up, he sat there dang near cross-eyed with his mouth gaping open.

"James, cut it out." I pinched up his hand, tossed it back to him. It scooted a bit, then stopped, stuck in mid-air. My hand waved in front of him. I faked a punch to his face. Not a flinch. Talk about crazy. James had retreated, gone fishing.

At once, all the smells of the theatre seemed to coalesce and stir into something worse: sour, bitter, full of rot, like the butcher shop's back alley. Gravity pushed down, suffocating, heavy. The film stopped. A stuttering frame displayed a man in a baggy suit, hands up in eternal surrender. From the frame's center, a dark pinpoint appeared, then spread outward, burning with a black crust of cinder. Then the blank screen faded into darkness, and I just knew I wasn't gonna like the next movie.

I turned around. The octopus couple had been cemented into place: arms entwined, lips smushed together, glued tight. Below, the movie herd had likewise fallen asleep with popcorn clusters lifted and drinks up to mouths.

Lights flickered from the projection booth, casting moving shadows over the balcony. The projector snapped, picked up speed: *click, click, click, clickety-clickety-clickety...*

On the screen, an image jumped to life. A cornfield. In sepia tones, silent like an ancient movie, jerky movement carried me deep into the field. While all cornfields look alike, I harbored no misgivings this was the Saunders' field. The cameraman filmed a familiar dirt path, the one I'd traveled several times.

The camera caught a pale fold of color, brighter than the surrounding dull field tones, and scooted in close on Tommy Saunders. Huddled on the ground, arms locked around his knees, he shivered up a scare. Suddenly, the camera swung left. Stalks toppled quietly, announcing Hedrick Saunders's arrival. Rage consumed his eyes as he turned in a circle. Sweat bled from his hairline, rode down angry lines demarking what might've been a handsome face in kinder times. His scythe swung through the air, slashed through corn stalks. The boy looked up, eyes wide, terrified.

Hedrick's expression crumbled. Softened into a different man, one hardly recognizable. He heaved his weapon aside. Stumbled toward his son and knelt. A hand stroked Thomas's hair as he pulled him into a hug. Thomas's thin arms reached around and hugged back.

The camera moved, jostled animatedly through the field. Leaves scratched at the lens, itching to get inside the camera. A flesh-colored blur focused into Hedrick's face, his eyes closed. The camera pushed in. Hedrick's bloodshot eyes jerked open. His jaw dropped. The camera pulled back to catch Hedrick slip from his son's embrace and fall into the dirt. His scythe stuck out from his back. Thomas, on his knees, arms still out, stared down at his father's body. He let loose an agonized scream, all the more horrible for the lack of sound. A shadow stretched across the boy, twin claws reaching, and finally engulfed Thomas into a blackness that swam into full screen.

Next to me, James hadn't moved a muscle, still lock-jawed and paw raised. An eerie stillness reigned, lacquered on thick.

Something ticked behind me. The smallest, most inconsequential sound and it nearly sent me through the roof. A sound I couldn't identify, tiny snaps, maybe the wet lapping of a dog's tongue? Kissing?

I turned around, curious, terrified. The red exit lights had gone belly up. A small, shimmering light from the projection booth provided scant illumination. Captured in mid-smooch, unmoving as statues, the couple behind me clearly hadn't made the sound.

Tek…skitch, skitch, smek…

Back in the corner, far left-balcony, last two seats, two people sat. Folks who hadn't been there earlier. The projection booth light limned the figures, blurry at best, my guess a man and woman. Wide shoulders spread across the back of a seat, a cap on the man's head. His companion occupied but a slice of her seat, a couple pounds beyond skeletal. A white bucket of popcorn glowed on the armrest between them.

Suddenly, a hand snaked out, dipped into the popcorn. The rest of the body stayed as motionless as the rest of the moviegoers.

Crnch…crunch…smek…

The woman fed popcorn into her mouth. Kernels crunched in her mouth, loud, louder, stringent as tree limbs coming down in an ice storm.

I hadn't an earthly clue as to the couple's identity, and I s'pected an earthly answer wouldn't be forthcoming, so I opted to leave.

Sidestepping James, I skedaddled to the end of the row, the right balcony exit my goal. At the door, I stopped. Braved another look. The woman's head wobbled, loosey-goosey on her neck. High-pitched laughter, familiar and awful, stopped me dead.

"You got work to do, girl," rasped Hettie.

"Help us rest." I'd never heard his voice before, but a harsh farmer's timbre matched the man's image I'd just seen on-screen.

Hedrick Saunders and Hettie took turns digging for popcorn, bones creaking, white hands working back and forth between bucket and unseen mouths. Their mass of shadow rippled like waves. In tandem, they stood, flowed over the theatre's seats, drifted closer to me. I saw—imagined I saw?—pale kernels slip between Hedrick's fleshless lips. The popcorn bucket swayed in the liquid darkness, bouncing merrily, carried by bone white, possibly skeletal hands. They moved fast. From one end of the balcony to the next they flew. I couldn't lock down their location, didn't want to; I just had to survive. But I couldn't move.

And the awful, toothless, wet *crunch, crunch, crunch* sound drew closer.

I closed my eyes. Forced my legs against their will. Moved a hand along the wall. My shoulder went through the door first, and I didn't open my eyes until well into the hallway.

The lobby hadn't escaped the big freeze either. Ever vigilant, Mr. Halloway stood tall, hands respectfully atop his ticket box. Behind the concession stand, one kid had his head stuck in the hotdog case, getting a bit hot under the collar, I imagined. Another held a cup beneath the soda dispensing machine, the liquid overflowing and soaking the carpet.

I broke into a run, then pulled up short beside the next concession customer. Angela, Suzette's top beast, stood there, insolent eyes rolled up (and I fervently hoped they'd stick that way), hand on outthrust hip. Undoubtedly poised between cruel words for the concession stand help.

There's scared, then there's opportunity that only comes knocking every once in a great while. I decided to answer the door.

From the counter, I grabbed the mustard dispenser. Not nearly enough to satisfy my artistic aspirations, I fetched the ketchup bottle as well. A two-fisted, condiment gunslinger, I commenced to decorating Angela's precious party dress. Added a few dollops to her hair, too.

Fresh, untainted air welcomed me as soon as I stepped through the

Starlight's doors. The lights in the lobby flickered once, twice, three times, then brightened the sidewalk.

From within the theatre, Angela screamed, a sound that thoroughly warmed my heart.

Chapter Twelve

As regular as the pigeons, Sunday mornings I could be found in Forton Park. Named after a man who didn't figure very heavily into anyone's sense of history, Frederick M. Forton's bird-spattered statue stood
at the head of the small, grassy island. His pride jutted out nearly as far
as his ballooned-up chest. His fancy duds bespoke a man in love with his
own importance. With a stone leg propped up on a boulder, he looked
as if he'd conquered Mars rather than set foot on a tiny hunk of Hangwell. And I still really never knew what Mr. Forton did. These days, I
wanted to limit my knowledge of local history.

The park itself wasn't much to sneeze at, not much more than a
couple of benches, a tree, and ol' Mr. Forton watching over his lands.
But it was my favorite place to think. Besides that, the best show in town
played out once the dueling churches let out.

Down the street, tortured bike wheels clacked. A dog panted to catch
up. Nope, not a dog, but pretty much the same thing. James raced toward
me, dying astride his bike. In motion, showing off, he jumped from his
bike while attempting to wrangle the handlebars. The bike had other ideas
and kept right on going. James ran, hands still glued to the handlebars.
For a grand finale, James tossed face first onto the road.

The bike raced ahead, bumped the curb, and flattened onto the grass not far from me. I laughed, applauded the bike. Always on stage, James hopped up, bowed.

"I meant to do that." His smile wavered a bit, kinda dizzy looking. "I saw you from my room." He gestured back toward the Lewis and Clark Hotel.

"Stop following me." I bit my upper lip to keep a smile tucked inside. Cad or not, it felt nice having a boy—a cute boy to boot—pursuing me.

"I'd follow you anywhere." He sat next to me, kicked his tennis shoes out. "And I got dibs on you."

It wasn't the first time I'd suffered through that hoary word-play on my name, but I imagined it'd seriously taxd James's brain. Giving it your all goes a long way with me. "No, you don't. And never say that again."

He sighed. "Dibby…why'd you leave last night? I thought…you know, I thought we were getting along."

"Apparently you aren't the same James that was annoying the tar outta me last night then. Your world must be a mighty odd place." Unable to comprehend sarcasm other than his own, he grinned and nodded. "What do you remember about last night anyway?"

"What? I dunno. We were sitting in the balcony, then I guess when I wasn't looking, you beat it."

"Sorta." I told him my accounting of things.

"Really? Wow. So…I was a stiff or something?"

"Same as always."

"And you thought Thomas's old man, Hedrick, killed the kid, but now you don't?"

"If anything, it seemed like Hedrick was trying to save his son. Then someone sliced him down with his own scythe."

"Man, that's…hairy. Hey, one other boss thing happened last night after you beat feet. You know Angela, right? Someone dumped ketchup and mustard all over her. She was a real mess, bawling her eyes out. Funny thing is, she said she didn't know who did it. Crazy!"

"Huh. Weird."

"Anyway, what're we gonna do next?"

"*We're* not doing anything. As president of the Find the Murderer

Club, I kicked you out."

"Well, I'm reapplying. Here's my card." He found his heart, patted it. "My derring-do belongs to you, Dibs."

"Don't you *ever* give it a rest?" I scooted over. He followed.

"Nah. I'm gone for you, baby."

Don't give in, don't give in, don't give in… Maybe a little giving in is *okay…*

"I want you gone. Now." Unfortunately, my shameless grin belied my words.

"I'm not going anywhere." He grabbed my hand. I yanked it back, our endless tug-of-war battle. Nothing would satisfy other than complete victory. "Dibby…things just haven't been right without you. Forget about Suzette. All that junk. She's not important. You are. I really wanna know what happened with your old man about your mom."

I didn't know if I believed him, trusted him. Then again, I doubted he was a good enough actor to muster up such conviction. Maybe I just wanted to talk to someone. I told him about Mom.

"So, your mom's cuckoo? 'Round the bend?"

"Show a li'l respect, dangit! Those are mighty hurtful words."

"Yeah, okay, sorry. She's, ah…looney-tunes?"

I'm so dumb. Not as dumb as James, but right next in line. I shot up, huffed away toward my bike.

"Wait! Dibby, hang on!" He ran after me, grabbed my shoulders. Turned me around and tortured me with his dreamy brown eyes. "I didn't mean anything. It's just…I've never met anyone who's…" He stammered, better than saying something ignorant again.

"My mom has a chemical imbalance in her head," I said, "or something like that. It's a sickness, nothing to make fun of."

"Honest, I wasn't making fun. It's just sorta…you know…" If he went for a twirling "crazy" finger around his ear, I fully planned to lay him out. "This is all new to me, Dibs. And, maybe…it makes me think about myself, you know. Maybe my own brain's kinda imbalanced."

His troubled eyes, his unsure mouth-set switched everything around. No faking, no showmanship, just a hurting boy. Someone who I understood, empathized with. In this big, ol', scary world, it's a bit of a comfort to have someone flailing right alongside of you.

I took his hand, led him back to my bench, the Dibby Caldwell Sunday bench. "James… There's not a day goes by I don't think I'm a bit tetched in the head. The thoughts that meander in and slip away leave their mark. The good news is I'm beginning to s'pect we're not alone. Maybe we're normal and it's…I dunno, some kinda stupid cosmic test we have to figure out. How to live, how to make sense of stuff… How to be who we are."

I had to clear James's bangs away to look into his eyes. He said, "You think even the football players…even Suzette has weird thoughts?"

"Even ol' Suzette," I answered.

"This might sound way out, but…do you ever wonder if Suzette and the rest think about…you know, ending it all?"

I've never given thoughts of suicide serious heft, not really. But on occasion—on a particularly bad day, when the weather's drippy like a runny nose, when I feel like I'm the only suffering person in the world, when I want my tormentors to feel horribly over their treatment of me— that mean and self-serving idea sometimes sneaks right up and pokes a finger inside my mind. And it scares the daylights outta me. Of course, I know suicide's stupid, know it's wrong. I know I shouldn't make a knee-jerk decision based on a stupid bully, or hormones, or a runaway mother who doesn't love me. Or give more than a fleeting thought to when I look in the mirror and wonder why I'm not like the popular girls.

"Yep. I suspect everyone's had those thoughts from time to time." I placed my hands aside his cheekbones, assuring his full attention. "It's normal. What ain't normal is acting upon those thoughts. You know that, right?"

He nodded.

"Someday, somewhere, things'll change for us, James. I know it. Feel it down deep. Just hang on. 'Cause I think life—the future's—worth hanging on for."

He got it all right, a bit too much. Eyes closed, lips puckered, he leaned toward me. I probably would've surrendered, too, if the Catholic church's bell tower hadn't clanged just then.

"Here they go again," moaned James. "No wonder I can't sleep Sundays."

"You shouldn't be sleeping 'til noon anyway, lazybones. Now, hush, you already ruined my show last night. You're not gonna do it again."

"What? I don't—"

Since words never worked, I clamped my hand down over his mouth.

"You gonna shut your hole now?" He nodded. "Fine and dandy, then. Just watch."

Folks flocked out of the Holy Mary Shrine of God Church doors, many of them strangers to me. The Holy Mary was the only Catholic church around, so Hangwell played host to Catholics from several counties.

Pastor Dobbins, he of mighty import to the Hangwell Baptist Church, took the Catholic invasion as a personal affront. Every Sunday, after both churches simultaneously released their congregations, Pastor Dobbins visibly boiled as Catholics swarmed the streets.

Not to be outdone, Father Lufton donned his fighting gloves as well. Those unfortunate souls who still bothered with town meetings were always treated to the holy men spatting over trivial matters.

By watching the Sunday showdowns, I learned a lot about Hangwell's inhabitants.

"What's going on?" asked James.

"Will you just hush and watch? I swan, worse than a kid."

The Catholic bell tower clanged its twelfth stroke. Across the street, Pastor Dobbins twisted up his face and carried on, his hands over his ears. Several of his faithful followed his lead.

"Now watch this." I nudged James, pointed toward the Baptist church.

Several of Dobbins's acolytes propped speakers into the church's open windows. With the aid of a very long extension cord, a man dragged a microphone stand out to the front stoop. Mrs. Dobbins, 300 pounds wrapped tightly into her floral dress, waddled to the stand. She cleared her throat, demanded attention.

I grinned, anticipated the caterwauling.

Mrs. Dobbins never disappointed. Someone, somewhere, apparently had told Mrs. Dobbins she could carry a tune, forty cats tossed into a wood-chipper be hanged. Enormous bosom thrust out, she belted through *Onward Christian Soldiers*, stuck in that one-note, glass-breaking, high-pitched shriek.

"Oh, man…too, too much!" James approved, bent over with laughter.

"Told ya."

Pastor Dobbins and his flock clapped along spiritually, smiling, some marching in place like the titular soldiers.

Across the street, Father Lufton grimaced, red beneath his collar. With a military roll of his hand, he ordered return fire. The Catholic's carillon system rolled into a hymn I didn't know. Since Mary figured prominently in the lyrics, I reckoned it'd been picked with the sole intention of getting under the Baptists' skin.

In their Sunday's finest, folks filed out of both churches, milling about on their respective lawns, afraid to cross the line into enemy territory. Nasty looks were shared, heads were shaken, stories were perpetuated about the unknown adversary lurking just across the street.

Suzette and her picture-perfect family posed on the Baptist church's lawn, duded up straight out of a Sear's catalog. On the other side, Odie— our postman and one of the few local Catholics—pretty much kept to himself. Most folks thought it odd Odie chose the bachelor's life. Some of the local busybodies used to try to set him up with the few eligible women in town. He declined. These days, I kinda thought Odie might be onto something.

Back at the Baptist church, Sheriff Grigsby (nearly unrecognizable out of his professional uniform) parlayed belly to belly with Mayor Hopkins, amazing they could even hear one another since their ample guts created a wide rift between them. Serious faces portended serious import, no doubt regarding Hettie's remains. Couple times their grave consideration fell upon me. Unable to stand up to such heat, I switched my head away.

Bank president Terrence J. Thomason and family, noses up in the air like show poodles, breezed by the Catholic church, not affording their adversaries a glance. Except li'l Terrence Jr., always free with his wicked tongue. "Mary worshippers," he spat.

A Catholic teen retaliated. "Stupid faith-healing frauds!"

"Dancers! You're all going to——"

"That's enough, Terry!" Mrs. Thomason snatched Terry's arm and dragged him away. His little legs toddled beneath fancy dress-shorts. Hard shoes clogged down the sidewalk as he skittered to keep up with his mother.

"Is it always like this?" asked James.

I nodded. "Once a fistfight even broke out. Wait…this part's always fun."

Both men of God strode to the center of the street, both angry as hornets. They didn't shake hands, didn't say boo. Just grimly stared at one another, mouths pulled taut.

Father Lufton began the ritual. Through gritted teeth, he said, "Fine morning, Pastor Dobbins."

His white cotton field of hair blowing in the breeze, the Pastor volleyed back. "It's a great morning, Father Lufton."

Their voices rose, competing with the dueling hymns of redemption.

"I had a wonderful congregation today," hollered the Pastor. "Near full house, one hundred and some change, I reckon."

"For your church, that's just fine," countered Father Lufton. "'Course, we were pushing one hundred sixty, give or take a soul or dozen."

"Lord, forgive them, for they know not what they do." The Pastor looked up toward Heaven, suffering scrawled across his face.

Father Lufton crossed himself, closed his eyes. "Oh, Lord, Jesus Christ, redeemer and savior, forgive their sins, lead them unto the right path."

They stared at one another, nostrils flared, fists bunched at their robes. Mrs. Dobbins set fire to another blistering verse. The Catholic hymn looped back to the beginning. I full-on expected guns to appear. Then the holy men would take ten steps, swivel, and blast one another to Kingdom Come. Which Kingdom they landed in would surely make for a lively debate.

Mr. and Mrs. Halloway breezed by me. The theatre owner tipped his hat. "Dibby, I didn't see you leave the Starlight last night. Was my movie too spooky for you?" Again, he wiggled crawly fingers at me.

"That it was, Mister Halloway. Not for the faint of heart," I said.

He laughed and rolled on his way.

In the street, the showdown grew more fevered. Now nose to nose, the pastor and priest looked ready to duke it out.

"I'm gonna put a stop to your Bingo night if it's the last thing I do," spat Pastor Dobbins. "The very idea! Gambling and what not!"

"I've already got the official okey-dokey from City Hall," said Father Lufton. "Half the proceeds goes to charity, the other half to city works."

Pastor Dobbin's hair whipped violently forward. "Feh. That's because the Mayor's secretary is a Catholic." He rubbed a thumb against his first two fingers. "A little payoff to sweeten your Bingo plans? I know how you Catholics operate."

"That's an outrageous insinuation, and I take personal umbrage toward it, sir!" Father Lufton thrust his barrel chest out, an old-time boxer. "If I wanted to be ornery, I might just ask the Sheriff to look into some of your fund-raising ways. How you're bilking your congregation outta their hard-earned dowry. Honestly, Pastor… Faith-healing?"

"At our church, we don't go in for such shenanigans! We—"

"That's not what Miss Billyews claims! She says you cured her rheumatism! For a generous donation, of course."

"That's neither here nor there! Your gambling and dancing and drinking will undoubtedly lead next to whoring!"

"There'll come a reckoning, Pastor, and then you'll see! You'll see! Mark my word! You holler about fire and brimstone 'til you're purple in the face, but you'll be proven wrong one of these days! In Hell!"

Sheriff Grigsby strolled up. "We all had a nice bout of religion this morning, fellas. Let's pack it in real peaceful-like, go our own ways, maybe do some reflecting at home." Chief Wakuna—who I don't believe belonged to either church, but always put in an appearance at noon—stood behind the Sheriff, ready to wake up if necessary.

"Hmph." Pastor Dobbins stalked back to the safety of his church's yard.

"Hateful, intolerant buffoon," hissed the priest. He rejoined his congregation, arms out as if ready to hug each and every one.

The crowds began to dissipate, ready to rest six days before the next Civil War reenactment. The bell tower hushed. Thankfully, so did Mrs. Dobbins. The sudden silence was at once calming and oddly unnerving.

"Hi, Dibby." The daughter of the town pharmacist, Mr. Simonson, stood before us, swaying in her red-dotted dress, an act adorable on young 'uns, deplorable on Suzette and her ilk.

"Hey there yourself, Libby." Libby always liked me, mostly because our rhyming names tickled her. "Libby and Dibby, zippy in Mississippi," I sang.

She giggled. Her father swooped in, swept her up in his arms. Without a word, he rushed her to safety, away from the vile teen smokers. Over his shoulder, he shot me a look of disgust. I imagined it'd take a while for him to forgive my wanton act of teen rebellion. One more reminder why I shouldn't be so willing to forgive James.

"So…what do you wanna do next?" he asked.

"Suit yourself. As long as it's in the other direction I'm headed."

"Come on! Where you going? Let me tag along."

With a deep sigh, I explained things slowly, as I would to a child. "I'm just not ready to trust you yet. That's just the way it is."

He lowered his face into his hands, growled. When he came back up, his hair stood on end like the Wild Man of Borneo. "What's it gonna take? I mean…I've never gone through this much for a girl! I'm sorry, sorry, sorry! A thousand times sorry! Suzette means nothing! I think of her like…I dunno, a kid sister! Not like you, Dibs."

He almost had me. But I couldn't go through it once more, not now that I almost felt human again. "I believe you, James. I think. Thing is… I can't help it. It's not all your fault, truth be told. I guess Mom had a sorta hand in it, leading me to distrust folks who I…" I nearly said "love," a mighty bold word to toss about, especially since I'd only known James a short while. "I just don't trust you."

"I won't do anything to lose your trust again, Dibs. Not now, not ever. Honest."

"That's all fine and dandy. But it's my decision, James. Not yours." I didn't want to leave him with no hope, all sad-eyed and downtrodden.

"Maybe with time. We'll see."

He brightened. "Fab! How long?"

"Slow down, hot-shot. I said 'maybe'."

"Right. So what're you gonna do next about Thomas and his killer?"

"Beats the tar outta me. I keep going back to the clue Hettie left me. The star on Dad's freezer door."

"Wait, wait, wait! Hold the phone!" He waved his hands. "Hettie gave you a clue at the Starlight last night?"

In between my busted affairs of the heart, I'd plum forgotten what I'd told James and what I hadn't. So I filled him in on Hettie's first ghostly visit. To rub salt in the wound—I knew he wanted to see a ghost, or at least *thought* he wanted to—I embellished the story, made it rival the best of Lovecraft.

"Dammit! I miss all the great stuff. So…what's the star mean?"

"Well… Remember what I told you about that night at Hettie's? How I saw her sitting inside a six-pointed star?"

"Sure. A Hexagram. What all witches use, right?"

James's knowledge of witchcraft rivalled my own. Our teacher? Horror films and comics. "That's what the motion pictures say, at least."

"But I still don't get it. What's a hexagram got to do with Thomas Saunders?"

I shrugged. "I got a hunch. Have to see how it plays out."

"What hunch? Spill the beans, Dibs." He scooted closer, excited.

"This is a lotta guesswork and all, but it goes to figure that if Hettie was a witch, then her sisters might be witches, too."

"Her sisters? Wait… Who're her sisters?"

I'd forgotten I hadn't told him that as well.

"Wow. I guess that makes sense. You know, with how weird the Sooters are and everything. Like how the blind one can really see and how they can talk to one another without words and stuff. So…you think they killed Hettie?"

"I don't know what I think. It appears the sisters and Hettie didn't much care for one another, that much I know. But that doesn't fit in regards to Thomas Saunders. And who killed his daddy, Hedrick. Unless there's more than one murderer in Hangwell."

"Hm." James rubbed at not-quite-there whiskers. "Kinda weird you saw Hettie and Hedrick's ghosts together at the theatre last night, though. Doesn't that sorta prove they were, like, connected?"

"Hettie admitted Hedrick had come to her, asking who Thomas's daddy was, so I suppose there's that connection. This dang…mess is so big, I can't see the whole picture. I need more information. From someone who'll finally talk to me for a change."

"You…you're gonna go talk to the Sooters?"

"Heck no! Their lips are sealed tighter than a tomb. Besides, I don't fancy a hex or evil eye or scythe in my back. Nope, tonight I'm gonna go visit ol' Boot Gundersen."

James's eyes grew big and worried, the way I like 'em. "That…creepy guy? Dibs, you can't! He might…who the hell knows what he'll do, but it'll be creepy! At least let me go with you!"

"No."

"No?"

"No." I suppose I felt like I had to do it on my own, not rely on anyone but myself. And with my mind all swimmy, James would just provide a distraction. Not knowing if I could trust him. Wondering when (if?) our next kiss might happen. "I'm gonna visit him alone. Besides, he didn't invite you."

Before we wasted more time bickering, I hopped on my bike and got up to speed.

"What if he's…a vampire? Or a ghoul?" James called.

"Then I'll deal with him," I hollered back with a wave. "And pack my wooden stakes!"

Fear shambled up, wrapped its prickly shawl around me. I deliberated, considered changing my mind. I surely would like someone else with me when I entered Boot's creepy shack. But I stuck to my guns.

Consumed by my thoughts, Main Street just sorta whizzed by me like a vista outside of a moving train car's window. As I flew by the Hangwell Public Library, the temperature plummeted. I slowed.

Fear and curiosity—two good kick-in-the-seat motivators—prompted me to look up at the library.

Attached at the hip, Yvette and Miriam stood on the steps, dressed head to toe in mourning black. They said nothing, unmoving, like those at the Starlight last night. Something appeared within Yvette's dark eyeglasses. Fire whipped around and around, swirling like dragon's breath.

I raised a shaking hand, a half wave.

No salutations, no acknowledgment, verbal or otherwise. Then Miriam raised a crooked finger, as crooked as ol' Hettie's, and pointed at me. Although blind, Yvette's withered digit also pinpointed me with accuracy. Accusing me of a heinous crime, something far worse than an overdue book.

Together they mumbled, indecipherable, reaching a near melodic duet. Putting the whammy on me.

I sped out of there. Terror burned a fiery trail behind me.

Earlier, I'd guessed the sisters were dressed as if in mourning.

Not for their sister, though. Rather, for me.

* * *

Dad had visitors, a good thing today. It'd keep him occupied instead of more grueling heart-to-hearts.

Sheriff Grigsby's hound of a pick-up overshadowed Mayor Hopkins's very mayoral Lincoln Continental. From the ticks and clicks of the cooling engines, I reckoned the autos hadn't been in the drive for long.

I parted the festival of cats and slivered through the half-open door. Just outside the living room where the men had gathered, I listened.

Dad's imaginative cursing dominated. Testier than a squirrel with a nut allergy, Dad gave the Sheriff and Mayor what for, flinging expletives like torpedoes. I almost felt sorry for the Hangwell lawmakers.

"Goddammit, I'm not done with the autopsy yet," hollered Dad. "I'm just at the tip of the damn iceberg! Sure as hell Hettie was murdered and in a shit-kicking horrible way, too!"

"Calm down, Oscar," pleaded Mayor Hopkins. Didn't take much imagination to know he had his politician hands up. One of Dad's irritants. 'Course, then again, everything about our mayor irritated Dad. "No one's asking you to do less than your usual stellar work. And by no means are we—"

"Then leave me the hell alone so I can get back to my job!"

"Oscar, for Pete's sake," said the Sheriff, "we're just asking you to keep a lid on things while I complete my investigation. That's all. We ain't looking for you to bend any rules."

"Coulda fooled me!" Dad's voice grew loud, soft, loud again as he paced the room. "You know goddamn well if I determine Hettie's death a murder, then I have to report it to County! And they'll want to see the body fast as I can turn it around! What kinda rinky-dink, shit-in-a-shoe politics are you trying to pull here, Mayor?"

"Hardly rinky-dink, my friend—"

"I'm not your goddamn friend!"

"Sure you are!" I heard a smack, no doubt the Mayor slapping Dad's back, a dangerous choice. "Of course, we're all pals here. Ain't that right, Sheriff?"

"Friendly as Eskimos in an igloo."

"If we're so goddamn friendly, surely you won't mind me reporting Hettie's murder to County," Dad snorted.

"And you will, Oscar, you will. I vow to you, you'll have every op-portunity to—"

"I know how much your bullshit vows mean, Mayor!"

"I say we all take a nice breather, have a sit down, and let cooler heads prevail." The recliner crunched beneath the Mayor's weight as he sat his cooler mind down. "Maybe we can all partake of some of that nice lem-onade."

"I'm not offering! This isn't a social visit, and I'm feeling less than sociable. Goddamn irritated at the both of you!"

Sheriff Grigsby sighed. "Oscar, listen to reason. After all's said and done, you can report Hettie's death—"

"Murder," corrected Dad.

"…Hettie's death to high Heaven and back for all I care. Mail her body to the North Pole and let Santy have a gander. I don't give a damn.

But right now—and I'm just saying for conjecture and all—right now I ain't so sure Hettie was murdered."

"Oh, holy hell! I've just started my exploratory investigation and have more than enough goddamn evidence that clearly points to murder!"

"Never minding that..." The Sheriff didn't even attempt to hide an elaborate sigh. "Give me time to look into it. You know how word gets 'round. If there's a murderer here in Hangwell, give me time to find him. If news of a murder gets out, everyone will have their say, point fingers at one another, want a look-see at the scene of the crime... Hell, Oscar, our slice of paradise will turn into hell before you know it. It'll derail my investigation, maybe put a stop to it completely."

"Sure. And we all know how intensive your investigations are, Sheriff."

"What the hell's that supposed to mean?" Boots clunked across the floor. For a big man, the Sheriff moved fast when he wanted to, which wasn't very often at all.

"I'm just saying a thorough murder investigation might be a helluva lotta work for you," said Dad. "Certainly don't want you going out of your way."

"I don't much care for the cut of your jibe," the Sheriff growled. Dad could cut deep with words, but I imagined he wouldn't last more than half a round in a physical fight with the solidly shaped Sheriff.

"Then let me cut into Hettie's body." Dad resumed pacing, walking off his mad streak. Calmer now, he said, "I'm not trying to run you aground, Bill. And I'm sorry if I came off as a bit...testy. I'm just trying to do my job. Do the proper thing by Hettie. The right thing."

"I appreciate that, Oscar," said Sheriff Grigsby, "but I'm trying to do my job here, too."

"There now," said the Mayor, "that's what community's all about. Coming together, everyone doing their respective jobs, working hand in hand like—"

"So help me, Mayor, if you start singing, I promise you I'll run for mayor myself next term." Silently, I cheered Dad on. "Why the hell are you two stonewalling me? If that was your mother or aunt or friend lying down there, you know goddamn well you'd want me looking inside her and getting to the bottom of things."

"No stonewalling here, Oscar." For all Dad's verbal attacks, the Mayor kept a cool, even keel. The sign of a knowledgeable—if not necessarily good—politician, I suppose. "Seems to me the three of us just want to do our jobs and serve the community as a whole. Not just one or two…ah, vocal citizens."

I could feel Dad steaming, ready to blow. Something he never unleashed on me. "Mayor, if you're referring to me as one of those vocal citizens, then you're goddamn right I am! Hey, everyone!" A window thrust open. Dad's voice sounded far away, his head stuck out the window. "Hey! Wake up, Hangwell! Someone's murdered Hettie Williquette! And no one gives a good goddamn about it either! Your Mayor—"

"That's enough, Oscar!" Shoes scuffled, boots chocked. The window crunched down with the finality of a guillotine blade. "Get hold of yourself," demanded the Sheriff. "Simmer down!"

Silence. Then footsteps, a softer tread. Dad's shoes. A blast of breath whooshed out of the sofa's upholstery as Dad collapsed into it. The sofa's wooden legs jumped.

Tired-sounding, resigned, Dad said, "I'll hold off calling Durham. Just a bit. I'll give you two days. I don't like it. It's not right. I want Hettie's killer brought to justice. Even if Hettie was the most reviled person in Peculiar County, I don't give a good goddamn… She deserves her proper due, same as anyone. But I don't want the investigation jeopardized either."

"That's the spirit, Oscar," said the Mayor.

But I didn't think so. Thought the opposite, matter of fact. They'd beaten the spirit outta Dad, and I didn't care for it, not one iota.

I didn't give a good damn—I'm my dad's daughter, after all—if it is an adult's world, they were just gonna have to get used to my being in it.

I whisked around the corner and into the living room. The three men sat at opposite sides of the room, each holding down their territory like solidly embedded tent-spikes. My place belonged in the middle.

"Well, hey, there, young 'un!" The Mayor scrunched up his baby-kissing face, all flabby cheeks and thin sentiment. "I didn't know you were about."

"I'm about," I said. "And I can tell you Dad's right about Hettie. About her being done up by someone."

The Sheriff chortled, then took his hat off to sway his red face. "Oscar, I think you'd agree such things ain't for children's ears."

Dad blinked, did it again. Carefully weighed his words before he spoke. Something he'd drummed into my head since I could talk. "Dibby may be young in age, but she's wise beyond her years. She's the one who brought Hettie's murder to my attention."

Even though the topic at hand was morbid, I beamed. Happy to be acknowledged. Now sitting at the big folks' supper table.

Of course, Sheriff Grigsby viewed it a might bit differently. "And we're gonna take a child's word—"

"Almost sixteen," I muttered.

"…a little girl's word on grown-up business? That ain't the way I police this town."

"Then maybe you better rethink how you're policing, Bill," said Dad.

"I've about had enough of this." The Sheriff stood. "You do what you want, Oscar. But I'm asking you, man-to-man, to keep hushed."

"Already said I'd give you two days."

"Well, if that ain't enough time, I'll be asking for more," said Sheriff Grigsby. "Hangwell elected me for a reason."

Smoking mad again, Dad hopped to his feet. "Bill, you were elected because nobody opposed you. For the umpteenth year running."

Sheriff Grigsby grinned, a bully's front. "Speaks for the fine job I'm doing. Needless to say, you'd be wise to heed your publically elected law-enforcement official."

"I don't much care for threats."

"No threats, Oscar. Just upholding the law as I was sworn to do. Without rabble rousers getting in my path."

"Goddamn it to hell and back, Bill! Now I'm a rabble rouser?"

Took him a while, but Mayor Hopkins managed to dislodge his girth from the grip of the recliner. The chair actually rode up with him, before plummeting back down. "Fellas, fellas, easy does it. Little ears and everything." He prodded a thick thumb back at my little ears. "We're all friends here, part of Hangwell's wonderful community."

"No problem here, Mayor," said the Sheriff.

"Just healthy discussion." But no matter what he said, Dad looked less than healthy, steaming like a bull ready to gore a matador.

"Now that we have that settled, fellas," said the Mayor, "I reckon we'll be moseying on. And Oscar? Them two days you asked for should be 'bout right."

"About right for what?" asked Dad.

"The Sooter sisters have been banging down my doors, wanting to claim ownership of Hettie's body. My assistant looked up the legalities and they have ever' right to do so. I'll let the gals know they can take ol' Hettie in two days."

"Even if the body's a part of an on-going murder investigation?" Dad raised his eyebrows, ready to raise the roof.

"That hasn't been proven yet, Oscar." The Mayor formed sad, cow-like eyes. "So, unless there's official proof and documentation, the sisters get custody of their dear, departed sister."

"This…this is *crazy!*" A word Dad insisted we never use, it banged the nail on the head. "You won't listen to the evidence I found! And unless Bill corroborates my findings within two days, the body goes to the Sooter sisters for God only knows what!"

"That's about the size of it, Oscar." Sheriff Grigsby patted Dad on the back, similar to the condescending pats everyone favored me with. I wondered how Dad liked it. Not very well, I could surely tell.

"So long, Oscar." Walking tall, the Sheriff hitched up his low-riding britches, grimaced as he stepped around me.

"We'll be in touch," offered the Mayor. "Keep up the fine work."

They were nearly to the front door when Dad ran to the hallway. "This isn't over. I'm going to do my job. I'm gonna do it for Hettie."

A slammed door answered him. Dad dragged back inside, resumed his spot on the sofa. I sat next to him.

"Goddamn red-tape, bureaucratic, lazy-assed, stupid-as-cowshit, no-good dolts." He looked at me, took off his glasses, tried to tame his mad hair. "Sorry, Dibs. I suppose it makes me feel better."

I smiled, letting him know it was okay. "Ain't anything I've not heard before."

"Don't say 'ain't'."

"Don't cuss like a drunken, stub-toed sailor."

The first laugh we shared in a while, and a darn full-on one to boot. Dad scooted closer to me.

"Look, Dibs… I know you don't want to talk about Mom, but—"

"Then don't."

"Okay. But will you listen to me for a minute?"

I nodded.

"I've made a real mess of things lately. In handling you, the situation with your mother…everything."

"A real goddamn mess."

"Dibby Caldwell! Do you kiss the boys at school with that mouth?"

"Dad!"

The laughter won out again. Cathartic, I believe, for both of us.

"Fine. I won't talk about your kissing boys—and I really hope you're *not*—if you don't start cussing like me." I said nothing, just sorta blushed, a full heat wave. I'd rather talk to Dad about any other topic—even Mom—than kissing James.

"It's a deal," I said. We shook on it, up, down, contact broken.

"Okay, here we go… I'm your father. I'm always gonna be your father. Pretty much everything I do, I relate it back to you one way or another. You're always on my mind, and I suppose the most important thing in the world to me is to see that you have a happy, healthy life and—"

"I'm healthy, Dad. You don't need to worry. So just…stop."

He shook his head. "That's just not going to happen. That's what dads do. What parents do. I know you don't understand now, but—"

"I kinda think I do."

"I know you think you do. And…intellectually, I have no doubt that you do. But I really think it takes being a parent to understand parenting. And I still don't always understand what I'm doing half the time. I'm still learning. Always will be, I suppose. Does that make sense? All of my babbling?"

"I reckon it does."

"So…I'm always going to worry about you. You're a very capable, mature young woman. I know that, even if it's sometimes hard for me to admit. In some ways, you'll always be my little Dibby, bouncing on my knee, and…" His voice went gargly, his eyes gleamed. He reached out a hand, ready to tousle my hair. But he reclaimed it. "I'm working on changing. Learning alongside you. It's what it'll take. But you're going to have to be patient with me. Okay? Can you do that?"

"As best I can, Dad."

"And when I ask you how you are…if there's anything wrong…this is hard, damn hard…" His voice rode high, nearing waterfall heights. "…I'm not asking because I fear for your mental health, Dibs. It's not because of your mother… Frankly, I can't think of another person who has a more solid head on her shoulders than you. But the reason I ask those questions is because I'm your father. My most important designation now."

"I know." I tossed my arms around him, anchored in for the long haul.

"I love you, Dibs."

"Love you back."

Baptismal tears flowed, washed away the problems between us. At least temporarily. But in my father's warm embrace, I felt it would last forever.

Chapter Thirteen

As far as the pantheon of Hangwell bogeymen ranked, Boot Gundersen came in third just behind Hettie and the town drunk, Hy Thurgood. I'd never heard a particular reason why Boot rounded up the top three, but I knew enough about the man that the idea of being alone with him gave me a severe case of the willies.

It'd taken time to build up courage, of course. All day long I'd puttered around. Finally, I just rushed toward the front door, hollered to Dad I was studying with James, and left, my courage still in hiding.

I pedaled up Oak Grove Road, the opposite direction I usually traveled. Dusk crawled in on dirty knees. Under other circumstances, the sleepy shades of blue shot through with magenta highlights on the horizon might've been pretty, but now they just reminded me how stupid I was not to have set out earlier.

Everyone knew Sunday was Boot's one day off from manning the telephone lines. What he got up to in his off hours provided ample grist for the gossip mill, and I tried to put such tales out of mind.

A mile-and-a-half down the road, I forked right onto Harrow Lane, otherwise known as the "Bad Side of Town." Out here, in the wooded boonies, houses were scarce, the land by and large considered unfit for living. Lotta folks used the area as a dumping ground. Deep in the woods, I spotted a worn-out sofa. Boxes and pipes and sinks and all the unwanted debris of homes lay scattered around it, very much like tornado fall-out.

The Santa Fe Railroad ran smack-dab down the middle of this wooded wasteland. Four times daily, the train chugged through the area, horn a-whistling, the only life willing to visit this No-Man's Land. At night, I always listened for the late-night train, its forlorn horn crying, a soothing lullaby of sorts. A song for those still awake, telling us we're not so alone in the night.

Although I knew a train wasn't scheduled now, Dad taught me well and I looked both ways anyway. Then I crossed the tracks. Just down the hill a jig, not too far now, sat Boot Gundersen's house, though calling it a "house" seemed mighty generous.

Boot's shack made Hettie's abode look like the Taj Mahal. Like our house, Boot had added on over the years, his construction material clearly scavenged from the surrounding dumping grounds. His newest addition, an abandoned Dad's Root Beer billboard, supplied a dandy, makeshift outer wall. Plywood, tin, abandoned building parts, car fenders, trash, you name it, Boot's shack looked like a work of modern art, a bird's nest of cast-off junk.

Contrary to his meager living means, however, Boot was well off, just swimming in money as rumor had it. He earned a mighty fine wage at the phone company, just didn't believe in banks. What he did with his money remained one of Hangwell's long-running mysteries, but everyone knew he could've afforded a fancy house up by Mr. Thomason, the banker.

But for whatever reason, Boot preferred his life as a hermit.

At the top of the hill, I hesitated. As Boot didn't drive, I couldn't tell if he was home. Maybe he was out in the woods tearing the throats out of opossums with his teeth, the way he gathered food, one of those tall tales I tried not to think about. After all, he rarely visited town to gather provisions.

Dusk decided not to stick around too long. Nighttime blew in like an ill wind. An owl hooted, impatient. Startled, my feet found the pedals and I coasted down the hill toward the shack.

I hopped off the bike, walked it the rest of the way in a nice and slow manner, hoping to forego a bellyful of buckshot. A lawn of weeds sprung up past my knees. Mites and other winged bugs swarmed. Not 'til I neared did I see ol' Queeg lounging on the warped porch. The three-legged German Shepherd's head rose. His tongue unrolled like a red carpet. His tail dusted dirt away, cleared a path for me.

"Hey there, Queeg." I leaned my bike against the porch. Hand out, I approached the dog. "Good boy. Good dog." Queeg gave me a sniff, licked my hand. I scratched his head, gave him a couple good, hearty pats. While ol' Boot seemed as cantankerous as a hung-over mule, the whole town loved his dog. A welcome sight on his rambling, hopping journeys through town, lotsa folks tossed Queeg food scraps.

Hinges squealed. The screen door ratcheted open. "Who the hell's there? Whaddaya want?" Boot stomped out, eyes narrowed. "That you, Dibby Caldwell?"

I straightened, felt like I'd been caught with my hand in the cookie jar. "Um, yes, sir, Mister Gundersen. Howdy."

"Howdy yourself." He strolled closer, bare-chested beneath his overalls. Tufts of gray chest hair bloomed out from behind his overall straps. The splintered floor boards didn't bother his naked feet one bit. He hooked his one thumb behind a strap, squinted up in the sky, then spat a wad of tobacco to the dirt. "I didn't expect you'd take me up on my offer, girly." He chortled, a weathervane squeaking in the wind.

"I didn't think I would either," I blurted out.

That made him laugh even harder. He pulled up a knee, slapped it a good one. "World's fulla surprises, ain't it?"

"Reckon it is, sir."

"Well, quit standing there, shaking in your boots, and come on in." He stomped toward the door, slipped inside. The screen door slapped shut. I considered dragging Queeg in with me for comfort.

Inside the shack, my jaw nearly dropped. The interior appeared a far cry from the patchwork exterior. Boot kept the large front room tidy, swept, clean. A nice sofa and well-lived-in recliner sat in front of a lovely, wooden coffee table. In the corner, a small gas stove, sink, and tiny round table comprised the kitchen. A large, old-timey radio provided Boot his entertainment, no television in sight. Along the back wall, hanging curtains hid two other rooms, presumably the bathroom and bedroom, neither one of which I had a hankering to visit.

Next to the recliner, a single lamp stirred the darkness. Shelves had been built into one wall, packed with photographs vying for attention. Even though Boot knew everyone in town's business, it seemed funny how little anyone knew of his. Every bit the loner as Odie, I sorta assumed Boot didn't have any loved ones. Or he'd outlived them all on his strict diet of orneriness.

Downright cozy and isolated, I kinda understood why Boot didn't want to leave his shack for a bigger abode. Comfort like this couldn't be bought.

"I like your place," I said.

"Yep. So do we." I hoped Boot meant Queeg and not a surprise shack-mate. I'd had my fill of shocks lately. "Sit yourself on down, Dibby Caldwell."

I sat on the sofa, keeping to the edge.

Boot flopped down in his recliner, the cushions molded to his lean frame. "Correct me if I'm wrong, but I seem to 'member our deal as being I'd tell you what I know about the poor li'l Saunders boy in exchange for a favor. That about the size of it?"

"That about fits."

"I gotta say, you're toeing in turbulent waters with your inquiries. Got no idea why you're doing such a thing, reckon it's none of my business, but the whole town's in a tizzy." While he spoke, he gestured wildly with his hand. The tapered stump beneath his right shoulder wagged along. Frankly, it was a might bit hard to keep my eyes from it. "Yes, sir, the whole town's got their knickers in a knot!" At first, I thought he'd stepped into a fit of sorts, coughing and bouncing all over his chair. But hellish laughter soon rose from the ashes, loud within the confining walls. "Buncha prissy ol' worrywarts. They'd just as much liken to sweep anything from the past under a rug, 'cause they don't wanna admit bad things happen here. What a town, what a town…" He wound down, out of gas. Reflecting a spell.

"Hangwell surely is something," I agreed. "Still, I don't have a clue why folks are so riled up."

"Oh, there's lotsa reasons for that, Dibby Caldwell, lots of reasons." He sat forward. The lamp's light caught his eyes just so, small embers flickering in them. "Nobody in this here town likes change. They want everything the same, hunky-dory as ever. Buncha goddamn hypocrites don't wanna think about the bad things. And Hangwell's got a bunch of dirt to hide, yesiree."

"That's what I'm finding out."

"Good! I hope to high hell you find it all out. Somebody needs to, dammit." Boot sat back. He scratched at his ever-present five-o'clock shadow, blinked wary eyes. "Now, before we get down to business, I'd like to collect on that favor."

I gulped, my imagination pushing me down a treacherous slope. I managed, "That's fine."

He sprung to his feet, bounded over toward the photograph filled shelves. On a small table beneath the shrine, he plucked a handful of flowers from a vase, a collection of poppies, peonies and sunflowers. Very much the Southern gentleman come a-courting, he lowered his head and offered them to me. "These here are for you."

Before things turned really ugly, I jumped to my feet. Much too young to become his kept bride, I visually plotted my escape route. My fists knotted. "Mister Gundersen, that's not the reason I came here. I s'pect you got the wrong notion about—"

"What're you yapping about? Take the goddamn flowers." He thrust them toward me. The stems poked into my arm. Anger rippled across his face. "Take 'em!"

I grabbed them, bundled them close to my chest, an impotent shield.

"Now follow me." Boot turned, stomped out the front door. "Come on," he hollered from the porch.

Glad to leave the prison of the small shack, I rushed outside. Queeg tore out in front of me, nearly tripping me up on the porch. Beside a gathering of trees Boot stood, impatiently tapping a bare foot. "You coming? Ain't got all day. Night'll soon be here."

The last surviving stretch of sunlight pulled. Tree limbs wiggled crooked fingers. A gust of wind forced the trees to shake hands with one another, a pact of darkness.

Boot stepped within the woods and all but disappeared. I considered high-tailing it toward my bike, but the promise of vital information ensnared me. One step closer to putting poor Thomas Saunders's soul to rest.

Owls hooted from all corners of the woods, an air-borne game of Marco Polo.

Suddenly, hair rose on the back of my neck. Chills skied down the slope of my back.

Someone else had joined us. Someone hidden in the woods, watching me. Felt it like a slap on the back. I turned, peered into the darkening woods. But I didn't look too hard.

As they say, "Better the devil you know." I took off after Boot, figured at least I could see him, outrun the old coot if it came down to it.

Once I entered the woods, the meager, remaining sunlight just up and went home. A heart-stopping spell of blindness froze me in place. Aided by small jags of purple light poking through the brush, my eyes got the hang of it. Ahead, I spotted the tip of Boot's cigarette, burning bright and red. I followed the tiny beacon, tracked the smoky smell down a rock-strewn path, the drop just deep enough to make for slow-going. Eventually, the path flattened and opened into a circular, man-made clearing. Even the trees overhead had peeled back, inviting in the last dim light of dusk.

Boot stood in the center, his back toward me.

Behind me, something snapped. Cracked. The following silence came too abruptly, unnaturally. I whirled. Saw nothing. But I surely felt the presence of something. Human or otherwise, I couldn't swear by. I hurried toward Boot. Chills chased me like a persistent flu bug.

In reverence, Boot fisted his hand over his belly and bowed his head. At his feet, a cross composed of two pieces of nailed-together wood jutted out of the ground. A heap of small pebbles and rocks sat in front of it, a smaller version of the skull-sized rock mounds found on top of the graves in Judge Wilbur's hanging cemetery. In red paint—blood?—the name "Richard" had been scrawled across the horizontal wood plank.

I stood next to Boot, followed his example. Folded my hands and looked down in silence.

"Go on," he said.

I hesitated, not having the foggiest.

"Go on, put them flowers down." Irritation crisped the edges of his voice. His arm stump gestured, just a small wag.

On my knees, I placed the flowers at the foot of the crude grave marker. Quickly, I got to my feet, uncomfortable with Boot behind me. I resettled beside Boot.

He said, "Richard. Li'l Richie. My grandson."

"Was he… Is he buried here?"

"Yep. Well…no. Not really. But he may as well be."

Up on the path, leafs snapped. Footsteps approached fast. Three of them. Queeg broke into the clearing and raced toward us. He sat down next to me, lowered his head, too. Used to the ritual.

"This here's part of what you're looking for, Dibby Caldwell." Boot's stump wiggled at the marker.

"I don't understand."

"'Course you don't, dammit! I ain't tol' you yet. Now if you'll gum up a minute, I'll explain." His voice broke a little, just a hair. A slice of the rising moon hooked into his damp eyes. He took a deep breath, let it out. Queeg seemed to mimic him, then settled into a groan. "About four months after Thomas Saunders disappeared, my grandson Richie went missing, too."

"I'm rightly sorry to hear that, Mister Gundersen. But I've never heard of—"

"'Course not! And don't interrupt adults when they're speaking!" He clucked, carried on a bit. "Some time ago, my daughter, Gretchen, went head over heels for Alvie Holmberg, a well-to-do Durham farmer. Wasn't long after that she married him and moved to Durham. They started raising a family of their own. Their first-born, Richard, was really something, really special. I loved that boy. Loved him like he was my own son. Hell, he looked like a Gundersen more than a Holmberg, too, I always said." He thumped his chest, jut his chin out.

"I'll just bet he did," I said.

"Used to bounce that boy on my knee. When he was old enough, I took him out on hunts. 'Course Gretchen thought him too young, but age don't matter for certain things, if you know what I mean."

I didn't, not really, but nodded like I did.

"Well… It was tragedy enough when li'l Thomas Saunders went to missing here in Hangwell. Whole town was on edge, the gossip flying left and right. I heard it all on the phone party line. And since the boy's father, Hedrick, had gone missing just a couple months earlier, tongues were really wagging, putting together outlandish stories. I heard all of them. All of them, I tell you, Dibby Caldwell!" He placed a finger beside his nose, winked. "But by then I learned not to give too much consideration to nattering. You hear it day in and day out on your job, it tends to not matter anymore."

"Wish more folks would turn a deaf ear on gossip."

"You're damn tooting! Anyway, I didn't give the gossip no mind. Until Richie went missing. Four months after Thomas Saunders. The law in Durham said Richie'd done run away, just like Thomas had. Same age, same situation. Now, I ain't a big believer in coincidences, a fool's game, you ask me." I nodded again. "I blew my stack. Refused to believe Richie would run away. Let me ask you this, Dibby Caldwell, how many eight-year-olds run away?"

I considered it. The several occasions I'd tried it, I hadn't made it farther than the woods and was home in time for supper. "Not many, I reckon."

"You reckon right. The kiddies go sit by the crick, climb a tree. Get scared and come home. And those are the kiddies who ain't had a happy upbringing, feel they got reason to run away. But Richie'd come from good stock. His folks gave him everything he wanted. No, sir, Richie didn't run away. Just like Thomas, someone'd killed Richie." His voice derailed. He gulped out great sobs. Lately, I'd taken to carrying around a wad of clean tissues and for good reason. I handed Boot one. He ripped it from my hand, honked into it, then finagled his arm stump into his eyes to dry them.

"Sorry 'bout that. I know it ain't very becoming to see a man bawl."

"It's all right, Mister Gundersen. Everybody does it now and then. I reckon it proves you're human."

To that, Boot laughed. "For a little one, you're wise beyond your years, Dibby Caldwell." He cleared his throat, rattling like he'd swallowed a can of nails. "No one would believe me. About someone murdering my grandson, I mean. The Durham sheriff just laughed me out of his office. Gretchen and Alvie, Richie's folks, were all bound up in blind faith. They overlooked the mean reality of it all, holding onto hope Richie would come home. To this day, they still put a light on in his bedroom at night. Gretchen even turns down his sheets before turning in."

"I'm sorry to hear—"

"Not half as sorry as me," he spat. "My daughter refused to give Richie a proper Christian burial. So—and I know it ain't right and all—I put together this here li'l memorial for Richie. Hoping he'd be invited into the gates of Heaven."

"I'm sure he has, Mister Gundersen."

"Well, I believe in doubling down, Dibby Caldwell." He turned toward me, his face drawing long as the outlying shadows. "I'm collecting on your favor. Get down on your knees."

"What?"

Boot could turn on a dime. Just seconds before I felt a great flood of empathy for him. Now it seemed as if the Devil himself had set up camp within Boot.

"I said get down on your knees!" I backed away. He came at me, arm outstretched. My foot rolled over a fallen limb, sent me tottering back. I hit the ground hard, my hind end absorbing most of the shock. Boot grabbed the back of my flannel shirt. With surprising strength in his one arm, he hauled me up. Wrangling me by my shirt collar, he shoved me toward Richard's temporary gravesite.

"Get down, goddammit, down!" He shook me like a rag doll until I dropped to my knees.

In the woods, something crashed. Limbs snapped, leaves crunched. Lowered on his front limbs, flange of hair raised, Queeg growled at the sudden intruder. A shushing sound grew loud, louder.

"Let her *go*!"

I whirled around.

Scratched, sweaty and red-cheeked, James raced his bike into the clearing. He sliced into a semi-circle, his feet dragging him to a stop. The bike crashed to the ground as James abandoned it. One fist pulled back, he ran toward us.

"Leave her alone before I kick you into next Tuesday!" James looked like he meant it, too.

Boot let go of my shirt and straightened. A howl of laughter erupted from him, sent up toward the moon.

Cautiously, I rose to my feet. James stopped, just sorta stood there, dumbstruck. His fists still coiled, he stared at them, clearly wondering if it'd be proper to sock a laughing old man.

"Well, I'll be dipped in shit and put on parade," hooted Boot. "Your li'l boyfriend here's come to your rescue, ready to take on a one-armed marine. You—"

"Not my boyfriend," I muttered.

"You still ain't no match for me, sonny," Boot continued. "Not even on my worst days! If that ain't the damnedest thing! Now I seen it all! The very idea… The best laugh I've had in a coon's age. Why I never, never, *ever*…"

From a dire situation to one I couldn't comprehend, I had no recourse but to listen as Boot wound on. Not to be left out of the merry proceedings, Queeg circled his owner, tail wagging, his missing back leg not setting him back a bit. No doubt the dog didn't see Boot in a giddy, back-slapping mood often. Birds cawed and fled, afraid of the unusual beast in their midst.

Finally, Boot's legs gave up on him, just dumped him into the dirt. He issued a bagpipe wheeze. "Sonny-boy, I wasn't aiming to hurt your little darling…"

"Not his darling," I said.

"I reckon I owe you my apologies, li'l lady," Boot said. "When it comes to my grandson, Richie…I just kinda slide a little to the bad side. A dark side I don't much like, picked it up in the war, but it's mine and I have to live with it. Sometimes…about Richie… Everything goes black…" He scratched his whiskers, looked either lost or ashamed, hard to tell. "It ain't much of an excuse, I know, but I s'pose I'm not all that good at one-on-one interaction with folks anymore. Since Richie's death, I've kinda become a hermit, sometimes forget how to be good to folks." He held a hand up. "I surely shouldn't have manhandled you, missy. I'm sorry. I rightly am."

"I understand how family matters can color one's view at times." I grabbed Boot's hand and tried to tug him up. He shooed my helping hand away, then managed to crawl to his feet.

Confused, James looked between us. He settled for matter over mind, what he knew best. "You…you just leave her alone, you hear me? Or I'll…I'll…"

The menacing storm had passed. Boot laughed again, lending James's threats the significance of a gnat's sneeze. Humiliated, James sunk into a cute bundle of silence.

But James *cared*. Inside, my heart flowered. Outside, I festered. "James…what're you *doing* here, dangit? I *told* you I'd take care of it on my own!"

He shrugged, put on his flash again. "I was worried about you, Dibs. I found out where he lived…" He jerked his chin at Boot. "…and thought you might need help. I was right."

"I downright handled this a bit sloppy, I reckon, but my intentions were clean." Boot pointed toward Richie's marker. "Dibby Caldwell, I'd muchly appreciate if you'd pray for Richie's soul. You might say I ain't been much of a righteous man. Done sinned with the worst of 'em. For all I know, my praying here might not be doing a lick of good. So I figured if I could get somebody righteous, somebody good to pray, it just might ensure Richie's arrival into Heaven."

A pickle of a situation, to be sure. Praying didn't come naturally to me, either. I hadn't prayed since…well, pretty much since Mom had left. And I hardly felt good, righteous folks went around socking their enemies in the mouth, either. Still, it seemed like it might put Boot's mind at ease and it surely couldn't hurt. Maybe for me, too. Besides, with all the un-explainable things I'd seen in Hangwell lately, it just seemed a bit short-sighted to rule out matters of Heaven just yet.

"All you had to do was ask, Mister Gundersen." I got down on my knees, beckoned for James to join me. "Next time you might try a softer touch."

Boot shrugged, a mighty peculiar gesture with only one arm.

James joined me, whispered, "I don't know how to pray."

I nudged him. "Shut your hole and follow me."

Down on one hand, Boot tucked his legs beneath him, then sidled up next to us. Together the three of us folded hands, closed our eyes. Queeg anchored the other side.

"Dear God in Heaven," I said, "please help the spirit of li'l Richie Holmberg find safe passage into Heaven and to live a good and peaceful eternal life." James lagged behind, occasionally repeating words and snip-pets. "Give his folks and Grandpa peace of mind and help them know that someday they'll see him again. Um…I reckon that's about it 'cept I'd like to ask that Thomas Saunders find his way there into Heaven, too. Maybe the boys can be friends, just having fun, fishing off their cloud, and what not. So…"

Boot murmured, "Ask for Queeg to go to Heaven, too. When it's his time."

"Oh, and dear God, help Queeg to hob-knob it up there, too. When it's rightly his time, of course. Amen."

"Amen," said Boot.

"Amen." James fumbled his way through a variation of the sign of the cross, although I figured the only Catholic thing about him was drink-ing and dancing.

First to his feet, Boot said, "Thank you, Dibby. Now…I'm plum-tuckered. Let's make our way back."

For a plum-tuckered man, Boot made short work out of trawling up the hill. By the time we reached the shack, James couldn't catch a lick of breath. We settled onto the sofa. As if chaperoning, Queeg hopped up between us.

"Reckon I don't have much in the way of refreshments," said Boot, "lessen you'd like some fish jerky. Water? Whiskey?"

All of that sounded about as appealing as an ingrown toenail. Whiskey seemed to light fire in James's eyes, though. I answered for both of us. "No thanks, Mister Gundersen. We're fine." I shot James a scowl. He looked down at his hands, a chastised school-boy. A look I liked.

"Mister Gunderson, what's the link between Richie and Thomas?" I asked. "Do you know who…took 'em?"

Boot got up, quickly walked toward his display of photographs. He snatched one up, and on the way back to his recliner, he dropped it into my hands. "Before we go on, I want to put a face to the name. You should know who you done prayed for. Who you're helping to put to rest."

The face didn't shock me, not really. "I know this boy," I said.

"That can't be, just can't." Boot shook his head solemnly. "Richie went missing when you were just a wee li'l lass."

"I know that, sir. But… I saw him in a vision. He was the other boy in the Saunders' cornfield." Since Boot had been forthcoming with me, I returned the favor, told him about my ghostly encounters, though I framed them as dreams.

Boot reacted unexpectedly. "The Saunders. Bah!" He spat on the floor. Queeg lifted his head, appeared to give his owner a disgusted look. "You wanna know what happened to them two boys, look no farther than your next door neighbors."

"What's the Saunders' connection with the missing boys?"

He tossed up an arm and stump. "I hear lots of things, Dibby Caldwell. Lots of things. Yes sir…" Boot began to fade, lost in a reverie.

"Mister Gundersen, please!" I clapped my hands. "What can you tell me?"

"I'll tell you one thing, missy… That ol' Evelyn Saunders? She ain't as innocent as she plays to be. Now, she likes everyone to think she's a frail, not-quite-right-in-the-head, poor, li'l thing who can't take care of herself. That's far from the mark." Boot closed one eye, stuck out his thumb and forefinger. Taking aim, he dropped his thumb, fired an imaginary shot my way. "But I got her number all right, yes, sir. Ol' Boot knows the score. Evelyn Saunder's a man-eating monster if there ever was one. Surely, she up and did away with her husband, Hedrick. And if she was capable of that, I reckon she did away with the boys as well. Sure as my name's Boot Gundersen, I know it for gospel."

"Did you actually hear it, Mister Gundersen? Did Missus Saunders say something over the phone?"

Boot scratched his cheek, worked his way under the chin and around to the other side. "Well…no. Can't rightly recall that she did. But I can piece things together all right."

"Like *what?*" Exasperated, I tossed my hands up. Boot's credibility as a source slowly slipped away, his age eroding memory's edge. James didn't help matters, fussing and fidgeting like he had better places to go.

"For starters, everyone knows Thomas wasn't actually Hedrick's boy. Well…maybe not everyone. But that juicy tittle-tattle kept the phone lines burning. Of course, Hedrick got around, too, if you know what I mean. Not that I put much stock into rumors, mind you, but Hedrick was having relations with…ah…that is…" Boot waffled, first time for everything. He looked at me, averted his eyes. I knew what weighed on his mind. And frankly, it surprised me I didn't give a hang.

"I've heard the rumors about my mom and Hedrick Saunders, Mister Gundersen. But that's not relevant right now. Who was Thomas's biological daddy?"

"I could venture some guesses, I s'pose, but that wouldn't be doing anyone any favors. That Saunders woman got around though, just couldn't keep her bloomers on. Now, she was careful, I'll say that for her. Always careful about what she said on the phone. She got a lot of calls from male admirers. A lot of 'em. But they spoke in codes of a sort, kinda like what I heard back in the Big War. Just short nothings, mind you, howdy-do's and the likes. None of it really of import. But I heard enough to know things weren't right. That she was cheating on her husband with half the men in Hangwell, seemed like."

Headed nowhere again, my frustration reared. "Did Evelyn *ever* come right out and fess up as to who Thomas's father was?"

Boot thought, absentmindedly scratched at himself. "No…can't say that she did. But from what bits and pieces I heard… I believe Hedrick found out about Thomas's heritage, then plum went outta his mind. So Evelyn killed him and covered it up. And if you murder once…I should know…" Boot's eyes turned dark again, scary and rooted in the past. "…it don't take much to kill again. Mark my word, Evelyn Saunders killed the three of 'em. One after the other. Probably accountable for all the other missing kids in Hangwell, too."

Boot dropped me right back to the beginning again. Even though he'd lured me to his shack with the promise of big revelations, he'd only given me gossip, scraps not hearty enough for starving birds. "Mister Gundersen, is there anything else you remember? Did the Sooter sisters have contact with Missus Saunders?"

"Them ol' witches? Feh. Far as I know, outside of their library, they don't even own a tellyphone. Communicate through smoke signals or some such hooey."

"What about Missus Saunders's men callers? You remember who they were?"

"Lessee…well, there were a lot of 'em. Mayor Hopkins, Odie Smith, Sheriff Grigsby, Daryl Mooney down from the gas station, Rod Simonson, the pharmacist…even ol' Hy Thurgood. Evelyn wasn't beyond tossing the town drunk a shag, shameless as she was. And, um….well, hell, Dibby… Sorry to say your daddy called on her, too."

Whenever my world started to ground itself (and contrary to Christopher Columbus's findings), it had a tendency to send me sailing right off the edge again.

Sick at the disclosure of Dad's involvement, I pitched forward, a hand over my mouth. I rose, raced out of the shack.

It all made sense now, a horrible sense that didn't sit well. Why Dad wanted me to stay away from Evelyn Saunders. He was up to his neck in everything.

I couldn't think, could barely see. From a distance, I heard James hollering after me. Atop my bike, I wobbled out of Boot's yard, made it onto the dirt trail. The world spun, my stomach twisted the other way. The ground raced up and things exploded with a cone of sparks.

"Dibby!"

Head pounding, I opened my eyes, looked up into James's worried face. I closed them again, wishing for everything to fade away.

"Dibby! Are you okay?"

That damn stupid question again…

"Go away," I muttered. "I'm sleeping."

Leaves scattered as James plopped down next to me. "Damn, Dibs, that was some wipe-out you took. Maybe we better get you to a doctor or something."

At the touch of his hand, I jumped. It felt cold, nearly dead. Or maybe I was feverish.

"Say something, Dibs! You okay?"

"I just wanna be left alone!"

"No."

"*What?*" My eyes popped open. James, wan-looking, stroked my forehead.

"Your old man will kill me if you've got, like, a concussion or something and I left you in the woods."

I sat up. Dizzy, but doable. "I'm fine. Quit your caterwauling. And get your hand offa me."

"You sure? I mean, I'll call for an ambulance or something."

"By the time it got here from Durham, I'd be six feet under. I'm okay, dang it." I tried to stand, wobbled a bit. James grabbed me. I shrugged him off.

"Hey, just trying to help."

"I don't need your help!" I brushed dirt from my arms, my backside. Brushed away any notion I needed help. "And you're not off the hook yet! I'm still mad at you for coming. Don't you ever listen? You almost ruined everything!"

"C'mon, Dibs. Seems to me I got here just in time. I don't care how much he apologized, that old codger was going to do something to you. He was—"

"I can handle ol' Boot. He wasn't gonna hurt me."

"Dammit! I just want to *help* you! *Why* don't you—" His mouth snapped shut. For a change, he thought first, then calmed down. "Sorry. It's just… I dunno, you're the most frustrating girl I've ever met."

"And I plan to stay that way." Surely, he didn't mean it as complimentary, but I took it that way.

Side-by-side, we walked our bikes down the dirt road. The owls had returned in full force, keeping one another appraised of our progress.

"You know, just 'cause Boot said your old man talked to Evelyn Saunders doesn't really mean he was, you know, having sex with her or anything."

I suppose James was right. But my anger was something I intended to hold on to for a bit. Lately, I'd forgiven folks too readily only to be betrayed by them all over again. Like James. And Dad. My heart could only take so much stomping on.

"I'm not passing judgment one way or another on my dad just yet. But the truth of the matter is, he pretty much lied to my face. As usual. And I aim to make it stop."

"How? You can't change parents."

I shrugged. "Same way I always do, I reckon. I'll make him tell me everything."

"Good luck with that. I can't even talk to my old man."

As if it'd suddenly keeled off a tree branch, an owl stopped midhoot. Pretty much used to the sensation by now, I still didn't like it. Somewhere a switch had been triggered. The woods had grown unnaturally quiet.

"Back there, at Boot's," said James, "you asked about the Sooter sisters. You know it's not possible for them to be Thomas Saunders's dad, right? Right?" He grinned, thinking he was cute. He wasn't that cute.

I swatted his shoulder. "Ow! Geez Louise, what was that for?"

"Don't be dumb. It's not becoming. And I betcha I know more about sex than you do."

He stopped. I watched as his face rolled through its limited display of emotions: dumb, lecherous, befuddlement, and finally, face-sagging insecurity. He said, "Wanna find out?" But his voice squeaked, a frightened child playing at big boy games.

I just laughed. "Let's not get side-tracked. I think there's a couple different things going on here. There's the unknown identity of Thomas's scientific daddy. Then there's the question of who killed Thomas and Richie. Hedrick, too. Not to mention ol' Hettie. My brain hurts! But I'm beginning to think there's more than one killer."

"Why?"

"I keep going back to the symbol Hettie showed me in Dad's freezer. The six-pointed star. The hexagram."

"Right. Witch stuff."

"Yup. I think Hettie was implicating her sisters. Even Boot called 'em witches."

"But…why would they kill Thomas Saunders?"

"Beats the tar outta me. Human sacrifice, maybe?"

"Maybe," said James.

Deep in the woods, something thumped. Something heavy. A second bump ground up through my boots' soles. Bats fled their nocturnal roosts. Leathery wings whisked away. Creatures fled, trotting briskly across the ground cover. Leaves snapped, then settled. Again, all sound had bottled up, sealed with a cork. Not a chirp, buzz, caw, anything.

Faster than a forest fire, something had emptied the woods.

The air weighed heavy, muggy. A sweat drop poked out at my nose's tip and dangled. Another ground-trembling throb knocked it off.

"What the hell's that?" whispered James.

"Danged if I know." I looked down, realized I'd grabbed James's hand. Didn't know when I did it, but it provided a bridge of comfort.

Whump…thump…thump…

From the dark of the woods, inhumanly heavy footfalls approached.

Thump…thump…

The unseen creature's pace increased. Not quite running, but determination drove its monstrous tread toward us.

"Let's go!" I dropped James's hand, hopped onto my bike. The bike bobbled back and forth, bumped across the pocked road. With speed, I straightened it out. I glanced back at James, saw him struggling. "Go, James! Dammit, come on!"

"I'm trying!"

Whump, thump, thump...

The creature broke into a heavy sprint. My bike vibrated. The handle-bars jack hammered in my hands. A spattering of collected rain spilled from treetops.

"I'm...coming..." James wheezed, falling farther behind.

Carelessly, blindly, I sped like mad, dipping in and out of potholes. If I hit a rock, one unlucky move, I'd go flying head first into one of the trees.

Behind us, the world's largest door swung open, moved back and forth, back and forth on great, creaking hinges.

Reet, ret, reet, ret...

A vacuum of hot air sucked back my hair, whipped my shirt tight around my bosom.

Whumph.

The ground quit shaking.

Ahead lay the railroad tracks. The moon glowed off-white, sick. I clattered over the tracks, not slowing, hell on the tires. James followed.

Above us, something flapped. Heavy wings spread out, spanning wide enough to blot out the moon.

I didn't want to look. But I had to. Above, a dark figure paced us—big, unimaginably big—wings whipping out, then folding back around its squat body.

The same hellish creature that had flown over us the other night. Suddenly, the beast's identity dawned on me, a scary and impossible and all-too-real notion.

"James, we gotta get outta the woods!"

"*Trying!*"

Past the railroad tracks, we plummeted down the dirt road's massive hill, speed to our advantage. Ahead lay one more terrifying, vulnerable patch of woods, the only way back to Oak Grove Road and blessed civilization.

I broke into the dark, blindly following the trail, navigating by gut. Tears of fear streamed back across my cheeks, then evaporated in my wind current.

Behind me, a thin knife of light snapped on. I shrieked, looked back. One handed, James fiddled with a pocket-sized flashlight, his bike drunkenly weaving. Awkwardly, he plugged the flashlight's grip between his teeth—his big mouth finally coming in handy—and reclaimed his bike's handlebars. The light bounced up and down, chaotic.

The beating of the creature's wings rose, ancient, rife with stone arthritis.

Flump!

Leaves fluttered down around us, new leaves not yet ready to shed. Branches tremored. Smaller twigs dropped, a sudden hailstorm. The beast had roosted in the tree tops.

The dirt road curved right, not too much farther to the fork delivering us to Oak Grove Road.

"Faster, James! Get your arse in gear!"

"Dibby…wait…" He'd fallen behind, his voice barely audible. Maybe now he'd quit smoking. If we lived for the chance.

I cut the bike sharp, twisted. My foot jagged down into the leaves, shushing through them.

The beast leaped into the treetop next to me. Limbs cracked. Leaves rained.

Head down over his handlebars, James had given up. But his shaking hand remained up, flashlight still trying to light my way.

The monster didn't move. Not an inch. But I knew he was up there. Felt his heavy, otherworldly presence, like Santa on Christmas morning.

I sped back toward James. Stupid, sure. But even if it meant an early end to my abbreviated life, I'd have done it for anyone. Except for maybe Suzette.

"James, it'll be all right." Everyone's allowed a white lie now and again. "Give me your flashlight."

He handed it over, dropped his arm like it weighed a ton. I straddled my bike closer to the beast-occupied tree and rode the beam up the tree. Other than a thick crown of leaves, I couldn't see anything.

"Yvette! Miriam," I hollered, not standing on proper names now. "I know it's you! I know you're using ol' Stoney to get me. You're too scared to do your dirty work yourselves, gotta use your gargoyle! Yvette, I know you're watching through Stoney's cement eyes. And Miriam! Are you listening through his horned ears? Well, I ain't afraid! You hear me? You may as well come on down, Stoney!"

James looked at me like I'd gone 'round the bend. Maybe I had, too. My brave words didn't match at all how I felt, nothing but lies.

A large limb broke, dropped. Inches from shearing James's arm off, it exploded on the ground. A sudden loud *whoosh* pulled branches up and sent leaves storming down. More limbs broke away, snapping like gunfire.

Fast as gunshot, I hightailed it back to James.

Thump, bump!

Stoney dropped to the ground.

He stood beneath the overhanging tree's umbrella of darkness. The flashlight couldn't catch a lick of the gargoyle other than his thick, gray legs. Of course I'd seen his clawed feet up close and personal many a time, but this was the first time they set me to shivering. One foot moved just an inch or so. The resulting crack sounded near to a dam breaking.

I got off my bike. Time to make a stand.

"You can kill me now if you want to, ladies. But it ain't gonna do you any good. I already told my dad and the sheriff you killed Thomas Saunders. Whatever you do, it ain't gonna save your hides from prison."

As far as bluffs went, it was a doozy. One I felt I sold, especially since I somehow managed to stay up on my feet. Never had I felt so adult and never had I so wanted to retreat into a mother's—who I didn't even know—arms.

Stoney stayed still, true to his statue origins. He grunted, just a single, deep-chested sound, an old dog with failing bones.

Suddenly, the beast squatted. His clawed fists dropped into view beside his thighs, then tightened into small boulders of stone. Knees bent with double cracks. Up he went, crashing through the tree's foliage. A barrage of limbs and leaves cascaded down, his departing gift to us. Across the night sky, he diminished in size until he flitted out of sight.

I nearly collapsed. James did. Just laid down his bike and flattened on his back.

"Was that…was that really the library gargoyle?"

"It surely was. The Sooter sisters' killing machine." I don't know why I handled the gargoyle's visit with such matter-of-factness. For once, I felt calm and in charge. A natural response, I suppose, after looking the impossible in the eye and living through it.

"But…why didn't it kill us?" Balancing a fine line over hysteria, James spoke reverently up into the trees, treating it almost like a religious experience.

"That's a mighty fine question. One I intend to get to first thing in the morn." I strolled over toward James, toed him a couple times. "Get up. I gotta get home."

Dazed, he sat up. "What're you gonna do, Dibs? You can't just go up to the sisters' front door, knock, and say, 'Hey, how come your gargoyle didn't kill us last night?'"

"That's exactly what I'm gonna do."

Chapter Fourteen

Soon as I stepped inside the door, Dad yodeled, "Dibby? That you?"

"Who'd you expect?" I answered. "Missus Saunders?"

Dad's recliner snapped back into place, his feet slapped the ground. Drink in hand—his usual bedtime modifier—he corralled me against the stairwell. "I'm sorry, would you mind repeating that?" He knocked back the rest of his cocktail, apparently fortifying himself for the battle ahead.

Frankly, I'd had enough fighting. For once, I just wanted to get to the point. Dispense with the emotional build-up.

"Dad, will you just tell me the truth? For once?"

Like his innards had caught fire, he winced, then sat down on the bottom step. "I'll do my best, Dibs." He studied his empty glass before setting it down. I sat next to him, not too closely. "What's this about? Your mother?"

"No. How close were you to Evelyn Saunders?"

Dad reacted as if he'd sat on a land mine. His eyes went big, his mouth blew open. "Ah…that's kinda out of the blue."

"That's your best?"

A good, cleansing inhale, then he expelled all the bad. "Okay. Where to start… Well, as you know, Hedrick Saunders went missing back in… 1953, it was. After that, no one saw very much of the Saunders' boy,

Thomas. Evelyn'd taken him out of school, said he was too saddened by the departure of his father to continue. The few occasions I saw the boy, he just seemed kinda dead to the world, not much life in him. Hardly how a boy his age should act. Not too long after that, Thomas vanished as well. At the time, I thought Hedrick came back and stole his son away. A lot of people thought that.

"And while all of that was going on next door…your mother's mental state was rapidly deteriorating. The Saunders' misfortunes seemed to affect her badly, and I couldn't understand why."

"How? I mean…how bad did she get?"

"I told you about her mood swings, her depression. One minute crying. At other times laughing and singing…"

"I remember her that way."

"Me, too, Dibs. It's natural to remember the best of people. But… she grew even worse. She started…seeing things that weren't there. Shadows that moved, even ghosts. Sometimes she saw creatures, things flying through the skies. Late at night, I'd catch her looking out the windows. Just sitting there, staring for hours. Almost as if waiting for something."

For a mother I barely remembered, we apparently shared a good deal in common. Either I'd soon be bunking with her at the Lackasaw Mental Facility or we both had an affinity for creatures of the night.

"It was only then I started realizing how deep your mother's problems were rooted. Not nearly soon enough." Dad pulled at his hair. "Stupid, stupid me. So damn stupid."

"Dad," I said, "most folks probably would've had the same reaction."

He nodded. "But I waited too long. By the time I started mentioning a psychiatrist to your mother, she left. Just took off one night. I was distraught, Dibs. Really upset. So…not knowing what to do…I called Evelyn Saunders. Without thinking, just picked up the phone and called her."

"Why?"

"Because I knew she'd understand what I was going through. I thought we could…support one another over the loss of our spouses. And maybe I could find out if your mom had truly run off with Hedrick.

I needed an answer before I could move on with my life. Of course, now I know the gossip of her departure was a bunch of hokum, but anyhow… I needed someone to talk to. So we did. Long talks, too. Then I thought it was kinda ridiculous carrying on long telephone chats with Evelyn since we were neighbors, so I started visiting her. Our talks lengthened, our friendship strengthened. And…secrets were shared."

He paused, closed his eyes again. Things were about to get bang-on pertinent. His voice dropped. I leaned in closer so as not to miss a peep.

"What secrets?"

"This is…difficult. Evelyn started rambling on, saying things that didn't make a lick of sense. I saw her sinking into a deep, dark hole of depression. Having gone through this with your mother, I recognized the signs. Naturally, I was worried for her. If I could do something to save her—unlike how I'd failed your mother—I'd give it my all. But Evelyn wouldn't listen to reason, pooh-poohed the notion of psychiatric help. Just like your mother, I watched her deteriorate. After a while, I couldn't separate what was true from her deluded babbling. One time, in one of her worst fits, she claimed she'd killed Hedrick."

"She admitted that?"

"Well, not so much a confession, nothing that would hold up in court. From what I can recall…" He cradled a knee, closed his eyes, deep into recalling. "…she said something along the lines of 'I didn't mean to do away with Hedrick. I really didn't. But it was out of my hands.' Probably not her exact words, but close enough. Then she snapped back to reality, just started talking about how her brother, Devin, was going to move in to help her on the farm. Like her admission of murder never happened."

He grimaced, rocked back and forth. "Dibs, I was really at a loss as to what to do. I didn't believe half the stuff she went on about. But on the off chance she had actually killed her husband, I couldn't just ignore it. I went to Doc Willoughby, explained Evelyn's mental condition. Then I slipped her confession in casual-like, using it to illustrate her behavior. Doc said it was normal behavior for someone who'd been through what she had and that I should keep an eye out on her."

"Did you? Watch out for her?"

"I tried. For a while. But…things got complicated."

That familiar ball of turmoil in my gut turned. But I had to know. "Dad, did you have…'relations' with Missus Saunders?" I hung heavy finger quotes, hoping they'd bear part of my discomfort.

"What? No! Of course not. But… full truth here, Dibs… I was tempted. Mighty tempted. Your mom had been gone for a while. I was lonely. Broken. And the more time I spent with Missus Saunders, well…the more such thoughts occurred. One afternoon, we kissed. A long—"

"Dad! Every little detail ain't necessary!"

"Don't say 'ain't'." He chuckled. "Sometimes I forget you're still a…" He almost said "little girl," I just knew it. But he managed to stop himself. "Anyway…I was still a married man. Legally, at least. And I always uphold the law. Or try my best, I guess I should say."

"Yes, sir, you do."

"Well, guilt got the better of me. After that one kiss, I told Evelyn it'd be wrong to pursue a romance. So…I visited less frequently. And she just fell deeper and deeper into whatever darkness was waiting for her. Started saying even wilder things about Thomas…about what had happened to him."

"What'd she say?"

"She said a monster got him. Ate him."

Immediately, the Sooters' gargoyle came to mind. "And you didn't believe her, of course."

"'Course not, Dibs. As a scientist, I know there's no such thing as monsters. But human monsters? That's a different story. I've seen plenty proof of them in my work over the years." He paused, frowned as if considering a late career change. "But back to Evelyn… I was at a real crossroads. I didn't know what to do. On the one hand, I wanted to help her, guide her into proper care. On the other? I thought maybe her claims should be properly investigated."

"What'd you do?"

"Tried to have my cake and eat it, too. Which we all know is damned impossible." Actually, I thought not but didn't want to derail Dad over semantics. "So I told Sheriff Grigsby about the things Evelyn'd been spouting off about. He regarded it the way he does everything, with little stride and a lotta laziness. Told me he'd look into it, but I shouldn't hang too much credibility on the rantings of a mad woman. Then I made one last attempt to convince Evelyn to seek help. She refused. Grew angry with me. Told me to get out and never come back. So that's what I did."

"Was that the right thing to do?"

"To this day, Dibs, I don't know. It haunts me. And truth be told, I had to get away from Evelyn. Her mental issues were weighing on me. I know it's silly, but I almost felt like they were contagious. I was in a vulnerable position myself, knew from experience how anyone could become afflicted." He tapped a temple.

"Anyone," I echoed.

"All these years later, I still wonder if there was an inkling of truth to Evelyn's confessions. And I've never come up with a solid answer, not one that satisfied me. I had no proof either way. But I knew enough to keep you away from Evelyn Saunders."

"I s'pose I understand that." Although I had no intention of adhering to that rule. Not now. Especially not now. "Seems like you did your best, Dad."

He worked a dry knot down his throat. "I try. But I'm only human." We sat in silence for a spell. "Why in the world do you want to know about this, Dibs? Again about the Saunders?"

Although it took some leg-pulling, he'd favored me with the truth. He'd earned some pay-back. "Because I want to find out what happened to Thomas Saunders."

"Why? It's not your place. You're a teenage schoolgirl, not a law-enforcement—"

"Because it *is* my place, Dad! The sheriff's not doing his job, even you said that!"

"That's true, but—"

"I've been…dreaming about Thomas Saunders. He wants me to find out what happened to him."

Dad straightened. Looked at me. Reacting carefully, measuring every move and word. Scared to set off the crazy girl, the one taking after her mother, the neighbor, a rampant crazy epidemic.

But this week, both of us had grown a bit.

With more quiet respect than usual, Dad said, "Dibby, I appreciate that. But you know you shouldn't put too much stock into dreams."

"Rightly so, but this is different. I've seen things that I shouldn't, things I know are the absolute truth. Pointing me toward Thomas's murderer."

"Dibby…there's no proof that Thomas Saunders was murdered. A monster certainly didn't eat him, either. He ran away." Dad rattled off the official line behind Thomas's disappearance, but in a dull monotone, one void of conviction.

"Do you really believe that, Dad? Deep down in your craw?"

"Well, as long as we're talking about craws …" He flashed a quick grin, then just as suddenly dumped it. "No. I don't think Thomas ran away."

"Hallelujah!" I nearly pulled a victory cartwheel. "Dad, it's not too late to help Evelyn Saunders."

Puzzled, he gave his head a little shake.

"Help me. Help me find out the truth about Thomas Saunders. Make things right. Not just for Thomas. For Evelyn. And maybe for yourself, too."

Silence stretched into an eternity. Dad retreated behind closed eyes. When he opened them, he brought along clarity. "Okay, Dibby, fine. But we do it by my rules. Everything aboveboard and legal. Nothing danger-ous. You don't do anything without my accompaniment. And you defi-nitely don't go calling on the Saunders. Agreed?"

"Absolutely." *Absolutely not.* Not after the highly irregular visit I had planned for the Saunders, one Dad or the law wouldn't abide by for a second.

Because, now more than ever, I knew—those dang bones acting up again—what Hettie had told me was right on the nose. Everything had started at the Saunders' homestead and that's where it would end.

* * *

Plum-tuckered and bone-weary, how my grams used to describe herself. Until now, I never rightly understood it, either.

It'd been a while since I'd treated myself to a nice bath, and by gum, I thought I'd earned it. Sure, it was getting on late—well after ten o'clock—but since Dad had his evening tonic to prep him for bed, I may as well let a nice, warm bath caress me into a relaxed state.

In the bathroom, I cracked the window just about four fingers high. I planned on building up a good head of steam. Heavy on the hot faucet, I drew the water.

Much older than me, the tub fit like a glove. The back lip rose high, perfect to rest my head. The opposite end lowered a bit, custom built for my feet to roost on when I slid into the water, immersing myself in deep water and thought. 'Course I never rightly understood why the tub had gold-plated lion paws hoisting it off the floor. Seemed a might odd combination: the white, porcelain body and paws that gleamed like costume jewelry. When I was younger, I'd asked Dad about the paws, absolutely fascinated.

"Why, they take bathers for walks," he'd said in an uncustomary, very non-scientific, flight of fantasy.

Near the faucet, I dumped a heaping handful of Mr. Bubble—a holdover from my childhood I wasn't quite ready to relinquish yet—into the water. A healthy head of bubbles grew, foaming, nearly overflowing. I cut the water, doffed my clothes on the floor, and slipped in.

Every bit as glorious as I'd wanted it to be, the water tended to my abused muscles, soaked my dirt-clogged pores, replenished me. Bubbles tickled my chin, my nose. At the foot of the tub, I tested the dexterity of my toes by flicking bubbles with them. With a wet and warm washcloth over my eyes, I relaxed.

And slipped down into the water.

And kept right on slipping.

I heard, then felt a hollow *thump*, similar to a large stone dropped into a pond.

Water sloshed above me, then volleyed back. I shot up. Inhaled deeply through my draining hair. Yet the tub's contents kept moving, sloshing this way, then that.

Dad had been right. Like a confused dog, the tub carried me in a circular pattern. Tongues of water lapped at the tub's sides.

Frightened, flummoxed, worried I'd fallen asleep—dreaming and most possibly drowning—I flailed my arms about, attempting to wake. But the water felt all too real, a tad on the hot side, cooking my skin into a baby's pink. The tub jagged away from the sink and cut a sharp turn before crashing into the door. Water splashed out onto the floor. My hands slipped across the tub's slick sides, failing to grasp a solid hold. The tub's nowhere journey hastened. My hind-end scooched down on the bottom, dragged my head back under the water. I reached up, finally latched onto the sides. A strain on my arm muscles, I pulled hard, broke the water. And gasped in a great, big breath.

Right before hands snatched my ankles and yanked me back under.

Inexplicable hands inside the tub with me.

I thrashed my legs, kicked up more bubbles. Prepared for the soap product's sting, I opened my eyes. I saw nothing, but felt the hands slip away. Only to return to my shoulders. Strong hands attached to stronger arms held me under. They moved up, slipped around my throat. I gripped the wrists, pulled at them. My feet lashed out, stirred up a whirlpool. I twisted, yanked at the hands. Dug my fingernails into my assailant's flesh. The iron grip held.

My lungs burned, ached for release. Dizziness took me, at first frightening, then strangely relaxing. Multi-colored dots paraded before me, dancing in the now-settling water. I'm not rightly sure when the hands released me, but they had. Everything calm, the turbulence passed.

Now I had a very clear view, one to make a mermaid jealous. The water deepened, and I fell with it. Above me, my view of the bathroom ceiling narrowed, grew small, blinked out. I sunk. Soon, the idea of a small, encapsulated bathtub of water just seemed silly. I had free reign, gave into it, and swam deep into a large body of water.

From a distance, something sharked toward me. Not something. Someone. In his underwear, Thomas Saunders fishtailed up in front of me. A few bubbles popped from his lips. His dark hair waved like seaweed.

The other boy, the blond I'd seen earlier—Boot's grandson, Richard—swam up behind him. His motions slowed by the water, Thomas raised his hand, gestured for me to follow him. The two boys took off, their feet kicking up a gentle current behind them.

I pedaled after them, no match for their speed. In the distance, they appeared no larger than flesh-colored tadpoles. The harder I tried to kick, the farther behind I fell, nearly at an irritating stand-still.

Darkness blotted over the boys, swallowed them like ink from an octopus. The blossoming black cloud rushed toward me, formless, massive, terrifying. Undisguised death.

The black mass expanded, swallowed the body of water, became it. Thick and murky like oil, it enveloped me, squeezed hard. I panicked, kicked, tried to scream, but I had no voice.

The substance encasing me hardened. Able now to fight against something solid, I punched at it. My tomb's walls flaked, crumbled around me. I clawed and climbed. Light poked through at the top, just a peep. I thrust an arm through and felt fresh, beautiful air cool my skin. I hauled myself topside and burst through the ground. Rolled over, inhaled deeply. And looked up into arms of cornstalks welcoming me. Clouds rolled across the moon, putting a face on it. Winking at me.

Back where it all started. Smack dab in the middle of the Saunders' cornfield.

Frankly, I thought I was dead. Instead of finding out what'd happened to the two missing boys, I'd joined 'em in death. While I didn't put too much stock into the notion of an afterlife, a cornfield left a lot to be desired.

But then I realized how badly my body hurt. My lungs burned, put through the ringer and finely abused. Surely, if I'd journeyed down the post-life road, my aches wouldn't have aches on top of them. I bit down on the space between my thumb and forefinger, gave it a good chomp. I yelped. Blood seeped from a puncture.

I rallied with a cheer. Pain was generally a sensation reserved for the living, I reckoned. Granted, I found myself in a mighty peculiar state and place, one I didn't know how to get out of exactly, but if I'd been saddled with a gift horse, I didn't intend to go exploring its mouth.

A familiar sound stopped my reverie, set my heart into overtime. Ground-shaking footfalls stormed through the cornfield. Nearby shrieks of hysteria rose. From both Hedrick and Thomas Saunders.

I parted two cornstalks, privy to a front-row seat of the tragedy about to unfold. Tonight, I'd finally witness an ending, I just knew it.

Across from me, Thomas cowered, tucked up inside himself. Stalks that touched him shook, spread his palpable fear.

The scythe cut through and Hedrick followed. Panting, sweating, eyes agog.

"Thomas?" He said, his voice calm, very human. "Tommy? Where are you, son?"

Thomas didn't answer.

"Come on out, son." Hedrick looked in all directions, then lowered his gaze. "It'll be all right. I aim to get us outta here. Just you and me, son. We'll be just fine. Tommy?"

Hedrick spotted Thomas. He heaved the scythe behind him, down the path he'd trampled. Dropped to his knees. Arms out, he beckoned to his son. "There you are. Come here, son."

At last, Thomas crawled out and into Hedrick's waiting arms. Hedrick hugged and Thomas gave back, the two of them fitting together natural as love.

In the shadows, a third figure crept out from Hedrick's forged path. The scythe rose, scarred the moon's face. The weapon swooshed down. Thunked into Hedrick's back, the sound of a watermelon chunked apart. Hedrick's eyes burst wide. Thomas shrieked. Hedrick fell forward. His face hit the dirt. Dead eyes glowered at me.

Thomas cried. He tucked his head between bent knees, wrapped his arms around them, and set to rocking. Shutting out the death of his beloved father and closing off the rest of the world.

A bad wind, riding shotgun with evil, spat through the field. Corn stalks rattled like bones. A whistle wheezed through the field, a train plummeting down, down, dead straight into Hell.

The killer stepped into the moonlight. No longer beautiful, Evelyn

Saunders had transformed into a monster, a mythical Medusa. Her hair lifted on the wind, snaky tendrils held aloft. Her big, wild eyes saw nothing. Through clenched teeth, she made a sound, not quite a cry, not quite a growl. The scythe dropped from her hands, thumped down at her feet.

Blood dotted her chest, spattered her skirt.

Along with the wind, Thomas's cries died.

Petrified to move, something itched on my forehead. I risked it, scratched. Pulled away a smear of blood. Hedrick's blood. Then the warm, rich liquid kept rolling down my face, soaking me. I tried to keep my eyes open, I surely did, but my vision tinted red.

Waves of flowing blood rolled into the cornfield. Soon, only the tips of the tallest stalks rose above the red tide, and I floated into the sea of blood. I let it take me, far downstream, away from the murder and madness. I closed my eyes. And sunk, seeking calm.

When I opened my eyes, the blood had turned clear. Water again. From a distance, the two boys waved at me. This time I had no trouble catching up to them.

Yet Thomas and Richard—still typical boys, after all, even while dead—aggravatingly played a game of water tag with me, always staying just out of reach.

Above, light filtered through the water. An unnatural off-yellow light provided by a bulb.

Thomas rolled over on his back, stuck his head up above the waterline.

Then his head flushed back under, held in place by two hands. One moved to grip his throat. Thomas's feet thrust out frantically. His small, weak hands gripped the killer's hands to no avail. The strong hands—a man's hands with tiny hairs floating on the knuckles—held him under until the life left Thomas's frail frame. His body went limp. Then drifted back and forth slowly, peacefully, falling like a feather. Falling down into the depths of darkness, until he resembled just a white speck on a black velvet landscape. Then—just like his sad, shortened life—he blinked out of existence.

I turned around. Richard, too, followed Tommy down the drain of life. Fading, fading, gone.

The man's hands withdrew from the water.

Damned determined to see who killed Thomas and Richard, I swam toward the light, the waterline. I burst through the water and gasped in a hideous sounding intake of air. Cool air slapped me.

I sat in my bathtub. Alone in my bathroom. I peeked over the side, ensuring the tub's lion claws were at a standstill.

Other than spilled water next to the tub, everything appeared as I'd left it. Before I departed on my strange trip.

Quickly, I jumped out of the bathtub. Breathing hard, eyes locked onto the tub, I grabbed a towel. Wrapped it around myself. Then sat on the closed toilet. I didn't imagine my future held many more baths.

My hand throbbed. Sure enough, my skin showed remnants of my teeth marks.

I didn't rightly understand what I'd just experienced. Didn't know if I wanted to, either. Part dream, part vision maybe, just like Thomas's cornfield visits.

Undoubtedly, though, I now knew who'd murdered Hedrick. But someone else had done away with the missing boys. Drowned 'em. A man.

Which tossed my Sooter sisters theory on top of the trash heap. Still, they were mixed up in the mess, and I needed to find out how.

Too exhilarated to go to bed, maybe a tad scared, I sat on the hard porcelain for a good bit of time.

Back in my bedroom, I grabbed the box off the top shelf of my closet—the box stuffed full of my childhood discards—and pardoned Rags, my teddy bear, from his stay in his cardboard prison.

Together, we tucked in and kept the bedside lamp burning the rest of the night.

* * *

A rooster beat me awake, but not by much. The early bird had nothing on me. I had places to be, people to meet, murderers to uproot.

The cool, early morning temperature sat right by me. The horizon bled from dark to light blue. In the dew-tipped grass, I walked my bike toward the road, avoiding the gravel drive so as not to wake Dad. On the road, I paddled slowly past the Saunders' homestead.

Wind ruffled through the cornfield, Thomas's purgatory. Leaves twittered, rattled like paper flags. They waved at me, a welcome, knowing full well I'd come back tonight.

Filtered sunlight struck the Saunders' barn, rendered it a darker, duller shade of red, blood red. Pink-dappled skies gussied up the house with a deceptively innocent color. On the top floor, a steepled attic, a curtain withdrew through an open window, then exhaled out.

A moan drifted out, rode the wind, then muddied into sobs. A woman's voice, Evelyn's voice.

Sadness gripped me, wouldn't let go. I couldn't really say why, either.

In fact, everything about today felt different. Menace hung in the air, a dangerous squall ready to unleash. No doubt about it, dark forces were at work, stirring things to a boil.

As I rode down the road, Mrs. Saunders crying faded like a forgotten dream.

At the Oak Grove Road intersection, I stopped. Just took in the tranquility of the early morning. Night wouldn't quite give up its squatters' rights just yet, spotty darkness still hanging on. Birds woke, sung to one another. Somewhere off in the distance, a cow lowed and sparked some imitators.

Down the road, I spotted a lone figure, bopping up and down, marching to his own beat. Boot Gundersen, dressed in his military clothes, empty shirtsleeve pinned to his chest, on his way to the telephone company. He raised his hand, and I waved back. Hand cupped around his mouth, he hollered at me, his words meaningless barks in the distance. Downright insistent he sounded, but urgency rimmed everything he said.

But I didn't have time for a long-winded chat with Boot. I waved again, got on my way.

I had an important meeting with a couple of witches to tend to.

This early, downtown appeared to be a ghost town. Just a couple of vacant autos lined the street. Sunlight struck the empty storefronts, dazzling diamonds in coal. As I rode past Mr. Simonson's drug store window, my reflection distorted in a funhouse manner.

Unimpeded by traffic and townsfolk, I sped through the street. Directly ahead, Stoney had returned to his natural perch, locked down where he belonged. Gently, I set my bike next to the block he sat on, said, "Morning, Stoney."

He just glared ahead, vacant gray eyes ignoring me. Innocently pretending like he hadn't been chasing us last night.

I walked up the steps, gave no mind to the *Library Closed* sign, and put my hand on the door knob. The door beat me to the punch and clicked. In exaggerated library silence, the door swung open.

Soon as I stepped through the double set of doors, the front door automatically locked behind me. The tiny snap echoed through the walls of books. Now I knew how a mouse in a trap felt. My breath buzzed in my ears. Every footstep I put forward ricocheted right back at me.

On the front desk, a black candle burned. Set into a brass holder, the candle's flame danced, formed a dark shadow of a woman on the wall behind. Behind the desk, the office door stood ajar, an invitation meant only for me. As if sleepwalking, drawn by the flame, I bumped through the swinging gate and headed toward the office, a room never seen but often wondered about.

The door handle nearly gave me freezer burn. I yanked my hand back, elbowed the door open.

Yvette and Miriam sat at the end of a long table. Another dark candle burned brightly in front of them. Clad in black dresses, the material on their shoulders poofed up. Considered mighty stylish back in ol' Salem days, I imagined.

Grim and dour—nothing new under the sun there—they remained as unmoving as Stoney.

"Good morning, Dibby," said Yvette. Miriam nodded her acquaintance. "Please have a seat." Miriam gestured toward the end of the table. "We've been expecting you."

I sat. My wobbly knees very much appreciated it.

Miriam grabbed her sister's arm, went through a routine of tugs and nudges.

"We would like to remind you to refrain from saying 'ain't'," offered Yvette.

Turned into a frog, my heart extracted through my ears, these things I'd expected. Anything but a grammar lesson. "Excuse me?"

"There's no excuse for improper grammar. Last night, when you confronted our gargoyle, you said 'ain't' twice. Extremely ill-bred." Yvette tsked. Miriam tried to.

"Well, I rightly apologize for that, ma'ams. But I kinda feel that doesn't hold a candle to your sending Stoney out to do me harm."

Miriam appeared on the verge of a seizure. Her head swayed in a trance-like circle, her mouth gulping like an obscene fish out of water.

Yvette interpreted. "Miriam finds that quite hilarious. She's beside herself."

"My lack of safety ain't…sorry, *isn't* very funny to me. Not from where I'm sitting, at least."

"Oh, Dibby, you're a curious girl. Lately, you've surprised us."

"Think I surprised myself a bit, too," I mumbled.

"Dear child…on what plain of existence could you possibly think my sister and I would ever want to harm you? Why, we're both actually very fond of you." They displayed their fondness by remaining stonier than their pet gargoyle. Miriam nodded three times, though, big show for her.

"Well, that feeling used to go both ways, ladies. Before you sent Stoney after me." I held my ground, yet not Miriam's unwavering gaze.

"For a moment, let's pretend such a preposterous idea is true, Dibby, and for—"

"It is. Witchcraft. Your witchery brought Stoney to life, and you sent him after me."

The right side of Yvette's mouth hitched. Miriam's left portion of her lips flicked. Between them, they formed a near smile. "You've been reading the wrong type of books, Dibby. Perhaps we should've steered you clear of such wild flights of fantasy as *Frankenstein* and—"

"Dagnabbit, let's just get on with it! Forgive my impertinence, but we all know you're witches! I'm not gonna spill your secret to anyone. I just want to know why you sent Stoney to kill me!"

The sisters turned toward one another. Finally, Yvette said, "Very well. We've always known you're a bright girl, Dibby. It's true, we are witches. And, yes, we sent our gargoyle servant after you. But, answer us this…did he hurt you?"

I paused. I'd never gotten past what I imagined he'd do to me. "I suppose not."

"Did he threaten you in any manner?"

"No. Gave us quite a fright, though."

"Yes, well, I suppose to the uninitiated, 'Stoney,' as you call him, might present a rather disturbing sight." Miriam shrugged, tossed up *Who's to say?* hands. "But, know this, Dibby… Not for one minute were you in danger from our servant. But you *are* clearly in danger from others. Which is why we took it upon ourselves to liberate our gargoyle to watch over you. As you surmised, I kept tabs on you through its eyes. And Miriam listened."

Stoney as a watchdog hadn't been something I'd considered. I felt dumb as a box of rocks, no offense to Stoney himself. "So…you were worried about me?" Twin nods. "And you sent Stoney to safeguard me?"

"He's excellent at keeping us informed. Unfortunately, his bones aren't what they used to be. Other than flight, he moves rather slowly, old age catching up to him. Happens to all of us. Isn't that right, Miriam?" Miriam entwined her fingers, flexed, and cracked a slew of knuckles. "So, our servant's limited in how much actual safeguarding he can do. But we've been keeping our eyes on you through him. Oh, yes, we have." She tapped her dark glasses.

"Why? Why not just come to me? *Talk* to me, dang it."

Miriam dropped hands onto the table, sulked. "Oh, dear, you really must watch your tongue, Dibby," said Yvette. "Truth of the matter is, we wanted you to abandon your silly Nancy Drew aspirations, particularly in regards to the poor missing Saunders boy. What we actually know as fact about the entire sordid situation surrounding that family doesn't amount to much more than an anthill of rumor. And as librarians, of course, we would never fall back upon rumor."

They beamed. Somewhere, celestial librarians blared trumpets.

"Of course," I said.

"One thing we *do* know for a fact is you're involving yourself in a dangerous situation."

"You don't say."

"Excuse me?" The sisters frowned, leaned forward.

"Sorry. Why do you reckon my peeking into the Saunders' affairs is so dangerous?"

"Dibby Caldwell!" Miriam slammed down her fist, the physical portion of her sister's indignation. "We do not 'reckon'! The very idea. It's uncouth." Miriam nodded, formal lower lip stuck out. "But it doesn't take a coven of witches to see the whole town's in an uproar over your antics." Again, Miriam lolled around on her seat, cawing silently to crows everywhere.

Once Miriam worked the hilarity out of her system, Yvette continued. "The entire circumstances surrounding Hedrick and Thomas's disappearances have always been subject to idle gossip. Most people—including your father, I must say—have suspected foul play for a while. But there are forces at work, those we can't intuit or divine, people who want the entire matter hushed." Miriam tsked. "They've done a fine job for years. Until you reopened old wounds. And might we ask why the Saunders family has become so crucial to you?"

"Thomas's ghost started appearing to me. I think he wants me to find out what happened to him."

The witches took it in stride, nodded, a ho-hum day in the dark arts of the arcane. "Now, that certainly explains a lot, doesn't it, Miriam?" I wondered if Miriam ever got tired of nodding.

"And I really don't understand why Thomas picked me. Or why he decided to throw me into this mess now and not before."

"The answer to that is quite simple, Dibby, something we've long suspected about you. You have the gift. Not everyone has it, but you've been gifted with the special sight that allows you to see beyond this world. It's something that comes with insight and age."

"Some gift...can I take it back?" The sisters responded to this request with grim silence. "Anyhow, I know I'm putting a lotta bees in folk's bonnets," I said. "Seems like everyone in town's got some say in the matter, but won't tell me boo about the truth. Would you ladies care to enlighten me on anything?"

"If we knew something of import, we'd surely tell you, Dibby. As we've said…we're rather fond of you and wouldn't like to see you harmed. But sometimes even witches can't uncover well-cloaked secrets. Who's to say why? Some things—*dark* things—are beyond anyone's ability to uncover, buried deep as they are. Be wary of everyone. Heed our words, Dibby Caldwell, *everyone*."

I nodded. "Words to live by, I reckon." They sighed at my faux pas. "So…I'm sorry to ask this, but…why do you think Hettie might've implicated you ladies in the whole affair?"

Their jaws dropped, aghast. "Us? Why…that's ridiculous! And what on earth are you talking about?"

"Um, well… After she died, Hettie visited me."

Yvette sighed. "I suppose Hettie's *still* trying to cause trouble for us." Naturally, Hettie's ghostly visit didn't confound them, but her prank from beyond shook the sisters to their core. "How, pray tell, did she implicate us?"

"She drew a six-pointed star on my dad's freezer door. A hexagram. I thought she meant a witch had done away with her."

"Hmph." Both Sooters tapped long fingernails on the table. In front of them, the candle whiffed out. No doubt Hettie's ears burning from the beyond.

After a long pause, Yvette withdrew a piece of paper and pencil from a folder on the table and scooted them toward me. "To the best of your memory, recreate Hettie's drawing. Michelangelo, she wasn't, after all." The sisters shared another creepy laugh.

As the image had been permanently branded within my brain, I drew the six-pointed star with ease. "There. A hexagram." I passed it to Yvette, who moved it toward Miriam. Miriam frowned, squeezed and tugged at her sister's long, black sleeve.

"Miriam says what you've drawn isn't a hexagram," said Yvette.

"Sure it is! It's got six points and everything!"

"Child, are you going to argue with actual witches?" Yvette's eyebrows lifted above her glasses, a spooky reminder of what lurked below.

"No, ma'am."

Clearly fed up, Miriam grabbed the pencil and paper and embellished my drawing. She held it up, rattled the paper. Yvette deciphered the hieroglyphics. "*This* is a hexagram." Miriam had added a circle around the star. "A six-pointed star is just a six-pointed star without the circle enclosing it. At least as it pertains to witchcraft. Did Hettie draw the circle?"

"No…"

The sisters sat back, their broad smiles pregnant with self-satisfaction. "Well, then, all this skullduggery has nothing to do with witchcraft after all. We've been exonerated."

Not really. But I wasn't about to argue. "But what else could it possibly mean?"

Yvette shook her head. "Dear child…one thing we know about our in-transit sister is she was a prankster of the first order. If she saw a way to pull the wool over someone's eyes, she'd jump at the opportunity. If you ask us…she was having fun at your expense."

I didn't think so, not by a country mile. Hettie seemed to have gone through a lot of trouble—even pain—to come back just to play a joke on me. "I don't know…"

"Sometimes a six-pointed star is just a six-pointed star," said Yvette. "Now…the library's preparing to open." She said it like the library would open on its own, a living entity. Didn't sound wrong to me, not this morning. "And we know you have school to attend. So…is there anything else we can help you with?"

"No, ma'ams."

"Then there's something you can help us with, Dibby." Again they leaned forward, hunkering over the table in grand inquisition style. "Never, ever, *ever* destroy library property again, young lady."

I gulped, taken aback. I thought they'd long forgotten the article James swiped. "Yes, ma'ams." I cowered back a bit.

"Are we sure we have an understanding?" Yvette's shadow stretched out onto the tabletop, across the room, and kept creeping. "Do we?"

"Yes!"

"Are you…ssssssurrre?" Half-cat, half-snake, Yvette dragged the word out with relish. And her shadow just kept on coming.

I didn't know what else to say. A fly caught in their web, I literally stood there shaking in my boots.

With great deliberation, Yvette slowly drew her hand up toward her face. Her fingers settled on her eyeglasses, prepared to whip them off, and stun me with her horrific, eggy eyes.

I screamed, "Yes, ma'ams! Never again! I'm so sorry, so very, really sorry! Anything I can do to help pay—"

"That's fine." Yvette withdrew her hand. Then she chuckled, actually chuckled! "That won't be necessary, Dibby. We'll take you at your word. Overall, you're a good girl."

"Yes, ma'ams!" I made to leave.

"Dibby?"

I turned. "Ma'am?"

"As your father told you last night…human monsters are the real threat." Stalled in time, the sisters didn't move. "Even though Hangwell may have its share of the more fanciful kind of monsters lurking just out of eye-shot…they're not the ones who'll hurt you."

Via Stoney or other means, the sisters had overheard my conversation with Dad last night. Shivers rippled down my back, rode up my arms, and camped out on my neck. I wondered if Stoney—and the sisters— had witnessed my haunted bath.

Miriam clapped her hands. Yvette stood, said, "Very well, Dibby. Tah-tah. Don't be late. We certainly hope to see you visiting the library once again now that we've cleared the air."

"I surely will." I hurried toward the office door.

"And let us know if you have any more visits from dear Hettie. If you do, there're some words we'd like passed onto her."

Not fancying to be their conduit to the dead, I nodded but didn't actually commit. But they reminded me of something that'd been bugging me.

Standing safely outside the office door, I leaned in, tentatively muttered, "Miss Sooter? And Miss Sooter? You mind if I ask you a question?"

"Go ahead," said Yvette. Miriam circled a permissive finger.

"What…um, what do you intend on doing with your sister's remains?"

"That's a question you may not ask," snapped Yvette.

The door slammed shut, missing my nose by but a hair.

Sure as shooting, the library began to wake up. Curtains pulled back in front of windows. Rings clawed over rods. Somewhere in back, a succession of doors shut, one after the other: *bam, bam, bam*! The candle on the counter extinguished. A ghostly thread of smoke curled up into an improbable question mark. Lights clicked on, buzzed, spread wake-up calls to their kin. Clouds of dust swept through the air, swirled, as if a mouth in the floor had opened up to blow them away.

I galloped toward the front doors. As a courtesy, the library opened them for me.

My gaze set on my bike, I scrambled down the stairs. Out of the corner of my eye, I saw Stoney sitting there.

I didn't want to look, absolutely couldn't look, so help me it was the last thing in the world I wanted to do was look…

I looked.

Stoney's head was turned toward me, not locked down in its usual straight-on position.

One heavy stone eyelid—an eyelid I never even noticed he had 'til now—dropped, then lifted quickly. A wink.

And I left faster than a wink.

* * *

Even though I'd tarried longer than I'd meant to at the library, I still got to school in plenty of time. I had a mission to formulate and finalize. Now I just had to recruit my team.

I waited by the bike rack until James finally pulled up.

"Hey."

"Hey, yourself," I said. "We got lots to catch up on." Hordes of students surrounded us, laughing, shoving, jostling for attention. For privacy, I grabbed James's arm and dragged him over to the side of the building.

We flopped down onto the grass. First thing, James dug deep into his pocket and plucked out a pathetic cigarette, bent around like a boomerang.

I grasped it, broke it, handed it back.

He stared at the destroyed pieces with the sad eyes of a mother bird hovering over a sick baby. "Dammit, Dibs, that was my last one!"

"You've been on your last one for some time now. Where in the world do you keep coming up with those nasty things? Nobody round here's gonna sell 'em to you. You a magician of sorts?"

"Mackleby the Magnificent!" He spread his hands above him. "Making cigarettes appear out of—"

"Hush. Won't do either one of us a lick of good if a teacher hears you carrying on about smoking. Now, listen…" He did, enraptured, a good audience no matter how crazy my story grew. Then I told him my plan. Of which he'd play an instrumental part.

"So…you're finally ready to let me back into your good graces, huh?" More than my tales of spooks and haunting and witches, all that seemed to matter to him was my forgiveness. Hardly a rational person's reaction, it warmed me nonetheless.

He grinned. I couldn't help it and served a smile back to him. "I don't have much choice. With your dubious skills, you're the best person for the job. Think you can handle it?"

"Does a bear shit in the woods?" asked James.

"First, that's just really disgusting. Second, I don't really have a need to know a mammal's bathroom habits. Again…can you handle the job?"

"Yep. Sure can."

"Fine and dandy. Come 'round tonight. Soon as dusk starts settling in, say about eight to eight-thirty."

"I'll be there. You can count on me, baby."

Our eyes locked. Just as they had the other night, during our first kiss. I felt more than knew what would come next. I wasn't ready. Not yet.

He leaned in. I counter-balanced, putting my spine to the test by bending inhumanly backward. I pressed my fingertips to his chest, put him back in his place.

"What's the matter?" he asked.

"Right now, James, I'm welcoming you back as a friend. We're gonna take things nice and easy, one step at a time, before we leap further ahead. So don't mess this up."

"Me? Mess things up?" He held splayed fingertips to his chest, an innocent look.

"Don't play dumb. If things are meant to work out between us, we'll let time chisel away at the rocky parts." Quickly, I stood.

All eyes were on us. At my feet, James rolled about in exaggerated grief, making quite the spectacle of himself, a spectacle of us. Usually, I'd have blushed red and withdrawn into myself. But maybe it was my time to shine. Maybe I needed to embrace some light. It felt so good, very right, and I wanted everyone to know it.

Still on the ground, James hollered, "You're putting me through the ringer, baby!"

I giggled, started walking away. "That's where you belong after everything you've done."

"Wait, Dibs!"

I turned around. Of course my cheeks set to burning. But today, instead of hiding, I chose to wear them proudly.

Up on his knees, hands folded, James pleaded. "Come on, Dibs! I'm gone over you!" His voice rose.

My hidden little schoolgirl ventured out for recess. I held fingertips to my lips, giggled. Like my classmates, I watched the show.

"What's it gonna take for me to prove my undying love?" he shouted, face screwed up in mock agony. "Dibby Caldwell, you're one primo girl! Be my main squeeze! I want the whole world to know how I feel about you!" His voice rose, hammy as Easter and louder than the Fourth of July. His hands thumped over his heart. Shot by Cupid. "You're the ginchiest, Dibby Caldwell, and I'm way, way gone!"

The first school bell rang, killing James's performance.

I could've watched more.

Completely unlike me, today I shared my smile with everyone who'd look. My head held high, I strolled past my classmates; classmates who'd previously thought I was a placeholder at best, classmates who looked at me in a different light now that the fab new boy had fallen for me. Just as James had, they viewed me with different, fresh eyes.

Nothing else mattered. For a brief moment, all things threatening and spooky and unearthly buried themselves back where they belonged.

Then I bumped into Suzette.

"Watch where you're going, Dibby!" Her sneer spread. She patted her hair, although it didn't really make a lick of difference seeing as how she sprayed cement on it every morning.

"Frankly, Suzette, I dunno how you can see where you're walking," I said. "Not with that poodle attacking your scalp."

Instead of our battle escalating as our typical ritual, we surrendered a laugh. She chortled, a sound she quickly tried to stifle. A wary truce had been met. Although I reckoned we both held onto a little ammo behind our backs, just in case.

"Hey, I'm sorry again for the way Angela treated you at the theatre the other night." Suzette didn't look me in the eye, just sorta side-stepped and curtsied into guiltlessness. "I told her to never do it again."

"I appreciate it, but it doesn't really matter—"

"You should've seen what someone did to her dress, though! She was covered in mustard and ketchup and—"

"I'm sure it suited her winning personality just fine. Listen, the other day you said you wanted to come over. See a ghost."

Her eyes grew round. "You mean it? Can I really—"

"I can't promise you a ghost. But how would you like to help catch a real-life murderer?"

Chapter Fifteen

The stage had been set. The players stood behind the curtains, an unlikely team. I'd never even wanted Suzette and James within the same vicinity again, but now I'd intentionally partnered them together.

Things change, I reckoned. Life moves ahead. Folks modify, or at least, try their best.

And plans develop.

"I still don't know why you asked that sosh, Suzette, to come with us," groused James.

"And here I thought you'd want her along. Maybe still sweet on her."

On our front lawn, he rolled over on his back. A real affinity to dogs, James had been spending an inordinate amount of time in the grass lately, it seemed. "Come on, Dibs, don't start again. You're the only one who floats my boat."

"Sing another tune." Although, honestly, I never tired of hearing this one.

"Only songs I know are the ones in my heart. Ones that rhyme with Dibby… Lessee. Dibby, you make me…squibby…"

"Stop already. Before I lob tomatoes and keelhaul you." I plucked the long strand of grass from between my teeth and flicked it away. I dropped beside him. "Now leave ol' Suzette alone. I need her special skills."

"She's got skills?"

"Sorta. She's the only one I know who can whine and cry and pitch a fit on demand and adults still find her adorable. I know I can't do that. Can you?"

"Wouldn't want to."

"Then hush and stick to what you know. As long as you can get me through the Saunders' back door, then I'll be done with you."

He grabbed my arm, tried to tug me toward him. "Aw, you need me for more than that, Dibs."

"Cut it out." I shirked away. "We need to focus on the job ahead."

James puffed out his cheeks. The air escaped in an annoying wheezy squeak. "So…what are you trying to do anyway?"

"Thought that was clear. Find out the truth about Thomas."

"Well…we already know Evelyn Saunders killed her husband. But since she's not a ghost and everything, she's not the one who cut your back, right?"

"I've been giving that some consideration. I reckon the scythe-wielder was just a manifestation from Thomas. As were the rest of the 'ghosts' in the cornfield. And that's why it sounded like a giant crashing through the cornfield. I suspect Thomas is a mighty powerful ghost, able to stir ecto-plasm and…" Based on James's lost look, that cute indentation folded between his eyes where brains should've been, I quit explaining.

"Wait. You think a ghost like Thomas can create other ghosts?" he asked.

I sighed. "James, I thought you considered yourself a horror fan. Have you ever read any of the classics?"

"Sure." He looked up, one eye shut. "*Uncanny Tales. Boris Karloff's Tales of Mystery. Tales from the Crypt.* You know, all the greats."

"I ain't talking about comic books!" I gripped a handful of grass, tossed it in his face. "But, yes, to simplify matters, I s'pose you can say Thomas made up all the other cornfield ghosts."

"Huh. Got it." Clearly, he didn't get it. "So…if Evelyn Saunders killed her husband, doesn't it make sense she did away with her son, too? Maybe even Boot's grandson for some wild reason?"

"You just don't listen to a thing I say." I thumped his head with a finger. "Evelyn didn't do away with the boys. A man did."

"Oh…right. The hairy knuckles. Who do you think they belong to?"

"I've been giving a lotta thought to that. I'm kinda leaning toward Evelyn's brother, Devin."

"What? That's bananas! Doesn't even make sense." James sat up.

"Purt near nothing makes sense anymore. But he's my best bet right now."

"I'm still not sure what you think is gonna happen with your nutty plan."

I shrugged. Frankly, I had no idea either. But on a wing and a prayer, I hoped we would do right by the missing boys. "I s'pose I'm hoping for things to go the way of TV shows. A confession would fit the bill nicely."

James nodded. "Things usually don't happen like those cop shows, though."

"Don't you curse us!"

"Geez Louise, sorry! Peace already!" Behind protective hands, he chuckled. "Dibs?"

"Hm?"

"When this is all over…you know, all the ghosts and murders and investigations and stuff… Would you go on a date with me? A real date, I mean."

I smiled, but not too sunny. "I'm still in consideration."

He groaned, fell on his back. Raised his arms to the unfair Heavens. "What've I gotta do? I've done everything, I've—"

"It's not what you've gotta do; it's what you already gone and done."

"Even your old man's keen on me! Why—"

"Is not! Dad's highly suspect of you."

"Well…he seemed glad to see me when I came over tonight."

"He let you in. That hardly rates as pig-in-a-pen happy."

"He let you know I was at the door."

"He wanted to get rid of you," I said. "He's got a lot on his mind what with Hettie in the basement."

James shuddered. "Has she…ah, visited you again?"

"No. But I'm gonna sic her on you if you don't behave."

A fancy-schmancy Chevy took its sweet time crunching down the road. In front of our house, it crawled to a stop, then turned into the drive. I didn't recognize the driver, a colored woman. But I surely recognized the mess of twisted, bouncy curls riding next to her.

"You gotta be kidding me," said James. "Suzette couldn't have taken her bike?"

"I betcha she doesn't even own a bike. Probably born in a Rolls Royce. They had to pry the silver spoon outta her mouth with a crowbar."

Suzette, dressed in a pink and white collision of frills and lace, stood by her open car door, chatting with the driver. The woman shook her head, appeared hesitant about letting Suzette out of her sight. Finally, the she-beast won out and the Chevy backed down the driveway.

Suzette spotted us, rolled her eyes, and approached. "Either of you boys seen Dibby? I was supposed to meet her here."

"My, oh my, you gave me a fright," I said. "We don't see too many clowns around these parts. Did the circus leave you behind?"

James ignored the verbal arrows and asked Suzette, "Was that your chauffeur?"

"No, silly," she tittered. "We don't have a chauffeur. That was our maid." She frowned, lips pouted out like chewing gum bubbles. "The nerve of that woman! She acts like she's my mother. Doesn't let me go anywhere without her. I swan!"

"You have a maid," James said dully.

"Of course, silly! Doesn't everyone?" Suzette wrinkled her nose, looked around. "It smells funny here. Is that all the dead people?"

"No, it's your perfume. Scent of skunk."

"Takes one to know one."

"That's mighty clever, Suzette," I said. "Even if it doesn't make a lick of sense. Did you tell your folks where you were going?"

"Are you kidding me?" Her face contorted into a rabies-stricken beast. "If Momma knew I was coming here, she'd ground me for life! I had to talk the maid into taking me."

"'Course you did. Now that our precious cargo has arrived, let's get to it."

By the time I laid out the plan again, full-on dark had set in. The time I'd been waiting for. The three of us climbed between the fence posts and duck-walked through the Saunders' cornfield. We set up behind the front row to view the house.

"Dang it to heck, Dibby, you didn't say I'd be crawling through dirt." Suzette clipped every syllable precisely, showing her good and annoying upbringing. "My dress is going to get filthy." She swayed her hands over herself like she was a valued Cracker Jack prize.

"Hush," I whispered, "we don't want the Saunders to hear us."

Suzette pouted a bit, hugged herself. Unlike us, she refused to squat and just sort of bent over behind the stalks.

Right on schedule, Devin Meyers stomped out onto the porch. Tonight, his tipped hat—always just to the right—wasn't the only thing tipped about him. He wove a round-about way to his pickup truck, scattershot as all get out. Before his weekly Monday night poker game, Devin had apparently been hitting the bottle, getting warmed up.

The truck snorted, banged an ear-jarring shot out its tailpipe. Then Devin swung the vehicle around and sped out of the drive. Gravel zinged up, hailed down onto the truck's body. A smoke trail hid the truck's departure, but the knocking of the engine eventually slipped away into silence.

"It's time," I said. "Suzette…go be more annoying than ever."

Clearly, she didn't catch on to my backhanded compliment. She grinned, shared her metallic lattice. Eager eyes jumped with anticipation. I imagined she'd never dipped a lacquered toenail into wild waters. Could be I'd uncorked the bottle and let the Genie out. I sorely hoped I wouldn't regret it.

She patted her hair, straightened her dress, and departed. Through the yard, she kept adjusting herself, itching as if she'd just stumbled into a wood tick party. In front of the porch, she stopped. Her shoulders heaved, her fists bunched. She repeated the motion several times until she lathered up a good head of tears.

Her baby-like *boo-hoo-hoo*'s traveled back to us in the cornfield, her silly talents finally put to a humanitarian cause.

Suzette bounded up the steps, her hands pressed at her sides so as to keep her skirt from flying up, and pressed the doorbell. Patience not one of her strengths; she kept banging away at the doorbell.

At last, the door opened. Evelyn Saunders stood there, dark glasses on, cigarette burning between two fingers, looking every bit the washed-up motion picture star from yesteryear.

I couldn't hear what Evelyn said, but Suzette's tirade rang out loud and clear.

"You've…you've…gotta help me. Please, ma'am. Please, oh please, can't you help me find Pockets? He ran away… I was just out walking him not far from here and…he got away from me. Oh, I don't know what I'll do without Pockets. He's my best friend… And my parents will tan my hide! I wasn't supposed to walk him, not by myself… But he needed to… Ohhhhh, please, Miss, can you help me? I just don't…"

Washed-up movie star met the brash, young upstart. Suzette gave the performance of her short, irritating career, and I almost bought into her act myself.

Evelyn leaned over, face to face with Suzette. She gave Suzette a reassuring, yet wary, pat on the back, turned, and vanished inside the house. Quickly, Suzette made the "a-okay" sign, finger meeting thumb to form a circle, smiled at us, then immediately resumed a scrunched up face.

Tissue box and glass in hand, Evelyn reappeared. She ushered Suzette toward the twin rocking chairs that I'd shared with Evelyn the other afternoon. They sat together, rocking. Worse than a suffering critter caught in a bear trap, Suzette's simpering drowned out everything.

I nodded toward James, and we cut left through the cornfield. Above, the moon felt robust tonight, gifting us with an ample belly of spotlight. The field traveled a ways beyond the back of the Saunders' house. Once cleared of the front porch, we broke cover and hightailed it toward the back door.

Three steps up and we stood on the scant back porch. James tried the doorknob. Locked. Usually, in the country, folks tended not to worry too much about burglars, so they left their doors unlocked. Unless they had something to hide, of course.

Hands cupped around his eyes, James peered through one of the door's small windows into the kitchen. He peeled off his jean jacket, wrapped it around his hand, and popped it through the lowest window. Glass tinkled and dropped inside.

Amazed, and not in a good fashion, I grabbed his arm and gave him a mighty shake. "Dang it, you said you knew how to get into houses," I hissed.

He shrugged, his mouth tipping slantwise. "Don't have a cow. We're in, aren't we?" he whispered.

"I thought you were gonna pick the lock, not destroy property!"

"Geez, maybe you want James Bond instead of James Mackleby."

I had a thousand things to say, most of 'em as colorful as Dad in a cross mood, but it seemed pointless; the damage had been done, and time was wasting.

James reached through the window, twisted his arm inside. He bit his lower lip, suffered through a contortion of sorts, then the lock clicked. With his retracted hand, he turned the doorknob. It swung inward.

"Like magic." He sprinkled invisible magic dust with wiggling fingers.

I tiptoed into the kitchen. James followed. From the kitchen doorway, beyond the living room, I made out Evelyn's silhouette, her back against the window. Suzette's sobs rode the air like a particularly foul bout of gas. Evelyn countered with an indecipherable, yet soothing tone. They'd be busy for a spell.

I held my finger to my lip, whispered, "Stay here. Keep an eye on things."

James nodded.

Slowly, nerves jangling, I tiptoed across the kitchen. Just like in our house, the linoleum squeaked. At every outburst beneath me, I winced.

That odd burnt smell smacked me again, haunting in a way I couldn't quite put my finger on. I imagined if sad memories—ones that had a tendency to overshadow life—carried an odor, they'd smell just like the Saunders' house.

Tonight, Evelyn had her burgundy curtains drawn back, allowing in a healthy stream of moonlight. Good news for my secret investigation, bad news if Evelyn happened to turn around to look inside.

The mountains of clutter hadn't been touched since I'd been there before, not that I expected it. Traversing a clear course around the piles proved tricky. I sucked in my gut, slipped sideways through two leaning piles of periodicals. One of them timbered a bit, then wobbled back into balanced complacency. My hip banged into a small table. Figurines wobbled, little sheep and children in prayer clicked against one another. Near the edge, a kneeling boy timbered, his pointed hands leading his dive. Too late, too risky for me to grab for him, I pulled in my breath. The figurine bounced once on the rug's edge, flit up, and landed on the hardwood floor. The clatter was miniscule, the figure unbroken, but I fully expected Evelyn to storm in, scythe above her head.

To my relief, Evelyn still sat bewitched by Suzette's inexplicable spell. Consoling the young girl with half-hearted clichés and phrases, clearer now.

I navigated toward Evelyn's photographic shrine to Thomas, the shelf above the fireplace, the only part of the house where dust carried no business. My hand traveled the rough-hewn shelf until it found the end. Close to the window I stood, just a couple feet away from Evelyn's back. Hand shaking, I grabbed the face-down frame. And lifted it.

I pretty much expected what I saw, a heart-breaking photograph of Boot's grandson, Richard Holmberg. The same blond boy I'd seen in my visions. But unlike in Boot's photo where Richie's aura glowed like a sunbeam, here he looked like hay gone to seed. Thin, unhealthy, cheekbones poked uncomfortably beneath his skin. Darkness around his eyes contrasted with the whites of his eyes. Once-vibrant hair looked dirty, greasy. Knees drawn to his chest, he sat in a corner where a bed met two walls. All of this I'd fairly expected.

What came next I never expected.

Water filled the bottom of the picture frame. The level rose. Sheets at the bottom of Richard's bed lifted atop the tide, floated like ghosts. Top of the waterline, items swirled around in Richard's room: sneakers, underwear, overalls, a teddy bear not too different from Rags, and Lord, did I wish I was back in my own bed with Rags!

Hypnotized, absolutely unable to tear away, my hands glued to the frame, I watched.

The water reached Richard. It lifted him, liquid hands carrying him toward me. Face in frame, Richard opened his mouth in a silent scream.

The glass in the frame broke. Water rushed out, splashed up my arms, soaked the front of my shirt.

I shrieked.

On the porch, Evelyn's voice rose. Footsteps pounded across the floorboards.

Shaking, shivering, I dropped the framed photograph. Watched it twist top over bottom. Richard's tiny hands jutted out from it, grasping for help. The frame smacked hard. In the blink of an eye, the photo snapped back to its original state, Richard on his bed. Nothing awry except the broken frame glass.

Outside, Suzette screamed, too. Her voice trailed off into the night as surely as she had, obviously running away to save her own skin.

The door opened.

Backlit by the moon, Evelyn Saunders stood in her doorway, shoulders up, sunglasses abandoned. Rage personified, her nostrils rose and dropped with each chest-heaving breath.

"You! You little…*bitch*! What…what do you…" She noticed Richard's photograph at my feet. Her gaze moved across the room. With an animalistic roar, she came at me.

"Missus Saunders, I'm sorry! Evvie! I—"

Her hands gripped my throat. She swung me around, a murderous merry-go-round. Magazines cascaded to the floor. Figurines bobbled, shattered to the floor.

I couldn't breathe. In a rasp, I managed, "Evvie, I just want to talk…" It came out garbled.

Our horrific hoe-down continued. The room spun in a sickening circle. Her fingers bit into the back of my neck, her thumbs pushed into my throat. I couldn't muster the energy to pull her hands away. Weak in the legs, I would've collapsed had Evelyn not been holding me up by the throat.

She screeched, ranted, raged. My world wavered.

"You come into my house and sully my Richard? Poor, sweet Richard! I'll kill you, you little bitch, for doing that to Richard! For disturbing Thomas! For—"

"*Mother!*"

The sudden, unexpected shout stopped Evelyn's mad cascade, but my world kept revolving. Evelyn released me from her grip. I toddled in an inebriated circle, then dropped to the floor, coughing. Sick to my stomach, eyes bleary, I looked up.

From the kitchen, from the shadows, James stepped forward. "Mother… It's me… Thomas, your son."

He'd doffed his jean jacket. Brushed back his hair. He wore his soulful puppy-dog eyes, the ones that weakened my will. And damned if he couldn't have passed for an older Thomas with his dark coloring.

"Thomas…" Evelyn hesitated, took a step toward James. "It can't be…"

"It's me, Mother. I've come home." In their beyond slow dance, James took another step.

"You've come home… Finally… I've prayed and prayed… And He's answered me. Oh my God, son…" Evelyn's legs gave out. She thumped down onto her knees. A split in her hose raced up beneath her skirt. She grabbed her head of blonde hair and tugged. A wig fell, leaving a patchwork of matted, shorn hair, anything but movie-star caliber. "Thomas… Come here, Tommy… Mommy needs you."

Never mind the fact she'd just tried to kill me, my heart bled for her. Sobs drowned meaning from her words, but I didn't need to understand them. The intent was clear.

James stared at me, raised his hands in a panicked "What do I do now?" look. I nodded, gestured. *Go to her.*

Unsure as I'd ever seen him, James took baby steps toward Evelyn. When he knelt next to her, Evelyn folded her legs beneath her, settled in.

"Oh, Tommy…"

The sobs just got worse, louder. Evelyn threw herself onto James. Her arms locked around him. Her crying rattled the windows, the grief in the room physical.

"You've come back to me, Tommy... At long last..."

Although I could see James squirming in his own skin, I let Evelyn work out her grief a spell. Even killers—sad killers—were due their emotional release.

Quiet as I could, I went toward them. Sat down. "Evelyn," I said. "I know you've been through a rough patch..." I kept my voice low, soothing as spring water. A trick I'd picked up from Dad's parlor room manner. "But now that Thomas has come back, it's time to get everything out. Get what's bothering you off your chest. Make a clean start of things."

She didn't look at me, just kept hugging on James. But she nodded, released a hand long enough to drag her wrist across her nose.

"Evelyn, what really happened to your husband, Hedrick? With Thomas?" Truthfully, I felt a bit like a heel, grilling a woman at her most vulnerable. As far as rotten tricks went, it was a doozy. But my allegiance lay with the dead boys.

"Hedrick... he found out Thomas...*you*..." She squeezed James harder. He winced and I understood completely. The woman had a surprisingly vice-like clutch. "...he found out that you...wasn't blood kin. That he wasn't your real father." She spoke to James, mouth to his shoulder and directly into his soul. I didn't even exist. "That goddamn ol' witch Hettie told him so! Hedrick, he...he just lost control. Started screaming about how he was gonna take you away from me. That I wasn't fit to be your mother. You...overheard it all." She leaned back, framed James's face in between her hands. "You remember that don't you, Tommy?"

James nodded. She pulled him to her chest, stroked his hair. "'Course you do, Tommy. You're all better now." She broke into a soft hum, rocked James.

I couldn't lose her yet. "Evelyn, what happened next? After Tommy overheard your argument with Hedrick?"

"Well, Tommy, he...*you* took off. Just started crying and running for the fields. Fit to be tied, Hedrick went after you. He grabbed the scythe by the tractor and followed after you. Oh, my Lord…I was so scared. Just petrified! Hedrick was off his rocker, wailing mad. I thought he might hurt you, Tommy… So I ran after the two of you… I caught up, heard Hedrick telling you how he was going to take you away. Take you away from me. My Tommy… I wouldn't have it." She paused, swallowed. Pulled James even closer and I suspected she never wanted to let go.

"Tommy… What happened next… It just happened. I don't even remember it, tell you the truth. Not really. Just…well, next thing I knew… I was standing over Hedrick. All the blood…too much blood… And I'm so sorry you saw it happen. So sorry…"

Evelyn froze, eyes dried up by terror.

"Evelyn? What happened next?" I prodded.

"I didn't know what in Heaven's name to do! So I called your birth daddy, Tommy. He always knew what to do. He helped fix things. But nothing could help fix you, Tommy." Her hands played over James's face as if she were blind. "You never were the same again… My boy… I'm so sorry, sorry for what I did to you, sorry for what you saw that sent you down into your darkness… I'm sorry I killed your daddy in front of you…" Evelyn's tale became non-linear. She repeated things. Spoke nonsense.

I tried to set her proper again. "Evelyn…What happened to Thomas? After he saw you…put Hedrick to rest?"

She looked at me, first time in a bit. Eyes wide and incredulous like I'd just stopped by for a surprise visit. "Tommy just sank into himself. Could barely talk. Wouldn't eat or sleep or play. Just kept moaning, repeating how I'd killed his poppa. Over and over and over and—"

"Of course, Tommy remembers those sad days, Evelyn," I said. "But what happened later? What happened to Tommy?"

Doubt troubled Evelyn's brow. She shook her head, searched inward. I imagined truth and fiction weren't being very companionable in her head. "Why, you ran away, didn't you, Tommy?"

Not a fast learner in improvisation, James looked imploringly at me over her shoulder.

I rolled out my hand along with a dose of impatience.

"Um, no, Mom," he said. "Someone killed me."

Kinda cold and knifing right to the point, but it's where we needed to go.

Evelyn shook her head violently, clamped her eyes tight. "No! That's not true, none of it! You ran away! That's what *he* told me, goddammit! That's why he got me another boy, too! To fill your place 'til you came back to me! 'Course, no one killed you! You're here now, aren't you?" With a tender touch, afraid to break her long-lost son, Evelyn separated from James. She studied him carefully. Her eyes cleared, nostalgia and sadness departed. Anger once again swam to the forefront. "Wait… I don't understand… Who—"

"Evelyn, *who* told you Tommy ran away?" Things looked set to implode. I raised my voice, raced my words together. "Who was Tommy's birth daddy? Is he the one who killed Tommy?"

Finished with James, Evelyn turned on me. "Who the hell are you? What do you want?"

"Missus Saunders… Evvie, it's me, Dibby Caldwell. Remember? I'm your neighbor who—"

"You're not supposed to be here." I don't know how she did it, but in her form-fitting dress, she smoothly and quickly regained her feet, remaining the proper lady while doing so. But there was nothing proper living in her hate-filled eyes. "What do you *want?* Why're you filling my head full of *lies?*" She whipped her head toward James. "You!" She thrust a finger toward him. "You're not my Thomas. He'd never lie to me!" Arms went up, claws out. Like a cornered animal, her gaze bounced wildly about the room. She whirled, whipped open a desk drawer. Light flashed off an object in her hand, a letter opener. "I'll show you both what I did to Hedrick!"

Like a gunshot, the front door bashed open. "What the hell's going on here?" Devin stopped short in the doorway. Out-of-breath, eyelids at half-mast, he surveyed the odd scene.

"Mister Meyers, it's me, Dibby! I'm sorry but—"

"Get 'em, Devin" screamed Evelyn. "They broke in, trying to hurt me!"

Devin roared. A bull in a china shop, he trampled into the room, knocking over everything in his path. He gripped James's collar, ripped it clean away. On rebound, Devin snagged James's arm, twisted it behind him. James yelped. I raced over. Between James's legs, I raised my boot and stomped down hard on Devin's foot. He howled, shoved James toward me. I twisted off James's body to the side. Devin's foot jerked up, and he grabbed it, cussing, hopping in a circle like a cartoon character.

"Run, James," I cried. "Get help!"

He hesitated. Wouldn't move. Devin and Evelyn stood between us, James close to the back door. I'd set my sights on the front.

"I'm not leaving you here." I barely heard James, his voice small and frightened. Inside the kitchen, he clung to the door jamb, half-hiding, half-ready to spring to my rescue.

"I can take care of myself, dammit!" I picked up the lamp to prove it to him. Before Devin could lower his injured foot down, I ran up, smashed the lamp down on his head. When he collapsed, the room shook. "Now go, James!"

James nodded, said, "I'll be back."

I turned, ready to make for the front door. I'd nearly forgotten about Evelyn.

She barred my way, lips pulled back from her teeth. Growled. Held up her fang of a letter opener, ready to bite.

"You need *help*!" I shouted it with the force of a launched grenade. My shoulder went into Evelyn's chest. She spun sideways. The opener jagged down, ripped through my shirt sleeve. I zipped by her and bounded through the open door. Fast as I could, I ran across the porch floorboards. A running leap took me down the three steps. My foot caught at the bottom, twisted. I didn't slow, burst into a mad sprint. Upon my next footfall, I cried out, only then registering sharp pain in my ankle. But I kept going.

Behind me, Evelyn clambered out onto her porch, shrieking. I shot a look over my shoulder. Evelyn's knees jacked high in pursuit across the lawn, her dress by no means hindering her dervish speed. The letter opener cut a deadly swath through the air.

The cornfield lay ahead. With my twisted ankle, my best chance at losing her. If I could get through the field, get to Dad…

I dove in, straight into the stalks. They tore and nipped at me.

The tall stems towered over me and seemed to keep growing. They blocked the moon's visage. Blindly, I battled my way through the field. My sore ankle caught, tripped me up. I plummeted, grabbed a handful of leaves on the way down. I whipped over, looked up, saw nothing.

I scrabbled to my feet. My face, legs, and arms stung, scratched to no end. Blood slithered down my cheek. Weakened, tired, I fought my way through the near-impassable field.

I stopped, listened.

Nothing. An uneasy silence where there shouldn't have been one.

Evelyn could be anywhere. Quietly hiding, ready to spring. Ready to cut me down like she'd done her husband.

My breath thundered in my ears. I held my breath, but my heart kept bashing away.

Then I heard something else. A deep, chesty rumble. In no hurry, tires chewed up gravel.

A car door croaked open, slammed.

Footsteps whisked across the lawn, heavy as heavy gets. Headed my direction. Someone crashed into the field. Stalks snapped, popped, and died beneath my pursuer's bullish chase.

I sucked in a deep, deep breath to keep from screaming. And ran for my life. Behind me—just as in my visions, just like what had happened to Thomas—cannonball footfalls bounded after me.

I pitched my knees up higher. Chugged my arms like pistons. Pushed my twisted ankle to the point where it numbed, just dead weight. Next row over, just ahead of me, stem tips shook, then yanked down. Neck in neck with my pursuer, we raced down our rows, on course for an inter-section crash. I poured on the speed. The roof of my house—my safe house—appeared just over the field.

The picket fence in sight, I ran faster. Right next to me now, the competing footsteps grew loud. Louder yet. Spitting distance.

Almost there.

An arm shot out.

I shrieked.

A hand snatched my wrist, wrenched my body up off the ground. Whiplash propelled my legs forward, my back smack dab into my pursuer's chest. His arms wrapped around my waist and held me against him.

I kicked and clawed and shouted and—

"Dibby, *stop*," he ordered. "Quit carrying on like a hell-cat and tell me what in hell's going on around here."

I stopped. Relaxed within Sheriff Grigsby's safe hold. For once, exhilarated to see him.

"You gonna behave now?" I nodded. "Fine and dandy, then. I'm gonna let you go. Then I want you to *calmly* tell me what's going on."

Calm, my foot. There was no way I could knit calm outta madness and murder. But I tried to be succinct, the best I could. I didn't want the Saunders getting away.

"Sheriff, Evelyn Saunders killed her husband and tried to kill me just now. And I highly suspect Devin Meyers killed the missing boy, Thomas."

I waited for the laughter, the derision, the disbelief accorded one my age and stature. For once, Sheriff Grigsby appeared to take me seriously. Granite set in his features, his big nostrils flared with tired righteousness.

He tipped back his hat. Looked solemn. Scared, even. Crow's feet walked through all the corners of his eyes. A side of his mouth hitched up. It wasn't a smile, not by a mile. More like a grimace recognizing the job that lay ahead.

A long sigh came next, one that just about never ended. "I've had my suspicions for some time now about the Saunders. Yes, sir… But I can't just go charging in there, Dibby, not without proof."

"Evelyn's off her rocker, Sheriff. She confessed to me and James she killed her husband. I imagine you'll find physical proof in there, too. Boot Gundersen's grandson's photo for one thing."

He scoffed, the familiar face I associated with him. "Boot? What in hell's that ol' coot's grandson got to do with any of this?"

It'd take too much time, too much effort to explain it all now. "Please, Sheriff, just go check it out. Evelyn Saunders tried to kill me!"

The Sheriff looked left, right, saw nothing different than I did. Weighing matters, I suppose. "What were you doing there anyway, Dibby?" I shuffled, looked down, didn't know how Suzette pulled it off. "Never mind. For now, you're coming with me."

"But Sheriff, I'm telling you—"

"And I'm telling you, you're coming with me. *Now.*" He took off, a might faster than usual. I followed his broad back, thankful he made easy work of blazing a trail. Winded, he stopped by his Sheriff's car, parked askance as if he'd been in a hurry.

"You just sit here in the car, Dibby. For your own good while I look into matters." He opened the passenger door for me and I climbed in. Before shutting it, he said, "Anyone comes close, you just lock the doors and lay on the horn. Don't open up for anyone, not even Jesus coming back to collect the faithful."

I nodded.

He swaggered across the driveway, every bit the Western motion picture hero resignedly headed toward a showdown. His hand played at the holster on his belt. Almost absentmindedly, he flipped the button from the latch, exposing the gun butt.

The stairs warped in the middle as he mounted them. At the screen door, his hand rose, curled, knuckles out as if to knock. His hand stayed that way a good spell before I realized what he was doing. Listening.

Suddenly, he whipped out his gun. Belying his weight, he slid through the door easily, stealthily.

Time ticked by, an eternity.

Voices rose. A scream. Followed by an agonized howl, no doubt Devin.

A gunshot cracked. I hopped in my seat, banged my head against the window. I double-checked the door locks.

The second gunshot yanked me down into the seat. My eyes barely overlooked the dash.

Seconds, then minutes passed. I held my breath, waited for the survivor to come out.

Waited several lifetimes.

If one or both of the Saunders had somehow overpowered the Sheriff, snatched his gun…

I was next.

Quickly, I looked for car keys, found nothing. I looked over yonder, just next door, where safety and Dad sat, just out of reach, a bit too far… I estimated the time it'd take to run back through the field, hop the fence, get home. Then I looked at the Saunders' front door. I'd never make it in time. And I surely didn't want to go back into that cornfield. Ever again.

I cracked my window, just a hair. Angled my ear toward the opening to hear better.

Footsteps sounded from within the house. Not the loud, take charge, and damn the torpedo clomping of the Sheriff's boots either. A slow, steady shuffling.

The door opened.

Sheriff Grigsby came out. Gun securely holstered. Fanning his hat in his face and sweating up a storm. Never had I beheld such a beautiful sight.

I heaved a sigh of relief and straightened up. Back to his usual leisurely shuffle, it took him a stretch of time to make his way back to me.

He opened his door, slid in. Tossed out a weary sigh and his hat to the back. The Saunders' front porch lamp caught in his eyes. They were moist.

"Dibby… You were right. They were done loco, the both of them. They attacked me. I had no choice…" His throat caught, clicked. That was it, just a momentary hitch, before he swung into the stolid voice of order again. "I had to put them down."

"Oh… Oh." Tears bit at my eyes. I didn't want the Saunders to die, never even considered it a possibility. For all their crimes—maybe just their mistakes, the kind anyone might be capable of under the wrong circumstances—they were only human. Tragically so.

"I know this all must be upsetting for you, Dibby." He slipped the key into the ignition and started the car. "I'm sorry. I truly am. Just couldn't be helped."

I nodded, fearful I'd cry if I opened my mouth.

"I'm afraid I need you to come down to the station. Sort this mess out. Get your statement and what not." As he faced forward, the seat squelched beneath his weight. The porch light caught on his sheriff's star, his shining star. Mesmerized, I stared at it.

"All right," I said. "But maybe I should go tell Dad so—"

"That won't be necessary, Dibby." He chuckled. Rubbed my hair into a mess. I sat and took it, wondered how old I had to be before adults quit doing that. "After all, you're not under arrest."

"Just thought he might like to know where—"

"We can call him from the station. I want your story nice and fresh. Dot all the i's and cross the t's, if you know what I mean." Arm draped over the backseat, head craned, the Sheriff backed down the drive. The porch light grew dimmer, now just a dull edge on the star pinned to his chest.

The six-pointed star.

I tensed. Quietly moved my hand up to the lock.

Calm. Stay calm.

"Sheriff, honestly, it'll only take me a second to go tell my dad. Then I promise I'll be right back." I tried to keep my voice steady, but it still sounded quivery. Surely, my uneasy smile resembled a child's scrawl.

"Nope. Sorry. Gotta do it by the books." The car kept moving. His headlights never came on.

"I have to tell Dad." I flicked the lock up. Reached for the door handle.

The car jerked to an abrupt halt. My head crashed into the dash, then I fell back into the seat. I looked at the Sheriff, opened my mouth to scream.

His fist collided into the side of my head, shutting down my scream and shutting off the lights.

* * *

Death seemed mighty peculiar, and I guess that's not much of a reach seeing as how I hung my hat in Peculiar County.

My head throbbed a native tom-tom beat. All the stars in the sky plummeted, a galaxy of shooting stars. I couldn't move my hands or feet.

A spray of something scattered next to my head. Grass blades gently bent as if touched by raindrops. It happened again.

Tshhhhrit.

A wayward chunk of debris bounced up, caught my mouth just right while I took in a breath. I recognized the taste every kid tries once: dry, bitter, acrid dirt. I spat it out.

Next to me, a flashlight sat on the grass, turned toward Sheriff Grigsby's upper torso. Either he'd had a sudden realignment of body parts or he was standing about four feet in an open grave.

I lifted my head and recognized my surroundings. Deep inside the Hangwell Cemetery, I lay in the gated-off section reserved for the Judge's victims. The area most folks avoided like the plague.

The Judge's tree's limbs scratched across the face of the moon. Crumbling and slanted tombstones—their inscriptions long faded—rose like iceberg tips around me.

Sheriff Grigsby had taken to humming. "Whistle While You Work" from *Snow White and the Seven Dwarves.*

The big man shoveled more dirt near my head. "You're awake. Frankly, I didn't reckon you'd lift your eyelids 'til you were six feet under." He let out a hardy "ho-ho," full of beans, everyone's favorite uncle.

I wiggled, tried to set sense into my paralyzed limbs. Rope snagged me tight, feet to wrists. When I coughed, my brain orbited around my skull. "You killed 'em," I said. "Evelyn and Devin. Did they even attack you?"

Grigsby paused, leaned on his shovel handle. "I don't reckon that's neither here nor there. Fact of the matter is, Evelyn'd been getting kinda mouthy ever since she'd gone 'round the bend. Before long, she was liable to spill the beans about everything. Just like her son tried to do. Like *my* son."

"You're…you were Thomas's daddy?"

"A-yep. Proud of the li'l bugger, too. 'Til he went crazy, just like his mother."

"They have…*had* mental imbalances! *Not* crazy."

He laughed, called to his fellow vultures. "That's a barrel of horse-shit if I'd ever heard one. 'Mental imbalances'. Sounds to me like you been listening to your daddy. Fact of the matter is, I loved Evelyn. Had for some time. She rode me good and hard before, during, and after her marriage. But Hedrick… Hell… Ol' Hedrick wouldn't give up his suspicions about Thomas's parentage. Took the stupid fool long enough to figure it out, too. Evelyn had him figured as sterile. Um…you know what that means, Dibby? Shooting blanks? Firing on—"

"I know what it means."

"'Course, you do; 'course, you do. Anyway, things would've been just fine had Hedrick just accepted the boy wasn't his. Hell, he got to raise him, something I was denied."

The Sheriff bent over into the grave, one elbow poked up. With a grunt, he hefted another shovelful of dirt my direction.

"So after Evelyn killed Hedrick, she called you to take care of the body."

"See what I mean? Evelyn gave you an earful, sounds like. Frankly, I shoulda done away with her years ago. But I couldn't. Part of me still loves…loved her. But you had to go and stir everything up, nosing around in goddamn business that ain't yours!" He struck the shovel into the dirt. Wiped his brow. Sweat blistered his face. Couldn't catch his breath. Heart attack ready and that suited me just fine.

"I tried to warn you away, I did," he continued. "Can't say I didn't."

"What'd you do with Hedrick's body?" I intended to keep the man chatting 'til dawn, 'til Hangwell woke up. Until someone ventured past this way. If they would.

"I reckon you'll be getting nice and acquainted real soon with ol' Hedrick." He grinned at his feet.

"Is that where Thomas is? Richard Holmberg, too?"

"Now, how in the wide world did you find out about the Holmberg boy, anyway?" His jaw fell, then settled into a slow nod. "That damn bigmouth, Boot. You really been getting around, Dibby."

"Ain't no moss on me."

"Not yet, at least. But soon, real soon. Then you can say howdy to Thomas, Richard…the whole gang. I've been getting a lot of mileage out of this here hole." He chuckled. "Stupid town's so damn superstitious, no one even sets foot inside these gates. Too spooked by ol' Judge Wilbur."

"How could you kill your own son, Sheriff?" The inhumanity smacked me worse than Grigsby's sock to my head. I couldn't even fathom such a thing. Tears, born of anger more than grief, colored my voice. "How could you do that? How could anyone?"

He paused. Looked a bit lost for a moment, as if his missing soul would come tapping on his shoulder. "Well… I certainly didn't wanna do it, mind you. But after Thomas witnessed his momma kill his daddy… the boy just gave up living. Became a ghost of himself, fifty pounds wet and with clothes on, if that. Only damn thing he did was take to chanting like one of them African tribes or something. Just kept saying, 'Momma killed Daddy, chopped him good, Momma killed Daddy…' Of course, Evelyn took him out of school right after Hedrick's murder. But it wasn't enough. Soon, social services would come a-calling, and the boy would open his yap, sure as shooting." He shrugged, spat. "His momma pretty much became just like him. A walking dead woman, just playing at living."

Again, he chunked his shovel into the dirt, let the handle stick up. He came to the edge of the grave, rested his elbows over the lip. "Thing is, now that Hedrick was outta the way, I had Evelyn all to myself. But I surely didn't want her that way, no sir. The thought of touching that bag of crazy turned my gut. I had to make her right again. So…one night when I came a-calling, Thomas was in the bath. Took a lotta baths, that boy. As usual, Evelyn wasn't much company, not much good for anything. Not giving any thought to it, I just walked right on up the stairs. I snuck up behind Thomas, my mind all cloudy and what not, put my hands on my son's shoulders, gave him a couple of loving pats. He didn't respond. And I just pushed him under. Boy didn't struggle a bit. After he was gone, I carried him down, plain as day—Evelyn didn't notice a thing— put him in the bed of my truck, tossed a tarp over him, waited a couple hours. Then put him to rest next to Hedrick."

"You're a monster." Just like Dad had told me, the human monsters were the really bad ones.

"Aw, you're gonna hurt my feelings. So, Evelyn… she finally notices her boy missing. I tell her he ran away. Well, that sorta backfired on me in a big way. She got worse, made up some cockamamie story a monster stole Thomas away. Jumping Jesus, I was beside myself. I figured the only thing that'd set Evelyn back to good was another son. So I did some poking around in other towns, found a boy roughly the same age as Thomas in Durham, grabbed him up and handed him to Evelyn."

"And…she just accepted him?"

"It took a lotta fancy footwork, but she was so far gone, it hardly mattered. I just told her it was her new son. I told her she had to keep him indoors, keep him quiet, lessen the monster might come for him, too. For a while, she was happy with her new doll. But that boy was more trouble than Thomas. Couple times he broke free from the cellar, took off running through the woods. Both times I was lucky enough to catch him. Third time, I'd had enough. Put him underwater over at Myrtle Creek and whisked him away to join his 'brother.' When I told Evelyn the monster took Richard, too, she just accepted it and crawled deeper into her hole."

"What about poor Hettie?"

"What about that meddlesome ol' bitch? Hell, she knew I was Thomas's daddy. I s'pected she might've known more. And since you decided to stir the pot again, I had to put things right." He jabbed a finger directly between my eyes. "Don't you judge me, goddammit! Don't you dare! Ol' Hettie's death hangs on your head, not mine!"

Something moved behind Grigsby. A shadow detached from the Judge's tree. Several shadows. They shambled, walked stiffly toward us. Two short figures flanked a taller one in the middle, their hands linked together. I had no doubt who they were: Thomas, Richard, and Hedrick.

I was wrong.

Not about Thomas and Richard. As they came closer, moonlight a-lit on the boys' wan faces. They released the hands of the adult, faded back into darkness.

But the adult figure was tall, very tall, so tall his upper body remained hidden in shadow, supernaturally tall. Not Hedrick, not by a long shot.

A white blob bounced about where the man's face should be. As he ambled closer, his gaunt head took shape, defined by harsh and angular lines. Under any other circumstance, I'd have been wetting my britches. Not tonight, not now.

"You're a horrible, awful person, Sheriff. It'd be damned easy to judge you. But tonight, I'll leave the judging to someone with a bit more experience."

"What the hell're you on about? You're as nutty as your mother. You just—"

Judge Wilbur's noose quickly tied off Grigsby's foul words. Stiff as a marionette, the judge wrenched back a near-skeletal arm. The rope tightened. Grigsby's eyes snapped wide. His face turned purple. Fat cheeks puffed out, ready to explode.

Hunched over, the Judge peered into the grave and grinned at his handiwork. His white hair hung down to his shoulders. A bald patch of bone crowned the top of his head. A hawkish nose dipped over his thin-lipped grin. His judge's robes hung in raven-black tatters. A gust of wind beat the remains of his ceremonial garb like a kite.

Grigsby's fingers dug at the rope tightening into the fat of his neck. His mouth gaped, his tongue lolled out. The judge straightened and tugged Grigsby off his feet. Grigsby's fat legs thrashed at the dirt walls of the grave, his hands still tugging at the rope. With each jerky movement, the judge's bones snapped and popped. One last, mighty exertion, and the Judge wrenched Grigsby completely out of the grave to look him in the eye. The Judge's joints creaked, but the rope creaked louder.

Slowly, the Judge lifted his head. His chin, his nose, his overhanging brow pointed at me. Assigning me as his juror. The grin grew into a wide, nightmarish smile. His thin lips never parted, but teeth shone through the decaying flesh. His head tipped. A bushy, white eyebrow lifted, questioning.

He waited for my answer.

I closed my eyes. Dropped my chin to my chest. Whispered, "Okay."

Grigsby managed to set free a scream. A shiver lodged in my back. I didn't dare look. I surely didn't want to.

The sounds were bad enough.

Grigsby's scream cut short, nothing more than a hiccup. With whispery sounds, his fat carcass sledded away through the grass. Judge Wilbur's bones kept scraping, groaning.

Wood split, a giant tree ripped asunder. Roots tore up with great cleaving sounds. The ground shuddered. Then, as if the earth swallowed up the Judge and Grigsby—and I fairly think that's exactly what happened—the ground below me shifted, actually shifted. A great breath of heat blew over my back. Beneath the dirt, the core of the world grumbled. Then settled.

Beautiful, sane silence.

I opened my eyes. Other than Grigsby's car and the half-dug grave, it's as if the Sheriff had never existed. He certainly didn't now.

A car rushed up, headlights on bright. Near full-on hysterical, I laughed as my cavalry, riding in on a hearse—a tad late—raced up the meadow.

The hearse's tires spat up grass. Inches from Grigsby's car, Dad shuddered to a stop. James hopped out first, followed by Dad. They ran toward me, yelling their fool heads off.

"I'm over here," I called. As my hands were indisposed, I wriggled my shoulders to no great note.

Wonderfully worried, they made a big to-do over me. Dad didn't even bat an eye when James produced a switchblade to cut my bonds.

"Dibs? Are you okay? Did Grigsby do anything to—" Dad hushed when I threw my arms around him.

I let him go, turned to face James. Consequences didn't matter, embarrassment seemed impossible. I leaned forward and pressed my lips onto James's. For better traction, my hands slapped his cheeks. He fell from his squat onto his back. Unbelievably, he pushed me away.

"Um, Dibs?" Blatant as a train crash, he kept jutting his chin toward Dad.

Given the circumstances, Dad reacted the best he could. He studied the night sky, doing his dangdest to look patient, cleared his throat, which apparently needed a lot of clearing. I'm sure he died a bit inside, and while we were at the appropriate venue, I wanted him around for some time yet.

Laughing like a loon, I stood and pulled both of my men into an awkward—for them, at least—hug.

Another voice nearly sent me screaming into the surrounding woods. "Dibby! I've been worried sick!" Fashionably late, Suzette scooted out of the hearse's backseat.

"You got a funny way showing it, Suzette," I snapped. "You just took off, leaving us to be murdered!"

"What?" Dad apparently hadn't been brought up to speed yet.

Suzette started crying as if she'd been the one who'd been put through the wringer. "I tried to find your dad…I went into your house…I got lost and…it was so big and so horrible and…I was so scared…and finally your dad found me…and…"

She was too pathetic to just leave standing there. "C'mon over, Suzette. I reckon there's enough room in this hug for you, too. Just don't give me any of your cooties."

* * *

There were a mighty lot of belated funerals in Hangwell and Peculiar County the following week, and Dad's business bloomed. I attended 'em all. Like it or not, funeral gatherings pretty much became my regular social outings. At least I had a date to escort me. James cleaned up pretty nicely in his single Sears-ordered suit. Even Dad seemed a bit astonished by James's Cinderella do-over, but, of course, he'd never let James know that.

The funeral I'd been most yearning to attend had been Hettie's, of course, but the Sooters kept their mystery memorial to themselves. Turned out I owed the Sooters a debt, though. Thanks to their stone-faced gargoyle spy, Yvette had phoned Dad, told him to hightail it fast to the Hangwell Cemetery. Once an adult had verified James's wild stories, Dad finally jumped into action. Some things never change. I didn't hold it against

Dad, though. At least he was trying, especially with the world changing radically every day.

Around town, a lot of speculation passed lips regarding what'd happened to Sheriff Grigsby. Thanks to surviving Devin Meyers—suffering a wound that'd landed him in critical care in Durham General Hospital for a spell—the truth had won out, the Sheriff implicated on all counts of murder. Turned out ol' Devin didn't know a thing about any of his sister's murderous past. That was his story, at least. Me, I don't rightly see how anyone could turn such a blind eye toward loved one's doings, particularly while sharing a dwelling.

Still, there was the question of what had happened to good, ol' Sheriff Grigsby. The official line, one I started myself, was that upon seeing Dad's car approach, our wondrous Sheriff panicked and dashed off into the woods, never to be seen again.

But the gossip spread like cold germs.

"He's down in Mexico!"

"He was a secret Russian spy!"

"Martians took him!"

"He ran off to join his secret lover, Dibby's mom, and they're having cocktails and sex on a beach somewhere."

Boot himself had told me of these wild flights of fancy, heard 'em over the phone. The first three I found hoot-worthy. Not so much the fourth. I didn't bother sharing it with Dad either.

The only person I ever told about what really happened to the Sheriff was James. I knew Dad wouldn't buy into it. And if he did, I knew him well enough to know that it'd just shake up his world of logic and facts and science. I let Dad hide behind his scientific mumbo-jumbo, a safer place for him.

But the Judge's Hanging Tree held the truth, if anyone dared investigate. A new knot had grown since the Sheriff's disappearance. One strangely resembling Grigsby's tormented face, screaming away in eternal silence.

Not many folks gave the Sheriff a second thought after that, such is the way of Peculiar County.

After Evelyn's funeral and Hedrick and Thomas Saunders' twin memorial, I attended my last one, the one in Durham.

Boot Gundersen had again donned his war uniform, empty sleeve fastened to his chest. For a man his age, he stood with a rigidly straight posture. Until they began to lower the remains of his grandson, Richard Holmberg, into the ground. Then he folded, crying, looking much more the senior citizen he was.

Boot did something then that surprised me. I reckon it restored my faith in humanity, dislodged me out of my jaded, seen-it-all funk of fifteen. He turned toward me, smiled. Wagged his hand for me to join him. I looked at James, who hadn't a clue either. I released my boyfriend's hand and quietly sidled up next to Boot.

By his side, he held out his hand. Fingers wagged and waited. I slipped my hand into his. He leaned over, whispered, "Everything you did for my Grandson, you got a right to be right up here with us, Miss Dibby. You're kin now."

He pulled his hand away, draped it around my shoulders. Pulled me in close. Although he smelled of tobacco, sweat, and something indefinably awful, I didn't mind one whit.

ABOUT THE AUTHOR

Stuart R. West is a lifelong resident of Kansas, which he considers both a curse and a blessing. It's a curse because…well, it's Kansas. But it's great because… well, it's Kansas. Lots of cool, strange and creepy things happen in the Midwest, and Stuart takes advantage of them in his work. Call it "Kansas Noir." Stuart writes thrillers tinged with horror and horror tinged with thrillers, both for adult and young adult audiences. He writes at the crossroads of horror and sneaky humor. *Peculiar County* is Stuart's fifth book with Grinning Skull Press. Stuart spent twenty-five years in the corporate sector and now writes full time. He's married to a professor of pharmacy (who greatly appreciates the fact he cooks dinner for her every night) and has a twenty-seven-year-old daughter who's still deciding what to do with her life. But that's okay. It took him twenty-five years to figure that out.

Stuart's blog can be found at http://stuartrwest.blogspot.com/

Drop in on him at Facebook at: https://www.facebook.com/stuartrwestwriter

For more young adult options, check out
The Witching Well by S.D. Hintz

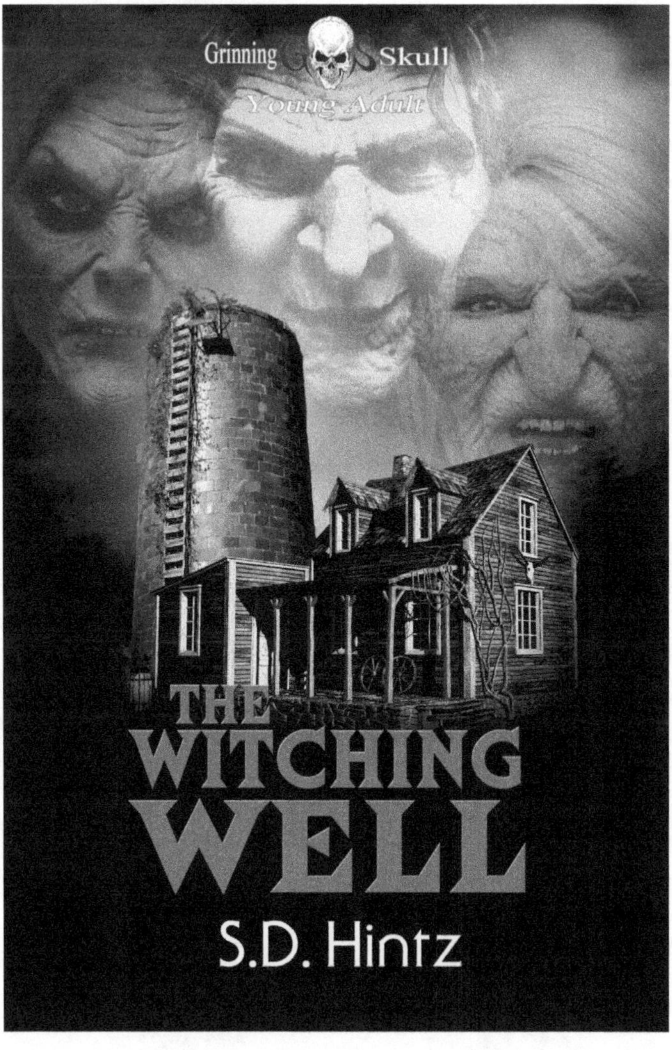

Chapter 1

After I slit your mommy's throat, I'm gonna cut her face off.

Murray blocked the image before it could drown him. A month of therapy only made the memories more vivid, every session reliving the nightmare. While wounds healed, scars remained. Maybe, with time, the mental preoccupation would fade. He doubted it. Relocating to his grandmother's home—courtesy of his mother's will—would surely be a constant reminder.

He gazed out the passenger side window, straining to distract his thoughts. Towering firs swayed in a green blur. Churches and bars vied for the locals' devotion. Rustic inns lured travelers every other mile. The surroundings gave Murray an eerie vibe. Suburbia had been his comfort zone. Now, smack dab in the middle of bear country, he hoped Grandma Anna's car ran like new.

He squinted through the windshield as the forest thinned out and four-foot crags lined the roadside. Dogwoods and spruces edged the limestone, providing glimpses of a glistening Lake Superior between branches. They neared a timbered sign posted in a bed of violets and cyclamen, perhaps twenty yards beyond a scenic outlook.

**Welcome to
Windom
"Port of the North Shore"
Population 79**

Murray frowned. "Twenty more than Rushford."

Flashbacks of his hometown blinded him. His mom's flower shop, Roses in Rushford. Trading comic books with his best friend, Gilby Wells. Shooting hoops at Eden Elementary. Saturday spaghetti dinners at Lon's Diner. The Saturday dinner his mom canceled. That was the last time he saw her. The last time he held her. The last time…

He fought off the memory.

Grandma Anna smiled. "And just about a three-hour drive on the nose. To think, I left here yesterday morning. It feels like I've been gone for weeks."

For Murray, the previous two days had passed in slow motion. He thought back on the wake, the funeral, and the reluctant goodbyes. At the time, they seemed neverending. Part of him had been eager for it all to end, while the other part refused to let go.

Tears welled up as he recalled his mom's casket being carried to the cemetery.

He wept for everyone and everything he left behind. His mom. His friends. His old life.

Grandma Anna squeezed his shoulder. "It's going to be

okay. I know it's hard right now, but we'll get through this together."

Murray dried his eyes and nodded. His grandmother's words dissolved in his tunnel vision. The setbacks seemed endless, seemed to bear down like an avalanche.

Grandma Anna decelerated as the Crown Victoria entered town, and seconds later she steered the car into a neighborhood. An odd development of multiple builders on different deadlines, it reminded Murray of Minneapolis; no two houses were alike. The car paused at an uncontrolled intersection. An olive street sign boasted Blossom Boulevard with the crossroad Philodendron Drive.

Murray stared out the window as they headed down the boulevard. He had never seen a more manicured block. On the left corner, a white picket fence encircled a quaint two-story house of the same hue, the lawn lime green and trimmed. A snaking row of flowering blackthorns coiled around back. A miniature picket fence edged a garden of sunflowers and lemon tulips. Welcome to Mr. Rogers' house.

Grandma Anna noticed Murray's interest. "That's Missus Muldoon's place. She tends her garden at nine o'clock sharp every day. It's her pride and joy. I wouldn't be surprised if it was surrounded by landmines."

"That's some hobby." Murray eyed the cantilever roof that extended from the front steps to the driveway. "How come she doesn't have a garage?"

"I guess she doesn't really need one. She rarely drives as it is. Probably why she's still alive and kicking."

"Weird."

"One thing's for sure, I don't go out of my way to talk to her, and neither should you. She's quite the oddball when she's not gardening. And I don't think she fancies children. I see her tear up those Pro-Life pamphlets all the time."

"Guess I'll keep my distance then."

Murray regarded the house on his right. Three stories of steel gray shutters and navy blue siding. Two twisted yew trees littered the lawn with blood-red cones and needles. The place looked haunted. An elderly woman stood in the broad bay window like a mannequin in a store display, staring at them as they passed by.

The thought of an old lady creeping in the curtains gave Murray the willies. "Who's that?"

Grandma Anna turned her head as if knowing precisely where to train her gaze. "That's Missus Vitikin. She's the town busybody." She paused and waved. "She loves to gossip, spread rumors, throw everyone under the bus. I do my best to keep the peace with her."

Paranoia seized Murray. "Does she know I'm coming?"

"Of course. She's my next-door neighbor. We talk every day, sometimes even have tea together. Well… This is it."

"*That's your house?*"

"*Our* house."

The four-story, rose-colored Victorian towered over the block. Red brick outlined the numerous windows and oak front door. Red and white roses graced the walk that stretched from the driveway to the front steps, which then wound a-round the side of the house through a vine-covered pergola. Blooming annuals encircled the trio of maple trees in the lush yard.

Murray gaped at the thought of relocating from a two-bedroom rambler to a mini-mansion. Maybe his new life wouldn't be so bad after all.

Grandma Anna parked the car, popped the trunk, and opened her door. "Let's grab your belongings. Then I'll give you a guided tour of the Macabe Place."

Murray unbuckled his seat belt. He gazed at the looming house. The Macabe Place. It sounded like a horror movie. It would surely haunt him with memories of his mom. He hoped the pain would pass with time, as his therapist implied. His suggestion of distracting the mind with work or a project possibly held weight and needed consideration.

Murray climbed out of the car and stretched. Standing never felt so good after sitting down for the last three hours. The warm breeze smelled of roses and freshly mowed grass. Again, he regarded the house. The sun peered over the left chimney and cast a glow on the third-story rose window. The whole setting possessed a refreshing air. Murray felt the vague sense of being on vacation at an extravagant bed and breakfast, which were more common than McDonald's in northern Minnesota.

He turned and headed to the rear of the car. His gaze drifted across the boulevard. An old, bald black man with wire-rimmed glasses casually approached the drive. He sported an electric blue suit and cream shirt with a cornflower bow tie. His black loafers glared more than his head. His greeting came with a deep voice.

"Need a hand, Anna?"

"Oh, hello, Cab. No, thank you. I think I can manage to carry one duffel bag."

"One duffel bag? Boy, if you plan on visitin' longer than the summer, my name's Cabot Linlith. My friends call me Cab; my neighbors call me Trouble."

He offered his hand. Murray gladly accepted it. "Murray."

Cab's handshake was firm, trusting. His hazel eyes twinkled. "Welcome to Windom. If you like shootin' the bull on the porch with raspberry lemonade, then I'm the man to see."

Murray grinned. "I'll see you soon then."

Grandma Anna shut the trunk. "After lunch." She pointed at Cab. "And you, young man, either forgot that Mass was yesterday or you have a hot date."

Cab bared a toothless smile. "Only with the sunshine, Anna. And Murray, if that's alright with you."

"Of course, but promise me you won't be gambling."

"Gamblin'? Why? 'Cause I'm on my way to church? No, ma'am. It's not bingo night. I made a deal with the Devil. I've got to help Reverend Regent with the potluck."

"Altar boy wasn't good enough?"

"He said I was too old. Imagine that." Cab shook his head. "Now if you'll excuse me, one can't be late with the Lord."

He waved and crossed the boulevard to his bronze Cadillac. Murray's anxiety eased. He dreaded the neighbors, especially after Grandma Anna's details concerning Mrs. Vitikin and Mrs. Muldoon. He knew the challenge of meeting new people, but what worried him most was befriending elderly adults. They always seemed so grumpy and needy. After encountering Cab, though, he wondered if he was being too judgmental, a quality he undoubtedly inherited from his mom.

Grandma Anna gestured toward the front steps. "Shall we?"

Murray nodded and followed her up the brick path. She stopped on the steps and unlocked the door, the brass knocker rattling against the solid oak.

Murray's eyes widened and lips parted. They stood in a large foyer, the floor hardwood and glossy, casting a mirror reflection. Oil paintings of bouquets and gardens decorated the apricot walls. A set of marble benches flanked a glass end table with a crystal vase of red roses set upon it. A sweeping oak stairway disappeared above.

Grandma Anna slipped off her black pumps. "You can set your shoes by the door for now. Your bedroom's upstairs. I think we'll head up there, and you can take some time to unpack your things. Once you've made yourself at home, I'll give you the grand tour."

"Okay."

Murray tailed Grandma Anna up the staircase, each step creaking. He could not wait to see his new bedroom. The thought of decorating it from scratch with comic book and movie posters excited him. He could even paint the walls if Grandma Anna allowed him the privilege. He had yet to test the boundaries of their relationship, but that would come in time.

An open landing of hardwood floors extended from the top of the stairs. More oil paintings of annuals covered the walls. To the left, a wrought-iron spiral staircase led to the third story. Grandma Anna headed right down a wide hall-way of four propped-open doors.

Her voice echoed down the hall. "The first room on the right is the bathroom. The other three are bedrooms. The last one on the left is yours. The one across the way was your aunt's and mother's."

"They shared a room?"

"'Til your mother was sixteen. Aunt Eva was five years older and out of the house by twenty-one. Speaking of which, she'll be stopping by tomorrow with a few things of your mother's." Grandma Anna sighed as she set down the duf-fel bag. "Well, here it is. It should do for now. It used to be your Grandpa Macon's study. The bed was your mother's."

Murray stepped inside. "Thank you."

"You're welcome. I'll let you unpack."

Grandma Anna left Murray to absorb the spacious room. Sunlight poured through the two double-paned win-dows, casting a glare on the floor. A pair of bookcases leaned against the far wall, plumb full of paperbacks and hardcovers. On the right sat an oak dresser with a large globe and match-ing roll-top desk. All remnants of the converted study.

Murray's eyes locked on the four-poster. Hand-carved across the headboard, roses intertwined a thorny vine. Grand-ma Anna had removed the canopy, surely so it looked less feminine, but the white lace comforter remained. Murray fought the urge to lie down and test the mattress. After the long car ride, an intended catnap would have him waking up at bedtime.

He unzipped his duffel bag and sifted through the contents. He filled the top dresser drawer with tube socks and briefs, the middle with his iron-on T-shirts, and the bottom with his Marvel comic book collection. He piled his folded pants and jean shorts on the desk, lacking the energy to hang them in the closet.

He shoved the duffel bag beneath the bed and plopped down on the comforter. He stared at the ceiling, his mind eagerly drifting. He wondered how many times his mom had lain in the same bed lost in thought. Certainly hundreds, if not thousands of nights. Had she ever felt alone, a young girl in a little bed against the entire world? Murray failed to ignore the feeling as it crept over him like a translucent body bag. Of course, Grandma Anna raised her through childhood. Motherless, he had…Grandma Anna. He closed his heavy eyelids and felt his mind running off without him. The ceiling turned to sky, and the comforter became a cloud. His room of loneliness filled with imaginary friends, and he embraced it wholeheartedly.

Chapter 2

"Murray, Murray. What's your hurry? You've got nowhere to run."

Clouded shards of memories flooded Murray like a deluge. His mom waving goodbye on the doorstep before walking to her killer's black sedan. The doorbell awakening Murray on the living room couch. The sheriff delivering the news and escorting him to the car. Sobbing in the backseat. Waiting at the police station for his best friend's parents, hugging his knees to his chest. Standing beside his mom's closed coffin, wishing he could see her one last time.

Murray forced his eyes open. He glanced from wall to wall. For a moment, he thought he was in his bedroom at Rushford. The decor of garden paintings brought him back full circle. He dozed off on his mom's four-poster.

Movement caught his eye. Grandma Anna stood to his right with her back turned. She placed a small brass lamp on the desk. Murray sat up and rubbed his eyes.

Grandma Anna turned at the squeak of bed springs. "Up so soon? You only napped for a half-hour."

"Had a bad dream. I can't… I can't stop thinking about

him. I see him every time I close my eyes."

Grandma Anna touched Murray's cheek lovingly. "You think you see him. Maybe you even want to see him. But you'll never see him here. He's buried far away at that."

Murray looked down at the satin sheets, the daymare still haunting him.

Grandma Anna hugged him tight and kissed him on the forehead. "You're in Windom now. No one's coming to get you. I won't let them. You're safe here."

Murray nodded as he met Grandma Anna's aquamarine eyes; they twinkled like gemstones, as his mom's had.

"So, Mister Macabe, would you like to help me with my garden? The fresh air might do you some good."

Murray sighed, still rattled. "I think I'd rather stay inside."

"Indoors it is. How about a tour of the attic instead? That's where I usually go when I need some time to myself."

"Okay. Sure."

Murray sidled out of bed and followed Grandma Anna into the hallway. He noticed she changed out of her dress into more casual apparel, salmon slacks, and a cream blouse. Her perfume wafted as she walked, smelling of roses and lilacs. She crossed the landing and ascended the spiral staircase.

Murray's overactive imagination took hold. Butterflies fluttered in his belly. He wondered what Grandma Anna had in store. Thanks to films like *The Changeling* and *Flowers in the Attic,* he always considered the top floor the creepiest room in a house. At the same time, he expected it to be a dusty disaster area, cluttered wall to wall with antique junk and family heirlooms. His heart thumped with every step. The staircase wobbled under their weight, unaccustomed to supporting two people.

Grandma Anna paused, regarded Murray, and then pointed over her shoulder. "When this door is closed, that means I want to be alone. No disruptions whatsoever."

Murray nodded with a furrowed brow. He bit his tongue as thoughts of Grandma Anna's private goings-on prodded him.

She noted his confusion and added quickly, "When it's open, you can come up here whenever you like. Understand?"

"Yeah."

"Good."

Grandma Anna turned and lifted the trap door. It creaked like a sealed coffin. She ascended the last few steps. Murray anxiously followed in her shadow. The moment he entered the room, sunlight blinded him, and a hint of incense smothered his sense of smell.

Taken aback, he scanned the attic, turning on his heels to take it all in. It exceeded his expectations. By far the largest room in the house, vaulted ceilings and double-paned windows eased the need for artificial light. The hardwood floor gleamed as if recently varnished, sparkling with a green and red kaleidoscopic reflection from the rose window above. Oil paintings of blooming flowers and majestic gardens decorated what little wall space existed.

Murray's gaze locked on the left side of the room, and his eyes widened. Before the corner window sat a blue easel and gray tray of paints, from which jutted a wood stool. A semi-circle of five red candelabras created a boundary line. A crystal chandelier dangled from the ceiling, surely spotlighting the space at nightfall. Murray suddenly felt the urge to paint, like back in middle school art class.

Grandma Anna withdrew a black matchbook from her pant's pocket. "This side of the room I call my gallery. This is where I spend most of my time thinking—and painting."

Murray approached a framed landscape of a field of daisies receding into a glimmering pond hanging between two windows. "Wow. These paintings are really good. Do you ever sell any of them?"

"Sometimes. A little extra spending money never hurts."

"You must be up here a lot then."

"That's not the only thing I do for a living, sweetie." Grandma Anna struck the match and began lighting the candelabra. "I used to be a registered nurse. I volunteer at the nursing home twice a week. It gets me out of the house."

Murray noted the right side of the attic. A black curtain undulated from the rafters, concealing the corner and a quarter of the room.

Murray pointed. "What's behind the curtain?"

Grandma Anna glanced at it and flashed him a stern gaze. "That's my dark room. I devote a good chunk of time to it. It is also the only room in the house you are forbidden to go. Your mother learned the hard way. I trust you'll respect my wishes."

Murray nodded reluctantly, taken aback, as Grandma Anna lit the last candelabrum.

She blew out the match and set it on the paint tray. "Now if you'll excuse me, I need to water my garden. If you'd like to test out the canvas, be my guest. I set out some fresh watercolors earlier. And believe me, painting is a nice way to clear your mind. I've found it's the best way to pour out all the feelings I bottle up inside."

"Maybe I'll give it a try."

"You do that. I'll come back up in a little while to see your masterpiece."

Murray smiled, and Grandma Anna disappeared downstairs. Seconds later, his curiosity wandered back to the black curtain.

What was the big secret? Was she hiding something illegal back there?

Whatever it concealed, his mother had known at one time. But only once from the sound of it. Grandma Anna had surely punished her for snooping. And truth be told, he wanted to avoid her mean streak. Like many adults, she probably detonated when you pushed her buttons.

A loud slam made Murray jump. He whirled. The trapdoor shut on its own. He looked to the windows facing the boulevard. The maroon draperies billowed in the wind, caught red-handed. He approached them and shut the window part way, paranoid the fiery candelabra might blow over next. He'd rather not burn down Grandma Anna's favorite room.

His eyes zoomed in on the easel. The blue paint flaked around the edges and fluttered in the breeze. Besides the obvious wear and tear, it otherwise appeared to be in solid condition. Years ago he painted on one. Back then he had to wear a smock and hairnet and use one of those fat brushes. Now he could paint in his regular clothes and create whatever he desired.

He rounded the candelabra, savoring the heavenly scent of cinnamon. Just as Grandma Anna said, a blank canvas awaited with a tray of fresh paints. He pulled out the oak stool and sat down, the legs creaking beneath his weight. He picked up a slender brush and scanned the watercolors. The circle of red paint glinted in the sunlight.

The color of choice. The heart of his anger and pain.

Red.

Blood red.

Murray plunged the brush into the open wound. Instantaneously, his heart bled through his fingers. His strokes slashed at the canvas like a knife. Red splattered and trickled, trailing onto the easel. His eyes welled up as his emotions took hold.

Concocted images of his mother assaulted him. Her face contorted as she struggled in a chokehold. Wailing with each stab wound in an alley on her knees. Her bloody hand reaching desperately over the lip of a dumpster.

A whimper escaped Murray's throat. His breathing became more labored with each lash. Tears spilled down his cheeks, splashing in the watercolors like a blood rain. The brush shook in his fingers, reluctant to stab again. It slipped from his grip and clanged on the tray.

Murray's shoulders slumped, and his head hung low as he sobbed uncontrollably in the afternoon sunlight.

✪ ✪ ✪

The trapdoor creaked open.

Grandma Anna entered the attic. "So, how's the Picasso coming?"

Unresponsive, Murray clutched the stool to keep his weary body from falling off. He stared straight ahead, his focus drowning in the watercolors. His lip trembled, struggling to form a word. He wiped his tear-stained cheeks with the back of his hand.

Grandma Anna placed her hands on his shoulders. "It's been how long since you last painted?"

Murray shrugged, cleared his throat. "I… I don't know." He looked up into Grandma Anna's smiling face. "You were right. I feel…"

"Relieved?"

Murray thought momentarily, then nodded. "Yeah, relieved. It felt good… to get that all out."

"It always does. Never hold back your feelings. Not only will they eat you alive, but they'll hurt the loved ones around you." Grandma Anna squeezed his arms. "Now tell me all about your painting."

"I… I don't know how to explain it."

"Is that blood everywhere?"

"Yeah."

"And that's his car?"

Murray nodded.

"So why is it so sunny?"

Murray regarded the giant yellow star in the cloudless sky. "Because…there's hope…somewhere after this."

Grandma Anna hugged him and kissed his cheek. "Well done. Now, all we need is a place to hang it."

Murray spoke his mind before he could bite his tongue. "How about in the dark room?"

Grandma Anna shared his haunted gaze. "But you'll never see it in there."

Murray shrugged.

Grandma Anna stared at the curtain. "That sounds like the perfect place." She rounded the candelabra and blew them out one by one. "Now go wash up. You look like you've been finger painting. I'll cook an early dinner at three since we didn't eat anything on the road. Hopefully, you'll find your appetite by then."

A grin cracked Murray's frown. "As long as it's not tuna casserole."

Grandma Anna raised her thin, silver brows. "Your mother learned that dish from me. It was one of her favorites. Consider yourself lucky."

With that, she chuckled and left the attic. Murray eyed his artwork one last time. He decided whatever he painted in the attic would remain there. The room possessed a special spirit. A means of therapy, a shoulder to cry on. It provided privacy and an outlet to let emotions run free. All the sunlight and shadows—windows to the soul. Whether Murray wanted to admit or not, the attic had seized him in its clutches.

He stood and pushed the stool under the easel. He regarded the dark room one last time. The curtain fluttered like a vampire's cape; the shadows wavered, teasing the sunlight. A ghost of a smile haunted Murray's face. Deep down he knew he shared more in common with Grandma Anna than a child should. He hoped it meant their relationship would grow stronger. At this point, Grandma Anna was all he had.

The telephone rang as Murray took his seat at the dining room table. Grandma Anna cut it short and snatched up the receiver.

Murray's eyes wandered around the dining room. French doors separated it from the living room. Two opposite paintings decorated the oak-paneled walls: one of a rose on a brick doorstep, the other a flowery pergola with a sunset backdrop. A crystal chandelier sparkled above the set table; the fine china and silverware gleamed in its bright glow. In the center of the lace tablecloth stood a white ceramic vase of pink roses.

Murray analyzed the aroma wafting from the kitchen. It smelled delicious, like Alfredo, definitely not the stench of tuna casserole.

The French doors slid open. Grandma Anna strolled in with a silver platter of fettuccine garnished with basil and lightly toasted garlic bread.

She set the food on the table. "That was your Aunt Eva on the phone. She's stopping by tomorrow with those things of your mother's."

Murray's eyebrows arched. "Like what?"

"She didn't say. She did, however, mention that she's been meaning to talk to you."

"About what?"

"She didn't say that either." Grandma Anna sat across from Murray and unfolded her napkin. "I do know she's hurting right now. Your mother was her only sister. Her best friend." She paused as she composed herself. She raised her napkin and dabbed a tear that threatened to fall. "She hardly ever comes up here to see me, you know? Once a year, if I'm lucky. I talk to her on the phone, of course, but…it's not quite the same. It doesn't help she lives three hours away."

As Grandma Anna dished out their dinner, Murray considered her comment. The extent of his mom's death sank in. Aunt Eva truly suffered. After all, she and his mom ran the flower shop together, working with each other on a daily basis. Best friends indeed.

Grandma Anna hurt even more. Murray noticed every time she mentioned his mom. He assumed since she was older she'd dealt with the passing easier. Unlike in his case, thirteen years old, losing the only person who loved him.

"Grandma? Why did my mom leave here?"

Grandma Anna ate a forkful of pasta, swallowing it before meeting Murray's gaze. "Did she ever talk about growing up in this town?"

Murray shook his head. "Not really."

"Well, she was a bit of a homebody, didn't have a lot of friends. But then again, there's always been a lack of children in Windom."

Murray's serving of noodles froze before his mouth. "Are there kids here now?"

"Not in this neighborhood, at least not that I'm aware of. Mister Linlith and Missus Vitikin have children and grandchildren, they just don't visit much. And trust me, I know how that is."

Murray's paranoia devoured his appetite. He couldn't possibly be the only kid in town. If true, what would he do with himself? No friends, no playmates. He would die of boredom!

He lowered his fork to the plate. "Where's the school at?"

"About twenty miles from here in Highland, same place your mother attended. That, in itself, made most of her friendships long distance. Even so, as she got older, she seemed more restless, more eager to get away."

"Get away? From who?"

"Oh… Everybody. Me. Grandpa Macon. Windom."

"But why? I don't get it."

Grandma Anna raised her wineglass and sipped. "When

your Aunt Eva left, that was inspiration enough. Your mother… Well, that's a day I'll never forget."

Murray's throat was parched, as if thirsting for the knowledge his mom kept secret. He grabbed his tumbler of water and took a gulp. He looked down at his plate.

"What happened?"

Grandma Anna eyed Murray, her jaw stiffening, clearly reluctant to share the information. After a five-second silence, she decided otherwise.

"She came home that night after seeing a movie and… and told us she was four months pregnant. She had just graduated high school and didn't have a job, and… and we didn't know the boy she was dating. We never did meet him. We all got into a yelling match, which I now regret…" She sighed and drank her wine. "She skipped town the next day, and your Aunt Eva took her in."

The story spun through Murray's brain like a Tilt-A-Whirl. His mom left Windom because of him. He had dismantled the happy family. The thought rattled him.

"So my mom left because of me."

"No, no, honey, not at all. It wasn't because of you. Don't ever think that. There were plenty of other reasons. Plenty. As she got older, we all banged heads a lot more. Argued, disagreed. I suppose I tried to control her too much. I just wanted what was best for her. And she—she wanted a life of her own."

"But why didn't my dad go with her?"

"She never told you that either?"

Murray shook his head. He knew little about his dad. His mom once said: "He's not here, that's all you need to know." Afterward, he avoided the matter. Obviously, the man disrespected her in some way. Her relationships seemed to bleed together. The last man… Murray simmered his bubbling anger and refocused on his original inquiry.

A flash of resentment passed over Grandma Anna's face. "Like the last man, he treated her like trash. When he found out she was pregnant, he gave her five dollars for diapers and bought a train ticket to Canada. That was the last we heard of him. I think that's what really made your mother want to get away from everything. Quite frankly, I never blamed her. I probably would have done the same."

Murray processed the information, letting his mind drift in retrospect. Reluctant to go out on dates, men approached his mom all the time. She typically declined, but over the years Murray could tell an umbrella of loneliness opened even on sunny days. She would often nurse a glass of wine in the late evening, embraced by the darkness of the living room, comforted by the murmuring television. He figured she eventually came to terms with herself and decided a kind man waited somewhere out there for her. If only she remained lonely, she would still be alive.

Grandma Anna noted the gloom in Murray's eyes. "Let's change the subject, shall we? How do you like my fettuccine?"

Murray stepped out of his mental closet and regarded his untouched plate. The noodles clumped on the fork. He brought the serving to his lips. "It's good. Tastes like a restaurant cooked it."

"Wait 'til you try my tuna casserole."

Murray grinned. "I think I'd rather have seconds."

"Already? Shouldn't you finish the firsts?"

Murray scooped up another forkful as his appetite returned with a vengeance. The tasty food also improved his mood. He washed down a bite and looked across the table. "Thanks for showing me the attic today."

Grandma Anna smiled. "You're welcome. What's mine is yours now, sweetie. You're not a guest. You're my grandson."

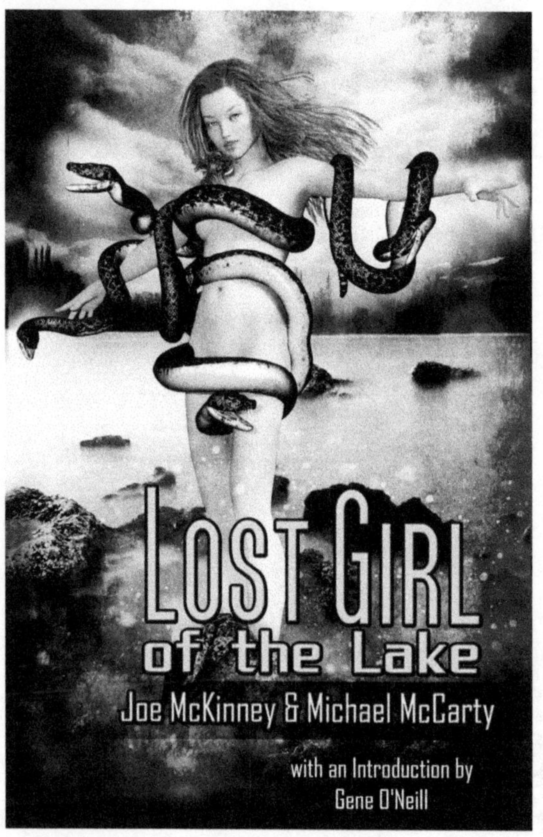

Lake Livingston: August, 1961

Mark Gaitlin is 15, the son of one of the wealthiest men in Texas, and on the most boring summer vacation of his life. His days are filled with the pomp and circumstance of country club life, while his nights are a parade of one embarrassment after another at the hands of giggling teenage girls.

But the piney woods above Lake Livingston are dark at night, and they hold many secrets for an impressionable youngster on the cusp of becoming a man. And one night, after skinny dipping in the lake with a mysterious local girl, Mark Gaitlin's life takes a crazy turn into the fire and brimstone religion of backwoods snake handlers and abandoned villages haunted by old family secrets. If he can survive the snakes and the ghosts and his own family's dark history, he just might make it out of the woods alive.

And something else…he just might become a man.